"This book is immediately gripping. I was invested every step of the way, and loved the visceral world of the ledge. The cold might not be alive, but these characters definitely jump off the page, and the enemies to lovers romance hit all the right spots. Stacey's debut novel is a triumph for all fantasy lovers, and I can't wait to see where this series goes!"

Raven Kennedy, author of *The Plated Prisoner* series

"The Maas mob will devour this trilogy. *Ledge* reads like Laini Taylor's lore set in Leigh Bardugo's Fjerda, penned with Katherine Arden's prose. The narrative pacing, playfulness, and deliverance will delight fans of Ilona Andrews' *Innkeeper Chronicles* and Holly Black's *The Folk of the Air*."

Angela Armstrong, author of *The Unflinching Ash*

"McEwan, a popular figure on BookTok, has written an ambitious fantasy debut. The plot and worldbuilding are thoroughly fleshed out and make this novel a great start to the Glacian Trilogy."

Library Journal

"A bold and gutsy epic fantasy debut... Lusty at times even rollicking, with formidable fighting, pops of powerful healing magic, and a heroic plot, *Ledge* will appeal to those seeking new adult romantic fantasy."

LoveReading

"Despite the icy setting, *Ledge* is a sizzling story filled with sexual tension, betrayal, and stolen heritage and a series to watch out for."

British Fantasy Society

Stacey McEwan

CHASM

THE GLACIAN TRILOGY, BOOK II

ANGRY
ROBOT

ANGRY ROBOT
An imprint of Watkins Media Ltd

Unit 11, Shepperton House
89 Shepperton Road
London N1 3DF
UK

angryrobotbooks.com
twitter.com/angryrobotbooks
The Chasm, it sings

An Angry Robot original, 2024

Copyright © Stacey McEwan 2024
Cover by Kate Cromwell
Edited by Gemma Creffield and Travis Tynan
Map by Thomas Rey
Set in Meridien

ISBN 978 1 91520 299 4
Ebook ISBN 978 1 91520 266 6

Printed and bound in the United Kingdom by TJ Books Ltd.

9 8 7 6 5 4 3 2 1

FSC
www.fsc.org
MIX
Paper from
responsible sources
FSC® C013056

To my husband – Michael –
you're despairingly non-fictional,
but holy shit, I love you.

KINGDOM
— OF —
TERRSAW

GLACIA

THE LEDGE

THE BOULDER
GATE

YENNES' CABIN

BALTISSE CABIN

THE FALLEN
VILLAGE

SALEM'S INN

CHAPTER ONE

Most of her body is bloodstained.

Old blood, dried and flaking in strange patterns. Dawsyn can trace the outlines. Landmarks on a map. It makes brittle ropes of her hair, and clings to the inside of her nose. It is all she can smell despite the rot on the walls and the fetidness of her own unwashed body. Nothing can mask the scent of blood that is not one's own.

Ryon's blood.

She bites down on her tongue. Each time his name rises, she tries to bury it like a body in water. But the thought is buoyant; it floats to the surface each time, the assault of memory with it.

A sword hilt glints from his chest and a creased hand wrenches it out; he is spilled out onto the floor.

"Lock her away," the Queen calls.

"No!" Dawsyn howls, and her body revolts against hands that haul her from the ground, dragging her away from Ryon. His glassy eyes do not turn to the sound of her call.

"Hybrid, get up! GET UP!"

"I am sorry, miss," whispers Ruby, the captain of the guard. The woman shoves a gag in Dawsyn's mouth and ties a band around it.

Dawsyn kicks and lands a blow to Ruby's shin, but the woman is sheathed in armour. She grunts but does not buckle.

Dawsyn looks her last at Ryon Mesrich, at the face she'll fail to carve from her mind. Then, she is pulled down a corridor, into a stairwell.

Dawsyn bellows and chokes out a promise, but the guards cannot hear it. The gag traps the vow instead.

"I will cut out her throat! I will cut your Queen's throat!"

She's learnt that the images dissipate quicker with pain – an infinite resource in her current holdings. Dawsyn scrapes her fingers along her cheeks, collecting the grime beneath her nails. She strikes her head against the wall, letting the crash of pain flood her senses, washing over the memory, dissolving it into the recesses. Dawsyn sighs, relieved.

It is dark, there in the cell where she waits, but her eyes have grown used to the shadows. She sees clearly, even if she'd rather not.

A dead rat lies in the corner. One of its eyes protrudes from where she stomped on it earlier. Bastard was brazen enough to gnaw on her toes as she slept. Dawsyn imagines the thing was used to encountering more dead prisoners than living, here below ground. The smell, which impregnates the very walls, lends truth to it.

Dawsyn is no stranger to captivity or dungeons, yet this prison is different – or perhaps she is. Thoughts of the ceiling caving in, of being buried alive, plague her. A useless preoccupation. One that will not serve her escape.

And escape she must. The blood, the rat, and thoughts of suffocating fill her with a darkening dread, and Dawsyn can't allow it. She has survived too much to be thwarted by walls and bars. She will survive this, too.

With a grunt she rights her posture, pushing her back from the wall. Her legs are stiff from too many dormant hours on cold stone, but she stands, and her stare finds the lock of the cell gate.

"This time, stubborn bastard."

She grips the rusted iron lock tightly. By now it is familiar. She closes her eyes, as one does in prayer, and she tunes out the smells, the voices. She forces a different string of thoughts to bind. She makes one singular bid loud enough to wake every molecule, calling to every corner of her body.

Summoning the magic.

Open! she thinks, shouts, pleads. *Open it!*

There. Slinking in the shadows of her being she feels it, dull and resistant. It does not crawl into her fingertips as it once did. Instead, it grips her edges and stays buried, a refute.

Dawsyn grinds her teeth. *Open the fucking gate.*

It doesn't. It grows ever distant, and she hears its silky voice as it turns away, breathing its answer back into her veins. *Release me.*

Go! she says, pushing, shoving at it. *Unlock it!*

The magic merely quivers. A laugh. A taunt.

Dawsyn shrieks. The sound clangs off the walls and ceiling, and her hands pound on the gate.

"DO IT! NOW!"

But she has lost sight of it. The magic has retreated into her depths, and it won't rise at will. She pants and shudders and continues gripping the iron, cursing and lashing and suffocating in her ire. She is aflame with it.

It's a mockery, the way her cheeks flush and her palms sweat. She has rarely known heat her whole life – born and raised on the icy Ledge, grappling for warmth. Now she burns. Her mind is fire. It rages.

But this fire – the *anger* – is preferable. It is a distraction, at least. While it scorches her from the inside out, it keeps other thoughts at bay. She'd rather stay there, burning to ash in her own inferno, but the fire is short lived. It chokes out quickly, and without it, she is left in the wake of all that she knows.

She has learnt this much in the past days of her imprisonment: when the fire ebbs, the drowning comes.

So it does now.

Her fingers, torn from their efforts on the lock, slowly slacken. Her shrieks become howls and her body folds to the ground again, her forehead resting on a wrung of the gate.

Ryon, she thinks again, only this time she is too weak to banish the name. Instead, she lets it come, she turns it over. Her howls turn to whispers; she feels the pain in her throat and does not try to swallow it. Tears make tracks through the blood on her face, and she barely notices how they blur her sight. She thinks of all the fights and enemies and words and touches and cannot make sense of them, cannot force them into straight lines or sequences she recognises. So, she drowns.

No wood to cut. No adversary to fight. No task to raise her from the bottom of herself. Just this unending cycle of grief. A different prison from the one she escaped.

She turns her gaze to the rat, red-eyed and rotting. "What can I do?" she whispers. "Please... tell me what to do."

Chapter Two

As a child, Dawsyn's grandmother told her tales.

When the Ledge hosted those blizzards of the hostile season and even the most keenly tended fire could not curb the cold, the stories would. Dawsyn learnt to stay the frost by letting it claim her body, but never her mind.

Within the mind is where the cold wins.

"Still your teeth, Dawsyn," her grandmother would warn her. "That mouth of yours rattles louder than a bag of coin."

Another strange word she did not know. She used to make a list of them – alien words that came often yet meant nothing: coin, mouse, clover, Terrsaw, drug, mint, pasture, tide, iskra…

"Dawsyn, sit with me, girl. I'll take those teeth out myself if you cannot quiet them."

Dawsyn slammed her jaw shut and frowned insolently. Still, she scurried over the wooden floor and into her grandmother's lap, the promise of warmth too great.

"There. Now, keep it out," she said, tapping Dawsyn's temple. "It isn't alive, after all. Is it, now?"

Dawsyn pushed the finger away. "I want a story."

"You've got some blasted manners."

"*Hush,*" Briar begged from where she sat before the hearth. Dawsyn's guardian – the only mother she knew – rocked a sleeping baby in her arms. Maya was only a month old and had already known a week of blizzards.

"All right then. Quietly now. Which story?"

"The one of the water."

"River, or ocean?"

"The ocean!" Dawsyn called, and earnt a scowl from Briar.

"Again?" Valma groaned, yet pulled her closer. She let Dawsyn's cold cheek rest against her chest. Dawsyn's teeth were quiet now. "So be it. Close your eyes, my Dawsyn. How will you see the water otherwise?"

And Dawsyn closed her eyes willingly, awaiting the familiar tale.

"In the valley is a river, a great channel of water that flows off the mountain and over ground. It cut a path through the forest a long time ago. If you keep pace with the water, it will take you to the edge."

"The edge of the world?" Dawsyn asked blearily.

"The edge of *our* world." Valma said. "A great big bowl, so gigantic it stretches as far as the bird flies. You cannot see where it ends. And at the bottom of the bowl rests Garjum – the ocean's prisoner. A huge creature with seven faces and forty arms."

"You said fifty last time."

"Fifty then, stubborn child." Valma's hand came to rest on Dawsyn's other cheek to warm it. "Garjum did not always live in the water. Once, before humans lived, he walked the ground. But a great storm brought a wave that reached the sky and crashed into the forests, up the mountain, and dragged Garjum back into the ocean's belly. It never let him go. Garjum has lived there ever since. He still tries each day to reach the land. He uses his mighty arms to grab the shore, pulling at the water, but the ocean is too strong. Each time Garjum pulls the tide back, the ocean breaks away, and the waves crash back onto the shore again. Garjum and the ocean battle over and over, even after thousands of years.

Still, Garjum never surrenders. Each day he wakes in that prison and faces the battle once more. He knows that each pull of the tide is one closer to reaching the ground. Each fight he loses, is one less until victory."

"Why does Garjum not want to live in the ocean? It sounds beautiful," Dawsyn mumbled.

"Beautiful? What about it sounds so beautiful?"

"It's blue," Dawsyn said. "And not frozen. I wish I could see it."

"Perhaps someday you will."

Dawsyn turned her face to her grandmother. "And Garjum?"

"And Garjum," Valma nodded.

Dawsyn seemed to consider for a moment, her eyes heavy. Then she turned back into her grandmother's arms, burrowing down in her hold. "Garjum might give up by then."

"Nonsense," Valma told her, smiling thinly. "Garjum does not belong in the ocean. All things find a way back to their home."

Even young Dawsyn knew what a lie that was. How many people had disappeared over the Chasm or into it? Not one had walked out again. But the words, true or not, did their job and Dawsyn slept, cradled against Valma before the hearth while the wind battered the Ledge outside. It would be seventeen years before Dawsyn found the ground, found the kingdom of Terrsaw, saw the ocean. It would take a little longer though, for her to realise that her grandmother, the crown princess of Terrsaw, was right after all.

She would find a way back home.

CHAPTER THREE

Even with her title, Ruby is not permitted to wander the palace at will. The guards at each entry will not allow even the captain of the guard to pass without Queen Alvira's permission. She trained them as such. The kitchens, she taught them, are the only exception.

Ruby lifts the visor of her helm. Beneath, her eyes show the wear of long days, and even longer nights. The guards, every one of them, are walking the line between exhaustion and duty. Since the night Dawsyn Sabar and her Glacian friend returned to the palace, the Queen has ordered more sentries, more archers, more presence throughout the Mecca than ever before. Ruby has had little time to sleep between her watches, recruit training, strategizing meetings, and, though it risks her position, slipping extra food to a certain prisoner.

She does away with her helm altogether and rubs her hands against her much-abused brown cheeks. The places where the body armour presses against her bones smart. Her feet are blistered and bandaged. Her head is heavy.

"Look after this, will you?" she says to one of the cooks, placing her helm on a chopping board. The palace kitchens are below ground, and thus, the Queens rarely venture near. Ruby and some of her more trusted comrades often find sanctuary

16

within its humid walls, stealing morsels from the cooks and resting their legs.

One such cook nods to Ruby as she swipes an unattended serving tray from the counter. "And where yeh be taking that tray, miss?" asks Darius.

"Never you mind."

"That be for Queen Cressida. You gon' make her go hungry?"

Ruby scoffs. "Her majesty has yet to spend a single moment hungry."

"Then you'll make a poor man double his labour?" Darius whines, his forehead spotted with soot from the brick ovens. Ruby has come to pilfer a tray every day for a week, and she knows for a fact that he purposefully left this one out for her. A man with a missing ear and barely enough words to string together, but detrimentally kind. Ruby has taken advantage, of late.

"Leave off, Darius. These feet haven't had respite in a year. I've earnt the meals of ten Queens."

"You ain't eating no Queens' meals. You be scurrying to the dungeons to feed that Ledge woman!"

"*Shut up!*" Ruby spits, her eyes wheeling to the other cooks. Thankfully they are too absorbed in their tasks to notice. "I hear you speaking lies like that again and you won't have a tongue left to tell them!" she hisses.

Darius smiles, the gaps in his mouth more prominent than usual. "Aye. Stop yer squealing, Ruby. I ain't gon' tell nobody. Just you be careful, sneaking round underground where you ought not be. And I ain't looking after no helm. Take it with yeh. You never know who be waiting to knock yer head off." Darius winks.

Ruby smiles at him. As captain, she should reprimand him, remind him of his place, but she finds when it comes to friends, her authority takes its leave. Ruby pats him on the shoulder, replaces her helm to her head, and leaves with her Queen's supper tray in her hands.

She takes the stairwell to the dungeon at a torturous pace, stepping as lightly as her garb allows. The armour at her thighs and chest clatters nonetheless and the sound is lobbed from wall to wall, higher and higher. There is nothing so indiscreet as a Terrsaw guard. Queen Alvira and her wife, Queen Cressida, will be in their living quarters at this time of night; but still, Ruby grows nervous. She thinks of her years of training, the years of grovelling and grinding in a world made for men. The small tray in her hands could very well make all that for naught, should someone become wise to it.

And still, she carries it. She descends the steps into the dank and the dark – to the woman of the Ledge, the one with the name of a royal. But by no means do the girl's current holdings infer anything of the sort.

A guard stands sentry before the gate to the cells, half asleep and slumped, but when Ruby rounds the corner, the man straightens. It is Grayson, this evening.

"C-Captain?"

"Grayson. Your meal is going cold in the kitchens. I thought you might be starved to death by now."

"Aye, but who will–"

"I'll take my supper here while you are gone. I could use the quiet."

Grayson sighs in obvious relief. "Aye. My thanks, Captain. I'll not be too long." He takes a set of bronze keys from his belt as he speaks, thrusting them into her waiting palm.

"Take your time," Ruby mutters, and waits for the guard to pass. Once Grayson's clamour on the stairwell no longer echoes, she scowls. Sometimes, she wonders if they are too easily persuaded. Perhaps she did not train them as well as she thinks.

Ruby opens the gate with care, balancing the tray and keys both. Inside, the keep is separated into several cells and only one is occupied.

Dawsyn Sabar sleeps in the corner of her confines, her neck bent at a painful angle. She still wears the garb she returned to the palace in a week before, only now it is a patchwork of stains. Her hair covers her face in knotted, black ropes. Opened knuckles. Fingernails missing. Each day, Ruby comes to find the girl has worsened. Each day, the captain feels sicker for it.

A Sabar, they say. A *real* Sabar. Ruby cannot help but look for assurances that it could be true. Her bone structure, brown eyes, black hair. She supposes they resemble that of the Sabar portraits that still adorn the palace walls. Ruby has stared at them a thousand times.

It is a miracle. The bloodline survives, and its survivor sits in a cell of her own palace, fading into something small.

Ruby finds it… uncomfortable. Each night, when she returns to her barracks knowing that a Sabar lives as a prisoner below ground, her mattress becomes one of thorns. Whatever skerrick of peace might be possible is thwarted by the resounding calls that echo through the alleys and laneways of the Mecca. News of Dawsyn Sabar's escape from the Ledge has been passed from ear to ear, and the people are rallying, desperate for the palace to confirm it. She hears them celebrating in the streets, swamping the palace gates, and calling for her to be brought forth. It turns Ruby's stomach to think of what they might do, should they learn the truth.

Sleep evades her. She wonders what will become of the girl – a girl who lived and grew as an offering to Glacians in her place, and in the place of every other Terrsaw citizen who was not born to such an unfortunate providence. How will she reconcile with herself should the Queens grow tired of keeping her? Queens who seem so ready to cast aside a miracle as unlikely as a true living Sabar. Ruby grew up with parents who prayed to the fallen king and his lost daughter each night; they would be ashamed of her now, to know she could only offer the last living Sabar a meal and no more.

"Miss Sabar," Ruby calls, letting the tray clatter on the iron rungs of the gate.

The woman jolts upward, her stricken face finding Ruby's

immediately, her feet already beneath her again, ready. An animal stirred by threat.

Impressive.

Ruby clears her throat. "Supper."

Dawsyn sags again. Her body rocking back to the floor.

Ruby slides the tray through the trap door and locks it shut again. The sound makes her cringe, but she shrugs it away and nods to the side. "There is a dead rat in the corner."

Dawsyn's expression remains unchanged. "It was being impolite."

The captain grimaces. Hesitates. "I could smell it from the stairwell."

"I assure you it smells only half as bad as me." Dawsyn gives herself a dispassionate glance.

She is a strange woman. Alien. Even removed from the garb and setting of a prisoner, Ruby imagines she would still note the differences between them. She is a contrast of sharpness and serration. Brutally defined in her movements. There is a clarity to her, even dulled as she is here. But even caged and reduced, Ruby suspects that an entire spectrum of instinct lurks beneath her surface. She is dangerous – it is immediately obvious to anyone with sense. Ruby suspects that surviving the Ledge would have required much more than mere aggression. She would need ruthless resolve, strategy, near-constant vigilance. Ruby can see all the facets of her savagery, and all that it took to hone it.

Dawsyn eyes the tray warily. "Do the Queen's prisoners usually receive two hot meals a day? If so, do not tell the people of Terrsaw. I suspect some would take desperate measures to acquire such privilege. No labour, and more food than one might ever see." Even her words are serrated. Calculated. Precise cuts to draw measured blood.

Ruby grimaces. She grew up on the fringe of the Mecca. She knows missed meals like the back of her sword. "Perhaps I find you intriguing."

"I'd try not to, Captain," Dawsyn says dully. "The last person I intrigued was dead soon after."

An image of the hybrid upon the throne room floor invades Ruby's mind. She still cannot fathom it, how this fierce woman – a Sabar, a prisoner of the Ledge – came to accompany a Glacian.

"Eat," Ruby mutters.

Dawsyn moves on her hands and knees to the tray and settles before it. Whatever pride she once used to straighten her spine before the Queens is now gone. She sits at Ruby's feet on the other side of the grid, eating potatoes from her fingers.

"Why do you come, Captain?" Dawsyn asks. "Will your conscience rest easy if I'm well fed before they kill me?"

Ruby tarries again. The girl has a propensity for bluntness, and it makes her stumble. If she's honest with herself, Ruby can admit the woman intimidates her. It does nothing to quicken her wits.

Ruby wants to think that Queen Alvira will come to her senses, but she must concede the unlikeliness of it. Those terrible things the Queen had said in the throne room still ring in her ears. Still keep her from sleep.

Such joy you would have brought the masses had they known you existed, had they known you had been brought to them. Those fools bow to the memory of your ancestors like they were gods. They would have supported you.

True words, but spat out like venom. Ruby had not recognised the voice behind them, had never seen Alvira's face crease with such hatred. A Queen who had erected monuments to the Sabars, led prayers for their resting souls. Two different Queens. Ruby has tried and failed to consolidate them. There is too much she does not know. Too much that no one will speak of. Ruby is the captain of the guard and no more than that. She has no business knowing more. Her only business should be protecting the Queens, the palace, Terrsaw.

And this night, Queen Alvira believes the kingdom's biggest threat sits here, eating potatoes.

"You may live yet," Ruby says, though the words are hollow. "No plans have been sanctioned for your execution."

Dawsyn actually laughs, bits of potato on her lips.

Ruby grabs the rungs with both hands. "You're a fool, Miss Sabar."

"How so?"

Ruby looks incredulous. "I know the Queens offered you a deal, *a way out*. Yet you refused them?"

"Yes."

Ruby slaps her hands to the bars. "*Why?*"

No answer comes. Dawsyn simply stares at Ruby. Calculating. Calculating.

The captain growls in frustration. "Then if you die in here, it is of your *own* doing."

Dawsyn leaps then, like a mountain cat – sharp and undefined, both at once. One moment she is hunched on the floor, next she has her eyes levelled with Ruby's, hands clenching the rungs. They clang threateningly with the sudden impact, making the captain lurch away.

"*No*," Dawsyn implores, her eyes rounding in their intensity. "Not my doing. The deeds were done long before I lived, *Captain*."

Ruby swallows. "Perhaps, but there is no changing them. The people on the Ledge will remain there whether you take the deal or not. You cannot liberate them in death."

Dawsyn says her words with exactness, each one a thin blade pricking her skin. "Nor can I liberate them while chained to the Queens."

"They do not *wish* to chain you," Ruby answers, exasperated. If she can just make her *listen*. If she can just make her see reason. "They are *afraid* of you. Afraid of the Glacians. But you could persuade them… prove otherwise."

Dawsyn shakes her head, sighing deeply, as though her

words are wasted exertions. "You do not strike me as a simple woman, Captain," she says, backing away from the grid. "You know as I do; they do not want my advice."

"I am the *captain of the guard*. I'd claim to know more about the Queens I serve than *you* do."

Dawsyn huffs a laugh once more, but her face is drained, drawn. "I am sure it comforts you to think so."

Ruby lifts her chin. "By all means, Sabar, please tell me what I do not know. You speak often, but say very little."

Dawsyn turns razor eyes on Ruby again, and it makes the captain blanch. Something inexplicable begs Ruby to avert her gaze – the dark depths of them, unflinching, bottomless.

"They fear me," Dawsyn intones.

Ruby sighs. "That I know."

"No." Dawsyn shakes her head. "You do not. Your Queens do not fear what havoc I may reign down upon Terrsaw. They fear I will take the crowns from their heads."

Ruby frowns. "They fear the Glacians, Miss Sabar. They vowed to protect the kingdom at all costs."

"All costs," Dawsyn murmurs, "have already been paid."

"They believe you and the half-Glacian, Ryon," – Dawsyn's fists clench at the name – "would bring the Glacians here, to Terrsaw. We cannot allow that to happen. These mixed-blooded Glacians... they can live in the warmth where the others cannot. They could very well come to conquer. That is why Queen Alvira keeps you here. She believes you would go to Glacia, tell them that Ryon was slain by our Queen, and lead them down to the valley. They could win a war easily, Miss Sabar. I am sure you well know it. I trained this army myself, but I am not fool enough to pretend we would not be decimated in a battle."

"Queen Alvira wants you to believe that the mixed-bloods are no different from the pure."

"Are they so different?"

"They are," Dawsyn says without pause. "They have no

desire, no need to swoop in and steal humans from the valley. They are free from King Vasteel's tyranny, just as we are, just as those on the Ledge are." Dawsyn's glare is murderous. "And yet the Queens have no interest in allying with them to save their own people."

"So, take the Queens' deal," Ruby presses, frustrated. "Persuade them!"

Dawsyn seems to consider her for a moment, her shoulders slumped, defeated. She sighs, turning away from Ruby. "They do not wish to listen," she says lowly. "They wish to silence me. Soon they will realise they cannot."

"Then *pretend*," Ruby hisses, her voice echoing despite it. "Just *pretend*... and live. Is that not better?"

Dawsyn lies down again, curling onto her side. "You still haven't explained yourself. Why do you come down here, Captain? You needn't. My death will not be on your hands."

Ruby's tongue sits dry and reluctant. She unsticks it from the roof of her mouth. "My parents... they idolised your ancestors, your grandmother. What would they think of me, knowing I helped keep you prisoner here?"

A silence stretches between them, but in the darkness, Ruby sees Dawsyn frown, sees her eyes shut, and though pain is absent in her voice, it is clear on her face. "I cannot sit quiet and do as Alvira wishes while those on the Ledge slip into the Chasm."

Ruby groans, smacks her hand against the iron as she turns to leave. "Your arrogance will be what kills you."

"Your Queen will be what kills me."

Ruby halts, desperation causing her to try one more time. "Unless she has your allegiance!"

"I will sooner die than kneel."

There is no swaying her. Ruby sees it in the jut of Dawsyn's chin, the pinch between brows.

"Then you shall die," the captain tells her. Ruby stalks quickly from the keep, ignoring the slow churn of her stomach.

CHAPTER FOUR

Her Majesty, the Queen of Terrsaw, observes the girl on the floor with something akin to desperation.

She is not *desperate*, of course. True leaders cannot afford to be – and she is, in fact, the truest.

The girl sleeps, or rather, she pretends to. Queen Alvira would like to think it is out of fear but knows better. The girl pretends to sleep in the Queen's presence out of petulance.

A dangerous prospect.

"Dawsyn, dear?"

The girl remains unmoving. It is… irksome.

"My apologies for disturbing you. I've come with gifts." One of the guards shadowing her brings forward a pile of fine fabrics and unlocks the gate. He places them inside and Alvira's nose wrinkles as the finery is laid upon the grime-laden stone.

The opening of the gate does not stir Dawsyn Sabar. No attempt at escape. Not a slither of curiosity.

Irritated, Alvira clears her throat. "Clothes, my dear. You could use more. We cannot soak in the blood of our past lovers for too long."

A twitch. Alvira cannot see the girl's face, but she imagines her eyes have snapped open. The Queen smiles. A thread to pull.

"It must hurt, knowing that the bothersome creature very nearly brought about *your* death as well."

A flex of the girl's shoulders.

"Even more so, to think that you cannot hate him for it, now that he is gone."

The prisoner pushes her upper body from the ground. Her face slowly turns. She glares at the Queen. Burns her. She is little more than a *child* with the stare of an ancient. A detail that hasn't escaped Alvira's notice. An... unfortunate detail.

"Or perhaps you've realised your own mistakes? The ones that led to Ryon's death–"

"Enough," Dawsyn Sabar calls clearly, stronger than Alvira would have expected or preferred. The Queen had ordered her to be fed sparsely, to weaken her. She knows from experience that it is difficult to persuade the sturdy and able-bodied.

"Come now, girl. You are old enough to know that deadly games earn deadly prizes, and the games you... *participated* in with that half-breed were as ill-advised as trying to murder a Queen."

"Stop."

"Did you think you would find love with him, dear? Safety? Did the two of you plot to take this palace from me? I did you a favour, Dawsyn. That accursed boy would have killed you eventually. You should be thankful I killed him firs–"

"All right! Stop, please." Dawsyn rises to her feet. Legs unwilling, she approaches the cell door, her hands up.

Queen Alvira smiles at her captive's slumped posture. *It is not so difficult*, she thinks, *to break a person.*

Dawsyn stops before her on the other side of the grid where the stack of clothes lies. She exhales, and with it, the rest of her resolve seems to leak away. The grime on her face reminds Alvira of the street urchins in the Mecca. *How quickly pride fades when you cage it.*

Dawsyn finally looks up at her, but instead of having the decency to look ashamed, she smiles and tilts her head. "I am embarrassed for you. Did you really think I'd break if you poked me?" She laughs then, low and tired. "Could you think of no more creative means of persuasion? People like you always resort to baiting."

The Queen's cheeks turn hot. *People like me?* she thinks. She blinks in polite confusion, though the back of her throat feels scorched, aflame with ire. "There *are* no people like me, dear. I am the Queen of Terrsaw."

Dawsyn grins. "You are a *thief.* Wearing a crown you stole won't make you more than that."

"I've given my life to this kingdom, you insidious girl!"

"No, you have given other people's lives – an entire *village.* And then you demanded that those who remained kneel to you."

"I am the reason *anyone* still remains!" Queen Alvira's voice echoes off the walls and back to her; she hears how shrill her voice has become, raking her throat as it bellows out. Her hands grip the iron bars before her, the rust biting into her palms. She does not remember placing them there.

And Dawsyn smiles still. "Look at that," she says. "Perhaps there *is* some merit to baiting."

The Queen fights to slow her breath, her skin aflame. "I do not have time for children's games, Dawsyn. And neither do you."

"By all means, you can see yourself out."

"Your execution has been set for tomorrow," the Queen continues, savouring the pleasure of watching the girl's jaw tighten. *There,* she thinks. *That's better.* "You will be hung before the people of Terrsaw, Dawsyn Sabar, for attempting to assassinate your Queen."

Dawsyn raises an eyebrow. "Is that why you have brought me these fine threads? Do you prefer to hang only the presentable?"

"You'll hang naked if you must, Dawsyn. It is no concern of mine how you die." There, the truth between them. Alvira lets it linger, lets her see how very small she is in her world. But not so small in the minds of others, unfortunately. "What

I've brought you, however, is an alternative. I could give you a life within these walls the likes of which you've never imagined. Clothes, banquets, your own quarters, guards, companions–"

"The very same thing you've offered me each day for a week."

"And is it not better than a snapped neck?"

Dawsyn considers the pile of clothes. "Tell me, Your Majesty, when did the people of Terrsaw learn of it?"

The Queen stills. "Learn of what?"

"That the last living descendant of the Sabars is a prisoner in your dungeon."

A silence stretches between the two women – one waiting, one calculating.

The girl knows far more than the Queen can allow, but who has informed her?

"You do not need to behead your guards, Alvira," Dawsyn intones, reading and interrupting her thoughts. "No one has betrayed you. The chanting on the streets echoes into my cell. It grows louder each day. It is why you've kept me alive, is it not? People are growing mutinous, or so it sounds. They're demanding to see me, to know how I escaped the Ledge. Stop me if I'm wrong." Her voice lilts at the end.

Denial is useless, the Queen decides. "They do not know you are a prisoner, Dawsyn. Only a guest. But, yes. They are… eager to see you." Eager is a vague substitution for the rallying feelings stirring in the Mecca. Restless was a better term. Disquieted, perhaps.

Dawsyn waits, those unsettling eyes tunnelling into the Queen, as though she were the one standing in rags and covered in blood.

"Do you see the unrest you cause, simply by being here?" the Queen continues, testing a different route, another way around the wretched girl. "And you are just one person. Imagine the upheaval if every soul on the Ledge were brought down the mountain."

"And what would you have me tell them, Your Majesty?" Dawsyn asks. "I'm curious."

The Queen does not dare grow hopeful. "You could tell them the truth," she says. "Tell them how you escaped. Tell them about the pool and the *iskra* if you must. But do not give them hope that the threat is gone. Do not give them hope that others on the Ledge can be liberated."

"Because you fear them," Dawsyn interjects. "Imagine what my people will do to you, when they learn you sold them like cattle."

The Queen says nothing for a time. She has, in fact, imagined what they might do. She has imagined a great many things, more times than Dawsyn Sabar could fathom. She has thought of every choice before her and the consequences of their inception. She has mapped each course forward and divined the paths that will etch themselves in a thousand directions, spawning a constellation of different endings, and there are very few that leave the Queen any better than she was before this iniquitous girl fell off that ledge and stumbled into her kingdom. "You will be brought before the town at dawn and accused of treason," the Queen tells Dawsyn now. "We will tell the people how life on the Ledge corrupted you, broke you. I will tell them you brought a Glacian inside the palace walls and the two of you tried to assassinate the Queens, and they will cheer as they watch you die." This last word reverberates from the stone ceiling, and she senses a guard shifting uneasily behind her. "Or, you can live. You can shut your damned mouth and look to the future. You can help me build a stronger kingdom, one properly prepared for battle should the mixed-blooded Glacians swoop into our valley."

Dawsyn collects the clothes from the floor, running a hand over the silken threads despite the muck caked upon them.

"Death," she says, "is preferable."

CHAPTER FIVE

Dawsyn is awake long before the guards come to collect her. The darkness of the dungeon does not allow for her to know the time; dawn seems to take an age to arrive.

Finally, the clanging of armour echoes down the stairwell and the iron gate rattles violently as it opens.

"Miss Sabar?"

The guards insist on calling her that. All seem reluctant to speak down to her, as one would expect of a captor to their captive. Even this, the simple rousing, is laced with hesitation.

Dawsyn looks her last at her dead-rat companion, its beady eyes long since dulled, and stands, legs aching. The chill of this cell does not come close to matching that of her home on the Ledge, yet it still feels cruel – that she should be born cold and die just the same.

She sighs and rubs her gritty hands against her gritty shirt.

The guards – four of them, Ruby included – stand before her cell. Their garb differs today. Ruby's chest plate bears the Terrsaw emblem: a sword splitting a mountain in two. A farce. The other guards have red embossed on their helms.

"Well," Dawsyn says. "You all look very shiny."

Despite the deep lines of her furrow, the captain's lips twitch. It quickly fades. Dawsyn watches Ruby swallow, a lump travelling the length of her throat. The spark of anger Dawsyn saw in her, admired her for, is now gone. It is a different strain that creases her forehead now. The captain holds her chin and shoulders like that of an admiral, but every other facet of her says something else entirely.

I am sorry, she mouths to Dawsyn, some unfathomable loyalty compelling her to do so, and Dawsyn suddenly feels responsible for whatever burden this woman carries for her fate. Of all the people that should shoulder the blame for her demise, Dawsyn is angered that this captain, a woman who has only carried out her duties and shown Dawsyn compassion, should be the one to feel its weight.

Ruby's hands tremble as she unlocks the cell door and slides the grid open.

Dawsyn reaches out into the open space and grips Ruby's fingers. The guards at the captain's back hasten to action, their own hands gripping Dawsyn's forearm, her shoulders. The sounds of their drawn swords fill the stale air.

But Dawsyn only squeezes Ruby's hand, a woman who has little need to be concerned with a prisoner like her.

Ruby's eyes, now afraid, meet Dawsyn's.

"You were kind, when you needn't have been," Dawsyn tells her. "This is not your doing." For a moment, their eyes simply linger on each other, intangible missives passing between them, and then Dawsyn's hands are tugged away by the guards.

Ruby shivers as Dawsyn is pulled back. She squeezes her eyes shut a moment, but when they open once more, resolve shrouds her. "Bring the shackles," she says clearly.

The guards work quickly to secure Dawsyn's wrists and ankles, and then they are guiding her out of the cell, up the stairwell. For the first time in weeks, the light leaks down to her, growing brighter as they climb. *At least there is this*, Dawsyn thinks – golden light drenching her just once more before she dies, making her forget the cold.

The path is long and twisting. Each step brings the taste

of fear on her tongue. It is useless to fear, she knows. Soon, every terror, every memory, every feeling will be snuffed, but looming death has a tenacity for dredging up every dark and terrible thought from the depths of the mind.

She hopes her neck snaps on impact. It is the most rational fear she can cling to. The idea of slowly choking makes her gag. The crowd watching her body rotate in a slow circle, her body twitching in vain, clawing for its next breath…

Perhaps Queen Alvira will sully her name with lies and the people of Terrsaw will stone her to death instead. Perhaps they will break through the guards and lunge straight for her throat. Anything seems preferable to suffocating by degrees.

Despairingly, not even these, the last desperate minutes of her life, are enough to rouse the dormant magic within her. As the guards lead her through the dark passages of the palace, she calls to it, over and over. And though she can find it, feel it curled into its corner, she senses how heavy it is, how tired. She cannot lift it.

The passage curves again, and at its end is a portcullis to a courtyard, dusty and bare but for the gallows that wait ahead and the jostling crowd before it. The guards stop before the portcullis, waiting as it rattles upward into its cavity above.

The courtyard falls silent.

Dawsyn's breath hitches.

"Ready?" Ruby whispers.

Dawsyn does not answer. How can one ever be truly ready to die?

The people on the Ledge are still trapped.

The pool in Glacia still churns.

Ryon. *Ryon.*

Ryon's death remains unavenged.

And there it is, that flood of grief that has tried valiantly to consume her. That sorrow for a man who has not earnt her last thoughts in the moments before she dies. But something in her still welcomes the memory of his touch along her jaw, the feel of his lips on her forehead. And if she's to die this day, then resistance is pointless. She closes her eyes to better see his face and is, for once, not perturbed by the copious tears that overcome her.

Perhaps there is sanctuary to be found in those gallows. She can finally follow the ones who left her here alone, and cross that unseeable bridge. Perhaps they will be there, waiting.

The guards lead her forward, slowing their gait to allow her shackled feet to keep pace.

Thousands of faces turn to see her, chained and dirty, her eyes squinting against the harsh sun. Beyond the crowd is the Mecca, now emptied of its people. So many of them, here in this desolate corner.

Dirt starts to collect between her toes. It occurs to her that this is the first time she has felt earth beneath her bare feet. She cannot even linger on the strange way it yields. There are so many things that will remain mysterious to her now. So many corners and facets of this world undiscovered.

The crowd continues its silence as she passes, the gallows looming ever nearer. When she blinks the dust away, Dawsyn can make out the people around her but cannot discern their demeanour. Are they curious? Remorseful? Exultant? What do they think of her, this escapee of the Ledge? Do they wish to see her dead?

As the captain leads their assemblage forward, the crowd parts to her presence alone. She leads the way through, her chin lifted, but Dawsyn can still see the way her hand trembles.

An eternity passes before they reach the steps. As it draws nearer, Dawsyn's heart beats in protest, crashing against her ribs. She takes the steps awkwardly, her shackles a hindrance. The guards have to lift her to the platform, and once upon it, the nausea swells.

Help me, she calls inward, desperate, afraid. *Help me.*

But the magic is as trapped as her. She can feel how it sticks to the sides, mired in fear.

Beneath the noose, the woman who escaped the Ledge is turned to face the crowd – scarred, barefooted. Wild.

Dawsyn finally sees them: the faces of the Mecca. Women in aprons and shawls and coats with shiny buttons. Men with dirty hands and clean faces. Gaunt cheeks next to fed bellies. Parents with children at their feet, on their hips, in their arms. People bent with age and illness, and yet they all are here, wide-eyed.

Confused.

Disturbed.

Enraged.

She can feel, then, why they have come. It is not to spectate.

A short horn sounds from above, and for a moment, Dawsyn is transported back to the slopes, running through a blizzard with Glacians at her heels. That sound always forewarns disaster.

The Queens, Alvira and Cressida both, appear on a balcony, the only one jutting from this corner of the palace walls. The silver threads of their dresses catch the sun and glisten. Queen Alvira's hands clasp gently before her stomach, a ring per finger. She meets the gaze of her people, a perfected mix of duty and contrition.

How Dawsyn wishes she could pull her over that banister.

The crowd turns their attention to their monarch, and the guards hold their right hands over their hearts in her presence. Dawsyn waits, eyes straight ahead.

"To the good people of Terrsaw," Queen Alvira calls, her voice ringing from those plum-stained lips. "Today we mourn, for before you stands a miracle: Dawsyn Sabar, the granddaughter of Valma, the fallen princess of Terrsaw."

A rumble spreads amongst the people, one of awe, and one of impatience. *So, it is true,* they seem to say. *A Sabar.*

"But that is not all she is… She is also a murderer."

Dawsyn's head whips to the balcony.

"Miss Sabar escaped by making a deal with a Glacian, and it

was this same beast that helped her away from the Ledge and led her to Terrsaw. But this was not before she killed some of her own people on the Ledge who would have stopped her. *Our* people. Our fallen ones."

The crowd stiffens in increments, growing stunned, then appalled.

Clever, Dawsyn thinks, watching the throng as it shifts. She waits for their shock to subside, for the fury to take hold.

"Miss Sabar and her Glacian were welcomed into the palace, and they turned their swords on us too. This girl came to take the crown for herself. She may bear the Sabar name, but she has inherited none of the virtue of her family long since passed. I am sure she has suffered much on the Ledge... and I fear it has corrupted her."

Dawsyn remembers the day she swept through the streets of the Mecca, the patrons backing away as she passed them with a blade in her hand, her face etched in murderous rage. She closes her eyes in defeat.

"I had wished, as you all did, that her presence would bring us hope. But I cannot allow you all to suffer under the pretence that others might find their way off that forsaken mountain. This girl is not our miracle. She is a monster, and I banished monsters from our lands long ago."

The Queen turns to her wife, and Cressida reaches out with trained movements, to place her hand in Alvira's. "We will protect you, our people, at all costs," she proclaims, her voice thundering over the heads of her countrymen, ringing down the streets of the Mecca beyond. "Prepare her," the Queen calls, her voice lower, softer once more. A well-executed trick.

Dawsyn is shunted backward. Suddenly her feet are stumbling over the loose timber of a trapdoor, and a ring of heavy rope falls over her shoulders. Automatically she lifts her hands to pull the rope away, but the shackles tug painfully at her wrists, and she cannot stop the guards from cinching the noose around her throat. *Wait*, she thinks. *Not yet.*

"Who was the informant?" a voice shouts from the crowd.

Quiet descends once more. Even Dawsyn's heart stops to hear it speak again.

"Who knew o' her misdeeds on the Ledge? How did yeh learn of it?"

The Queen squints down into the crowd, her jaw taut. "Who speaks?"

"I do." And from the crowd steps Salem.

Dawsyn's breath stutters. Her throat closes.

Salem, his nose reddened and bulbous as ever, his paunch prominent and height more so. He stares, steely eyed up at his Queen.

Stop, Salem, she thinks, panicked to see him there alone. *Please, be quiet.*

"I'll ask again. How could yeh know anythin' o' the Ledge?" Salem bellows to all, but his eyes are fastened on Dawsyn's.

"Don't!" Dawsyn shouts at him, her head shaking. "Salem–"

"Seize him," the Queen says calmly, regretfully. "I will have no man nor woman corrupted by this girl."

Guards descend on Salem, pulling his arms to his back, pushing him to the ground.

"NO!" Dawsyn shouts.

"He only asks a question!" someone calls, a voice Dawsyn does not recognise. "For what reason will he be detained?"

The crowd rumbles. More shouts. A woman, tears streaming down her face, clutches a baby and yells, "Show us this Glacian! Show us!"

"The girl may know a way up the slopes!" another calls.

"SILENCE!" the Queen roars, but it does nothing. The crowd is roiling, the undercurrent shifting. Their clamour begins to fill the air. Fists rise, bodies shift with agitation.

"Let her live!" Some call.

"Grant her pardon!"

"A Sabar has returned to us!"

The crowd converges, moving closer to the platform, to the

palace walls. And all the while their demands unify to become a single chant – the same call Dawsyn heard from her dungeon cell, the call that could not be drowned out by earth or stone.

Bring her home!

Bring her home!

BRING HER HOME!

"PULL THE LEVER!" Queen Alvira calls, her eyes wide with alarm, spit flying from her lips.

There is no sound to reach Dawsyn's ears beyond the tumult of the people, the screams of the women, and shouts from the men. The floor disappears from beneath her feet, and she falls into the dark space below.

Before the noose snaps taut, she meets the eyes of the Queen, feels her blood slither with hate. She gives a silent promise of revenge, in whatever form she may take in the afterlife.

CHAPTER SIX

She dangles.

The noose does not break her neck like she'd hoped. There is nothing to hear anymore and nothing to see. Vessels in her eyes have given way to strain, her airways are crushed, and despite it, her body still fights for air. Her jaw struggles to open, her hands clench and release in vain. Where her mind has departed, the rest of her still claws for life uselessly.

Spasms take her chest first, then the rest of her. As she spins for the audience in a hapless circle, her body convulses and quakes until it begins to give in. The spasms slow. Her bare toes, earth-sodden, give their last twitch.

It is just as Dawsyn's body stills that the people of Terrsaw finally overrun the guards barricading the gallows. They swarm in a titanic wave, swallowing the shine and polish of the guardian's armour in one mighty heave. The guards fall below the crowd and not one of them raises a sword.

A woman, cloaked and slight, darts between the fists and feet and finds her way over the wooden platform, to where Dawsyn twirls and twirls at the end of the noose.

The mob behind riots, too busy to see the woman take her palm to the rope and snap it with nothing but a squeeze. They do not see how the trapdoor came to close itself again before Dawsyn Sabar could fall.

Dawsyn herself does not know how she came to be sprawled upon the wooden planks, her lungs gasping at the air, her head and palms and feet burning with the return of oxygen.

"Get up!" a hiss in her ear demands, "Now!"

And before she can, heavy fabric envelopes her, blankets her. It is tugged over her head, its hood bracketing her ears – a cloak. Hands pull at her underarms, heaving her to her feet.

"This way!" the voice hastens, deeper, more urgent than before, and Dawsyn stumbles forward, choking, eyes streaming. She pitches her body off the end of the platform, blood pounding back into her brain. The hands at her back thrust her along the outskirts of the crowd, where the young and the old spectate as the riot builds.

Together, the two women run the length of the courtyard walls and out into the Mecca, where the streets are hollow but for the sounds of rebellion at their backs, and not a person they pass stops to glance at the cloaked girl from the Ledge, now the girl missing from the noose.

Down the cobblestone alleys they run, their path adjacent to the palace. It towers over the Mecca's many roofs and spires. Dawsyn's legs and feet are leaden but somehow they move quickly, keeping pace with the dark figure who leads the way out.

Dawsyn's hood falls to her shoulders, but she cannot spare a moment to conceal herself again. What little she sees of faces pressed against windows pass too quickly. She does not know if those faces will recognise her, if they will reveal her escape to the Queens.

The road becomes nothing more than dirt, and soon the buildings begin to bunch, their roofs sagging. Dawsyn recognises the outskirts. Beyond, green fields unfold to the forest line and as she and her saviour sprint into the dew-slickened grass, the sun breaks through the cloud and meets Dawsyn's shoulders.

It takes only minutes to leave the Mecca behind. A handful of moments between death and freedom. Soon, she is far away from the castle and the courtyard, where a cloud of dust is stirring, mudding the Queen's face.

CHAPTER SEVEN

The bedlam in the courtyard only worsens as they meet less and less resistance. Already, the Queen's guards fall back, their shields just barely holding the people off.

Cut them down, Alvira thinks. *Just a few. Make an example. The rest will heed the warning.*

The balcony is not all that far from the ground. Any bastard could climb to it should they possess the gall.

A guard at Alvira's back pleads for her retreat inside the castle. "Your Grace," he implores. "Keep clear of the balustrade."

She ignores him. Her eyes flit between her subjects, raising their fists, their faces twisted and vehement. How ungrateful they all are. She should send them over the Boulder Gate. Let them see how they fare within reach of the very beasts she shields them from.

"Come, dear," says Cressida, taking Alvira's cold fingers in her hand. "Don't spare them a glance."

But the Queen of Terrsaw resists still. She hears the commands of her most favoured guard call for her soldiers to retreat. She watches them back into the safety of the palace gates, and a cold fear invades her.

How quickly it can all fall, she thinks.

Finally, Alvira turns her attention away from the mass of bodies, hands clenched around her bulbous rings, eyes glistening with rage. As she makes to leave, those eyes fall to the empty gallows, the cut rope swinging to the beat of her people's chants.

Bring her home!

Bring her home!

The girl.

The girl!

"Where is she?" snarls Cressida beside her.

"She's... gone," murmurs a guard, dumbfounded and useless.

But Alvira is already spinning, her skirts catching and tearing on the armour of the guards as she barrels past.

"Find her!" she shouts. And then another order: "And bring me that iskra witch!"

CHAPTER EIGHT

The high cornstalks snatch at the skin of her cheeks. The soles of Dawsyn's bare feet are laced with shallow cuts as they crush the broken shoots.

Will the guards come already?

Will the mob buy her a moment more?

The forest line is ahead, over the last knoll. There, the grass will not claw at her face, but the forest floor will prove even more unforgiving. She sprints toward it, her muscles resisting.

A little further, she wills them.

Her chaperon crashes through the bracken a moment before Dawsyn. She gasps painfully, her body leaning toward the sanctuary of ground, ready to surrender. How weak she has become in such a short time. She places her hands on her knees and gulps at the air, struggling to look up at her guide, her saviour.

"Who are you?" Dawsyn demands.

The cloaked figure turns, and Dawsyn looks at the place where a face should be. Instead, only shadow fills the hood of the cloak. It unnerves her.

"Show yourself," Dawsyn says now, squaring her stance.

A slow laugh. "Not even a word of thanks first?"

The voice... It is familiar. It brings to mind flashes of brilliant white light, the bitter taste of wine, the slow, seductive smile behind red lips. "Baltisse?"

The woman's hand passes over that faceless hollow, and as it lowers, the mage is somehow uncovered, her molten eyes churning just as Dawsyn remembers.

"You are as demanding as ever," the mage says, lowering the velvet hood to her shoulders. Her golden hair falls down her back and chest.

Relief, heavy and choking, shudders through Dawsyn, and she laughs. A familiar face.

Baltisse approaches. "You're laughing," she says blankly, nose wrinkling with distaste. "Did those Queens break you?"

Dawsyn's sighs, her chest still ragged with exertion. "It is likely. I've been conversing with a dead rat for the past week."

"A more scintillating conversationalist than the likes of Esra and Salem, I'd imagine," she remarks with a sniff. "We have a ways to walk and no time to linger. We are still too close to the palace. May I?" Baltisse holds out her hands.

"May you what?"

"Heal you?" Baltisse's fingernail caresses the side of Dawsyn's neck, and she flinches. Only now can Dawsyn feel the acute ache in her throat, the broken skin.

"Since when do you seek consent?"

Baltisse grins darkly. "You've been touched enough by unwanted hands for one day."

Dawsyn swallows and winces at the stab she feels along her airways. She braces herself. "Do it."

The mage's hands grasp Dawsyn's neck gingerly. "Close your eyes," she warns, and then there is a shock of white light.

Dawsyn groans at the shudder of power she feels snaking through her, down her throat to her lungs, her fingers, her feet. Her muscles press back as though resistant.

When the light beyond her eyelids recedes, Dawsyn opens them and finds Baltisse's face close to hers, the churning of her irises now a solid, gleaming gold.

"Odd," the mage murmurs, observing her closely, she then looks to her shuddering fingers. Dawsyn wonders if they beat the same unfamiliar pulse Dawsyn's do in this very moment.

It is not the first time Baltisse has called her strange. She does not dwell on it. The soles of her feet no longer protest the ground they rest on; their flesh is restored. Her throat is blessedly free of its aching, and she is here. She is out.

Freed by *Baltisse,* no less. And...

"Salem..." Dawsyn murmurs, seeing again the guards that pushed his face to the ground.

"Salem will be halfway back to the inn by now," Baltisse says easily, not a hint of concern in her tone. "He looks and speaks like an oaf, but he kicks like a fucking mule. There was a plan in place, sweet. Esra had a horse and cart waiting."

"How did you know?" Dawsyn asks. "How did you know where I was?"

Baltisse waves the question away. "Every man and woman in the kingdom knows, sweet. It's been the talk of town."

Dawsyn nods.

"And," Baltisse continues, "we heard of... of Ryon." Her voice wavers. "I am sorry, Dawsyn."

Dawsyn's throat tightens uncomfortably. She looks away to the ground and doesn't respond.

"It must be–"

"Thank you for saving me," Dawsyn interrupts, unable to bear the woman trying to articulate the way Dawsyn must feel. Baltisse herself was Ryon's ally. A friend. Dawsyn is sure she would not care to hear the way Dawsyn truly feels. "I'm grateful for the risks you all took."

It is more than just a diversion. Dawsyn is indeed grateful. All three of them, plotting to free her? It is... baffling. Such risk for a person they owe nothing to. On the Ledge, small favours had to be repaid ten-fold. A scrap of food would often cost more than she had to give. For a moment she feels wary of what debt she now owes, but then she remembers Salem's vehemence in the courtyard. She thinks of Esra's open face and considers that they likely saved her out of… loyalty.

Dawsyn's hand reaches out. It grips the mage's, her long fingers resting limply in her palm. Dawsyn is not well-versed in offering affection, but the mage is even more inept. Baltisse's hand grips mechanically, with a muscle memory long since faded. She allows Dawsyn to grasp it for a moment, and then pulls it back. "I asked your consent, and you could not return the favour?"

Dawsyn smirks. "Thank you, Baltisse."

"Do not thank me, Sabar. There is more ground left to cut those feet on." And with that, she turns on her heel and strides away, into the trees.

They push through the forest and do not break pace for much of the day. Dawsyn is oddly light. She wonders if the mage's magic cures the ache of the mind as well as the body. Or perhaps it is the air, unsoiled by the dank and damp of the palace dungeon, freeing her at last. Perhaps it is the small sounds of life in the trees and on the ground, the distant whispers of water as it cuts its well-worn path through the kingdom. Whatever the cause, she is, for this moment, blissfully unburdened.

Baltisse never once glances over her shoulder; Dawsyn doubts she would need to. The woman seems to possess senses outside the realm of humanity. Every so often, her hands outstretch and she drags her fingers across the trees, leaves and petals within reach, stroking them with the careful affection that she withholds from people. She seems familiar with them, and they with her. It reminds Dawsyn of the way her own feet knew the gradient of the Ledge, the way they would counter-balance with each step. The way they expected the parting of snow as her boots sunk, or the density of ice underneath. Months have passed since Dawsyn left the Ledge, and still her legs tilt, leaning her body away from the Chasm.

Baltisse lifts her hand to a rope of hanging ivy and it seems to shy away to let her pass. In fact, her palms seem to unconsciously seek all foliage within her reach without any observable purpose. It is a strange thing to watch. Is it the habit of a mage to be connected to wild things? She seems oddly at home here in these woods – not something Dawsyn would have predicted. The only part of Baltisse that seems fitting of the wilderness are her eyes – catlike and predatory. The rest of her is in contrast. Her hair, blonde and straight, glistens so brightly Dawsyn wonders if it isn't charmed. Her skin is flawless, body lithe, clothes regal and unmarked. If there is a scar or scratch anywhere, Dawsyn has never seen it – not befitting for a woman of the forest, so unlike Dawsyn herself, whose body is nothing but the wear of her labours.

And yet, the forest glows as Baltisse passes, the sun finding ways through the canopy to brush her shoulders, her cheeks. The branches and leaves stretch on the breeze toward her, then deflate once again in her absence.

Baltisse stops amongst a copse of trees ahead and smells the air. It seems to rattle in her lungs, as though she is tasting it, dissecting it.

"We will drink here," she says. And with that, she pushes aside the woven vine to reveal a small pond.

Dawsyn approaches and eyes the layer of green that covers the murky water. "It does not look drinkable."

Baltisse's lips slide upward. "No, it does not." She bends to the forest floor and turns to look up at Dawsyn. "Most pure things in this world are disguised."

The mage turns back to the pool, and pushes away the moss and slime, making a hole in which to cup her hands. She rises to her feet and holds the water out to Dawsyn.

It is not clear or pure. It is muddy. Dirt whirls in spirals.

"It is possible to separate the pure from the impure, but the impurities have value. The sediment enriches the water, the inhabitants enrich the sediment. There is nothing so undesirable here that it does not have its uses." As she speaks, the water in her palm clears, but not with magic. The dirt falls, collecting against the mage's skin, and leaves the water atop clean and inviting.

Baltisse drinks from her hands quickly and shakes away the dirt.

Dawsyn kneels to the earth and cups her palms in the warm water, watching the dips and darts of the living things within it and marvelling. Goodness can hide amongst the bad, just as evil can wrap itself in righteousness.

Dawsyn drinks, and then looks to the pond's surface, watching her reflection distort and then settle, but instead of herself, she sees the face of a person she does not know. It squints when she squints, gapes when she gapes. A beggar woman appears. A face lined and weathered far more than her own. Eyes grey, not brown. Lips thin and brittle.

She startles, rising from her crouch, spinning around wildly.

"Dawsyn?" Baltisse asks.

Dawsyn's eyes swing left to right searching in vain. "There was a woman–"

"There is no one else in these woods."

Dawsyn turns back to the water and looks again, down to its still surface. Again, the face of a stranger peers back at her. Dawsyn lifts her hands to her cheeks and feels her familiar curves and valleys. "Is... is that me?"

"No," Baltisse says. "Pure things generally come disguised."

"I am far from pure."

"Yes," Baltisse says easily. She reaches for the cloak that still shrouds Dawsyn's frame and lays her hand to it. The reflection in the water ripples, turning from beggar-woman back into herself. "But you are not so ruined that you can't be found."

"You disguised me?"

"The cloak did, actually," Baltisse says. "It is nearing dusk. Come."

"Where do you plan for us to hide?"

"I do not hide," Baltisse scoffs. "We will take shelter in my house."

Dawsyn follows, interest piqued. What would a mage's den comprise? A vat of stewing animal bones? Vials of poison? Spirits of the underworld?

"Not the first two," Baltisse says suddenly.

Dawsyn frowns. "Must you read my mind?"

"I do not have to if you can keep me from your thoughts."

Is that how it works? Dawsyn thinks. *Do you only hear my thoughts if they are of you?*

"Yes," Baltisse says. "I tire of it. Although, it has helped over the decades to weed out those who wish to burn me at the stake."

"And what happens to the ones who wish you ill?"

"I wish them ill in return," Baltisse answers, trudging on through the darkening wood. "Although *my* wishes tend to come true."

Dawsyn smirks. She supposes they would.

Night has fallen when they reach the cabin. The towering trees on all sides seem to hold up its walls. Indeed, if it weren't for Baltisse guiding her, Dawsyn is sure she would have walked right by.

Baltisse enters through the arched door and steps within, Dawsyn following.

The imagined cave of wicked invention is nowhere here. The small home is mostly ordinary. There is a table and chairs, a bench, a bed, a fireplace, wall and windows and a ceiling. But the ceiling is obscured by shadow, and only when a fire appears in the hearth does Dawsyn recognise the shelves of jars, the bunched greenery, swinging from low-hung rafters all over.

"Herbs?"

Baltisse nods. "And other things. You must be hungry."

"No."

"We have travelled all day and you've not eaten."

"I do not want to eat."

"Are you fasting for penance?"

Dawsyn scoffs. "From whom would I need to seek penance?"

"Yourself," the mage says, her eyes falling to Dawsyn's stomach. "I can practically hear that battle in your belly, turning you inside out."

Dawsyn stills. It is only then that she notices her own pacing, her restless fingers.

"It must be very painful," Baltisse says. Mild. Impassive.

Dawsyn scoffs. "I've been far hungrier."

"Not the *hunger*, sweet. The confusion."

Dawsyn's jaw twitches. A blossoming discomfort fills her.

"It is a strange thing, to be so filled with loss and heartbreak and wrath, all for one person. Impossible to consolidate, I've found."

The discomfort grows. Blooms. So too does the roiling of her stomach. Her hands sweat. "I do not need your consult."

"Ryon betrayed you. Did he not? I heard your mind earlier. It is plagued by him. Your thoughts are so tangled even I could not unravel the parts of you that break and burn." Baltisse regards her. "Whatever he did, Dawsyn. Whatever happened, he had reason to do it."

Reason.

The beast in her belly raises its head, bares its teeth.

"You hate him as much as you care for him."

"Stop it."

But the mage forges on. "That hate is misplaced, Dawsyn. Ryon is not your enemy."

"He is not my *anything* anymore."

Baltisse takes Dawsyn's measure, eyeing her critically, and smiles. "He is the reason you are still alive."

And with that, the beast surges, overflowing her, pushing every cell to breaking point. *"He is the reason I almost died!"*

Dawsyn shouts, each word laced with venom. "I will not listen to one more person discredit me in favour of a man."

"Not even a man you love?"

Dawsyn's palms begin to burn with trembling energy. "You mistake admiration for love. And I no longer remember him as admirable, either." When she looks down, she finds her hands coated in a filigree of ice, white shimmering patterns covering her skin. It barely registers in the flourish of hurt.

"You were drawn to each oth–"

"*He bartered my life!*" Light explodes from Dawsyn's hands, filling the room. The pain that has multiplied and fouled within her now fights its way to the surface. The sentient thing that she has failed to summon now expands with the wrath. The floor beneath Dawsyn's feet shakes, the widows rattle, and the light blinds.

For a moment, Dawsyn is stunned to silence, to stillness. How she had struggled to wrench this magic to the surface these past days, all for it to flow so easily now that she does not need it. The light recedes slowly, lingering on her palms, and she shivers, her body quaking.

Baltisse watches that ethereal glow, entranced.

But Dawsyn does not allow the things inside her to be left unsaid. "That hybrid made deals to trade my head for an alliance with the Queens. Even if he could not bring himself to do it in the end, he deceived me, and then he *led me* back into their palace. I do not care if his conscience was greater. I do not care if he changed his mind. He is no better than Alvira."

Baltisse continues to watch her, study her. "Is it easier, Dawsyn? To hate him?"

The light finally dissolves into Dawsyn's hands. With it, her body sways, spent. She is exhausted. She goes to the bed and sits on its mattress uninvited, feeling the magic beat its last in her fingertips before it retreats back into the recesses.

The mage watches Dawsyn's shoulders curl inward, her

blinks lengthen. The blood that heated her cheeks in her outburst is gone, her face now void of any colour.

Baltisse tsks. "You do not have a hold on this magic."

Dawsyn laughs weakly. "I do not have a hold on anything." Already Dawsyn's head is slipping sideways to the bed, her eyes wide and far-away. "I trusted him," she says, to herself it seems. "Stupid of me."

Baltisse kneels beside her. She takes the hand that hangs off the side of the bed and inspects it, turns it over like a map. "You do not fool me, Dawsyn. I saw something in you and something in him. It stumped me. I've lived many years, seen many things, but I have never seen a tether between two souls as sure as the one between you and that Glacian."

"I don't want it," Dawsyn whispers, a tear slipping free. "I do not wish to be tethered to anything."

Baltisse squeezes her hand as her eyes shut. "It was never for you to decide."

A shuddering sigh, and then Dawsyn slips into a fitful slumber with Baltisse watching on. The mage sees her eyes roll wildly beneath their lids, watches her breath catch and stutter. She watches the frost creep into her palms and recede again and again, and wonders at its intentions.

With one finger, Baltisse touches the centre of Dawsyn's palm. She feels again that strange muddle of power and iskra and hate running over each other like cascading waves.

She shivers. "So many battles still to be won," Baltisse murmurs to the girl of the Ledge, and it sounds like a curse.

CHAPTER NINE

Through the windows, Dawsyn watches the morning sun cast its light through the forest canopy. The mage sleeps and Dawsyn has no need to wake her. She leaves the cabin, closing the door lightly behind her, and steps out into the dappled glow. She notes the way it warms her eyelids when she raises her head, the way she sees gold even with her eyes shut.

She thinks of the people on the Ledge, who will step outside as she has just now and feel nothing but cold, all the way to the bone.

When she re-enters the cabin, it is with arms full of tinder.

Cut the wood, light the fire. Boil the snow, let it cool.

Her hands feel useless without their usual purpose, but she can at least light a fire. She can find water. She can do the next task, and the next, and maybe she can occupy her mind enough with menial busyness that she'll forget all the bad things that have happened, and all the bad things that will come.

"There is no need for kindling in a mage's house," Baltisse mumbles from her bed. She sits up slowly, hair spilling across the mattress. Dawsyn is momentarily mesmerised by it; when she looks back to the hearth, a fire spits and flickers, with no wood to feed it.

Dawsyn frowns at it. "You can conjure fire, but we must drink water from a puddle?"

"Fire consumes. You must replenish it constantly," the mage yawns. "It takes from the earth. Water is different – we will eventually return the water that we take."

Dawsyn scowls. "Yet you could blink water into existence, ready to drink?"

"I could, but no mage ought to conjure more than they need. The Mother gives us more than enough."

"How spiritual of you," Dawsyn mutters. "How old are you, Baltisse?"

The mage stands, letting her skirts fall to cover her feet. "I do not know."

"Hundreds of years?"

"Perhaps."

Dawsyn eyes her warily. "Is it only obstinacy that keeps you living, or something else?"

Baltisse smirks, dipping a clean rag into a full basin upon the bench. "I do not drink iskra, if that is what you mean."

Dawsyn hadn't thought of iskra, though it would make sense. "I find it odd that a mage can halt aging just as the Glacians do. Do you sacrifice humans, then? Eat their organs? Drink their blood?"

"Only the ones that annoy me."

"Tell me how it works," Dawsyn presses, curiosity besting her.

"Why? Are you scared to grow old?"

"I'm merely ensuring you aren't some demonic heart-eating forest dweller."

Baltisse's lips twitch. "It is no great secret, Dawsyn. I was the daughter of a mage. It is the mage blood that keeps me from aging."

The tension collecting in Dawsyn's shoulders melts a little. She'd never much thought of Baltisse having parents. Or a childhood.

"How do you feel?" Baltisse asks. She scrutinises Dawsyn in the way that only she can, like she is stripping the flesh away and peering within. As she watches, the mage unbuttons the front of her dress and disrobes, leaving only sparse underclothes. She retrieves a cloth from the basin and runs it over her collarbone and down each arm, her pale skin pebbling.

Dawsyn assesses herself, flexing her fingers experimentally. "I feel… spent."

"Do you feel any lingering power in your palms?"

"None."

"Hm," Baltisse murmurs, gaze distant and searching.

Dawsyn looks down at her hands to confirm – no different from usual. Dry, lined, callused. "I cannot control it," she mutters. "This magic. It does not come when I need it. Why?"

Baltisse turns to face her, her lips dipping at their corners. "It is the greatest mistake of us all to believe we can control magic."

"*You* can." Dawsyn frowns. "You use it at will."

"I call it, and it comes," Baltisse counters, raising her palms before her. She closes her fingers inward and the candle wicks that line her windowsill flicker to life. "But I do not control it. You should look at magic the way you would look at an animal. It is wild and sentient. It has its own motives, its own language. You can teach it to trust you, to serve you. But it cannot be done by force, it cannot be owned or ruled."

Dawsyn hesitates before responding, mulling on the words. "I called it to my palms in the Glacian palace and it unlocked the gates. But it would not help me when I was imprisoned in Terrsaw. I pled with it, and it would not listen."

"Yes. An animal is most wary of those who have abused it."

"I did not *abuse* it."

"You forced it to do your bidding in Glacia," Baltisse says calmly. "And now it shies away from you."

"It came out last night. Why?"

"Of its own accord, I presume. Unless you called to it?"

Dawsyn only remembers the anger boiling through her and suddenly out. She hadn't controlled a single thing in that moment. Not the pounding of her blood or the shaking in her hands. Not the light that had exploded from her, nor the ice that had coated her skin. "No," she mutters.

Baltisse nods gravely. "It fed from your anger and rose in the chaos. You should be very careful, Dawsyn Sabar," she says, eyes alight with unmasked curiosity. "If you feed that animal inside you with wrath and hate, it will tear everything down before even you are given the chance."

Dawsyn's magic roils inside her, as if in approval. She shudders. "Who taught you to use magic?" Dawsyn asks slowly, wondering if the mage will answer.

"My mother," she says, walking to a tiny closet, extracting a robe within. It seems so very human, the act of washing and dressing. Not at all like a creature of the underworld.

"Watch your thoughts, Sabar. Unless you would like a *personal* tour of said underworld."

Dawsyn grins. "Take no shame in it, mage. I came from nothing better."

"No," Baltisse allows. "I suppose not."

"You said your mother was a mage. Are there many mage bloodlines?"

Baltisse eyes her carefully, those liquid irises delving uninvited. Dawsyn finds it difficult to look away once they capture her.

"Not anymore," she says. "But once... Once, there were many."

Dawsyn senses reluctance in the mage's tone, but she pushes a little further. "Are you the last mage in Terrsaw?"

Baltisse rolls her eyes. "No. But you will not find the others."

"Why?"

"They do not want to be found," she says simply, and offers no more. The words are defensive.

Dawsyn does not dare delve deeper. But still, perhaps another line of questioning? Dawsyn finds her interest piqued, her curiosity unending. She knows very little of the mage after all. "You once told me that my ancestors saved you. Is that true?"

Baltisse grins wryly. "Is this an inquisition?"

Dawsyn shrugs. "Something of the sort, but you needn't answer if you wish to guard it."

Baltisse chuckles mirthlessly. "My history is no secret, Dawsyn," she says, and takes a seat, readying to tell the tale. "When the Sabars took the throne in Terrsaw, witch hunting was outlawed."

"I thought you were rather more than a witch."

"I am your worst fucking nightmare," she says, and when Dawsyn becomes entranced once more by Baltisse's stare, she believes it. Something primitive tells her that Baltisse could squash Dawsyn's entire existence between her fingers with a single thought.

"What happened to the mages before the Sabars reigned?" Dawsyn asks now.

Baltisse's eyes turn cloudy. "Burned, mostly. It is... difficult to kill a mage. But not impossible. My mother was thrown into the ocean with her fingers cut off and her feet tied to a stone. I still remember it clearly. Terrsaw celebrated for days at having finally thwarted her."

Dawsyn's throat tightens, cloying with anger. "I am sorry."

"Don't be. She was an awful woman. Truly a thing of wickedness."

Dawsyn is brought up short. "How old were you?"

"Old enough to give her whereabouts to some very skilled witch hunters."

Further questions die on Dawsyn's lips. What a thing to do, to rid the world of your own mother?

"Though, still young enough," the mage continues, unperturbed, "that I could not gather the courage to kill her myself." Baltisse turns away then, finally releasing the grip on Dawsyn's stare. "I've since rectified that."

Dawsyn stays silent for a long time, her thoughts a maelstrom that Baltisse can likely hear. There is one particular question, however, that rises to the surface.

"Yes," says Baltisse quietly, still turned away, her hands leaning against the bench.

"Yes… what?"

"You want to know if I hated her. My mother. The answer is yes."

Dawsyn nods, and bites back the urge to ask why.

Then, unbidden, "I loved her too, though," she says, and a perceptible weight befalls the mage's shoulders.

It is a strange thing, to be so filled with loss and heartbreak and wrath, all for the same person.

Warily, Dawsyn brings another question to mind.

This time, she sees when Baltisse hears it. The muscles in her neck tighten. Her shoulders tense. "No, I do not hate Terrsaw."

Not the answer Dawsyn expected. The mage has been outcasted. Vilified. Dawsyn could understand a hatred of the kingdom. It would be justified. *Expected*, even.

"But… they tried to hunt your kind into *extinction*," Dawsyn states, as though Baltisse need be reminded of her own story.

"Many years ago, yes. But not now."

The mage's voice remains calm. Indifferent, even. For some reason it rankles Dawsyn.

"Some might still," she presses. "If given the chance. Hate is resilient. Fathers pass it on to their sons."

And doesn't it rile her, to think of what they took? Doesn't it rot her slowly from the inside?

The mage only sighs. "Mages and humans are no different in that regard. Some are bad. Some deserve to be burned alive, but not all. I do not blame the people of this kingdom for the misdeeds of their ancestors."

"You do not want revenge?"

Another sigh. "No."

"Why?"

"Enough questions."

"What about the Queens?" Dawsyn asks anyway, her eyes

on the back of the mage's head, her voice low and careful. "Do you grant them the same mercy?"

Baltisse laughs once, low and mirthless. It sends a stroke of malice down Dawsyn's spine, pricking her skin.

"Them?" she sneers, eyes sparking. "I will gladly hold them down while you remove their fingers and weight their feet."

Chapter Ten

Outside, Baltisse lifts the fainting stem of an edelweiss flower, coaxing its wilted face back toward the sun. Dawsyn watches as the petals lift in response.

She spent much of the day trailing the mage uselessly as she went about what seemed to be her usual habits. Collecting water, cleaning clothes, stewing broth, setting traps, and – presumably – now communing with the plants.

Dawsyn eyes the flower dubiously. The mage had used a paddle to beat the dust from a rug, but she will use magic to save a flower? *Why bother?*

"Sometimes you need to reteach a thing its loveliness," the mage says, not turning to look Dawsyn's way. "There are too many questions in your head, sweet. Pick one."

Dawsyn chews her tongue, marking the mage's hands, dipping and bending as she meanders, not quite touching the wild tangles of vine and shrub and bracken, but rather dispelling the air around them.

"These woods know you," Dawsyn starts, not a question at all.

"They know us all."

Dawsyn laughs dryly. "There are no flowers on the Ledge, mage. No ponds or streams or vines. These woods could not know me."

Baltisse continues her leisurely pace, a pail in hand. "You are wrong, dear. A thousand humans have walked this path before you. You are not so different from the rest." She points to the branches overhead. "I have never seen these leaves before. They are newly unfurled, but they aren't unfamiliar. I know them well."

"Poetic," Dawsyn quips. "But tell me, why does it respond to you the way that it does?"

"It?"

"The *woods*."

Baltisse looks around her, at woodlands that seem to belong only to her. "Mage magic is born of nature, just like anything else. Nature is entwined, interconnected. It recognises itself."

"And how do you harness it?" Dawsyn presses. "The magic?"

Baltisse stops walking down the sodden path, muttering about interruptions. She turns and regards Dawsyn for a moment, perhaps considering how much to share. Eventually, she gestures Dawsyn closer.

When they are eye to eye, the mage turns to the tall shrubs by Dawsyn's shoulder and lets her hand hover over the fruit on its stems. Without a word, the berries pull away from the bush, detaching gently. They follow Baltisse's palm obediently, letting her lead them through thin air. She brings them to a halt before Dawsyn's eyes and lets them hang there, the sun gleaming through miniscule veins on purple skin.

Dawsyn has never seen magic like it. She exhales in a gust, laughs, unable to stall the wonder in her any longer.

"Magic is nature-born, Dawsyn. The two are alike. There are times when it is dormant and quiet, but it can be vengeful, too. It lurks and waits before it pounces. It devours its threats and seeks safe harbour. It is not so different from you or I. If you want to harness it, you must know it first. Study its movements. Look for what makes it flinch and retreat. Learn what it craves. You cannot control something without intimacy. My magic was born with me, and I have lived a long time. It trusts me. Yours, however, differs in more ways than one. You took it from the pool. You pulled it from its source. You will need to work much harder than I ever did to earn its alliance."

Dawsyn swallows awkwardly, loath to ask of her what she must. "Will... will you teach me?"

The berries fall to the earth. The mage tilts her head. "Why? How will you use it?"

Dawsyn frowns. It ought to be an obvious answer. "I'll use whatever I can to get over the Chasm and free my people."

Baltisse appears unsurprised but remains silent as she peers into Dawsyn's eyes. "This magic is not powerful enough for *that*, sweet."

Dawsyn juts her chin. "Then I will use it to threaten those in Glacia. And make them do it for me."

Baltisse smiles with sinister glee. Her feline eyes burn brightly.

Dawsyn feels discomfort stroke the back of her neck. Her palms sweat. She feels the presence of the mage invading her mind. Dawsyn pities her for what she'll find. "Will you teach me, or not?"

Baltisse sees the gooseflesh along Dawsyn's wrist and grins. She turns away, sallow hair fanning out into an arc. "No."

Dawsyn blinks, suddenly absent of the strange disquiet in her mind. The mage is disappearing down the path, and Dawsyn hastens after her. "Why not?"

"I sense you'd make a lousy student."

"From the mouth of a lousy tutor, no doubt."

This gives Baltisse pause, of course. For all her blistering tongue is worth, the mage's ego is the size of a mountain. Dawsyn could smell it on her the first time they met. Baltisse may be powerful, but ego is weak and easy to press. It is the most simplistic manipulation. Dawsyn herself suffered the same vulnerability.

The memory of Briar's previous warning rings in her ears. *"Don't get cocky, my girl. There is an inch of difference between confidence and arrogance where the sword errs to one side, and arrogance always bleeds out first."*

She had never quite mastered the lesson.

Dawsyn pushes the thought further from her mind, lest it reach the mage. "I am returning to Glacia sooner or later," she says now, standing firm. "I'd much rather depart knowing this magic can aid me when I need it, but if you do not know how to show me–"

"There is no *showing* you," Baltisse snarls, "and there is very little to be taught. Magic is instinctive."

"Ah, I see." Dawsyn nods, walking toward her, and then past her. "Well, teaching is not a challenge that I ever expected you to take on, truly. But it was worth asking."

From behind, Baltisse huffs, "I've taught entire *covens* of mage offspring, Sabar. A lungful of iskra would not best me."

"It is not a familiar brand of magic to you; I can understand that. Forget it."

Baltisse laughs. One loud, dry, barking crack, and it makes Dawsyn turn to look. The mage's face is to the sky, glowing with dark mirth. Slowly, slowly she lays her glare to Dawsyn. Even the forest seems to lose its nerve, shrinking inward, darkening as a cloud passes over the sun.

"Some genes cannot be diluted," Baltisse says in her cryptic way, voice low and deadly. "Very well, Dawsyn Sabar, girl of the Ledge, conqueror of the pool. Let us bring the magic forward and see if those smart words will help you." The mage raises a hand and curls one finger inward. "Come, princess. Call it forth."

"I'm not a *princess*," Dawsyn bites, and regrets giving the words passage. The mage smiles in response to her quick anger and Dawsyn grits her teeth.

"Call it forth," Baltisse says again, coming closer.

"How?"

"Find it first. I assume by now you know where it hides?"

Dawsyn nods, for within her body is an ever-present

weight, a useless heft of matter. She feels it in the centre of her, burrowed tightly into itself, cinched and impenetrable.

"What does it feel like?" Baltisse asks, a hairsbreadth from her now. Dawsyn resists the urge to step away. Instead, she closes her eyes. She lets her mind wander to the magic in her core. She reaches out to prod it, but the magic ignores her.

"It feels... unyielding," Dawsyn whispers. "And cold." She opens her eyes, and sees the mage give a nod. "But it burns, all the same," Dawsyn continues. "So cold that it burns."

At this, Baltisse hesitates briefly. "Does it pain you?"

"No," Dawsyn answers immediately, for it doesn't. "It is... satisfying."

The mage's eyes narrow, she seems contemplative. The molten gold of her eyes, so wild just moments ago, now turns still.

Dawsyn frowns. "What is wrong?"

"Call to it," the mage says, as though Dawsyn hadn't spoken. "Do not beg or demand it."

"If I cannot beg or demand, then what can I do? Invite it out to stroll?"

"Yes."

Dawsyn's derisive huff bathes the mage's face, still so close.

Baltisse grasps Dawsyn's wrist and raises it in the remaining space between them. The movement is so sudden that Dawsyn has no time to react. It unsettles her. She did not know the mage could move so quickly.

"It is a creature, Dawsyn Sabar, remember? Already you are proving to be a slow learner. If you beg the magic, it will think you weak. It will not rise from its slumber. If you demand it, force it, it will bite. If you want the magic to rise at your will, then you will find the ways to coax it out. So yes, all-powerful girl of the Ledge, I want you to extend an invitation. Invite the thing out to play, and let it learn the boundaries of your leash."

Baltisse's eyes rise to Dawsyn's hairline before returning to meet her glare. "You think I am the most arrogant of all?" she asks, her voice resonating in the open space. "I am not the one debating the mechanisms of magic with a seven hundred year-old witch."

Dawsyn feels a chill sweep over her from head to toe.

"Mind your thoughts, Sabar," the mage whispers, and yet it rings loudly in Dawsyn's ears.

She refuses to let Baltisse see how disturbed she is. In her mind, her grandmother's sharp voice calls her a fool for underestimating one as ancient as the mage. Dawsyn closes her eyes, loosens a captive breath in her lungs, and focuses once more on the imposter that sleeps inside her.

This time she does not poke it, or pull at it with her mind. With doubt in every word, she speaks to it, and awaits its response. *Come out,* she tells it. *Let me show you the way.*

At first, that glowing mass does nothing, but then... a flicker.

Come with me. Dawsyn coaxes again now, encouraged. *Come and see...*

Where? It hisses, reluctant still. *Where?*

I will show you.

The gleaming mass fills her body slowly as it wakes, stretching, feeling its way along her limbs. Dawsyn feels it move with rapt interest this time, her attention not marred by anger or urgency. She feels the prickle of chill as it moves within her. She notices the way her body reacts to its cold caress. Her blood rushes to heat the places touched, burning away the frost of the iskra into something pleasant. It is not the iskra that burns her, but a... balm. A cure. Something other. A natural reaction of her body, perhaps.

Dawsyn's eyes open. Frost collects in her palms first, as before, slowly spreading to her knuckles and nails and wrists.

"Good." Baltisse nods, barely glancing down at the hand still in her grasp. "Now, let it go back again."

"What?" Dawsyn blurts. "I've yet to do a single thing with it."

"And you won't. Not today."

"Then how am I to use it the next time I am locked in a dungeon?"

"A smarter woman would not find herself in dungeons so often." Baltisse turns to leave.

"Show me how to use it, Baltisse! We are not done!"

"Yes, we are."

Dawsyn feels the frost begin to retreat from her fingertips, disappearing from her skin. She boils, infuriated. *No!*

Yes, it whispers.

Suddenly, Dawsyn cries out. At her attempt to wrench the iskra forward once more, an abrupt bolt of pain lances through her belly, squeezing until she collapses, her body falling to the forest floor. She lies panting, her face pressed against the damp, rotting leaves. The magic licks its way back to its resting place, becoming nothing but a small, heavy mass once more.

Baltisse's fingers sweep away the hair that half covers Dawsyn's face, and watches with apparent interest as her breaths slow and her limbs slacken. "I told you it would bite," she says, and holds out a hand.

After a few seconds, Dawsyn takes it, letting the mage help her from the ground, brushing the dirt and debris from her clothes with shaky hands.

Baltisse tsks. "Your desperation will not help you in your quest to rid the world of evil."

Dawsyn groans, suddenly worn. "I need to get them off the Ledge," she says, her breath still heavy. "And I have no way of crossing the Chasm. No other who will help me cross it. Now that…" she stumbles.

"Now that Ryon is not with you?" Baltisse finishes for her. "You think this magic will help in your crusade?"

"I have *nothing* else," Dawsyn says then. "Not wings, not leverage. Not even a fucking *ax.*"

"You had no wings or magic when you ran down the slopes, or when you killed the Glacians who came for you."

Dawsyn shakes her head. "I had weapons. I had…"

"Ryon," Baltisse offers, saving her the need to voice the name.

"Yes."

"And now you have only me," Baltisse says, smiling wickedly. "A most powerful sorceress. And yet, you complain."

Dawsyn rolls her eyes. "And you argue your arrogance?"

The mage only smiles serenely.

"You do not wish to accompany me to Glacia, surely?" Dawsyn questions.

Baltisse tilts her head. "You are surprised?"

"More than ever," she responds dryly. "Why would you possibly care to?"

Baltisse smiles. "For what reason do you think I cut that rope from your neck, sweet? I told you once that you would decide what you were born for, and it seems you have made your choice."

Dawsyn watches her for a moment, awaiting a hint of reluctance, or a sinister glint of motive perhaps. When nothing reveals itself in her expression, Dawsyn hedges. "You wish to help me save the people of the Ledge?"

Baltisse does not waver. "I do. I did not come to your rescue out of mere affection."

Dawsyn eyes her suspiciously. "The journey will be long. Unforgiving."

The mage's eyes turn amber and tumultuous. "With me," she says, "it needn't be."

CHAPTER ELEVEN

In the Terrsaw palace, a guard descends the stark stone staircase to the dungeons, his feet aching. It seems an age has passed since he last rested, yet it will be longer still until he can.

"Drew?" a voice calls to him from below.

It is Brockner. The fellow guard sticks his head into the stairwell, hair stuck at wild angles, rubbing his eyes.

"The one and only. Were you sleeping, soldier?"

"Do not tell the captain," Brockner says. "I'm already in grave danger of finding her blade at my neck."

"What did you do that would warrant it?"

"Woke her with my snoring, or so she says." He grins.

Drew reaches the floor and returns the smile. "The hazards of entangling yourself in the captain's sheets, I'm afraid."

"I won't pretend to complain."

Drew watches the man's smile curve with the familiar sickness of forgone lovers and groans. "Lucky bastard."

Brockner laughs.

"I have a message for you from your beloved. She says to prepare to move. The Queens want us scouring the kingdom for the Sabar girl."

Brockner's features darken. "When?"

"Tomorrow," Drew says. "I'm to join you."

Brockner swears, spitting onto the stone floor. "We'd be

better to let her go. Truly, I do not see the threat. She no longer has her Glacian to protect her."

Drew shrugs. "Perhaps she has more of those strange half-breeds stowed away."

"Perhaps." Brockner sighs. Collecting his lance, he juts his chin at the locked gate to the keep. "Are you to take sentry until dawn?"

"I am," Drew replies, propping his own lance against the stone wall. "Weep for me, brother. I'll have had no sleep when we set off tomorrow."

Brockner raises his eyebrows. He looks once more into the keep, where a lone form lies unmoving on the cell floor. "I got a few hours in. I cannot imagine you'll see much trouble from this one. Hasn't moved an inch since I took my post."

Drew grimaces. Whether the shape moves or not, he is loath to take his gaze off a Glacian.

"Go find your bed, brother," Drew says. "Give my regards to our captain."

The figure on the floor remains unmoving for another night, and the guard allows himself some sleep. It will be another day before the captive rouses.

The captive is, however, aware. He can hear the guard's even breaths. He can smell the stench of mildew and piss. He can't move. Can't speak. Can't fight. But he can hear. He can think. Ryon Mesrich never truly lost consciousness at all.

Had he been felled? Instantly.

The Queen's sword had thrust deep enough to sever any ability to fight back. He had not felt the shatter of his knees on the mosaic floor. The tether between his mind and body had already frayed, softening the ordeal of death. He lay with a hole in his chest, knowing his end had come, and waited for everything to become nothing. But his mind, in all its obstinacy, did not fade entirely.

He could not see, but he could hear.

He heard her voice.

He heard her scream.

He knows now how sound can hurt. Where the hole through his chest had seized him, paralysed him, that wail made him want to rip away his skin, tear through the blackness. Find the surface.

Did they hurt her?

Who hurt her?

He could not count the times she'd known pain in recent days. Too many. He remembered the way her body had felt in his arms as he'd dragged her from the river, small and cold. Again, when her blood had been riddled with the Glacian poison. He had promised himself not to let anyone touch her again, sworn it.

But then she was screaming, like a thousand hot pokers were being held to her skin. Yet he could do nothing to change it. The pain of enduring those screams was more excruciating than any wound.

Now, it is the dread that keeps him awake. Immoveable and unrested. Days and days of wakefulness where his body is not his own.

He wonders at times if this might in fact be death. Frozen in a static body, reliving his trauma through the sound of his memories. He commands his body to move, over and over, but nothing works. It reminds him of the Pool of Iskra, suspended in the viscous liquid until a voice lulled him to a sweet, numb end.

But this mustn't be the end. He can still think. He can battle against the dark in his mind as it tries to drag him under for good. He pushes back, searching for a way out of this limbo.

At times he can't discern, voices reach him. Guards, mostly. Quiet, meaningless conversations. He only catches fragments. Sometimes they mention the Queens, or Dawsyn, and he revolts from within.

"*Ryon*, you say?" a muted voice sounds. A careful one, but he hears it clearly. This speaker – a female – is closer than the guards were.

"A half-breed," comes a voice much more familiar. Queen Alvira. "How much do you know of them?"

A hesitation, and then, "Some."

"He seems rather unwilling to die," Queen Alvira says offhandedly. "I assume it's the nature of his kind. The beasts are most difficult to kill."

"No," says the stranger. "I do not think so. They are not so different from us."

"He'll be killed eventually, of course, regardless. But not until I get the Sabar girl back. She seemed attached enough to him that she might be lured."

"You... you will bait her?"

"Perhaps. But it isn't for you to know, witch. I've brought you here for your very specific area of expertise. So, let's begin. Does this Glacian have the iskra magic?"

A pause. Whoever the witch is, she weighs her response before answering. "He must. He would be dead otherwise."

"Can you rid him of it?"

"No."

"Then awaken him. I wish to see how he might aid us."

"Your Majesty. I do not think–"

"I did not *ask* what you think. Can you awaken him or not?"

A sigh. "Yes."

"Will his iskra magic be a hindrance?"

"Perhaps," says the voice, so small and inconsequential, it is almost disturbing to hear it beneath the Queen's. "But not for long. These... *Glacians*, they absorb the iskra. They were made from it, after all. It must be replenished. This power within him likely weakens as we speak, helping him cling to life. Truly, you needn't be so worried."

A sigh of relief. "Quite. Wake him, then."

"It will take some time. His wounds–"

"Time is of the essence, witch. Unless you would like me to parade you through the Mecca and have them see what you are, I would mind it."

The sound of footsteps leads away, solid heels glancing off the stone as they disappear. Moments later, iron squeals against rust – a gate opening.

A hand lays gently against his cheek.

The first sensation of feeling in eons, in an eternity. The warmth of human skin on his. The stroke of careful fingers.

"Be well," says that fragile voice, that disintegrating tenor.

And then something stirs deep within.

Chapter Twelve

It is a glistening creature in his blood. It slides through him into every limb, reaching for the tips of his fingers, the soles of his feet. It stretches and turns, twists and runs, touching the very ends of him.

Finally, he can feel the tether that was missing – a tie between his mind and his body that was broken but is now fixed. He moves his toes, curling them inward. It takes a while longer for the pain to begin.

It comes as waves do. Swelling and crashing, relentlessly ensued. With the re-joining of his body and mind comes the awareness of every gnashing pain. He shouts and bellows but can't be sure if his lips ever open. His chest is a pit of fire, burning him alive, and the iskra in him meanders through at leisure, slowly knitting the wound with its thread. It is painstaking, almost reluctant, as though it would rather Ryon had conceded to death and spared it the task. It goes about its work like a sullen child, and Ryon burns all the while.

He feels the snap of the last thread in his chest, the last tear stitching together and the burn mercifully fading. The crashing waves tame into something duller – a throbbing. He blinks several times, and suddenly he can see.

He is in a cell. As he thought. And she is not there.

The ache worsens. It has little to do with his wound.

Ryon looks down to his chest and sees endless red. His clothes are thick with it; blood is stiff in some places and sticky in others. A hole gapes in his shirt at a place just below his ribs and he sits to inspect it. He pulls back the fabric gingerly, his fingers slow to respond, and beneath is a mottled, pink scar, angry and prominent against his black skin. This is where the sword entered – it should have torn through his lungs. It should have killed him.

And yet he lives.

Ryon frowns. He is insatiably thirsty. There is a bowl, chipped and stained, sitting upon the floor and filled with water. It is only a few feet from him but might as well be a mile away. He has to drag his body toward it, and it is desperately unwilling. It needs rest. Every small movement sends stabs of pain directly to his chest.

"Fuck," he groans, feeling sweat bead along his forehead. He manages to stretch one arm to the bowl's lip, and drags it toward him. He pushes against the ground to sit up, breathing like he had just flown the length of the valley. He goes to drink, but even his lips seem uncooperative, spilling the water down his chin and neck. His hands shake, and when most of the water is wasted down his chest, he throws the bowl away weakly. It does not even have the decency to break.

Ryon's head falls back to the stone floor and his eyes shut. He trembles with each shuddering breath, the newly spun threads inside him threatening to fray.

He cannot escape in this body. He cannot find Dawsyn if he can barely move. He can be of no use to anyone like this.

Where is she? He cannot think her dead. Just the idea invites a consuming rage, taunting him to break down every door, buckle every window, set fire to all of Terrsaw.

"If they took you from me," he mutters, grappling with his mind as it slips back into its dark reprieve. "I will break them all."

* * *

It is days before Ryon wakes again. Before then, he dreams. He dreams of the Colony in Glacia, where a hand reaches out to capture a younger version of him, traipsing toward the woods.

"Ryon! Damn it, deshun. You're mighty close to the slope for someone with wings as valuable as yours... You're practically begging them brutes to cut them away!"

Ryon struggles, pulling his thin wrist in vain. "Lemme be, Ditya. I'll only be a moment."

Ditya curses again. Ryon has only ever known him to curse and spit and mutter under his breath, so it doesn't indicate any real threat. The mixed-blooded male is small, laughably so. The others have only ever called him 'Ditya,' meaning 'child' – if he has a real name, it has long been forgotten.

"Those wings ought to be clipped anyhow, for all the trouble they cause. Should let you fly off down them slopes and be done with you!" But Ditya does the opposite, and tugs Ryon away from the boundary between the Colony and the wooded slope, where none are permitted to be. "Do you not get flogged enough already, Ry? You need to get back to your bed. Now."

"Might as well make it worthwhile," Ryon mutters, but he stops fighting. He lets Ditya guide him back into the maze of the Colony. Ditya's hand on his wrist doesn't relent when they get there, and it is only then that Ryon notes the alarm in the man's furtive glances, the quickened stride. He pulls Ryon again, hastening further still.

"Ditya?" Ryon asks, and the man ignores him. "Ditya, what–"

"The brutes are coming," he says, and Ryon's stomach turns to stone.

"For me?"

Ditya grimaces. "Likely. You'll be hiding inside, understand?"

As they turn a corner, a figure steps out of the darkness. "Ditya!" it hollers. "You found him."

The mixed-blood before them is much taller than either, less lean, but wingless – many mixed are – but on him it seems strange; a mixed-blood so big and menacing would typically be equipped with wings just as big.

"Adrik," Ditya huffs, coming up short. He pulls Ryon closer to himself.

"I can take him to the stocks," Adrik offers, his hand proffered. "The brutes are already waiting."

Another penance, tonight? So soon after the last?

Bile rises from Ryon's stomach to his throat. The boy tries not to let his fear show. He holds himself tall, rolls his eyes. But his wings retract of their own accord, unwilling to be within reach of the King's swords. His hands tremble and he swallows, willing the contents of his stomach to stay put.

"No," Ditya grunts. "It is too soon. His wounds are barely healed from the last. I can hide him."

"And what then, my friend? They will look. He will be punished further for having kept them waiting. Even worse if they believe he tried to evade them. There is no other way." Adrik looks to the slope over the boy's head, eyes distant, and then down to Ryon. "I am sorry, deshun."

Ryon shrugs, teeth gritted.

"Come. Bad things are better done quickly."

Ryon tries to go, but Ditya's fingers do not loosen their hold. Instead, they grip tighter, they pull him back. Ryon looks back questioningly at the man who currently houses him, keeps him fed.

"We should be doing something... fucking anything," Ditya snarls, the ever-present spit collecting rapidly in the corners of his mouth. "We can refuse. We should deny them!"

Adrik sighs. "You know as I do, as Ryon does, that there is no escaping it, Ditya. Let the boy go. He will heal, as all warriors do."

Ryon tries to tug his hand from Ditya's, his chest tightening at the sight of the small man, eyes wet, furrow lined in desperation. "Let me go, Ditya," Ryon tells him with a confidence he does not feel. "I will return."

Ditya's thick fingers slip slowly from Ryon's wrist, reluctant. He takes a mollifying breath, and turns away. He cannot watch Ryon at the Kyph. He never can.

"Come, deshun," Adrik calls, a hand on his shoulder, turning him. "You will look to each of the brutes and remember their faces. Each cut

*will be another to their own skin when you are a man. One day, you
will hold the sword. Do you understand?"*

*The same words each time, but Ryon listens still. He nods and
squares his shoulders.*

*Adrik turns a corner through the Colony. The shelters lean away
here, leaving a small, circular opening – the Kyph, as it is known by
the mixed. It is laden with snow. At the centre is a row of stocks of
varying size, wooden and marked with lashes and scorches.*

*Before the Kyph, several pure-blooded brutes stand. King Vasteel's
finest. The white of their skin rivals the snow that falls upon it, so
pristine, so untouchable. Demonic, even.*

*"The bastard son of Mesrich!" one hollers, sloshing the contents of
his tankard onto the snow. The others share similar glazed eyes and
leaning postures, jeering and slurring as they watch the boy approach.*

*From the shadows and corners of the space, mixed faces hover,
lingering just out of sight. None dare come out into the open of the
Kyph lest they find themselves its spectacle. But they will stay on the
outskirts in solidarity. They will come to pack his wounds with snow
and feed him healer's tonic when the brutes leave. They will carry him
to a soft bed and not flinch when he cries in the night.*

"You doing the honours again, Adrik?" one of the brutes asks.

*Phineas is not amongst the brutes. He never is. Ryon wishes he
would come. He wishes Phineas would stop them.*

*"Tie him up, then, Adrik. I have a nice surprise for these fine men
here." The tallest Glacian slams his tankard against his companions',
and they laugh and hoot their approval.*

*Ryon turns his face to the stocks, letting his cheek find the cool,
smooth wood. He sees it as a friend, rather than an enemy. Ryon has
embraced it on each night that ended like this. Adrik ties his hands
somewhat loosely around the timber. The brutes are too drunk to
notice and Ryon is not stupid enough to run away, so it matters little.*

*"Here!" a brute calls from behind him, and the cheering grows
more raucous. "Let's see how the boy's skin fares under this."*

*Ryon swallows, cinches his eyes shut and waits. It is the worst part
– not knowing what will come. A lash? A stone? A knife? He turns his*

mind to the brutes behind him, just as he's been taught. He imagines them beneath his talons, at his mercy, their pale eyes pleading.

A sound of sizzling fills the air, and Ryon freezes.

Adrik is suddenly at his ear, whispering quickly. "Do not let them hear you scream," he tells the boy.

"Hurry up, Adrik," a brute calls. "Unless you'd like to be tied next to him."

Adrik holds the burning metal to Ryon's skin, gripping his shoulder as Ryon butts his head against the wood, but keeps his lips sealed.

"Wake, Glacian. You've slept long enough."

Ryon's eyes blink toward the voice and a shape comes into focus. The cell is so dark there'd be nothing to see but for a lantern flickering from the hand of a woman. One of the guards... *Ruby*, he thinks.

But it is the figure beyond Ruby that Ryon wants. The rest are casualties. Unfortunate of them to find themselves in the wrong place.

"Remarkable, is it not, Captain?" Queen Alvira says. "He is resurrected." Her papery skin lifts into the imitation of a smile.

The captain nods. "Remarkable, indeed."

"I had the inspired idea to observe the Glacian creatures," she says, eyes raking the length of Ryon as though he were an exhibit. "They are far more powerful than we knew."

Ruby's eyes twitch. "I see," she says quietly.

The Queen tilts her head at Ryon. "The more informed we are of these beasts, the better we can defend ourselves against them."

Beasts. Creatures. As though he is the unfeeling one. The callous one.

His wound is not nearly healed, but it is healed enough for this.

Ryon lunges from the ground to the gate, ignoring the flame erupting beneath his ribs. His chest collides with the grid as his arm thrusts through the rungs. He grips the velvet collar of the Queen's robe in his fist and yanks her forward, slamming her body to the rusted iron. Her forehead cracks against it in a most satisfying manner.

There is a flurry of action in response.

"*Stop!*"

"Halt!"

"Drop your hand! *Now!*"

"Do not kill him!" Alvira pants, teeth gritted. Her cheek mashes so tightly against the gate that her words are muffled. The tips of her toes barely reach the floor. This close, Ryon can see her clearly. Her veined skin beneath the powder on her cheeks; the sagging, hooded lids, pink with broken vessels; the lines on her forehead so deeply etched they could be scars. An old, decaying woman, hiding behind painted veneer.

"Where is she?" Ryon says lowly, voice gravelled – a quiet warning. The hot fury of his breath bathes the Queen's face.

He watches fear bloom in her eyes. She gasps, struggles.

"*Release her!*" A guard orders.

"Cut his fingers free!"

Their voices are no match for his. "WHERE IS SHE?!" Ryon roars, a thunderous call all the way across the valley. It silences them. The Queen, for all her temerity, has the wherewithal to flinch.

He could break her bones in an instant, and he can see she knows it. It takes restraint not to, but there will be no need for control if Dawsyn is dead.

And his intentions, his train of thought, must be obvious to them all, because a voice suddenly says, "Don't! Dawsyn is *alive!*"

He stills. It is not the Queen who spoke words so sweet, but the captain of the guard. Ryon turns his fierce gaze on her. *Let it be true,* he prays, though he does not dare to hope yet.

The young woman raises her hand to her chest. A vow.

"Dawsyn Sabar is alive. I swear it," Ruby implores, and perhaps she is lying, but Ryon somehow doesn't think so. Her stare does not waver from his. Something in her expression exudes sincerity, however desperate she might sound. "Let go," she continues. "Please. Any harm you do here will not serve you. *Let the Queen go.*"

Ryon tilts his head at Ruby. "Bring her to me."

"You make demands?" the Queen hisses between rattling breaths, her face still pressed against the grid. "You dare to command my guards?" she spits. "Command *me?*"

Ryon considers crushing the sound of her voice between his hands, but not yet. Instead, he pulls the woman tighter, incrementally so. Enough for the terror in the Queen's eyes to shine a little brighter. Enough to remind her how close she is to a painful end.

"I said," – Ryon's grip twists – *"bring her to me."*

The gate creaks with the added pressure, and the Queen gasps. "She is not here!" Her voice is a shrill, strangled cry. "I swear it! I swear to you. Now let me go!"

"She has escaped!" Ruby offers. Her hands fall atop Ryon's, prying at them uselessly. "She ran! We do not know where. Let the Queen go, Ryon, please. If you don't, you'll never see her again."

Ice begins to coat his hands. It lights his palms and crackles along his fingers until it reaches Queen Alvira's clothes, and then her throat, wrapping around it like a noose.

"Captain! Cut his hands away!" calls a guard.

"No! Do not move," the Queen gasps, her breath fogging the space between her mouth and Ryon's. "I can let you go to her, half-breed," she whispers. "I can unlock this cell today. Now. And you can walk free. But kill me here, and you'll never see daylight again."

"Go ahead then," Ryon jeers, his teeth bared. "Unlock it." And though the fire in his lungs burns on, the wound throbbing its own pulse, he feels the threat before him burning hotter in his grasp. He unfurls his wings, stretching them to the ceiling, filling the space.

As one, the guards stutter in their movements. They retreat, eyes to the expanse of his Glacian heritage.

"Mother above," one mutters, mouth agape.

Ryon flaps down once in a heavy stroke, and the musty air in the room displaces violently, throwing the guards back another pace. Ryon's feet leave the floor, and with him comes the Queen. Her body slides against the iron gate as they rise slowly, her gasps turning to small cries. Ryon hovers a foot above ground, holding the Queen tightly by her luxurious robes, relishing the sound of the seams beginning to split.

"*Unlock it,*" he commands.

"N-No!" the Queen splutters, her face growing red. And Ryon has to give credit to her endurance. "Not until you unhand me."

She is not one to yield. Even suspended in mid-air at the hands of a *beast,* she is resolved. Ryon, meanwhile, feels the burgeoning pain in his chest beginning to splinter him from the inside. "RELEASE ME!" he roars.

"NO!" the Queen shouts in return.

And though he wishes for nothing more than to snap her neck, he knows he cannot kill her. Not if he wishes to live. He will not be freed should he become responsible for her death. He has very little with which to barter, and he feels his energy waning quickly. A lancing pain suddenly strikes him, and he is forced to shunt her away, letting her fall to the ground on top of her guards. There is a clamour as they try to support her fall, checking her for injury.

It gives Ryon time to set his feet to the ground, his body curling inward to the stitched hole in his chest. His wings vanish, spent. The magic holding him together retreats, tapped and useless. Rage can only get him so far in this condition.

"Open the fucking gate."

Queen Alvira growls, ripping her arms out of the guards'

reach. They crowd her, not allowing her to come so close to the prisoner again. "I should have you quartered," she seethes. "Vile *beast!*"

Ryon throws his hands to the iron rungs, making them shudder. "*Try it,*" he spits.

The Queen runs her fingers hastily through her frazzled hair. "Or," she says acidly. "Perhaps I'll have your lovely Miss Sabar found first."

Ryon's hands tense. He turns cold.

"My guards are searching for her as we speak, and I dare say they will find her. What is the name of your accomplice again? Salem? Shall I have my guards pay a visit? The punishment for harbouring a fugitive will be great indeed. I do hope, for his sake, he has the sense to hide. Him and any other in this valley who seek to help her."

Ryon's teeth grind. *A despicable excuse for a queen,* he thinks. Would she really raze innocent households in search of one woman? Dawsyn knows no one in Terrsaw, save Salem. If she ran in search of sanctuary, it was likely to him, to the inn.

"Just how loyal do you think your friend will be to his new fledgling?" the Queen continues. "Do you think he would *die* to protect her?"

The Queen has learnt of Salem, perhaps Esra and Baltisse, too. There is no telling how much the palace knows, how readily his friends will be killed for their alliance with him.

"But I needn't disturb another soul," the Queen adds. "If I had some direction on which course she may have taken. Perhaps I could be guided away from those who needn't be harmed. What say you, half-breed? Should I have the guards ransack every house and establishment until I find her, or could you save them the tumult? These things have a habit of leading to accidents, false accusations... tragedy, even."

Ryon watches the Queen's guards grow uncertain. Restless. He wonders if the Queen usually speaks so fervently, so candidly in their presence.

"Where is she, Ryon?" the Queen presses, inching closer, despite herself. "You know her, do you not? Where would she go? Tell me, and no one else need suffer for her or you. Is she with that lout, Salem? Would she take to the seas?"

A memory impedes his thoughts then – a tumultuous current, a tempest crawling to shore. His hands itching to wrap Dawsyn up in himself and carry her toward the horizon, toward safety and peace.

Not yet, she had said.

Ryon's eyes close. He knows it will not be sanctuary she seeks. It will be the Ledge.

Not yet, she whispers again, her voice so clear to him.

He opens his eyes. "You think I would give her up so easily?" Ryon asks, the deep timbre of his voice reverberating off the walls.

The Queen's eyes flare. "What if I sweetened the deal?"

"I'll make no deals with you."

"Not even for your own life?"

"*Especially* not for my life!" he growls, and the guards blanch once more. "You once tried to make a deal with me to kill Dawsyn Sabar. I allowed you to keep breathing that time, I will not be so generous the next."

The Queen's lips tremble with her indignation, her rage. "Then I will find her without you, and I will have you watch as she dies by my hand."

But Ryon only laughs, low and dark, and the stale air is drenched in his bloodlust. "I'll take pleasure in watching you try."

Her hands hit the bars with remarkable force, the metal clanging in its stone recesses. She shrieks like a child, skin aflame with ire.

Ryon hears her quaking breaths as she fights to regain her composure. He enjoys the spectacle – seeing every refined facet of her shattered into something inhumane.

Queen Alvira snaps at her guards. "Shackle him," she says.

"Captain, bring a horse and cart. You will take him to the town square. Let us see if we can dangle him and tempt the girl out of hiding. In the meantime, the people of Terrsaw can redirect their energies. If it is justice they want, perhaps a half-breed will suffice. Make sure you bind him tightly to the *Fallen Woman*. Cut off his wings if you must." Her bosom heaves, eyes wild. "Let the people hack their piece of retribution from him."

CHAPTER THIRTEEN

Wind lifts Dawsyn's fur hood and tries to pull the hair from her scalp. It is unbearably familiar. Her eyelids push valiantly against the gale but can't open. Her ears are a chamber of wind, beating against her eardrums, demanding entrance.

Suddenly, it is silent.

The squall dulls without warning, and she can see again. Dawsyn blinks against the flurry, and shapes that were distorted by the blizzard begin to take form.

The sound of cracking makes her look down. The ice beneath her toes is splintering, streaking bolts of lightning across its surface.

No.

The sound of splitting accelerates. The air is full of its groaning. She staggers back as the ice starts to crumble away, feet skidding. On instinct she turns and dives, her shoulder catching her weight in the snow a second before the edge falls away. There is no sound of destruction as the ice meets the end of its fall – for the Chasm is too deep.

She stands at the lip of the shelf, the Ledge at her back, Glacia ahead and the Chasm between the two – a great gaping maw, mocking her isolation.

Dawsyn does not usually dare stand quite so close to its mouth. It must be stupidity that brings her here, tempting death. Sense tells her to back away, and if it weren't for the voice, she would.

*For the Chasm… it sings. Words rise from its black belly. They carry
on the wind, weaving verse into her ears.*

Make your soul unto itself,

Break the bone and cure.

*A lament. The people of the Ledge sing it when the blizzards will
not desist, when the mountain traps them inside for days. They sing
it when the time between Drops spreads thin and their limbs even
thinner.*

For when you lie within the mouth,

The cost will be no few'r.

A song of resignation. Of yielding.

Seal your eyes and sleep,

Still your lips and cease your breath,

Better than the ache. Better than the ice.

Lie where sorrow dares not be,

Free from the hands of death.

*Again and again the verse tangles in the wind, and each time the
sound grows sweeter. It begins to sound like a promise. She begins to
believe it. There is nothing in the Chasm, Dawsyn is sure, but darkness.
No sorrow. No pain.*

*As though caught in the current of the Pool of Iskra, her feet carry
her toward the precipice, seduced by the simplicity of falling, the ease
of ending. It is irresistible, this pull. And she lets the voice guide her
over the edge, spreading her arms as she falls. But for the lurch of her
stomach, she is at peace. She is free. She is flying.*

Dawsyn awakens to the sensation of falling and gasps.

There is a cool burn pulsing in her palms. Frost covers her
from wrist to fingertip. As soon as she holds her hands up to
inspect them, the magic recedes, its glow dulling.

"It looks for ways to seep out of you," comes Baltisse's voice,
and Dawsyn jerks upright.

The mage perches on a wooden chair before the hearth,
eyeing Dawsyn in her cot with apprehension. Dawsyn pushes

the covers off her legs, blinking away an imaginary wind, ridding her mind of the dream.

"The iskra seems not only resentful, but fearful, too," Baltisse murmurs, eyes distant.

Dawsyn isn't completely sure if she is speaking to her or not, but accompanying the mage's uneasy words is the blossoming darkness of the woman's irises. The ink within them unfurls slowly, eclipsing her eyes completely. A precursor to cataclysm.

Indeed, the mage looks troubled – and not for the first time.

"What did you dream of just now?" Baltisse asks sharply, her disturbing stare returning to meet Dawsyn's.

"Ah," Dawsyn defers, unwilling to share the image of the Chasm. Even less so, her ready self-sacrifice to its depths, or the ease with which the voice had persuaded her to fall. But as the dream plays over in her mind, Baltisse's eyes narrow keenly, and Dawsyn knows that the mage sees it too.

"Stop," Dawsyn says firmly – to her mind and to Baltisse. "Stop intruding."

"What was that?" Baltisse asks, ignoring her request.

Dawsyn stands, turning to neaten the bedding. "No business of yours."

"I saw ice falling away, beneath your feet. Was it–"

Dawsyn sighs, resigned. She places her hands onto the mattress. "The Chasm."

There is little point keeping thoughts from the woman, it seems. Trying to keep her out of one's mind only seems to invite entrance.

"Who was that... the one who sung?"

"No one," Dawsyn says. "A... voice of some sort."

"It was calling you into the Chasm?"

"Yes," Dawsyn says begrudgingly, avoiding her gaze.

"You shouldn't listen to it, Dawsyn Sabar," says Baltisse, voice oddly stern.

Dawsyn gives a huff of derision. "It was only a dream, Baltisse."

"No. It was the iskra distracting you so that it might roam free while you slept."

Dawsyn pauses, then she turns to look at Baltisse.

The iskra… invading her dreams? Had the sweet lure of the voice not felt familiar to Dawsyn? Had she not likened it to the unshakeable call of the pool?

Dawsyn looks to her palms again, now warm and human, and swallows past the harsh sting of her throat. "Can it do that?" Dawsyn asks quietly, shakily. "Can it escape me?"

"No, not fully," Baltisse answers, her chair scraping along the floor as she stands. "It can act beyond control, but it cannot detach itself. And yet…"

"And yet?"

"And yet… it tries to."

Dawsyn has the answer already. "It does not trust me, as you said."

"No," Baltisse says, her head shaking. "It is more than that. It is… preservation, perhaps."

"Preservation? It believes I will destroy it?"

Baltisse does not answer immediately. Her jaw ticks, as though she is biting her tongue, and then she says, "I do not know."

But it seems to Dawsyn that the mage knows a great many things, and only shares a morsel.

Dawsyn scrubs her face with one hand, pushing her black tendrils from her forehead. "You are annoyingly secretive."

Baltisse scoffs. "And you are abrasive."

"There is little point in not speaking my mind if you'll invade my thoughts, regardless."

The mage laughs, and the sound seems to take her by surprise.

Dawsyn grins, despite herself. "I don't suppose you have a brush?"

The mage points to a cupboard below a small window. "You should bathe, too. If you'd be so kind. It's bad manners to smell as you do in one's home. I prepared a bath while you slept," the mage gestures to the large basin in the kitchen, big enough to sit in. "The water is still warm."

Wearily, Dawsyn undresses in the mage's cabin, peeling the soiled fabric away like shedding skin. It has been a while since she saw her body. It feels smaller, somehow. Less significant. She takes the washcloth Baltisse hands her and steps into the bathing basin. She rids her body of the feverish sweat that coats her skin, cups water in her hands and douses her hair. The water is fragrant, smelling of the same blossoms that perfume the woods around them. The sudden feel of bristles against her scalp makes her stiffen for a moment, but it is only Baltisse who kneels behind her, sweeping the brush from Dawsyn's crown to the middle of her back methodically.

"Your hair is a thicket," Baltisse grunts, running the brush through the tangles over and over, until they relent. "My mother used to brush my hair this way as a girl."

Dawsyn too can conjure a thousand memories of Briar, standing on the wooden floor beside a wooden bucket not large enough to sit in. She would rub oil into Dawsyn's hair to free the tangles, cursing softly when her fingers could not free the more stubborn knots. "Mine, as well," Dawsyn murmurs, unease spreading through her chest because, if not for the green forest through the window, this could be a cabin of the Ledge, and the brush might be the fingers of the woman who raised her... and then left her.

"Did your mother not die when you were an infant?" Baltisse asks, the strokes of the brush slowing.

"She did. I was speaking of Briar. My mother's sister."

"What did your birth mother die of?"

"The cold," Dawsyn answers simply, cupping water in her hands. She watches it dwindle away through the breaches. "As most of them do."

"And Briar?" Baltisse asks, the brush pausing.

Dawsyn sighs, throat tightening again. "She gave up."

Dawsyn lifts herself from the tub, taking a scrap of towel from the bench to pat herself dry.

Baltisse passes Dawsyn a fresh pile of clothing, clean and dry. "Not a common trait," she mutters.

"Amongst mothers?"

"Amongst Sabars," Baltisse corrects, not bothering to turn her back as Dawsyn dresses. There is a tone in the mage's voice – one of... disappointment, perhaps? And it chafes.

"You say you've lived a long life," Dawsyn says mildly, hiding the anger simmering beneath the surface. "But I doubt you endured a mite of Briar Sabar's suffering."

"And this suffering... it led her into the Chasm?"

As Dawsyn relives the memory, she knows Baltisse must see it too – Briar pressing her lips to Dawsyn's forehead and then lurching herself onto the ice, over the lip. For a moment, Dawsyn feels herself there again, alone on the Ledge for the first time. Unsure if she shouldn't just follow that slick, promising path over the edge. Unable to rise from the snow and journey back to her den of girls. Unwilling to live out the rest of her days on the Ledge by herself. She remembers how very desperately she wanted them all back. She didn't want to be alone. Now she doesn't know how to be anything else.

"Briar answered the call and followed it into the Chasm," Baltisse says, and Dawsyn suddenly realises how close the mage has come, how her hand hovers over Dawsyn's but does not hold it.

"She was tired," Dawsyn murmurs, and she can feel it too – that tiredness, handed down, bone-deep. Her shoulders curve downward with the weight of it. She has only just awoken, and already she wants to return to sleep, as she does every day. Her body aches with a phantom exhaustion, with the expectation of what awaits. Each morning steals another share of her stamina, the pressure slowly sinking her. She knows that before she carried this millstone, Briar must have carried it too, and her grandmother before that. It is no wonder that Briar only wanted to rest. She only wanted to sleep.

Seal your eyes and sleep.

Baltisse's hands are on Dawsyn's cheeks now, pulling her face around to meet her molten gaze. But the mage is blurred. She can't find her. And Dawsyn feels her cheeks grow wet.

"You will not follow that call, Dawsyn Sabar," the mage says slowly, firmly. "You will not listen to it."

It is not in either woman's nature to embrace, but Dawsyn imagines this is the extent of Baltisse's affection – stroking her cheeks with the pads of her thumbs, taking away her tears until Dawsyn's head is clear. Until the howls of the Ledge fade.

Dawsyn lets the mage's strength imbue her – the truest power between women. In Baltisse, she can see the sliver of connection she still reaches for, after all these years. That tether of solidarity. Her den of girls.

"There are things to be done," Baltisse says, and the words are firm, bolstering.

Dawsyn nods. "Yes, there are."

"We start today," she proclaims. "We need to see Salem and Esra. They'll have what we need."

"How long will it take to get there?"

"That depends, sweet." The mage grins.

"On what?"

"On whether you agree to another lesson."

Dawsyn pauses. "And what will that lesson entail?"

"We will fold," the mage says plainly, her smirk growing.

"I do not speak witch." Dawsyn sighs. "How does one *fold*?"

"Like this," Baltisse quips, and then she disappears.

Chapter Fourteen

The women – one mage, one fugitive – appear suddenly at the front door of a sagging inn. The fugitive immediately bends at the waist and heaves her breakfast onto the stoop.

The mage lifts her skirt away from the mess, wrinkling her nose. "They *always* vomit," she mutters. "Sabar? Stand straight. You embarrass yourself."

"Fuck you." Dawsyn, back still hunched, sucks breath at a violent pace. "I am never doing that again."

"You will," Baltisse says darkly. "And you'll show more fortitude next time. These things take practice. Preparation."

It is true, Dawsyn had not been prepared. The second the mage's hand had clasped around her forearm, the world had collapsed. Or... not collapsed, but rather... compressed, as though the parts she was made of were mere walls. She had felt her body condense, bones shrinking, organs folding. Cell squeezed into cell, until the pressure was too great, until she wanted to roar from the unbearable strain. And then, like a latch opening, she unfolded again. Expanded. She found her feet on a familiar stoop, before littering it with the contents of her belly.

She rights herself, trying to slow the air that races to refill her lungs after every ounce of breath was squeezed from them. She turns and spits.

"You are disgusting," Baltisse says sweetly.

"Hush, witch," Dawsyn returns. "Next time, if there ever is one, I'll be aiming for your shoes."

No noise seeps through the cracks of the door. Salem's inn is often devoid of staying patrons, save for Baltisse at her leisure, and, of course, Esra on his extended liquor runs.

Suddenly, a clamour comes from within – the sound of breaking wood and shattering glass.

Dawsyn's stomach drops.

Without delay, the women crash through the doorway at the same time, their shoulders colliding. Dawsyn hears a loud groaning coming from the dining room, and with haste, they both fling open the twin doors, eyes wheeling for their quarry.

In the dim half-lit dining room, Esra lies upon the rubble of what was once a wooden table, his eyes scrunched either in pain, or from the exertion of shouting expletives to the heavens.

"Oh, *holy fucking mother of the mountains!* I cannot *breathe,* Salem!"

Salem rounds his bar, throwing a rag to the floor in anger. "That'd be the bloody day, yeh bastard-born half-wit! Yeh broke me fuckin' table!"

"Alas, the table has broken me in return, Salem. Oh, *bloody fucking hell, my arse!*"

Salem raises his hands in exasperation. "That's what yeh bloody get, yeh bog-titted moron. I've told yeh a hundred times, don't go dancin' on me tables."

"*Trickery and deceit,* old man! You challenged me, knowing how weak these decrepit tables are. Knowing how delicate my frame is!" Esra rolls from side to side, hands cradling his backside.

"I did no such fuckin' thing!"

"You proclaimed me too weakened by last night's drink to walk straight! Practically begged me to prove you wrong."

"Aye, and bolly to yeh." Salem huffs. "Yeh've proved me right. An' now yeh owe me a week's worth o' liquor."

"Oh, my arse!"

"Mother above," Baltisse intones, walking in a straight line to the bar, disregarding the man on the floor atop the wreckage, who finally turns to notice the presence of her. "Salem, I thought we agreed to lock him under a trapdoor until at least noon each day?"

"Aye, but it's hard to get a decent grip. He's always bloody covered in silk." Salem speaks to the mage, but looks to Dawsyn, eyes sparkling, lips curving upward. "Miss Dawsyn... love..." he says to her. The man, balding, hulking and rough, takes a hat from his head and grips it tightly in his fists before him, seeming unsure of what more he should say. He smiles gently at her, eyes welling, and Dawsyn cannot help but smile in return.

"Dawsyn! Finally, a woman of mercy! Please spare me from these compassionless, heartless–"

"Esra, you show all too much of your thighs for this time of morning," Dawsyn interrupts, stepping over the debris of splintered wood to Esra's sprawled form.

Esra looks down, and indeed, his dress has ridden up into his lap, his black, muscled legs revealed. "Oh," he says, unabashed. "Not quite the show I was aiming to provide."

"It was entertaining enough." Dawsyn smirks, holding a hand out to him.

"No, leave me here, Dawsyn, dear. Your sympathy is all I need to heal my broken arse. Though I fear it may not ever be the same."

"With a pretty face like yours, one needn't be concerned by the state of their arse."

"Ah, poetry," Esra murmurs, his eyes closing in a drunken stupor. "It has always been my vice." And with that, the man begins to snore, his legs bent at an angle that begs discomfort.

Feeling inexplicably lighter, Dawsyn stands, turning to Salem who waits by the bar. "Should we leave him here?"

"He weighs a tonne, lass. Best to let him sleep it off."

The pair smile at one another, and there is much that she wishes to say, but Baltisse clashes bottles and glasses from behind the bar and the words remain unsaid. Instead, Dawsyn contents herself with looking over his face and arms, happy to see no marks worth noting. He is well, just as Baltisse said he would be.

Baltisse groans. "Salem, did you let that imbecile drink my wine?"

"I've never *let* either o' yeh drink *anythin'*. But alas, the two of yeh tend to do as yeh please, even if it means puttin' an honest workin' man out of business."

Baltisse only rolls her eyes, and Salem turns back to Dawsyn. "Have yeh eaten, lass? I could fix yeh somethin'? Yer the only one who waits to be asked."

Dawsyn sighs contentedly as Salem walks away to the store cupboards beyond the bar, not waiting to hear her answer.

It is evening before Esra awakens, and in the time before it, neither Dawsyn nor Baltisse do anything to prepare for their journey. Instead, they linger, bothering Salem, lounging in his dining room.

Eventually Dawsyn rises to light a fire, and then again to follow Salem out to his vegetable patch. She helps him chop wood, till the soil, feed his chickens and listens to him spin tales about Esra's many, many exploits over the years. Dawsyn laughs. It feels odd to laugh. It thaws her, somehow. Releases the vice on her lungs, makes breathing easier. She buries the burden of the coming days and turns her body away from the mountain, basking in the warmth of Salem, of the inn instead.

"The bloody git nearly got himself killed at least a thousand times. Once he came runnin' and screamin' up the path, hollerin' out to all an' sunder. Behind him came two guards, both with their swords drawn. It were a sight. Esra flouncin' away in his skirts, with those two soldiers barely keepin' pace.

He'd lit one o' the pubs on fire, yeh see, back in the Mecca. Tipped over a whiskey barrel. Knocked out the knees o' a man with a holy book and a candle. Stopped his preachin' right quick."

Dawsyn laughs again and Salem seems to delight in it, but his smile fades some as her laughter ebbs. He looks past her, over her shoulder, to the mountain, looming all too close.

"It was Ryon who saved his sorry arse that time," he continues, voice careful, quiet.

Dawsyn's pitchfork hovers for a moment before carrying on turning over the soil. She shoves it into the soft earth again, a little harder than before.

"He came out and those two guards stopped in their tracks, what with a big behemoth comin' toward 'em." Salem smiles sadly. "He told 'em he'd pay for the damages personally, but that Esra weren't goin' nowhere. Told 'em Esra was his simple-minded brother, and that he would ensure it wouldn't happen again." He barks a rough laugh then stops quickly, making Dawsyn look up. "He was a good man."

Dawsyn gives a heavy breath. "He wasn't a man at all, Salem." She makes her tone gentle, for his sake, but her eyes are anything but. "Not all that good, either."

Salem seems stunned. "How can yeh say that, lass?" he breathes. "I thought... I thought yeh... the two of yeh looked so–"

"He made a deal with Alvira to kill me, and he didn't even have the gumption to confess once he'd decided against the idea," Dawsyn says, all in one breath. "Whether he changed his mind before or after I fucked him, we will never know." With that, she throws the pitchfork prongs into the soil and turns her back on the inn, on Salem, and beholds the mountain, its slope climbing into the clouds and all the way to the Ledge. "It matters little," she says, as much to herself as to him. "I didn't like him for his goodness. I liked him for his honesty." She sighs. "I made a mistake trusting him. And it almost killed me."

"Aye," Salem agrees. "But he ain't here to defend his actions, Miss Dawsyn. And I know that boy. He woulda died regrettin' his mistakes, just as yeh live regrettin' yers."

"It does not matter," Dawsyn repeats, despite the ache in her chest, despite the emptiness that gnaws and gnaws endlessly in her gut, no matter how she fights to subdue it. "We are all bad and good, are we not? The fools are the ones who try to separate the two."

"Aye," Salem says again. "But some o' us were born fools, lass. No hope fer me, I'm afraid. Yeh won't convince me that it ain't mostly good yer made up of." He wipes his nose. "Same as that half-man." Salem grins, eyes wet, and Dawsyn almost gives in at the sight of the man beginning to cry. She almost folds to the pressure of keeping her grief silent. Almost lets the name wash through her mind.

Salem had known Ryon for years more than Dawsyn. He'd forged a friendship more tried and tested than hers. And it is not for her to tell him whether his friend was good or not.

She wants to take back the words and let the man remember the hybrid in a way that brings him peace – an impossible feat. So, instead she takes Salem's muddied hand in hers. She waits until he can meet her eye before she says, "I owe you my life, Salem. If it were not for you, Terrsaw would have watched me hang. Thank you."

Salem shoos her away half-heartedly, blinking away his tears. "Leave it, lass. It was Baltisse who saved yeh."

"It was both," Dawsyn presses, letting the man back away. "And one day I will repay you."

"You'd better not," he warns, pointing a finger threateningly. "I'll not have a young woman puttin' her neck out fer an old codger like me."

Long after night falls, Baltisse gives Dawsyn a meaningful look, and the latter nods. They have lingered far longer than needed. The second Dawsyn had stepped over Salem's stoop, her reluctance had grown. She found that she wanted to stay here, at this bar, with Esra's jewelled fingers poking her ribs in jest, Salem grumbling in a steady stream, Baltisse rolling her eyes and helping herself to the wine. But the night was wearing thin. Staying meant taking a bed for the night, and whilst there were plenty on the floor above, she knew how plagued the place would be with recollections of Ryon, pushing into her, lowering his mouth to hers. So, she stands and pushes away her tankard, amid Esra's protests.

"It's the middle of the night, you simpletons! Stay! I have a rather scandalous story I've been dying to share. It involves bed mites and Salem's backside."

"ESRA!"

"Mother save us," Baltisse mutters, downing the last of her wine. "Glacia is surely the better choice. Sabar, we will gather what we need."

Esra sighs, dejected. "Fine," he mopes. "Why does no one ever wish to howl at the moon with me anymore, Salem?"

"Because more often than not, yeh end up bawlin' like a baby with yer pants 'round yer ankles and yer head in a barrel. None of us are all that decent, Es, but I reckon we don't deserve to see such a sight."

"You are an incurable bore, old man."

"Esra," Dawsyn interrupts, though she wouldn't mind listening to their squabbling until the night bled into morning. "Could I trouble you for some weapons?"

"Good god, woman! Weapons? I am but an honest liquor proprietor and I have absolutely no dabblings in–"

"Oh, shut up, Es," Baltisse calls as she leaves the dining room.

"Right," Esra returns, standing abruptly. "Let's get you all kitted up then, shall we Dawsyn darling?"

Dawsyn follows Esra into the hallway, and then to a familiar storeroom. Built into the floorboards, Dawsyn knows, is a trapdoor – one that conceals a small cellar beneath. She watches as Esra heaves it open and remembers how dark it had been hiding down there in that black hole while Glacians raided above. She recalls the cold – not from the air, but from Ryon's fingertips as his Glacian blood ran wild.

"Here we are," Esra says, lighting a lantern, and without an ounce of fear, he jumps into the depths below.

Dawsyn makes to follow, but before she can, his black shaven head reappears, and he begins hefting objects through the hole, letting them clatter at Dawsyn's feet. Swords first, then knives, sheaths of arrows, and finally a singular ax.

A battle ax.

Dawsyn bends to examine it while Esra grunts and curses his way out of the hole. Its handle is like none Dawsyn has ever held. Reinforced with steel halfway down the neck and etched with the Terrsaw emblem. It is ancient. The wood at the handle base has been worn smooth by a ghost's hand, grooves where fingers once held it a thousand times to win a hundred battles. The twin blades still gleam, though they are thin. Countless passes through stone have shaved them down. They will pass through wood and flesh as though they were water.

"Dawsyn," says Esra, his tone softer, more docile than she has ever heard it, and it makes her look up. "Is there anything I can tell you that will make you stay?" he asks. His shoulders are already slumped in defeat, the debate already won. She has already cast aside his concerns.

"I'm afraid not," she tells him.

Dawsyn rises with the ax in one hand, four knives of various size and utility in the other.

"An *ax* of all things?" Esra shakes his head, exasperated. "Take a sword, darling, or take the bow and arrows."

"It's a fine ax."

"Its heavy and gaudy and you'll not fell even one man with it before you keel over from back pain."

Esra continues to rant, but Dawsyn only looks down at the

ax, perfectly placed in her hand, and when Esra's voice grows draining she spins it over in her palm.

In a flash of glinting steel, the ax flies through the air, bypassing Esra's nose. It buries into the wall.

Esra does not finish his sentence. Instead, he chokes on the words as though they stick to his throat. He peruses her anew. The Sabar girl, the woman of the Ledge.

There is no malice in her stare, no quiver in her hand. Merely resignation, duty.

"Fuck me," Esra murmurs, voice quivering.

"I thank you for your concern, Es, truly. But we should agree that you do not have the slightest inkling of how many men I may or may not fell. I've grown familiar enough with the ways to use an ax. For example–" Dawsyn comes closer. "This place here," she touches a place below his ear, "is where the blade heel enters when I want to separate one's spine from their mind. Imagine a simple girl of the Ledge, knowing such things. She could only know it if she had seen it – first-hand, I believe they say. She knows it only because it has proven effective a dozen times."

She steps away again, turning to where the ax is fixed in place, meaning to retrieve it.

"Dawsyn, darling, I do not mean to underestimate you," Esra says softly. "I only mean that you should leave prepared."

"I am as prepared as I will ever be," she answers, wrenching the blade from the wood.

"But what you are trying to accomplish cannot be done alone!" There is a tremor in his voice, but he seems determined to say what he must. "You must know how likely it is that you will die? If not on the slopes or in Glacia, then on the Ledge when the blood runs bad. I may not know what you have planned, but I suspect you'll place yourself in the middle."

He slumps slightly, as though he himself feels the weight of Dawsyn's burden. For all his bluster, Dawsyn can see that beneath it, he truly worries. "You've suffered enough," he says quietly.

He is right. She has been starved and beaten and left alone, hauled over the Chasm and chased down the slopes. She has endured worse than few could withstand over a lifetime.

"You could find yourself some peace now, Dawsyn," he pleads, eyes beseeching her. "This quest needn't be yours."

Dawsyn sighs. She places a hand up on Esra's cheek, wiping away the evidence of his good nature. "I don't think people like me get to find peace, Es," she says. "Though if anyone in this world deserves such a thing, I think it might be you."

He nods, having said all he can, knowing it would do nothing to stay her course. He sniffs and covers her hand with his own. His eyes, warm and familiar, become fervent. "Then, be sure to cut out the spines of those who dare to think you simple."

Dawsyn grimaces down at the strange ax in her hand, etched in Terrsaw markings, knowing she will have very little choice in the matter.

CHAPTER FIFTEEN

Baltisse awaits her in front of the inn, donned in fur and boots.

Dawsyn is dressed similarly, having done away with Baltisse's robes in favour of borrowed trousers from Esra's stash. The man in the dress had wrinkled his nose as she pulled them on. "They do nothing for you, my darling."

Dawsyn had simply smiled.

Salem rummages within a large sack at Baltisse's feet.

"I knew yeh bloody sneaked some, yeh thievin' old wart! What fuckin' use do yeh have fer wine? Yeh hikin' up a fuckin' mountain, woman!"

Baltisse regards Salem's stooped form a moment, her brow furrowed. Then, her hand quickly rises and Salem is suddenly thrown onto his backside, the thud reverberating beneath Dawsyn's feet.

"*Ow!* Baltisse, yeh insufferable–"

"Leave the wine where it is, Salem," she says, sounding bored. "And we won't be hiking up the slopes, will we, Dawsyn?"

A shiver climbs Dawsyn's spine.

"No?" Esra asks. "Got a dragon stuffed in your skirts somewhere, Baltisse?" He turns to give Dawsyn a conspiratorial look. "I always sensed an inordinate amount of heat coming from her under carriage whenever I walked–"

But like Salem, Esra does not get to finish the sentence

before he ends up flat on his back, groaning soundly. "*Argh*, not my arse *again*! It has known enough suffering!"

Dawsyn sighs and steps over him. "When will the day come that you men learn to say less?"

"Oh, I hope it never comes," Baltisse replies, smoothing down her fur sleeves. "What a bore."

Dawsyn reaches Baltisse and takes the supplies over her shoulder. She grins as Esra and Salem come to stand.

"So long, then, yeh pair o' witches," Salem barks, already limping back to the inn.

"Thank you," Dawsyn says to his back, and smiles when he waves a hand over his head in reply. Dawsyn winks a goodbye at Esra.

Baltisse takes Dawsyn's forearm in her long fingers. "Deep breath, sweet. We will both need it."

Before they fold, Dawsyn has enough time to see Salem turn and give the women one fleeting look of fear. She sees Esra's face quietly darken, both stricken behind the façade of their banter.

Before Dawsyn has time to turn back, the air is sucked from her lungs, her body, the world. The universe coalesces, pressing in with such force… she is sure she will die.

The mage was right in insisting that Dawsyn would be more prepared.

Right and wrong.

Dawsyn did at least know what to expect – the insurmountable pressure, the unbelievable strain, followed by the abrupt unspooling, where her bones re-calcify, her organs swell and every nerve ending shrieks indignantly. But though Dawsyn anticipates it this time, her experience is very much the same. She vomits as her feet hit the snow. Her hands bite into the drift before she can tumble forward. She heaves violently.

"*Argh,*" Dawsyn spits, sweat beading her forehead. "*Fuck!* I'd rather take my chances climbing the mountain."

There is no reply from Baltisse – the mage is likely too disgusted.

Dawsyn focuses on the powdery snow mere inches from her eyes and counts her breaths, willing her stomach not to revolt again.

It is several moments more before Dawsyn looks up. She expects the expanse of the Glacian Colony to undulate around her – a dizzying network of shelters in their crooked lanes. Or else, perhaps Baltisse has folded them straight to the Glacian palace, its monstrous granite towers and turrets throwing the small kingdom into perpetual shadow, a beast all its own.

But Dawsyn sees neither.

Instead, she sees the rapid incline of the slope, the thick spruce trunks towering like shadowy giants into the night sky. She sees the undisturbed drifts of snow, painfully white.

Not Glacia, then. Just the slopes.

"Baltisse?" Dawsyn calls, turning to question her.

But the mage is not there. In fact, she is nowhere. There are no marks in the snow in any direction.

Dawsyn draws her ax from her back, her pulse spiking. "Baltisse?" she shouts, louder now, but no answer comes.

Ravens disturb the pine branches above and Dawsyn grips the ax handle reflexively, watching their black wings glide between the trees, soaring low to the forest floor and over the lip of a cliff.

Dawsyn's eyes widen. "*Fuck.*" Her breath fogs as she runs, her boots slipping down the decline to the cliff edge. She slows as she nears. "Baltisse?" she calls again.

The drop is a short one, but still threatening enough. At its end lies a crumpled figure, barely discernible in the darkness but for the contrast against the snow.

"*Baltisse!*" Dawsyn shouts, but it might as well be a call into the Chasm for all the effect it has. The mage's form remains still.

Dawsyn gasps once with indecision, eyes darting to all corners of the forest for a way down. But there is nothing. Not a tree nor jutting rock to clamber down. There is nothing else for it. She heaves her supplies over the edge, letting it fall that short way to the snow below and watches it sink into the drift. Next, her ax. It too disappears into the white, the depths of which is indiscernible – a foot or five?

Dawsyn closes her eyes. Her heart pounding, she sends a singular prayer to the sky that the powder below is deep enough… and then she jumps.

The fall is a quick one, and she tucks her body as she comes to land, but the snow is mercifully deep and she sinks to her knees, pain radiating up her legs. But nothing has broken, and in that, luck sides with her.

Dawsyn crawls from the snow to where Baltisse lies, a curtain of hair shrouding her face.

"Baltisse!" Dawsyn calls, wiping the hair away awkwardly with her gloved hands. "Be alive, witch, please!"

A shallow gasp, and then. "Do not… call me… 'witch.'"

Dawsyn sags in relief, letting her forehead touch the snow briefly. "What happened?"

The mage coughs as she tries to speak, the splutters wet and choking. Dawsyn helps her roll to the side, where she spits blood onto the white powder. Just like the people of the Ledge did, days before they succumbed to the sickness in their lungs.

No. Do not die.

"Do not be so dramatic, Dawsyn Sabar," Baltisse gasps, but she has begun to shiver, and each moment they linger on the snow will see the frost steal in.

"Can you move?" It is difficult to see the state of her limbs beneath the heavy clothing.

Baltisse grimaces, as though she means to bite back a retort, but then she swallows, humbled by pain. "Not far," she admits.

Dawsyn curses and looks around. The rock face is solid, and

there are no caves. She'll need to scout a place to camp – a warren, perhaps.

"I'll return," Dawsyn says, pulling off her coat, but the mage has closed her eyes once more, lids unmoving in sleep. Only small puffs of fog give away her breath.

She pulls Baltisse's head away from the snow and lays her coat beneath it, wrapping the excess around Baltisse's ears and the side of her face.

"Stay the frost," she tells the mage's still form. Then, she grabs her ax and rises from the ground.

Dawsyn's feet pummel through the deep drifts as she runs downhill. She had been more than willing to make this journey back to Glacia alone, but the presence of Baltisse has brought her something she only now recognises as comradery. Loath as she is to admit it, she does not want to be left alone. Not again. *Do not die,* her mind bids the mage. *Do not die.*

The snow thins enough that her legs are no longer ploughing, and she stops at the sight of a cropping of great boulders leaning together, almost invisible beneath the snow. At its base is the black mouth of a cave.

She knows it might already be occupied by the creatures of this mountain. A mountain cat, perhaps. But she'll be lucky to haul Baltisse even this far to reach shelter. She cannot afford to run farther. She has little choice.

Dawsyn wastes no time. Finding a rock large enough, she carefully approaches the cave mouth and hurls it inside, listening to the way it clatters against the walls. She waits. Nothing within stirs. Good enough.

She grits her teeth and makes haste back the way she came, following her tracks in the snow. The path feels easier twice trodden, but her legs still struggle against the drift. She uses her hands when she needs to, running, crawling when she must.

She climbs one incline, and then another. Each time her throat tightens to see her tracks before her, continuing upward.

How far has she come? How will she carry Baltisse back here?

A distinct sound makes her halt.

A snap.

On the Ledge, there are keen differences between sounds signalling danger, and knowing them is vital. The sound of cracking ice is the worst. There is little one can do when ice gives way. The sound of cracking skulls is a hazard of the ice; it too becomes familiar when one lives atop it. But the crack of a stick underfoot is a distinct warning. It carries none of the volume or urgency of the former, but the threat is just as real.

Awareness skitters across her skin. Licks of instinct on her neck say she is not alone.

In her centre, the sentient magic awakens, undulates.

The forest quiets, as though aware of an intruder as well. Slowly, she slips her fingers to her waist.

The wind stills, her fingers grip the blade handle, and she spins.

When the blade leaves her fingers, it turns, end over end. It cuts through the air to the place where a man stands, sinfully dark against the white.

Before the knife hits the ridge between his eyes, he raises a hand. With a precise swipe, he snatches it from the air. As though he'd been expecting it.

"Malishka," he says.

CHAPTER SIXTEEN

It took four men to transport him into the back of a wagon.

His legs and wrists were shackled, and he was held at sword-point – several of them, in fact. Though the guards could not know it, they had no need to fear his attack. An escape attempt was useless down here in this keep. If he meant to escape – and he did – his best chance had just been offered by Queen Alvira herself.

Ryon went willingly out of the keep. He allowed himself to be pulled and shuffled above ground, and then through a tunnelled exit. When the guards shunted him into the back of the enclosed wagon with barred windows, he made no attempt to stop them.

He heard the scramble of activity outside the wagon as the guards readied the horses and strategized their impromptu excursion to the town's square.

"Keep the wagon surrounded at all times," the captain's voice instructed. "A walking barricade on each side, understand?"

"Yes, Captain," came a chorus of answers.

They set forth, the wagon swaying and lurching across the uneven ground. It would take very little time to reach the statue of the *Fallen Woman*. Ryon knew that the time for escape was now, while the wagon ambled on, and the guards were focused on the destination ahead.

He was cramped, his neck bending at an odd angle to fit within the small space. It would be difficult to manoeuvre himself without attracting the notice of the guards, but that was not his biggest challenge. His shackled wrists were locked to the bars on the walls. He would doubt his ability to simply break them. That is, of course, had they not chained him to a bar with a precariously loose bolt.

It rattled quietly, barely discernible beneath the clopping horse hooves and rattling wheels. Still, it seemed too obvious an escape. It couldn't be a trick, surely? And yet, he had to wonder why he would be shackled to the only faulty bar in a row of many. Was it mere luck?

It took the smallest attempt to pull the bolt free, a moment longer to pull it away from the wall and slide his shackles free.

The irons around his wrists could be dealt with, but the ones around his ankles were problematic. With his strength so depleted, the hole in his chest so newly mended, he could not depend on his wings. He would need to run.

He began inspecting the chain, looking for separated chinks, rust, anything that might signify weakness. Yet again, it was a far easier task than he could have imagined, for the cuff on his right ankle still held the pin that would unlock it.

Ryon almost laughed. He would have, if he wasn't overcome with suspicion.

"Slow!" came the captain's voice again, and the horses were pulled to a steady walk. Ryon could hear the hustle of the Mecca around the wagon, glimpse flashes of it through the windows. They were close.

He pulled the pin free and unclad himself from the irons – first his ankles, then his wrists.

"Steady! Make way!"

He crawled to the back of the wagon.

"By order of the Queen, make way!"

Ryon took a fortifying breath against the burn in his chest, and with all his might, he slammed his feet into the back of the doors.

They burst free. Ryon with them.

"Halt!" came the voice of a guard, and then, "Captain! The prisoner!" But Ryon's feet were already hitting the cobblestone and carrying him away. He sprinted through the Mecca, dodging around carts and horses, the people traversing the busy lanes in throngs. He weaved amongst them, barely hearing their gasps of shock as he flew by.

The guards were in pursuit behind him for a time, giving chase in their heavy armour, shouting for pedestrians to move. Even in his depleted state, they were no match for him. He heard the clamour of them growing evermore distant as he ran and ran. By the time he reached the fringe, he could hardly hear them at all.

Ryon did not stop until he reached the forest. By then his chest was a burning pit, fraying at the edges. He found a tree to lean against, doubling over to catch his breath. *Mother above,* he thought. *What now, Mesrich?*

He wiped the sweat from his eyes. One thought arose: the same name that always came to him, rebounding, pulsing, even when his mind ought to be elsewhere. *Dawsyn.*

Where was she?

He was sure he knew where she was going, but as for her exact location? That would require something more than mere instinct.

Ryon reached into his pocket, fingers finding the smallest of treasures buried within its seam. He held the ornament skyward, watching the sunlight refract from it, for a moment praying that it would prove useful. An unimpressive bauble, slightly bent and gaudy, but charmed by a powerful mage. He pressed Baltisse's ring to his lips and slid it onto his third finger, vowing that when he saw the mage again, he would vow eternal servitude.

Flexing his fingers, Ryon turned toward the mountain.

CHAPTER SEVENTEEN

He had walked all day and well into the night to reach her.

Each time he thought the course was set, the charmed ring would suddenly tug him in a different direction, as though Dawsyn were changing her path.

In a moment of doubt, Ryon thought the mage's charm might be failing. He resorted to using his wings in his desperation – a stupid mistake. They merely carried him part way over the Boulder Gate before collapsing and sending him crashing onto the mountainside.

But he has found her. She is here.

And she is blessedly, divinely whole. She is well.

He exhales in a rush of triumph and feels the hole in his chest grow smaller.

Her raven black hair swirls in the weak wind. Her cheeks glow red with cold, lips cracked but still hers. She stands tall, proud as ever. Eyes widening in shock, breaths quickening.

Within him, the dam of his fear – that leaking wall that had pooled every drop of dread – breaks. Acute relief floods him. He laughs.

She is alive.

She is as short and furious and maddeningly beautiful as he remembers, and he wants to go to her. He wants to fight off the fists he knows will rain down upon him and take her into his arms, press his lips to hers again... finally.

He steps toward her.

Dawsyn flinches. It is a small, subtle movement – a twitch between her brows, a lift in her shoulders – but it is enough. He has never seen Dawsyn flinch.

Seconds suspend between them, and he watches as her expression turns from shock to fleeting relief, confusion. And then... unfettered, blinding fury.

Ryon raises his hand. "Malishka... don't–"

But it is too late. She slips another knife from her side and throws it at him.

He ducks with inches to spare. *"Dawsyn! Wait–"*

But she throws another and he rolls as it pierces his tunic, ripping a hole in the sleeve as he retreats.

He rights himself, only to see her closing the distance between them, an ax in her hand.

"Fuck."

He retreats further, his back suddenly slamming against the trunk of a tree, and he realises too late that she has pinned him there on purpose, chased him to this exact place... where she will likely split him apart.

"Malishka, *stop!* Will you not even let me explain before you kill me?"

She halts her advance, not close enough for him to make a move to disarm her. She isn't so easily beaten.

For a moment, their eyes lock, hers screaming from some unnameable turmoil, and it almost breaks him to see it. He almost kneels in the snow and surrenders to it.

But he cannot let the Queen win.

Dawsyn pulls the ax back over her head, forearms shaking, vacant of reason. With a cry of agony, she hefts it forward, and Ryon closes his eyes.

There is a heavy, crunching thud. Pine needles shower Ryon's face and shoulders. But there is no pain.

He opens his eyes.

Above his head, buried into the trunk, the ax shudders from the force of the collision, concerningly close to his scalp.

Ryon sags. Exhales. Cursing, he rests his hands on his knees, his chest heaving. He looks up warily, expecting to see her bearing down on him, murderous, or perhaps pacing. Instead, he finds her kneeling in the snow, face hidden in her hands. She shudders all over, overcome. Though they are quiet, he hears the sobbing, muffled by her hands. And he understands now, why wars are so often won and lost upon the promise of mercy, because here is his heart, wrenched outside of himself, twisting before him in the snow, and he'd give entire kingdoms to ease the torment.

Look at her, he thinks. *Look at what you have done.*

He waits until the shuddering slows, reticent though he is, not to take her into his arms. When her breaths begin to even, he lowers himself beside her, ever so carefully.

Tendrils of wayward hair hide her face, and he reaches out to brush them back. "Is that all, malishka?" he asks hesitantly. "Any other blades hidden under there?"

He'd once said something very similar to her, on this very mountain, but if she remembers, she gives no reaction. She only draws shuddering breaths, the air fogging in violent whorls before her.

"Malishka–"

"Do not call me that!" she screams, finally lifting her head. Her bottom lip trembles.

Ryon swallows his retort. He has earnt this much, he knows. But she might as well have thrown the ax into his chest. "One day, I will earn the right to say it again."

"Go!" she yells, and the word is so full of venom that it strikes him. Another blow. "Go from here!"

He expected this. Did he not? He has worried over it, every step of the way. But he won't be cast aside so easily. "I cannot be where you are not, Dawsyn."

"You will have to try!"

Ryon knows that if he must follow her from the skies or hidden away in the tree-tops, he will. "You know I *can't*. You... you know me."

Dawsyn stands, towering over him, but her lips do not cease in their trembling. "I do not even recognise you," she spits, the words quiet and filled with anger. Worse, they are – as they always are with Dawsyn – horribly, cuttingly true.

CHAPTER EIGHTEEN

She says nothing more, has no air with which to say it.

How can he be here? How is it that he lives? How can he stand before her, here on this mountain, whole and well?

And he *is* whole. The midnight eyes, the keen stare, the dark stubbled jaw. The place where his eyebrows bunch as he frowns, the way the skin along his throat pebbles when he looks at her. All of him is here... alive.

All of him is shockingly, inexplicably well.

All of him betrayed her.

Her mind collapses and rebuilds, over and over. Unimaginable relief, followed and overthrown by crippling fury.

He watches her carefully. No wings nor talons. Just Ryon. The hybrid. A man she once thought of as hers. Does he feel the pull that she does? Do his hands and heart and stomach ache? Does it feel like an illness to him? An infection? Does he feel the urge to cut it out as she does?

There is a tear in the sleeve of his shirt, a smatter of blood droplets stains it. Even this... this small wound feels intolerable to her. She cannot kill him. Can't so much as cut him.

And she despises herself for it – that she cannot cut him away, however much he might deserve it.

"Ask me," Ryon says, jaw ticking. "Ask me if it is true."

Dawsyn stills. Dread befalls her. She shakes her head. She cannot speak.

Ryon advances. "Ask me if what the Queen said was true, Dawsyn. Ask me if I made a deal to kill you."

But Dawsyn cannot hear the answer. She cannot hear his excuses and spend her life wondering if they are lies. Even more so, she doesn't want to hear that it was true – that everything Alvira told her was real.

"I saw it," she breathes. "I saw your face, hybrid."

He does not respond.

"The Queen offered you a deal. She asked you to kill me."

"Yes," Ryon says, now without hesitation. "She did. Now ask me if I took it." He watches her with a pleading stare, willing her to listen, to see.

Dawsyn turns her face away. She allows herself another moment to crumble, where he cannot see it this time. Then she swallows the pain, swallows the relief. "Whether you took it or not is only half of your betrayal," she spits. "You kept it from me. I need not know more."

Dawsyn begins to stride away. She means to leave him there in the snow, lost and alone as she was before they met, before she left one prison for another. The wind carries his voice so that she cannot hear what he says, but she is unable to block it completely.

"Mal – Dawsyn, wait!"

She won't. She wants to erase his dark stare from her memory.

"*Fuck*... Dawsyn, stop. Listen! Someone comes!"

She stops abruptly and turns. "*What?*"

Ryon halts below her, his hand raised. "Listen," he implores, gesticulating to the cascading slopes behind them.

She narrows her eyes, searching, hearing the faint sounds of footfalls in the distance. "Who?" she asks, voice turning to steel.

"Guards, I presume," Ryon answers. "The very ones I escaped."

Dawsyn pierces him with a glare. "Are you so incompetent?" she asks acidly. "You led them here?"

He grits his teeth, swallowing some smart retort. Wise of him. "So it seems."

Dawsyn fumes silently. She has many questions. How did he escape the palace? How is it that human guards have managed to track a man with wings? But if those guards are about to descend upon them, only one question matters: "How many?"

"Five, maybe six."

Dawsyn's shoulders settle. "Simple quarry. They will be weary."

Ryon nods, looking down at his hand. In it, he holds her ax. In her desperation to flee him, she must have left it behind. Some small part of her mind notes that this is a first. Like a gesture of truce, Ryon holds it out to her.

She closes the distance between them in seconds and snatches it, a scowl on her face. "I should leave you here to take care them yourself. You led them here, after all."

"Would you believe me if I told you that I needed your help getting rid of them?"

She stares at him, baffled.

Ryon sighs. "It is the truth."

"The truth is not something I can trust from you."

From out of the mist below come the guards. Their ridiculously weighted Terrsaw armour glinting in the weak dawn light, immediately giving away their position. Out here in the elements, they are hardly seasoned fighters. They could be outsmarted in seconds.

And time is of the essence. She cannot afford to tarry. "Baltisse is hurt," Dawsyn tells Ryon, without preamble.

Ryon's eyes widen. "Baltisse? She is here?"

"She came with me," Dawsyn says. "She needs help."

"Damn it," he grunts, then holds out his hand. "Will you lend me a weapon?"

Dawsyn takes a small blade from her belt and flings it at him with deliberate carelessness.

He catches it anyway, then grimaces at its size.

"Let's make this quick," Dawsyn says, advancing forward.

The Terrsaw guards branch outward at the sight of Dawsyn and Ryon's advance, though neither have their weapons raised. The expressions of the soldiers show how unaware they are of their disadvantage. Dawsyn and Ryon have the higher ground, and neither of them slip on the slope the way the guards do, their feet so unaccustomed to the tendencies of uneven terrain.

Dawsyn does not pause in her approach, and so the guards pull forth their swords, shouting for her to halt. The guard in front, the only one with the foresight to don a thick hood, calls loudest. Her voice is feminine. Familiar. "Dawsyn Sabar, wait–"

But one guard foolishly storms the hill alone toward her. With barely a look in his direction Dawsyn ducks and slices the side of his thigh with the corner of her ax blade.

The next guard roars at the sight of his downed comrade and swings his sword through the air toward Ryon. The Glacian steps back and then lunges forward, catching the soldier in the chest and easily knocking the sword from his hand. Seconds later, the guard is tumbling downhill, Ryon holding his weapon as a prize.

Dawsyn swings her ax toward another who hesitates, his feet inching back and forth with uncertainty. She remains still and tilts her head at him as he dithers, a wolf observing its kill. Then she raises the ax in line with his head.

"STOP!" shouts the leader, her sword drawn, but her feet edging backward. "I said halt!"

They all freeze. The remaining guards, who have yet to engage Dawsyn or Ryon, back away, their weapons raised, but obviously reluctant.

Dawsyn eyes the leader, shifting the butt of the ax toward

her. "I know you," she says, her voice dispassionate. "Ruby, yes?"

The guard raises her hands, dropping her sword into the snow. Dawsyn stares at it, surprised. Perhaps Terrsaw soldiers are not half as courageous as she imagined. Or maybe they have more sense than valour.

The soldier lowers her hood, and the captain of the guard meets Dawsyn's eyes, swallows. "Peace," she says.

Dawsyn tsks. "Was Queen Alvira so willing to see me recaptured that she would dispense of her finest soldier?"

Ruby grimaces, hands twitching. Her discomfort at being unarmed is clear. "You underestimate how threatened Her Majesty is by your escape."

Dawsyn nods. Good. "And how threatened will she feel when the captain of her guard does not return to the palace?"

The woman's face darkens. Her defiance surprises Dawsyn. "I cannot allow you to kill me, Miss Sabar. Nor any of my soldiers."

"Then perhaps you shouldn't have come so far." Dawsyn keeps her ax trained on her target, but Ruby holds her stance. "Go. Now," she barks to her men. "Take Oslo. He is bleeding."

"Captain–"

"That's an order!" Ruby calls, her voice echoing off the mountain. "Fall back. All of you. Tell the Queen I have been taken hostage."

There is a moment of hesitation before the guards respond, their swords lowering in confusion.

"*GO!*" Ruby yells once more, and finally, reluctantly, the guards move. Backing away slowly at first, and then turning and running when they stumble on the decline.

Dawsyn smirks without a sliver of true amusement. Foolish of them. They are easy game, scurrying animals free for the taking. Who would she be if she allowed them to leave unscathed? Just so they could return another time, stronger and better armed?

Dawsyn raises her dagger, preparing to lodge it into the base of a retreating skull.

"*Wait!*" the captain of the guard yells, hands desperately outstretched. "Spare them and take me. I wish to journey with you… to Glacia. To the Ledge."

Chapter Nineteen

Dawsyn laughs, the sound stilted. This time, her amusement is genuine, her eyebrows arched in surprise. Dawsyn will give the captain credit for this – she gives her pause, at the very least.

Shaking her head, Dawsyn prepares to throw her dagger once more, the retreating backs of the guards grow ever distant but they have not reached safety yet.

"I said, *stop!* Please! In the name of Valmanere Austrina Sabar!"

Dawsyn's eyes snap back to the captain. She has not heard her grandmother's name in its entirety for many years.

Well played, she thinks.

In the mist down the slope, the guards can no longer be seen. *Damn it.*

The captain pants, hands now shaking from cold rather than beseeching. "I meant what I said," she implores. "I would journey with you."

Dawsyn groans, suddenly exhausted, tired of playing games with a kingdom she does not understand. Just seconds ago, the captain had been stalking this mountain to hunt her down, only to throw her white flag between them so readily? For what purpose?

"I was rather under the impression you had brought your

men here for my recapture," Dawsyn says dryly. "Had I known you only meant to accompany me, I would have offered... a more *polite* welcome."

"I believe what you said before... about the king of Glacia," Ruby presses, her words urgent. "If there is a way for the people on the Ledge to be freed – if the people in Terrsaw are truly no longer in any danger..."

"A convenient change of heart," Ryon rumbles, his stolen sword glinting in the weak light.

"A familiar concept for you, I would think, hybrid," Dawsyn snaps. "Do me the great kindness of being silent. I do not need your help."

Ryon sighs audibly, and she almost throws her ax at him again, but there is no time for sport. She is not one for negotiations. Baltisse lies in the snow somewhere above, growing weaker each second, and Dawsyn will not tarry a moment longer with a deceitful hybrid and the fucking captain of the Terrsaw guard. "Enough."

Dawsyn takes several sure strides downhill. In the face of her advance, Ruby stumbles backward, fleeing, and Dawsyn marks each step. With a swift kick, she knocks the captain's feet out from under her.

Ruby's back slams into the snow, her eyes widening in fear as Dawsyn leans to press a knife to her throat.

"I'll decline your offer now, Captain."

"I was kind to you!" Ruby shouts into Dawsyn's face, her breathing laboured and unsteady.

"You were," Dawsyn cedes. "And then, as I'm sure you'll recall, you led me to the gallows."

Ruby growls, eyes wild. "Who do you think got word to your friends beforehand? Who ensured the inn owner saw no punishment for inciting that riot? Who pulled the guards from the gate to the city, so that you might run free?" The captain raises her head from the snow, pressing her own throat more firmly to the blade edge, spit bubbling at the corners of her mouth. "But perhaps you are not as worthy of saving as you seem, *Dawsyn Sabar*. Perhaps I have misplaced my loyalty."

Dawsyn nods. "You most certainly have."

"I freed you, too, *Glacian!*" The words come strangled, desperate. "Or do you believe that pin was left in your shackles by mistake?"

Dawsyn doesn't much care for Ruby's notions of claimed heroism and presses the blade down an inch to prove it, ready to silence her, as she ought to. Ryon, however, suddenly grasps Dawsyn's wrist, holding her still.

"You did that?" Ryon asks Ruby, dubious.

"Of course!" Ruby gasps.

"And what of the inn owner then?" Ryon growls. "How did you find him?" His voice, the authority in it, rankles Dawsyn once more.

She peers down at his hand still wrapped around her wrist. "Let go of me," she warns him.

With a grimace, he pulls his fingers away, his expression stony.

"Why don't you spare me your interruptions, hybrid, and go where you might be wanted. Find Baltisse. I do not need your help here."

Ryon dithers, torn. "And what will you do with the captain?"

Ruby's eyes flit between them, her breathing erratic.

Dawsyn considers the woman. "It won't be difficult to dispose of her."

The captain blanches. "I... I helped you!"

"And you have yet to give a convincing explanation," Dawsyn replies. "How am I to believe that the Queen's captain has truly shifted her allegiance?"

Ruby shakes her head. "If my aid in both of your escapes is not proof enough, then I can only ask for your trust."

Dawsyn shakes her head at the woman, bewildered. "What possible desire could you have to follow me up this mountain? Are you running from something?"

Ruby shudders beneath Dawsyn's hold. No doubt the snow is beginning to bite her exposed skin. The woman grimaces. "It seems I am possessed by some moral obligation. I just… I must see for myself. I cannot keep guarding the Queen if she is what you say. If I've spent my life in servitude to a tyrant, then I must know."

Moral obligation. Dawsyn knows that madness well. Still, this could be trickery. Some concealed intention likely lurks where she cannot see. Dawsyn just can't quite grasp it.

Ruby splutters again. "The mage! You said she was here, somewhere, did you not? You may ask her if what I say is true. When we made our plans, she did not think me ill-intended. She can confirm what I did to help!"

Dawsyn narrows her eyes. It is a compelling thought. If anyone were to glean this woman's true intentions, it would be Baltisse and her mind reading. "How could you have possibly *found* the mage? How could you come to know of her existence?"

Ruby hurries to explain. "Once the Queen became aware of you, she ordered that I learn where you might stay. I sent a guard to tail you back to that inn in the forest where you had lodgings. I went back there myself looking for accomplices, and I found Baltisse, the inn owner, and a rather peculiar man in a blonde wig."

Salem. Esra.

Ruby continues, grasping for anything that might save her. "The mage told me things! Entrusted me with them. She told me about your necklace! She asked me to ensure it was not taken from your neck."

As one, all three look to the simple silver chain that can only just be seen at Dawsyn's throat – the necklace Baltisse had gifted her before Dawsyn's capture and imprisonment.

"She said that you would be wearing a necklace. She said that it had been charmed so that one could track it!"

Dawsyn narrows her eyes. "Liar. The necklace has not been charmed."

"It has," Ryon murmurs.

Dawsyn's fingers loosen ever so slightly from the blade. She turns and inflicts upon Ryon a most sinister glare. "What did you say?"

"I had Baltisse charm the necklace before we left for Glacia. I needed a way to find you if we were separated. The captain tells the truth."

Dawsyn glowers with a ferocity to rival a god, searching for deception in him. There are flecks around his irises, and they disappear as his pupils dilate. His eyes become nothing but black, depthless holes – easy to fall into. The hybrid does not even have the decency to look ashamed.

"You've had me *tracked*, this entire time? Like an animal? A pet?"

Ryon holds a hand aloft. Glinting on his finger is a worn silver band. An unimpressive onyx stone in its centre.

"*You–*"

"It was precautionary," he interrupts. "Only for your safety and only meant for my use." He tears his gaze from Dawsyn to address the captain. "It was not knowledge to be entrusted to someone like *you*."

Even Dawsyn can feel the black malice seeping from him. From them all. The air is full of it – a thick, poisonous odour of mistrust between the three.

"The mage said to tell you–" the captain utters, halting as Dawsyn pushes the blade against Ruby's throat once more. "She said to tell you, Dawsyn, *you will decide what you were born for.*"

She is desperate, clearly. She will say anything to have her life spared.

And yet she says this.

The captain's eyes blink furiously, her lips quivering. The very same guard who had brought her food, still warm. The guard that had shown true remorse at keeping her prisoner. She is alone, now – not particularly threatening. Her soldiers scamper back to the Boulder Gate, likely breaking their necks along the way.

Dawsyn lifts the blade from her neck. She decides that she cannot – despite her wiser inclinations – cut out her throat. Not yet, at least.

There is still cause to believe Ruby is her adversary, but there is no need to take her life so soon, certainly not before she can ascertain a few things. Baltisse can reveal the truth.

Baltisse. Somewhere above them, surely fading.

There is no time. Few options. Nothing left but undesirable choices.

Dawsyn rises from the ground, swinging her ax around her head and letting it fall in an almighty spray of snow, covering Ryon's and Ruby's faces in powder.

"If I find either of you in my way," Dawsyn seethes, "I will kill you both and sleep soundly after."

A lie. Mostly. Perhaps imprisonment has softened her disposition.

Without looking at either of her unwanted companions, she sheaths her knives, picks up her ax once again and stows that too.

Without further preamble, she turns to Ryon, already detesting the need to ask a favour, even one as necessary as this. "Fly me to Baltisse," she demands. *"Now."*

CHAPTER TWENTY

"I cannot."

Dawsyn must have misheard. The hybrid stands before her, hands up in surrender. An almighty dark beast of the mountain. Apparently flightless. "You jest?"

"Now doesn't seem the time for jesting."

"Tell me you fucking *jest*."

"You don't seem in the mood."

Dawsyn growls, turning to throw back her hood. "Why? Did they cut the wings from your back in that dungeon?" She says it with cold callousness, but as the words leave her mouth the thought that the Queen may have done such a thing fills her with venom. It awakens the iskra.

"If you'll recall," Ryon intones. "I was run through with a sword."

"And yet here you are."

"Yes, death did not take."

"A shame."

"But it has been... challenging, even so," he continues, ignoring her aside. "I am still too weakened to fly."

"You came this far on foot?" Dawsyn asks. "Tracking me with that fucking witch's necklace?"

Ryon does not answer. The silver on his finger glints, goading her. It is ordinary in appearance, yet Dawsyn suspects that it does not sparkle from mere sunlight. Upon revealing it, the chain around Dawsyn's neck begins to pulse meekly, beating out of synch with her blood, and Dawsyn grinds her teeth. She turns.

"Get up," Dawsyn barks, kicking the captain's leg as she barrels past her and up the slope. "Move quickly!" Dawsyn does not bother to look over her shoulder to see if she is followed. They can both tumble downhill and wash up along the Boulder Gate, should they fail to keep pace.

New snowfall begins to obscure her original tracks up the mountain, and so she finds herself half running, half stumbling to retrace them.

In her haste, she carelessly sinks into a deep drift, and Ryon's hands appear at her waist before she can react, ready to lift her out.

"*Don't!*" she says, wrenching free of his hold.

He steps away, hands back at his sides. "My apologies."

Dawsyn does not acknowledge him, does not even look at him. Instead, she continues to lead them to the flat expanse at the base of the cliff, where Baltisse lies eerily still. She is far more difficult to see now, fresh-fallen snow camouflaging parts of her.

It is what the mountain does, Dawsyn knows. It steals away the idle, quickly claiming those who linger upon it. It buries you and all your traces as though you were never here at all.

"Baltisse," Ryon utters, then rushes beyond Dawsyn, coming to his knees before the mage.

Dawsyn, too, sinks to the snow before Baltisse's head. Gently, she begins to uncover her wrappings, swallowing hard.

Be alive.

The mage's breaths are shallow but steady, her cheeks pink and untouched by frost. The rest of her, however, remains to be seen. The cold knows pathways to the skin and creeps into the breaks and crevices like water finding the ocean.

"Wake up, Baltisse," Ryon calls, his fingers tapping the mage's cheek.

Her lids open and shut, eyes rolling beneath, but she is too weak, too weary even to scold Ryon for daring to lay a finger on her.

"We must move," Dawsyn says. "Can you lift her?"

But he already is. Ryon hefts the mage from the ground, the snow tumbling from her body, and brings her to his chest.

Dawsyn has never thought of Baltisse as small in stature, but in the half-Glacian's arms she looks slight. Breakable.

"I saw a place–" Dawsyn begins, but Ryon interrupts her, already striding away.

"There is a shelter nearby. Come."

Dawsyn swallows the urge to lash out at him. The way back to the cave she found earlier is long, and Baltisse must be brought out of the cold as soon as possible. So Dawsyn follows, watching as Ryon treads with sure steps away from the rock face, and despite the ire she feels, she is undeniably relieved.

They journey a much shorter distance than the one Dawsyn had intended, and by the way the sweat trails down Ryon's neck, it needn't be longer. Though the mage is not so burdensome, the hybrid does indeed appear weakened.

Dawsyn makes the captain walk in front of her, but Ruby gives no trouble. She follows Ryon obediently.

They arrive at an opening – another hole on the mountain side where the rock and ice have crumbled away, leaving a cavernous space in its wake.

Ryon leads the way inside, bending in half to fit. The captain follows, her expression uncertain, and then Dawsyn. She ducks her head as she enters, the smell of earth immediately assailing her. The sound of wind abates, and she feels her skin sing in relief at its absence.

Ryon lays Baltisse along the cavern floor and Dawsyn

crouches beside her. The mage's lips are bloodless, but she appears otherwise unharmed.

"What happened to her?" Ryon asks.

"I don't know. I found her like this."

"You weren't together?"

"We were, but we folded here, and then she was just… gone. I found her at the bottom of that cliff."

Ryon's mouth parts, but it is a moment more before he speaks. "She *folded* you both here?"

"Yes. She was supposed to take us to Glacia."

"So far?" Ryon asks. "Fool. She has not extended her magic in such a way for a very long time. She is unpractised."

"I am not deaf, Ryon," Baltisse says suddenly, her voice a whisper, eyes still closed.

Ryon sighs. "No, not deaf. Worse. Defected by your own arrogance."

"I am merely depleted," Baltisse murmurs, words bleeding together. "It has been an age since I folded into the realm."

"It looks as though the realm spat you back out."

Baltisse scowls weakly, one eye finding Ryon. "I will recover."

"And then we will journey the rest of the way on foot. If you had any ideas of flexing your magic again, you can forget them, at least until you have built up a tolerance."

But the mage has returned to sleep before he finishes and does not utter a word of agreement.

Dawsyn takes Baltisse's hand, removing a thick glove, and then the other, spreading her fingers apart to check for frost. She does the same with her boots to check her feet and then returns the clothing quickly. Baltisse still has Dawsyn's fur wrapped around her neck; Dawsyn removes it, laying it flat beneath her head.

Ryon's voice suddenly fills the cave, and it assaults her – assaults because it is still difficult to believe that he is here, speaking at all. "She once told me that to fold, a mage had to sacrifice a piece of their power. She said it was like tearing a muscle each time."

Dawsyn feels guilt wash through her. "She told me nothing of it. I didn't know."

"Fold?" Ruby asks from the cave entrance behind them. "Does she mean... disappear? Like in old mage lore?"

Ryon eyes her warily and then nods.

"Huh," Ruby exhales. "A true mage-born."

"And one that has been, by all accounts, outcast by the court you defend," Ryon adds.

His hand brushes over Dawsyn's as they both reach to adjust Baltisse's cloak. The touch pulls her in two directions. It makes her feel ill.

Dawsyn stands awkwardly, the disquiet spreading within her, climbing her throat. With Baltisse now tended to, she suddenly feels the compulsion to flee Ryon re-emerge, begging her to create distance, to free her from torment. With her head lowered, she brushes her way past him and out of the cave.

"Dawsyn? Where are you going?" Ryon asks carefully.

"We need wood and kindling for a fire," she says, the words disjointed. She pushes roughly past Ruby without acknowledging her presence. She cannot breathe for fear of vomiting. She cannot stop her heart from thudding. She hears blood crashing in her ears, ready to burst free from her.

She flees.

Dawsyn makes her away across the slope, one leg bent on the incline, the other aching with each sink into the powder. The ax is in her hand, and each time she rotates it, the steel glints menacingly.

She need not have come so far. Any tree would do, and the wind is picking up again.

She is a coward. Running away. Like a child. She stops

before a small spruce and begins hacking at its trunk, without finesse, shame slithering through her.

She let him touch her. She let him get to her again.

So quickly circumstances can change. Swift as wind. Dawsyn has weathered its assault before, yet she is rooted in days that dragged with perpetuity. Days and weeks and months of sameness, the Ledge barely changing but for the patterns of snow drifts and the unlucky ones hauled across the Chasm. Days that looked no different to the ones before, or the ones that would follow, and Dawsyn's limbs would grow impatient with the relentlessness of it. She would wish for something to break the unbreakable patterns.

But one day she awoke, and her grandmother lay wide-eyed and sightless.

One day the Glacians came, and Maya was taken.

One day Briar walked her to the Chasm, and Dawsyn watched as she slipped away.

One day, she met a hybrid.

One day, he died.

One day – this day – he appeared again.

It was foolish of her to have ever wished for a life of variety. Change has rarely offered its blessings.

"Dawsyn?"

She shivers. That damnable voice. Mother save her. "What do you want?"

Ryon stands ten paces back. Downwind, but still, she must be truly rattled not to have heard his approach.

He eyes her ax warily, chances a tight smile. "Well, you aren't trying to kill me. That's a start."

"Nothing is starting," she snaps, and walks on. "Leave me be, hybrid." But she hears him immediately keep pace behind her.

"I'll help."

"I do not need your *help*."

"You never do," he mutters, but he has gained on her, and she hears it still. The rumble in his tone hurts. The knowledge that he is so near to her; it is a torment not to turn and look her fill.

Her mind and body are at war. It is why she cannot be in the cave with him. She wants to demand things from him – the truth, answers, apologies. She wants to kick and punch and claw at him. She wants to hurt him. She wants to cut ties. She wants and wants and wants.

She walks ahead. She is dangerously close to snapping, and she knows that if he has the poor sense to reach for her, she might just throw herself over that internal edge. Anything to relieve herself of this chaos. All her thoughts of him are tangled in a web of her own self-loathing. She was an idiot, a blithering fool.

"Do you know what a fool is, Dawsyn?"

"What?" she asked her grandmother.

"A fool is a woman tricked into entrusting her life to another."

Dawsyn takes the ax and hauls it over her shoulder before letting it arc. It thuds violently into the side of a spruce, the sounds of its shudder scattering across the mountain.

Ryon has halted behind her. He seems to wait, as she does, for the echoes to dissipate. She can feel how close he is. His breaths seep through her hair to her scalp, raising gooseflesh along her neck.

"Dawsyn," he pleads. "I'm sorry." His voice slips over the skin beneath her ear.

"For what?" she asks, not nearly as sharply as she intended. Instead, her voice sounds hoarse, fragile. How she hates it. "For hiding deals to kill me? For allowing me to walk back into a palace of those who wished me dead?"

Ryon huffs a tired breath. "I made no deals to kill you, Dawsyn. Surely you've deduced that much."

"So Alvira asked, and you declined." Dawsyn rounds on him, widening the space between them. "You are truly a gentleman. You even made me come a few times after the fact. I should be thanking you."

His expression hardens, jaw ticking. "Don't."

"Don't *what*?" she challenges, squaring her shoulders.

His eyes turn violent. "Don't try to turn what we had into something as base as *fucking*."

The words are forceful. They hit her directly where she is weakest. She hates that she feels it breaking her, pulling her apart. Hates that she feels at all.

She hates that Ryon looks so lost, unhinged. His eyes afire, the planes and slopes of his face taut and agitated, fists unfurling and retracting uselessly. "I *couldn't* tell you," he continues in her silence. "Your very survival depended on your ignorance. I declined the deal, and then I swore to her that you were unaware of your lineage. I told the Queen that I was there by order of King Vasteel, and that I would return you to the Ledge myself." The air fogs with the urgency of his tale. "I thought I could hide you away at Salem's."

"But you learnt," Dawsyn interjects, "that I am not the kind that can be stowed away and kept safe, and you chose to keep your secrets anyway."

Ryon closes his eyes, and when he opens them, they are filled with torment. "I had little idea of the depths she would sink to, Dawsyn. I thought it was merely fear for her people that motivated her. Truly! Now I know that it is something entirely self-serving."

"You *died*," Dawsyn accuses him. "You left me there, *alone!*"

It doesn't make sense, this particular betrayal, and she knows it. But she feels it still. Of them all, this infraction hurts most keenly. "They *all* died. One after the other. And you *vowed* to me that you *wouldn't!*"

She doesn't know why these words should come now, nor why the faces of her grandmother, of Briar, of Maya, mixed with Ryon sinking to the palace tiles, eyes wide and unseeing, should echo themselves. She forgets the root of her argument, her fury. For a moment the feeling is misplaced, divided. She struggles to hold onto it. She blinks and shakes her head to dispel the images.

He takes her face in his hands, palms overwhelming her cheeks, wiping away tears she didn't feel fall. She closes her eyes.

"I came back," he says softly, ardently. His fingers implore her, try desperately to comfort, to reach her. "Dawsyn... I am well. Don't cry."

But she has little say in the matter. The very feel of his hands, warm on her skin, only serves to reduce her further. A singular sound escapes her lips. A small fragment of her pain.

"*Don't*," Ryon begs again, and presses his lips to hers.

Such sweet relief it is, for a moment, to feel his mouth on hers, to smell his scent, feel him draw breath.

His arms encircle her waist, collecting her, swallowing her into the wall of his chest.

How easy it would be to dissolve herself, let him consume her again. She remembers, now, how the cage of his arms felt like a sanctuary. It is heady, this toxin. Perhaps that is what he has been all along. A drug. A deception. A temporary suppressor of her judgement.

Fools entrust themselves to another. One must hold a clear divide between their mind and their body, but with him, when she is too near, it blurs. He has already made a fool of her once. She will not let it happen again.

Fools entrust themselves to men, and idiots to Glacians.

She pushes him back.

He stumbles, stunned, breathing too hard, eyes dazed and searching.

"No," she says. She raises a hand to ward him off, but it wavers. If he ignores it – if he comes to her again... "Whatever... *exists*... between us," she breathes jaggedly, "it will die here. Now." She pauses, regaining her breath, pulling herself up to her full height. "We are done."

"Dawsyn–"

"We are *done!*" she says again, her voice truer this time.

Ryon's hands run over his head, down his face. "It isn't that simple."

"It *is* simple," Dawsyn returns. "It wasn't before. I was confused then. It was difficult to hate you and grieve your death at the same time." She clenches her hands, forcing the trembling in them to subside. When she meets the hybrid's eyes, she ensures he will find no indecision in hers.

"But you are no longer dead," she says, coldly. "And now? It shall be easy."

CHAPTER TWENTY-ONE

Dawsyn ensures the mage is interrogated as soon as she seems lucid enough to provide answers, though it takes much of the day and night.

When she hears the sound of Baltisse's body shifting with wakefulness, she pulls Ruby into the mage's view and holds her there until Baltisse confirms that her intentions are pure.

"Leave her be, Dawsyn," Baltisse mumbles. "She is no threat to you. Quite the opposite. Though I am surprised to see you here, Captain. What happened to your unswerving loyalty to that Queen?"

The captain merely grimaces. "It swerved."

The mage's eyelids close, but she smiles ruefully. "It will cost you dearly, you know."

Ruby only nods with morbid resolve. "I do."

Dawsyn huffs, satisfied, for now, by Baltisse's reassurance. She can admit to herself that she is relieved. She had not wanted to kill the captain.

"How do you feel, Baltisse?" Dawsyn asks. "We might try to return you to Terrsaw, to Salem, perhaps. If–"

"Salem?" Baltisse chuckles, but it sounds hoarse. "Might as well throw me to his pigs."

"A healer, then?"

"And who will carry me? I merely need a day's rest or two,

Dawsyn. There is no need for dramatics." But her voice slurs and her body gives a delicate shudder. When Dawsyn lays a palm to her forehead, she finds the skin slick and hot.

"What if the hybrid could fly you back to the valley? Would you go then?" She deliberately refrains from addressing him directly, though she knows how close he is, listening.

The sound of his answering voice rumbles within the small space. "Need you be reminded that *the hybrid* has lost the use of his wings?"

Dawsyn continues to stare ahead. "Perhaps the hybrid can use that iskra inside him to put it right. If it was enough to bring him back from the dead, then it might as well bring back the wings too."

A pause, and then, "It can't."

"No?"

"It is gone."

Dawsyn finally turns to face him. He lounges in a corner, the long lines of his body stretched out, showcased perfectly, like some artist's depiction of a god. "What does that mean?" Dawsyn snarls. "It can't be gone, surely?"

He can't seem to meet her eye. "It was spent healing a rather large hole in my chest."

"Spent?" Dawsyn wheels back to the mage, the woman's eyes just barely opening. "Can iskra magic truly be spent?"

"It can if you only drink it," Baltisse says.

"He inhaled it."

"Did he?" she asks, her voice fading. "Or did someone press their mouth to his and shove the iskra down his throat?"

Dawsyn grits her teeth. Indeed, she had just replayed that woeful memory in her mind. "Stop watching my thoughts, witch."

"They are hard to ignore," she mumbles, eyes closing again, not truly awake at all. "So loud now, since Ryon returned."

At the mention of his name, Dawsyn makes the mistake of sliding her eyes over to the hybrid again. Ryon now scrutinises the cave floor with studious indifference. But there is a lift at the corner of his mouth. Slight, but visible.

Dawsyn abruptly returns to the slope for more kindling.

She spends much of her time doing this over the next two days. Though the threat of Glacian hunters is gone, she cannot help but look to the skies often as she goes about her work.

Within the stretch of those hours, she plans, though she knows very little about what has become of Glacia since the battle. For all the turmoil Ryon's presence brings her, she knows he will be of some benefit once they reach the kingdom's palace. Ryon is the leader of the Izgoi – the mixed-blood resistance. If she wishes to ally with them in her quest to free the people on the Ledge, she will need Ryon's influence there. The likelihood that they will listen to the pleas of a human, even one such as her who led them to their victorious revolution, is scant.

Dawsyn finds an outcropping of snow-laden boulders to perch on as she continues to plot, devising the right words, said in the right way to convince the mixed-bloods in possession of wings to fly the Chasm.

Admittedly, words have always presented a challenge for her.

"Miss Sabar?" comes the voice of the captain.

Dawsyn does not deign to glance over her shoulder. Minutes ago, she heard the unmistakable trudging of someone inept on this terrain, so she is not surprised by Ruby's arrival. "What do you want, Captain?"

Ruby approaches, carefully lowering to her backside in the space beside Dawsyn. For a moment the woman only looks out to the expanse of the forest around them, stretching in all directions.

Dawsyn wonders what a sight it must be for her, someone born of the Mecca. The towering pines, trunks as wide as a house. The perfect, undisturbed blanket of pristine white that covers it all. The quiet, dampened sounds. It snows now, but only lightly. The wind makes the flakes perform stunts in the air.

It is, Dawsyn supposes, beautiful in its way.

"It rarely snows in the Mecca," Ruby voices, soft and undulating. "We are too close to the sea. I've only ever seen it when I guarded the Boulder Gate."

This gives Dawsyn pause. "You guard the Boulder Gate?"

"Not any longer." She shakes her head. "The day I was proclaimed a grown woman, I was sent to the Gate to guard it with the other novices. It is part of initiation for the Terrsaw battalions."

Dawsyn frowns, looking back to the view ahead. "And at what age were you a woman?"

"Thirteen, on the day of my first cycle. I walked from the fringe to the palace that same morning and signed my servitude to Queen and kingdom. I was sent to the Boulder Gate a week later."

Dawsyn chews on her tongue. Despite herself, she is intrigued. "It must have been very bleak."

"Absolute torture, actually," Ruby answers, her brown eyes lost in the memory. "There was nothing to defend the kingdom against, of course. The Glacians hadn't been seen in Terrsaw in nearly half a century. No one dared pass to climb the slopes. It was… a test, I suppose. We stood in the snow for three days and three nights. Unable to sit or rest. Water, but no food. Horrendous. But nearing the end of it, I started seeing things – *visions*, Her Majesty called them. She was delighted when I told her. I saw a winged monster fall on my sword and the Queen proclaimed me a true warrior. She said it was a prophecy of my glory. And I believed her… at the time." Ruby lets loose a breath that sends the floating snowflakes into a flurry. Her complexion turns sallow. "I was pushed through the ranks faster than the others. Much faster. I worked to prove myself worthy, of course. I devoted every part of me to the guardianship. It became my entire world." She shivers. "Now, however, I know the vision I saw wasn't a vision at all. It was merely hunger. Exhaustion. Fatigue. A hallucination, as were the *visions* of every other initiate guarding the Gate. One of the lads saw a siren lying naked on a boulder and wept at his good fortune." The captain laughs, though her eyes remain hollow. "Our visions were the delusions that precede death, not predictions. That boy never found his siren. In fact, he died in a tavern brawl by way of a broken bottle. And I... I am not the one who will bring glory to Terrsaw," she says, catching Dawsyn's gaze. "That, I believe, was meant for you."

Dawsyn presses her lips into a tight line, considering the captain's proclamation. It is both like and unlike her own beliefs. Dawsyn believes she *must* be the one to free the Ledge, but not to fulfil a prophecy. She must go, because there is no one else who will.

"You are wrong," she finally answers, tone dry, glare pronounced. "You speak of my destiny as though my loyalties lie in Terrsaw. As though the goal I seek is in their name, their honour." Dawsyn shakes her head, bemused. "If I bring glory to anyone, Captain, it will be to my people on the Ledge. I will sooner free those who stole my wood, pushed me into the snow, dove over me for scraps of rations or snatched them from my hands, than defend the valley who condemned us to live that way. I am not one of them."

"Aren't you?" Ruby asks carefully, and Dawsyn frowns, confused by the question. "Their voices could be heard for days following your near-hanging," she explains. "Your name was on every tongue, in every ear, all over the Mecca and into the villages, calling for your pardon." She begins to tremble from the cold. "If you knocked on any door, begged sanctuary from any Terrsaw man or woman, I'd wager they would grant it."

Dawsyn scoffs. "Do I look like the kind of woman who begs?"

Ruby laughs. "No," she concedes. "You look like a Sabar."

Dawsyn does not know how one like Ruby could claim to know such a thing, but understands that the captain is extending a branch of truce, however thin. She remembers the persistence with which Ruby had come to the palace keep, attempting to persuade Dawsyn to stay alive, by any means. *I am sorry, Miss Sabar,* she had said, and then, apparently, orchestrated her escape.

Dawsyn gives a long-suffering sigh, resolving to, at the very least, consider the idea that the captain might be decent.

"This place reminds me of my initiation. It is even colder here than it was then."

"It will grow much colder yet," Dawsyn mutters, but eyes Ruby's stance with dismay. The woman is truly shaking now, from her hair to her boots. "Get off your ass."

"What?" Ruby exclaims, taken aback.

"Get. Off. Your. Ass," Dawsyn says again, drawing the words out, pointing to Ruby's rump. "My guess is that you've lost feeling in it by now."

And indeed, as Ruby makes to rise onto her feet again, she sways, unstable. She mimics Dawsyn's position instead, holding herself in a squat, where her backside does not reach the shallow powder. Ruby's legs shudder in this position for a few moments, and then the captain swears soundly, and falls to one side, her legs giving out.

Without giving it thought, Dawsyn laughs, and the sound feels misplaced, unsolicited here on this mountain, in such company. With it, her chest loosens a fraction – a singular inch. She watches Ruby roll onto her back atop the flattened rock cropping, groaning and cursing.

"I hope you're a quick student," Dawsyn says, rising from her crouch. In a gesture of no small importance, she extends a hand to Ruby, who doesn't see it, too busy defaming the Holy Mother and all the spirits.

Rolling her eyes, Dawsyn reaches for the woman's coat front and heaves her upward. "Your first lesson, Captain, is to keep your body off the fucking ground. Anything more than a few minutes and the frost will find its way in."

Ruby ceases her grunting and pays attention, her large eyes widened. "Noted. And what is the second lesson?"

"The next will undoubtedly come," Dawsyn tells her grimly, wondering how long it will take for Ruby to realise the gravity of her decision. "For now, you just stay the frost."

"Stay the frost," Ruby repeats. "Easy."

Dawsyn barks another laugh, the sound stirring the birds in faraway trees. "We shall see."

Despite Ruby's confidence, there is very little about their situation that may be called *easy*.

By evening on the first day, Baltisse is able to at least stay awake long enough to hold a conversation, before falling back into a deep slumber. On the following day, as Dawsyn and Ruby re-enter the cave together, she is sitting upright, eating and drinking from their supplies.

Through the daylight hours, Ryon rarely leaves Baltisse's side, and for that much, Dawsyn is grateful. He crouches beside her in a ridiculous effort to make himself smaller, repeatedly swapping out furs for snowpacks as her fever spikes and ebbs.

Dawsyn knows he does this for her sake as much as Baltisse's. Since Dawsyn drew the line between them, he has attempted to stay on his side of it. He does not meet her eyes, does not address her unless necessary, and Dawsyn in turn acts as though he does not exist at all.

The performance is for nothing, however.

Merely stepping into the cave brings her a rush of awareness. Being near Ryon signals something within her, and it goes against every fibre of her instinct to ignore it, like a tie she cannot sever.

It terrifies her.

The very sight of him – here, alive – baffles her still. Even as she fights to avert her eyes, she wants to stare at him. She wants to ensure that every small detail of him that she traced for weeks, months, in her memories, remains the same.

When he thinks she cannot see, he watches her. But Dawsyn

feels his eyes on her every time. It is possessive. It rattles her. She resents it. But she knows if he were to look away, she would hate that more.

This will fade, she tells herself in the night, where his presence is most potent. There in the impenetrable blackness of the cave, it is easy to forget that Baltisse and Ruby exist at all. It is just him and her, as before. She hears his breaths, and they are in time with her own. She shifts to find comfort, and so does he. Even with the captain sleeping between them, the world might as well fall away. The distance between them dissolves. She imagines moulding her lips against his once more. Staying silent, detaching herself from him, does not curb the need.

A hollow in her chest burns and burns. The iskra stirs insidiously, curling cruelly in her belly, telling her what she really wants. She wants him to find her in the dark. She wants him to take away the burden of indecision.

In the day, she is a fortress. She will not be dissuaded. But her will always wanes with the light.

"This will fade," she whispers to herself, aloud this time. Then she sends a silent bid of thanks to the sky for the safety of night, because the tears come now – and they come, and they come.

But she will never let him see.

Chapter Twenty-Two

When the sun rises on the third day, Ruby awakens before anyone else.

The last few nights, she has not slept well. The cave floor is frozen to an unforgiving degree, and though they keep a fire lit and burning throughout the night, tending to it every few hours, Ruby still cannot find comfort enough to allow for any deep rest.

Today, though, she awoke to warm stones between the layers of her chest and stomach. Dawsyn must have placed them inside her furs during the night. She feels more rested than she expected.

There hasn't been a day since her initiation into the Queen's guard that Ruby did not rise early – chores to perform, drills to lead. But, as it is, there is very little for her to do here, and falling back to sleep would be an impossible task. The fire still smoulders gently beside her, and Ruby supposes she could stoke it, set it alight once more, and boil some snow for water.

Thanks to the mage's supplies, there is a small iron bucket with which to pack the snow. It is with this that she sets out into the dim morning, the night only just beginning to yield.

She has not grown used to the sheer brilliance of it – the mountain forest. Her mother told her stories of the slopes as a child that made her imagine a menacing landscape, a plane of nightmares. But Ruby's mother had failed to capture the purity of this place in her tales – the absoluteness of the cold, the blankets of perfectly fallen snow, the pines that soared endlessly into the clouds.

A short way down the slope, a tawny hare traverses the snow drifts, expertly avoiding the deeper pockets, furrowing only in shallow depths as it searches for food.

Ruby stops to marvel at it. Such an insignificant creature, surviving with much more grace and resilience on this mountain than she. The captain smiles.

A sudden whistling sound whips past her ear. A knife soars downhill, and the hare falls lightly to the powder, a small spray of its blood fanned across the snow.

Gasping, Ruby turns to see Dawsyn approaching her.

"He might come in handy," Dawsyn says.

"You startled me."

The black-haired woman says nothing back, only tracks the span of the slope below them, perhaps searching for other game.

"What was it doing out here?" Ruby asks now. "Shouldn't it be hibernating?"

"Hares do not hibernate," she answers simply. "And even if they did, it is the fertile season. The weather is warm."

Ruby gives a huff. "Warm?"

"Yes," Dawsyn says turning back to her. "You'll need to get your wits about you, Captain. You have not known the cold yet."

The very idea that it would get colder worries Ruby. Upon leaving Terrsaw, she had donned extra layers beneath her furs and guard's uniform, doing away with the hindrance of the armour, but it seems she had severely under-estimated the fierceness of the mountain. Already, she is struggling to keep her gloves and socks dry from day to day. Dawsyn keeps reminding her to 'stay the frost,' but she does not know how to walk on the slopes in a way to stop the snow from slipping into her boots.

Dawsyn begins trekking down to where the hare lies, her back to Ruby. This, at least, is a positive development. The woman is lending her a modicum of trust. If only Dawsyn knew the true lengths to which Ruby went to ensure she lived. The intricacies of the planning, the risks Ruby took to see her freed. She has betrayed her Queen, her kingdom. Her family will likely be told she is dead, and they will suffer. Such steep costs for the sake of honour.

And yet Ruby knows, whether sensible or not, that she will not live alongside herself without it.

"What is your plan, Miss Sabar?" she calls to her now, voice trailing down the slope.

Dawsyn pauses, perhaps weighing the risk of confiding in Ruby, but then she takes the hare by its feet, letting it dance by her side as she begins to retrace her steps upward. "We go to Glacia," she calls back, panting slightly. "We negotiate with the mixed to help us free the people on the Ledge. I had hoped to offer them entrance into your Queen's territory in return–"

"She is no longer my Queen," Ruby reminds her, and the words are… freeing.

Dawsyn stops to look up at her. "My pardons. Your uniform is misleading."

"Shall I strip naked to show my true allegiance?"

Dawsyn smirks. "Be my guest."

The pair stand-off, still ten paces apart, and eventually, Dawsyn chuckles and looks away. "Ryon will help to sway them. For the most part, the mixed do not care either way if those on the Ledge stay trapped. They have no need for them now, and they only seek their own freedom. They do not survive on iskra from that fucking pool."

"And the… pure-blooded?" Ruby questions, her mind only having put together pieces of the full picture. "They took the *souls* from the people on the Ledge? The *iskra*, as you say?"

"Yes," Dawsyn answers. "There is a pool of strange magic that takes one's iskra, and when consumed, it gives the drinker immortality."

"So, these mixed-bloods… they age and die as humans do?"

"Yes. They are more human than not."

"Then surely they will help us? They will fly over the Chasm?"

"If they are persuaded correctly, they might," Dawsyn answers, but Ruby hears the uncertainty she means to hide. The Sabar girl is unsure of herself.

"And are they likely to listen to Ryon?"

"Yes. And, despite everything, I at least know he will help me with that." She stares down at the lame animal in her hand. "But he is only one."

Ruby watches Dawsyn resume her trudging up the steep terrain and reconsiders what she must have endured just to reach Terrsaw to begin with, only to feel her own conscience drag her back.

And yet her Queen, the one who swore to aide and protect her people, has never entertained a single thought of rescuing those on the Ledge. As the captain of the guardianship, Ruby knows that the topic of the Ledge people is not one welcomed in meetings of security and policy. It is only recently that this has struck Ruby as cold, and quite antithetical to the pledge of a monarch.

How long do they intend to ignore their own citizens, their fallen village?

The answer, Ruby has recently deduced, is indefinitely.

Dawsyn has frozen.

She is coiled, ankle deep in the snow below. Her head tilts to the side, braided black hair training down her back, cheeks pinkened by the cold, listening. It puts Ruby on edge.

"What–?"

"Do you hear that?" Dawsyn's eyes trail to the left, further up the slope.

Ruby listens. She only hears the faint call of birdsong. The hollow sound of wind travelling downhill. "What is it?"

But Dawsyn doesn't answer. Instead, she reaches for her ax, eyes locked in place.

Ruby tries to follow her gaze. Searching for whatever disturbance has turned her rigid, primed for recoil.

The mountain climbs away from them, disrupted by its foliage, and looking completely ordinary. White and glistening and unspoilt. Except... except for the faint imprints of something large that can only be seen when the sun disappears behind the clouds. Without the white glow of the daylight reflecting off the millions of shards of frost that lie on the ground, Ruby can make out the tracks. They lead a path downhill, before coming to a stop, twenty paces above them. At first, it looks to Ruby as though the tracks simply stop, right there in the middle of the slope. But when she blinks, squints, she can suddenly make out the difference in texture in the snow, the pinks of two ears. The black pupils of two watching eyes.

The animal huffs through its nose, and fog rises into the air.

"Take out your sword, Captain," Dawsyn murmurs slowly, carefully.

Ruby barely hears her. A mountain cat creeps forward in its crouched position, almost imperceptible against the snow. But stark against its white coat, its dark eyes, wide and predatory, follow the captain's every move.

"Ruby, take out your sword."

Ruby's hands shake. She reaches over her shoulder to grasp the sword handle.

"When I say so..." Dawsyn tells her. "Run."

Her neck bristles. The cat, possibly twice her size, stalks painstakingly closer. The only sound it makes is that of its breath.

Dawsyn lifts a miniscule blade from her waist by degrees. "Ready your wits."

The animal suddenly raises its belly from the snow, increases its pace.

"Run!" The blade leaves Dawsyn's hand, but Ruby does not turn to see where it flies, she is already staggering downhill, trying to fight her way through the snow, trying not to fall down the decline.

An almighty snarl pierces the air, sending birds into the sky, and Ruby looks over her shoulder to see the great cat baring its teeth, throwing its head into the air in pain. But still, it charges for them.

"Go!" Dawsyn yells, meeting her side. She moves quicker, already pulling ahead. "Faster!"

But Ruby's leg suddenly sinks deep into a drift and her body lurches forward. With a gasp she falls to her belly.

"Ruby!"

She is already scrambling, pulling her boot free, desperately regaining her feet. "Go!" she shouts to Dawsyn. But she can feel the cat behind her, hear its great paws against the terrain, now too close to outrun. Its heavy breaths are at her back. Any moment those claws will rake the skin from her shoulders, tear her apart.

She whirls, sword in hand, in time to see the wall of white fur bearing down upon her. The mouth of the cat opens wide to reveal its daggerlike teeth. Ruby thrusts the sword forward.

The entire weight of the creature falls upon her, sinking her, burying her in the snow, and she is suffocating, slowly splintering, her bones screaming for relief. But she is alive.

The cat is unmoving. Hot liquid spreads along her chest and belly from the place her sword pierced it. She cannot move an inch. She can hear voices, shouts, but Ruby can only muster the wherewithal to panic as the wall of her chest trembles beneath the pressure, her lungs fighting against the slow caving of her ribs.

And then suddenly, blessedly, she hears a heavy grunt, and the cat moves, the weight rolls away; light and air find her again, and she gulps, stealing lungfuls of it.

"Ruby?" a voice says. Not Dawsyn's, but the half-Glacian's. Ryon.

She gasps, finding his face, as well as Dawsyn's, hovering over her. "Are you hurt?" the latter says.

"I–" Ruby stammers. "I d-don't think so."

"Can you stand?" asks Ryon, lending her his hand.

Ruby winces as she reaches forward, grasping his wrist. He pulls her up gently. Helping her climb from the hole that would have been her grave had he not arrived.

The mountain cat lays unmoving on the snow, its white fur stained red by not one, but two wounds. The sword in its side, and the ax embedded in its head.

"Well," Dawsyn says. "That's one way to fell it." She pants heavily, her hands on her hips. But her eyes peruse Ruby's body carefully, checking for injury.

"Was…" Ruby says, swaying slightly. "Was I truly just attacked by a giant cat?" And had she really survived such a thing?

"It seems to be a rite of passage on this mountain," Dawsyn mutters, she and Ryon sharing a meaningful glance. Dawsyn looks away quickly.

Ruby puts her hands on her knees and bends forward gingerly, spitting onto the snow. She glances up at Dawsyn through the matted strands of her dark hair. "Was that the second lesson?" she asks.

Dawsyn chuckles. "I'm afraid not, Captain. Though if it were, you surely passed."

The mage's strength has returned.

With the new morning, and the smell of meat on the fire, Baltisse appears lively, talking brusquely with Ryon about the risks of folding to Glacia.

"Folding this far very nearly killed you," the half-Glacian says, his tone even, posture slumped casually along the cave wall. Ruby watches him closely. His eyes seem to keep wandering to Dawsyn as she tends the fire. Each time, his hands clench.

"It depleted me. I was not *dying*," Baltisse sneers.

One of Ryon's eyebrows rises. "No?"

Ruby is a novice in mage lore, such things are no longer spoken of very often, but she is almost certain that folding is a coveted skill. The old books associate folding with the most powerful of sorceresses. She imagines such a skill would be delicate – not one to be discarded and then picked up again so easily. But then again, this is the same mage who read her mind and demonstrated the ability to crush her, should Ruby prove a villain in their plans to release Dawsyn. So, perhaps this mage is capable of much more.

"I was… building resilience," Baltisse explains.

"Ha!" Ryon says. "And now the all-powerful witch wants to fold all the way into the Glacian kingdom, with not one, but three others to carry?"

Baltisse smacks him over the head, but Ryon barely flinches. "Why would I carry you through the realm when you've got those horrendous bat wings. You'll take Dawsyn, see if you can't sweeten the sour look on her face."

"I will do away with you both, and walk the rest of the way alone," Dawsyn says easily, but the mention of being alone with Ryon has made her shoulders bunch.

"I will fly us all," Ryon says. "I should be recovered enough for that. And you can think of more helpful ways to die, Baltisse, if you insist. Or else, build up your tolerance for folding smaller distances first. Old women such as yourself need to take c–"

Baltisse's eyes flash, and Ryon is suddenly hunching over his stomach, panting desperately. "All right!" he says, eyes scrunched shut. "All *right!*"

Abruptly, whatever pain possessed him seems to release, and Baltisse wears a wry smile, sweat sprouting along her hairline.

Dawsyn, however, has drawn a knife and does not return it. Knuckles white, eyes wild, stare locked on the mage.

Baltisse is staring back with something like supressed amusement. The corners of her mouth threaten to lift. Ruby gets the impression that words are being passed between the two women – one furious, the other entertained.

"There she is," the mage murmurs.

Ruby suddenly feels the same thrill that ran through her back in the palace, when Dawsyn Sabar had threatened the Queens' lives. She feels violence coat her tongue; she smells blood in the air.

Ruby watches Dawsyn place the blade slowly back into her furs and feels the potent desire to flee from this woman and all of her wrath.

A glow catches her eye, and Ruby's stare shifts toward it. There is a dulling but definite light emanating from… Dawsyn's hands? It is slight. Like the moon behind a blanket of cloud – muted, but compelling.

A low curse comes from Ryon.

"It is rising to join the chaos again, Dawsyn Sabar, and you are giving it a doorway," says Baltisse.

Ruby's eyes wheel between the two women, her confusion likely comical. *Of what do they speak?*

The faint light of Dawsyn's palms grows weaker, until it is barely there at all. It could be a trick of the eye, perhaps.

"I have a question for you, witch," Dawsyn says, switching focus. "You seem recovered enough now to answer it."

"Then make your ask, girl. Mother above knows, you will ask it anyway."

Dawsyn smiles faux sweetly, and says, "How do you know so much about iskra?"

Silence befalls the cave.

The half-Glacian stills, eyeing Baltisse warily.

The mage smiles, and one might see it as a goad, an acknowledgment of challenge to whatever this line of conversation might entail. But Ruby, who does not profess to know the nuances of deception, still gleans that the mage is... hesitating?

"All magic is alike," the mage says easily.

"You've said that before. But how would you know that to be true?" Dawsyn pushes.

The mage tilts her head, listening intently – to Dawsyn's mind, perhaps. "You think I have not gathered *some* knowledge of the Glacian magic, in all these years?"

"So, this is not your first journey to Glacia then, is it, Baltisse?"

Silence follows once more, thicker now, and Ruby notices Ryon's quiet reproach. Not for Dawsyn, but for the mage. The Glacian frowns at Baltisse, who is slow to answer.

"No," says the mage, finally. "It is not my first journey."

Dawsyn nods, understanding filling her stare. "Tell me how the Pool of Iskra came to be. You are the ancient keeper of all knowledge, after all."

Baltisse rises, her short stature allowing her to stand upright inside the cave, and if Ruby quailed at Dawsyn's quiet fury, it is nothing in comparison to the ire of the witch. Waves of some unnameable energy ripple in the air, raising the hair on Ruby's head. It makes her mouth turn dry to be in its presence.

"I would not make demands of me, Dawsyn Sabar. I've come on this forsaken quest of yours to assist. I have already proven my allegiance to you. If you try to turn me into your underling, I will take the hands from your body and have them do my bidding, just to prove a point."

Ruby would rather be anywhere but here. She wonders, and not for the first time, if her decision to leave Terrsaw was foolish. It seems anything but wise to have pushed her way into the middle of a trio such as this.

But she is here now. And she needs to know what they all seem to know already. She must see for herself, this *pool*... The Ledge... the people on it.

"So then, perhaps you know nothing at all," Dawsyn says, seemingly unfazed. "And you merely speak as though you do."

Baltisse's jaw ticks. "I know that it is centuries old, and I know it shall not survive another year," she says, when it seems the tension is a rope pulled taut enough to fray. "That it still remains is all the knowledge I need."

"And of what consequence is it to *you*, should it remain?"

"Dawsyn, you can trust Baltisse," Ryon says now, his voice careful.

Dawsyn closes her eyes at his words, and when she opens them again, they say plainly what her lips do not: that she trusted *him*, and he made a fool of her; that he ought not speak, should he wish to keep his tongue.

Dawsyn's glare hits them all in turn, again and again, her suspicion plain to see. "Keep your secrets," Dawsyn says to the mage, to the Glacian, to Ruby. "But if I sense your knives nearing my back, I will draw my own."

Chapter Twenty-Three

Ryon stares at Dawsyn in the same manner he once stared into the Chasm: with the absolute certainty that it could swallow him whole. She has always seemed immoveable to him. A towering tree born in the soil of this mountain, shifted by no element, and certainly not by him.

That is true now more than ever, but there had been a time – albeit a short one – where he had held the privilege of guiding her. Swaying her. He had spoken and she had listened, eyes gouging into his soul, relentless but curious. He had gained a place at her side; somehow. He'd found a foothold.

Now he was firmly ousted.

Dawsyn looks unperturbed on the surface, but he can see the pulse at her throat, thrumming the same beat as his. She is not unaffected by him, and somehow that makes it worse. She is, he knows, entirely aware of him, just as he is overrun by her.

He knows that he hurt her; he knew it before he set eyes on her again. A woman who was taught not to trust, not to surrender, gave herself to him. And Ryon fumbled that gift.

The curiosity in her stare is gone. Distrust is the only thing left. Each time he sees it, he wants to beg her forgiveness, her absolution, but he knows the look she would cast if he did: the disdain, the burning fury of her soul.

He did not protect her enough. He should have told her everything. This is the price he pays.

"Dawsyn, I won't drop you," he vows, arms rising toward her.

They need not tarry any longer. Baltisse has recovered fully, Ryon is strong enough to fly, and their location will be known to the Queens by now. But Dawsyn stands looking at him, regarding his arms with something like distaste. She lets her boots sink further into the snow rather than have them touch her. He realises that it is not falling from the sky that she fears, but simply being at the mercy of his hands.

A stone sinks into his stomach. He sighs, defeated and ashamed that he must reassure her of his intentions, that the words would even have to be spoken. "I would never touch you that way without your permission."

She swallows, but does not answer, her eyes glazing momentarily before turning away from him, and Ryon sees that he has misunderstood once more. It is not his *touch* that she fears, but something else. And he wishes he could siphon the meaning of her expressions and gestures now, but he can't. Somewhere along with losing her favour, he has lost the ability to read her as he once did. She is both tormentingly familiar and completely new. He is now a stranger to the scape of her, unsure of the terrain they both move on.

Ryon's arms lower, throat tightening with guilt, longing. "One day, I will earn your forgiveness," he tells her, tells the sky, tells any spirit who lingers nearby. "But I won't coerce you. There will be no tricks. I won't try to force you to love me as you did before. You have my word."

"You believe I loved you before?" Dawsyn asks. Each word cuts, slices. "Then perhaps it was I who tricked you."

Ryon doesn't miss it, the recoil behind the bravado. Some inward reaction that wouldn't be present if she was, in fact, so indifferent to him.

"It was merely lust, Ryon," she says. "Nothing more."

"Then I promise I won't try to seduce you."

"Seduce me?" Dawsyn scoffs. "You disgust me."

Ryon bites his tongue, swallowing a rebuttal. He holds his arms out once more. "Then you have nothing to fear," he says, "but mere revulsion."

Dawsyn heaves a breath, black strands of her hair blowing across her face with the wind. When she looks up again, she is resolved, eyes hard.

She walks into his arms, stiffening when he lifts her into them. She wraps her arms gingerly around his neck, and for a moment he just stands there and pretends. He pretends that her arms embrace him for comfort, not from necessity. He pretends that she still needs him for something not so perfunctory.

Finally, he summons his wings, letting them stretch wide and lift high above. With one downward stroke he leaves the ground, Dawsyn against his chest, and feels, once again, the pull of the wind against his wings, a prospect that should have died with him.

Ryon takes his time before landing, circling above Glacia.

In part, it is to prolong the feel of Dawsyn so near to him, but he is also searching. He wants to see what the expanse of the kingdom looks like now, in the hands of the Izgoi. He flies in a wide arc from the Colony's boundaries to the Chasm, but gleans nothing of importance, it seems.

Perhaps he expected the Colony to have been abandoned, the mixed-bloods now assuming the households in the pure village. But he sees moving bodies between the lean-tos in the maze of the Colony, and it looks just as it did. It seems that even without their oppressor, many have chosen to remain in the corner to which Vasteel had condemned them.

There are those within the pure-village too, its bold stone structures towering the shelters in the Colony, the Izgoi milling between the two. It fills him with a deep satisfaction to see how freely they move.

Dawsyn's face has risen from his shoulder, and Ryon realises that while his eyes scan the Glacian Kingdom, hers remain locked on the Ledge – a plane of oppressive mist in the distance, the prison beyond the Chasm.

Somewhere within that cloak of mist, her people exist. Somehow surviving. Her face turns bloodless, her jaw clenches.

Ryon wonders how much courage must be needed to return there, to that frozen hell.

He brings them to a gentle landing in the village that the pure once inhabited, directly before the Glacian palace. It was in this exact spot that Dawsyn and Ryon had rallied the Izgoi before leading them inside. Here, Dawsyn had asked him not to die, and her voice had stumbled under the weight of her fear.

If Dawsyn fears now, she conceals it well. She extracts herself from his arms at the first available moment, then turns in a circle. "Where are Baltisse and Ruby?"

As if she had summoned them, they appear. They approach accompanied by Tasheem, a striking black woman with hair braided to her hips. Her wings vanish at the sight of Ryon and Dawsyn.

"Good to see Baltisse didn't smite you," Ryon tells the mixed-blood, an easy grin alighting him. He had flown Baltisse and Ruby to the palace earlier, finding Tasheem and dumping them in her charge. Of the many members of the Izgoi Council, there are few he trusts more.

"Ah, she's a cheery thing," Tasheem quips. She elbows the mage lightly and winks, earning a chuckle from Ruby. The mage scowls menacingly at them both.

"I wouldn't prod her," Ryon warns Tasheem.

Baltisse has turned her sneer on Dawsyn. "We may as well have brought Esra."

But Dawsyn shakes her head, a smile threatening the corner of her mouth. "Tasheem's balls are much bigger than Esra's."

"A misfortune," the mage retorts, eyeing Tasheem from head to toe. "I loathe the brave ones."

Tasheem smirks at Ryon, her good humour unfailing. "Can I throw her into the Chasm?"

Ruby sniggers.

"If there was a way to do so without her respawning, I might consider it."

"Oh?" Tasheem asks, looking back over Baltisse with renewed interest. "Is she some kind of nymph?"

"A mage," Ryon corrects, wary of the fire churning in Baltisse's eyes. "Not a very forgiving one."

Tasheem's face brightens, teeth shining. "Mother above! How the fuck did you find yourself a *mage*, Mesrich?"

Ryon does not get the opportunity to answer. At her words, Baltisse's irises solidify and Tasheem keels over, screeching in momentary pain. For a moment, her back arches against the icy ground, and the next she is laughing, her breaths thick and panting, eyes cinched shut.

"He did not find me, sweet," Baltisse quips. "I found *him*."

Tasheem takes a moment to right herself, chest heaving, eyes sparkling. "I like you, tiny mage. He's always attracted the scary ones." She nods, brushing herself off.

Ryon winces. He knows the pain of Baltisse's administrations all too well. "That was unfathomably stupid," he says to Tasheem.

Ruby, for once, does not look lost. Her eyes are glued to Tasheem, permeating awe.

Dawsyn shuffles restlessly at Ryon's side, breaking his reverie. Straightening, he vanishes his wings and turns to the palace. He wonders if this time, he can enter it as a being of proportionate status, or if it will still feel like a tomb.

"Tash," he says. "Please, take us to Adrik."

CHAPTER TWENTY-FOUR

When Ryon first showed signs of becoming full-grown, Adrik insisted that Ryon live with him. Leaving Ditya's tent hadn't been easy, but Adrik had plans for Ryon. The young Glacian knew well what they were and was eager to prove himself. He did not hesitate to accept the offer.

The Council leader was a god to Ryon then, the only one in the Colony fortified enough to bear the delivery of Ryon's "penance" at the Kyph. Others had tried to share the burden with Adrik over the years. When the brutes came, one mixed or another had stepped forward with teeth gritted, apology in their eyes. The brutes then demanding they strike Ryon, or burn him, or cut him. Their grit was always short-lived. It was Adrik who picked up the whip when they could not continue.

Ryon had reached that fissure in time when a boy has the confidence of a man but the trust of a child – a malleable child. Adrik offered to mentor Ryon at this specific interval of his growth, and Ditya protested.

Ryon had reassured Ditya that he desired this change. He knew that Ditya worried for his safety, for his rebellious nature. Ryon challenged him nightly with his conquests into the forest, into the skies, into dark corners with females.

But Adrik was the Council leader, after all, and so Ryon left

Ditya's shelter, and as he had done so often, he went elsewhere to burden another.

Ryon soon learnt that Adrik could rarely be found. At first, the young Glacian revelled in his solitude. Ryon had space and privacy, and when he didn't, he could sit in on the Council meetings. He was quickly appointed as a member, despite his adolescence. It was quite the honour – one unheard of in the Colony.

When Adrik and Ryon were alone, the older male would tell Ryon things a full-grown male should know. He spoke of war and glory. He fed Ryon his hopes for the future of the entire Colony. He spoke about Ryon's father, and professed the truth about Thaddius Mesrich's insidious nature, something that no other had ever shared with him. Then, he spoke about women, about sex, and Ryon felt like Adrik's equal. He spoke to Ryon like he was a man already.

Adrik would bring females to his tent, and Ryon would leave, rather than listen to the sounds of their bodies in the dark. "A smart man would listen closely to the sounds, deshun," Adrik would say, laughing easily. "You might learn something valuable."

The women did not bother Ryon. He was used to slinking through the Colony at night. Sharing space with others his whole life had taught him the value in making himself scarce when needed. If Adrik was taking company, Ryon readily afforded him the privacy he never seemed to ask for.

Ryon didn't feel at all discomforted with this arrangement until the night Adrik brought *two* females to the tent. One was a familiar mixed who frequented their living space, and the other was Tasheem.

Tasheem, with her beautiful, flawless skin and bright stare. She was nearing adulthood herself. She had a tendency to throw stones at Ryon whenever he took flight. He'd never taken much notice of her, other than to shout names at her from the sky.

"For you," Adrik had said simply, winking once to Ryon. Then he pulled the other female down to a cushioned pallet, already pressing his lips to her neck.

Ryon and Tasheem had looked to the grown pair, and then to each other, revulsion lining their young faces. Without a word, Tasheem took off out of the tent, and Ryon followed close behind, a steady flow of nausea filling his stomach.

He ducked his head through the tent flap and into the night air… and was hit with a blow to the side of the head.

Tasheem was standing several feet away, her hands full of small stones she always kept stashed in her pockets. "Get away from me, Mesrich!" she yelled, hand raised. "I am not your entertainment this night."

In truth, Ryon had not experienced *entertainment* as Tasheem had called it. He had kissed girls, but it had gone no further. He had certainly not kissed Tasheem, nor did he want to.

"*Ow!*" he grumbled. "Wouldn't want it, even if you were offering, Tash. Put the fucking stones down!"

"Adrik told me there was a special meeting happening in there!" Tasheem spat, pointing to Adrik's shelter. A moan escaped from within the tent at that moment, and after a short pause, both Ryon and Tasheem muffled their laughter in their hands. "Very special, it seems," she added.

It was the first time Adrik had ever left Ryon feeling… inadequate. He was almost full-grown, after all, should he not match the proclivities of the other adult males of the Colony? If he was one of them, should he not act so?

But there was that sense of wrongness, too. A sickening dread in his stomach. Why would Adrik push him to participate in such things, as though they were a measure of his maturity? What of Tasheem, who so very clearly held no desire toward him?

Ryon and Tasheem spent the night taking turns at flying over the Colony's boundary, seeing who dared go the furthest into the woods before losing their nerve. When Tasheem yet again threw a stone at Ryon mid-flight, he pelted snow at her retreating head.

Eventually someone had alerted Ditya to the ruckus they were making, and he came to corral the two youths back into the safety of the Colony. He sent Tasheem back to her mother, and Ryon followed Ditya back to his home with a quiet sense of relief, of safety.

For once, Ditya did not scold Ryon for his recklessness. Instead, the man smiled and patted Ryon's shoulder twice before returning to his own bed.

The next time Phineas came to visit Ryon, he told the pure-blood all about Adrik and his teachings. Phineas listened intently, his scowl growing by the second, and promptly ordered Ryon to stay with Ditya. Ryon did not argue. Though he understood very little of Adrik, he appreciated the profound relief he felt in his absence.

The next body entrapped at the Kyph was not Ryon's, but Adrik's, and his back was soundly sliced by the switch.

The portcullises that once barred entrance to the Glacian palace are open, allowing any being to come and go. It brings Ryon a sense of peace as they pass through the tunnel, a reminder of what they accomplished. Finally.

Tasheem leads them, a torch in her hand to light the bleak path.

Ryon feels Dawsyn near him, his neck prickling, and his hand outstretches of its own accord as though he means to take hers. He pulls it back to his side before she can sense it there.

Tasheem guides them to a gentle incline, until the glow of sconces can be seen ahead, and then she stops.

"There you go," she says, gesturing to the open archway into the palace halls. "Adrik will be in the old King's chambers, I'd imagine. You would know where those are, Ryon?"

Ryon frowns at Tasheem, who is already retracing her steps away from the entrance. "You won't accompany us?"

"Not I," she says, and Ryon detects a note of sourness. "I've been tasked with duties elsewhere."

His frown deepens. "Tasked by who?"

"Adrik, of course," Tasheem answers. It is difficult to see her expression, though Ryon knows her well enough to read her tone. He imagines her eyes dulling, her jaw tense. Fighting to hide her frustration.

"I need you here," Ryon argues. "We have matters to discuss." Adrik might be considered the highest elder of the Council, but Ryon is the leader of the Izgoi rebellion. It counts for something.

Tasheem hesitates only a moment before her grin returns. "Oh, fearless leader, our good fortune that you've returned."

"Shut it," Ryon mutters, shoving her ahead of him.

"Although we hardly expected your return to take this long," Tasheem adds, leading them through the palace's stone halls. "I take it the Queens were not interested in your deal?"

Dawsyn laughs bitterly behind Ryon, and it seems to tell Tasheem all she needs to know. She smirks and walks ahead, sparing Ryon further questions.

A sense of dread befalls him as they continue through the palace, entering King Vasteel's old living quarters and coming closer and closer to the receiving room. Ryon has walked this path a thousand times as a servant to the fallen king – delivering messages, accepting demands, no matter how heinous. Now he walks it freely, not heeding the summons of his enemy. It should feel liberating, satisfying; and yet, it only feels... wrong.

They turn the last corner to find a human – thin, pallid, and dressed in the garb of the slaves – shutting a door behind him. He meets Ryon's eye and, frightened, diverts his gaze to the ground instead, shuffling past the group with a tray in his hands.

Like nothing has changed at all.

"Gerrot?" Dawsyn calls suddenly, her hand outstretched as though she means to stop him.

The man hesitates, his frail arms unsteady beneath the tray. Dawsyn wears a look of confusion. "What are you doing? Whom do you serve?"

There is a loud clatter, then riotous groans and cheers alike from beyond the door. At the sound, Gerrot hastens away.

Dawsyn makes as though she would follow him, but then looks back to Ryon instead, and penetrates him with a glare that promises blood.

Mother above, help the one who puts that look on her face, he thinks.

Ryon hesitates before entering the receiving room, Adrik presumedly on the other side, in the old king's living quarters.

As though a new king now claims it.

"Ryon?" Baltisse queries, perhaps gleaning pieces of his mind. He pulls away from the tumble of his thoughts, and realises that his companions are staring at him, waiting on him. Most of all, Dawsyn, whose gaze is not only curious, but concerned. Wary. He can almost hear her voice, read her mind. *What is happening?*

Ryon straightens his shoulders, lifts his chin, and nods to Tasheem, who knocks upon the receiving room door, as though she needs permission to enter.

Ryon's skin grows cold.

Within, the room is as Ryon remembers. There is a drawing desk, high-backed chairs. The shelves that once contained old Glacian weapons and relics now contain only dust and the occasional abandoned chalice. The receiving room is full. At least a dozen members of the Council and Izgoi lounge on the furniture, drinking ale and laughing. A casual scene, one of merriment, and yet it draws attention to Tasheem's stark discomfort.

She remains by the door, straight-backed and tight-lipped.

She looks purposefully away from the men within. These are her comrades, her *friends*. She has drunk and celebrated with this lot for years, alongside Ryon. What could cause her such stress to see them here?

"Mesrich!" comes a voice. It booms above the raucous laughter of the others, halting their conversations, and all turn to Ryon, their faces ruddy with drink.

Adrik rises from his seat behind the desk – the king's seat. He strides to Ryon, great feet clunking across the floor, arms wide. "You're alive! You elusive son of a brute!" He turns to another man. "You owe me that drink, Sailus. I told you he'd return."

Adrik clasps Ryon's shoulders. He huffs as the weight of Adrik's hands fall on him, heavy with drunken carelessness. At the contact, there is a small tendril of awareness that raises its head – the last remnants of Ryon's fading iskra, perhaps. Why it stirs now, Ryon cannot understand.

"Are you well, Mesrich? What's the matter? Did the Queens extend their hand in friendship and welcome you and our lot into Terrsaw?" He chuckles soundly.

"I am well," Ryon says, mind stuttering. He observes Adrik's bleary eyes, the tankard in his hand, the stains down his front. "Though the Queens would have me otherwise."

"Ah," Adrik nods knowingly. "I'm no prophet, Ryon, but even I had guessed your attempts to negotiate with them would not go well."

"And they did not," Ryon admits. "It seems I gravely misjudged the Terrsaw Queens nature."

Behind him, Dawsyn snorts, and Ryon grimaces.

"Never mind it, deshun! We have what we suffered for, after all. Glacia is ours! Is it not, fellows?" he shouts, turning to the room at large, and the gathering calls back to him, their shouts slurred and indiscernible.

This difference in desire is one Ryon has long argued with Adrik. The man had only ever wanted to seek freedom within

Glacia, and on the mountains. He had no care for venturing beyond it. But Ryon had been travelling beyond for years. He felt a pull to life in the Valley. He sought the feel of level ground, of pastures and oceans and warmth, and he was not the only one. Many in the Colony had long ago grown tired of the confines of the mountain. Many had longed to know a place away from the precipice. In at least that sense, they were no different to those imprisoned on the Ledge.

Ryon, raised in the Colony by the good of the mixed-blooded alone, would see them free to choose where they could settle, and it need not be within grasp of Glacia.

Another flicker of annoyance ran through him, cooling his blood further. How quickly Adrik dismissed the freedom of their kind, detaining them to the mountain.

But Adrik did not lead the mixed.

"The mixed will one day be free to choose the course of their lives, whether the Queens are agreeable or not," Ryon says easily, though his eyes narrow. "I am not so willing to give up that cause."

"A waste of your time, Mesrich, I say," Adrik barks, his hand waving dismissively and sloshing drink to the floor.

"I need to speak with you and the Council alone, Adrik," Ryon says above the talk and laughter, the room having long since returned to their discourse.

Adrik waves him off yet again. "They are busy, deshun. Drink with us. There will be time for talk later."

Time to talk later, as the people of the Ledge cut their wood and scrape for food. As the human slaves within these walls bring drinks at Adrik's whim. As the gathering in this room grows louder, rowdier, while the members of their Council return to the Colony to undo all its wrongs.

Ryon watches Adrik reclaim his seat behind the King's desk, raising his feet atop it and throwing his head back in careless mirth, an oddly assuming position for one who played little part in the defeat of the court.

Ryon remembers the night of the siege, and the absence of Adrik in the throne room. Ryon, Dawsyn, Tasheem, and the Izgoi had overwhelmed the pure-blooded, cutting them down one by one. Adrik had left them, taking to the palace halls in search of King Vasteel himself, only returning once the bloodshed subsided. And now here he sits.

A man hollers from the corner of the room, knocking a sconce from the wall as he raises his chalice. "Tasheem!" he calls, eyes hazed with drink. "Fetch more wine for us! We are poor, weary fighters!"

Another few of them roar amenably, holding their own cups aloft.

But Ryon's blood abruptly turns to ice.

With careful calculation, Ryon strides across the room, pushing his comrades aside as he goes, until he is immediately before the man with the dumb tongue and empty cup. His hand closes around the man's throat. With a force far greater than he intended, he hurls him backward over his plush chair, the crack of his head against the wall sending the entire room into a deadly silence.

Their laughter now dead, breaths shallow, the faces in the room sober in increments as Ryon turns on them. "I hate to turn this into an argument of rank," he says, barely tempered. "We were once all in agreement that the ruling of Glacia would not fall to just one, but to the many. However," Ryon continues, stepping through them, watching them shy away, "if it must, then I will remind you that Tasheem has my authority to pull you apart, limb from limb. And I will gladly help her do so should any condescend to her again." Ryon takes a crystal chalice from a stunned Izgoi and throws it at the wall opposite. The resounding shatter makes them all flinch. "Put down your drinks. Get the fuck out," Ryon says evenly, voice barely above a whisper.

But they hear it.

Every one of them.

His wings extend, appearing of their own accord, stretching high and wide. "Now."

The gathering stands as one, eyes averted.

Each man darts around Tasheem who lingers by the door and takes their leave, all but the one lying crumpled on the floor, the one stupid enough to speak down to a member of the Council.

Ryon shoves the overturned chair aside and bends to the male, who groans, a hand clutching his head. "Xavier, isn't it?"

Xavier's eyes widen in fear as they find Ryon's, and he nods.

Ryon promptly grabs the man's shirt and heaves him upward. He tightens his grip as Xavier's feet scramble to find purchase, his toes just barely touching the floor. "You owe your esteemed Council elder an apology," Ryon tells him, watching closely as Xavier's face grows increasingly red. "And then you will find some rags to clean up the mess in here. Tasheem will be the one to ensure you miss nothing."

He shoves the man toward the exit, watching with repulsion rather than satisfaction as he mutters an apology to Tasheem, and scuttles away.

Now, Ryon turns on Adrik.

The great mixed-blood does not look in his direction. Instead, he lifts the tankard to his lips and downs whatever remains. He gives a world-weary sigh as he replaces it to the tabletop, and says, "You should learn to live a little, deshun."

"Is this the way it will be now, Adrik?" Ryon demands.

Adrik raises his hands to the room, beholding it. "Celebrations? Recklessness? Joy?" He leans back in the chair. "I'd rather hoped so."

Ryon's fists clench to see him there. "Why do you sit in that chair, as Vasteel once did?"

Adrik gives a dramatic frown. "Who else, if not I?" he asks. "You? Or perhaps, Tasheem? Would you deny me the right to sit wherever I please?"

Ryon finds the answer evasive. Defensive. "Perhaps the

more important question is why you sit at all, while the rest of the Council have been delegated elsewhere? There is much to be done, Adrik. Imagine my disappointment, returning to find you and your *friends* drinking yourselves into a stupor, disrespecting our Council." He looks to Tasheem, whose eyes have blackened into pits. "And ordering the humans to serve you."

"Deshun, we only mean to have a little f–"

"I am *not* your son," Ryon retorts. "And you are no one's *king*."

For a moment, Adrik stills. His face, blotched by drink, turns suddenly colourless. He seems to chew on an answer, mulling it over without breaking his stare. Finally, he sighs once more, his great shoulders rising and falling with apparent exhaustion. He stands, slapping his thighs as he does so. "You are right, of course. I have let our success carry me away. I can admit it. Our defeat of the brute king has been something I've longed for. We all have. I saw no harm in letting the Izgoi celebrate a little longer than was warranted. An oversight on my part, I'm afraid. Now," he says, clasping his hands together. As though there is nothing else to be said, nothing further to explain. "Who have we here, deshun?" Adrik looks to Ruby and Baltisse, the former looking baffled, and the latter...

"Forgive me your first impressions," Adrik continues, not waiting for an introduction. "I am Adrik, the head of the Council."

"Self-appointed," Tasheem adds, her voice venomous.

"Oh, come now, Tash! I've invited you to our get-togethers many times! Though I am sorry about that lout, Xavier. He was improper."

Tasheem looks as though she would say more, but doesn't – a behaviour entirely uncommon for her, and once more, Ryon feels off-balance, perplexed.

He looks to Baltisse, whose eyes churn with unmistakable violence.

Listen, Baltisse, he calls to her silently. *Listen to his mind, please.*

"This is Baltisse," Ryon says, gesturing to the mage. "She is a friend of mine." He does not elaborate, and mentally implores Baltisse to follow his lead. "This is Ruby, another… friend."

"And this," Adrik interjects. "Is the woman I've longed to see… Dawsyn Sabar," he says, stepping toward Dawsyn with his palms raised before him, as though he would clutch her hands in his.

Dawsyn does not look to Adrik's hands, but instead stares up into his face, as though she means to turn him inside out.

"I'm relieved to see you have also escaped the Queens. Though, with your recent improvements." Adrik looks to Dawsyn's hands, which have begun to glow dully. "I'd assume escaping from humans would not be so difficult."

"What has become of the Pool of Iskra?" Dawsyn demands. Her tone is low, quiet, and her eyes flicker back and forth, watching Adrik's face. Searching. Always searching…

Adrik waves a dismissive hand. "The pool remains, for now."

"Is it sealed?" Dawsyn pushes.

"Not yet, my lady, but you need not–"

"Then you have failed to uphold your vow," she says, her tone sharpening further, "when Ryon did not. He went to the palace in Terrsaw. He sought an alliance between kingdoms to free your kind from this mountain, and you have been play-pretending in his absence."

Adrik's lip curls. "It was poor judgment on my part–"

"You have drunk from the pool," Dawsyn interrupts, withdrawing a knife from her side. "I can feel it."

Ryon becomes still, his throat closing, eyes taking in Adrik with this new understanding. He recalls the awakening of his own iskra moments before, and now realises what it meant. But Dawsyn, who has not laid a hand on Adrik herself, stands sure and unflinching, certain in her convictions.

Baltisse hisses something obscene beneath her breath, but Tasheem merely glowers, the knowledge clearly not new to her.

"I would ask you to tell me it isn't so, Adrik," Ryon says, his voice deadly. "But I'd be wasting my time, wouldn't I?"

There is a pause before Adrik answers. "The pair of you are well matched. Both prone to dramatics, I see. Come now, deshun! I had little choice. How else was I to ensure a way through the portcullises without the iskra to unlock them? With you and Dawsyn gone, someone needed to possess the magic to enter the palace. I did what was needed."

Perhaps, Ryon thinks, though Baltisse will soon convey the truthfulness of the claim. "Dawsyn," he says, and waits until her eyes meet his. He shakes his head once, watches her eyes flash indignantly, then sends a silent thanks to the Chasm that she takes heed. She lowers the knife slowly, her dissatisfaction clear.

"You will call for a meeting with the Council," Ryon says, turning away from the man who so many years ago had filled his head with dreams of freedom. "We will meet in the throne room as soon as they can be found. I will not stay in Vasteel's living quarters a moment longer than I must."

With that, Ryon exits the room, eyeing Xavier as he passes; the man's gaze is to the floor, arms full of cleaning rags.

CHAPTER TWENTY-FIVE

"Will you find some rooms for the others? Please?" Ryon says in an aside to Tasheem.

There are some things Ryon needs to do before the Council meets, and he can't have Dawsyn, Baltisse, and Ruby following him through the palace corridors. He must see to them on his own.

Tasheem's eyes narrow in his periphery. "Why? Where are you going?"

"Please, Tash," he mutters. "Will you? They could use the rest."

A moment's pause as the woman assesses him, and then nods. "And what of you?"

Ryon looks ahead, to where a spiralling staircase might take a weary traveller up to the bed chambers – it is an inviting prospect, fatigue beginning to burn brighter than his rage. But then his eyes move further down, to the corridor that leads all the way to the dungeons. "I'm to see an old friend."

The recognisable tang of rust and stale air grows more pronounced the lower he goes. Of all the halls and corridors and rooms of the palace, this stairwell and the keep it leads to is the most familiar. He and Jorst both were put to the task of keeping the Ledge prisoners secure, bringing them to Vasteel each season, and dealing with the empty shells the pool left behind. Season after season, he would watch them fall into the pool's clutches, and then send their unfeeling bodies into the Chasm. One after the other. He would bring them to the lip and nudge them over. Their limbs would spread wide as the wind caught them. They didn't scream. The soulless never do.

Then Dawsyn came.

Ryon's boot finds the keep's stone floor. He sighs and takes a heavy step, exiting the stairwell. Ahead, a long row of iron gates secures the cells within. Dawsyn had been held in the very last of these. He remembers the first time she lifted her weary head to look at him, face marked and bloodied, hair hanging limp around her damaged shoulders. She'd regarded him with confusion, as most humans did when they first saw his Glacian frame and human skin.

And he'd regarded her with pity. How stupid of him.

He hates this chamber. It is visceral. He can feel his body tensing and twitching at each scent, each echoing sound of movement. Within the dungeon cells, he sees that the pure-blooded who were not fortunate enough to escape, but were lucky enough to live, are chained to the walls.

Ryon looks in on each, noting the prisoners as he passes. Kilter, Maars, Vellis... he knows them all, has been taunted and ridiculed by each at some point in time. Now their hands and talons are shackled, their skin mottled with inflictions of fights lost. They are slowly fading, becoming what they made of the humans they stole from the Ledge.

Ryon smiles. He and Dawsyn did this to them. They tipped the scales. They evened the odds. Whatever other foolish mistakes he made, at least he knows this.

In the last cell, sleeping with his head resting awkwardly against the stone, is Phineas.

His white skin looks grey, here in the dark. His ashen hair now gritty, bloody and untied from its usual binding.

He looks near death.

"Wake up, Phineas," Ryon calls, and then, when the Glacian does not respond, he kicks the iron grid and lets it rattle loudly within its recess.

A heavy groan sounds. Phineas lifts his head as though it were weighted. His colourless eyes blink, struggling to find focus.

"You once told me not to turn your eyes from the foe," Ryon says, awaiting the moment Phineas comes to and realises the peril before him.

Phineas peers blearily at Ryon, barely conscious. He expels a huff of air – derision. He lets his head fall back down. "You are no foe of mine, deshun."

"But *you* are mine," Ryon says, his tone empty of anger, of anything at all. "You gave my whereabouts to Vasteel. You chose to have me captured, rather than to simply lie, to protect a friend."

"And allow you to tear down our kingdom?" Phineas rebukes, voice gravelled. He looks back into Ryon's eyes now. "The one I had fought and challenged and bargained with until it finally opened a door to you. I taught you to fight, to serve the king. I barracked on your behalf every chance I could to save you from the Colony, and you squandered it."

Ryon squats, so that his face is nearer to Phineas's. His guardian. His father's closest friend. But a brute, nonetheless. Still prone to the acts of a conceited race. "I squashed Vasteel's court between my fingers," Ryon murmurs, blood cooling. "I would sooner die in the fucking Kyph of the Colony, than serve your fallen king another day. Though, I *do* owe you thanks. Without your persuasions, I would never have learnt all that I needed to know about the palace – all of its secrets, all of its weaknesses. Without you, I would never have been able to rip it apart."

Phineas's eyes cinch shut. He appears pained, yet resolute. "This place… still stands, deshun."

"I am not your son," Ryon bites. His tone is dangerously cold, his temper hastening.

Phineas continues, "This place still stands, and so does the Pool of Iskra, and there will always be one who seeks to control it."

"Not as Vasteel did," Ryon counters, his control waning. "No one will reign in terror as you and the rest of your fucking court once reigned."

Phineas meets his stare wholly. No vestige of sleep remains. His face twitches, and Ryon realises that the Glacian is fighting tears.

"I used to tell you to keep your distance from Adrik, did I not? I tried to lead you away. I even threatened him. I thought I had succeeded. I thought... I tried to help you... for Thaddius."

The mention of his father's name makes Ryon flinch.

"I saw you on that mountain, with that human, and it was like seeing your father once more, clinging to some moronic hope that you would find a life that defied the one you were born to. I knew then that I had failed. I knew I had not separated you from Adrik... from the fate of your father."

Ryon frowns, struggling to find the meaning behind the words.

"Do you remember what I told you, deshun? I told you that your father... He was a good man, but he was without any power. In the end, he could do nothing to save himself or your mother."

Good. Bad. Ryon has heard so many renditions of his father in his life.

"You are no different, deshun," Phineas continues. "You are good, but you are... so much less powerful than you know."

Ryon rises to standing. Perhaps it is the remorse in Phineas's voice, the nostalgia. Perhaps it is the disquiet he feels, being warned of powerlessness by someone chained and caged. Whatever the reason, Ryon abruptly turns away. Despite the intention he came with, he escapes the smell and feel of the dungeon, leaving Phineas, his betrayer, his foe, still very much alive.

The Pool of Iskra churns resolutely, and Ryon finds it difficult to tear his eyes away. There is a fragment of iskra left within him. A small wisp of it, faint and fading, but it still sings at the nearness of the pool. It begs him to re-join it, and if he were any less dutiful, he might be tempted.

The meeting with the Council is thick with tension as they discuss their many undertakings. Many of the dozen are weary, stricken with the labour they have endured in the past weeks. Rivdan, an auburn-haired male, has bandages tightly wound around each hand. He insisted that each of the fallen Izgoi be buried, rather than thrown to the Chasm. Blisters were the price of his decency. Tasheem and several others have been relocating the mixed into the pure-village, treating the wounded, guarding the brute prisoners and the pool. The rest have organised groups to hunt in the mountain ranges, providing food and supplies for the kingdom. They have unified to protect and serve their people, and it brings Ryon no small amount of comfort.

It seems only a few have failed to lift a finger, and one of them is Adrik.

Ryon is the leader of the Izgoi, but not the Council. Even so, he knows that a certain weight of responsibility for Adrik's failures lies on him. In his youth, Ryon had been taught by Adrik that he would be the key to their glory, that his middling blood was the answer to their troubles. Adrik had ensured the Council was taught the same. As such, they revered Ryon, in some ways. They held him in esteem. They prayed he would grow to fulfil this prophecy.

With the hope that his success carries the weight of persuasion, Ryon raises his voice over the others who talk of task delegations and sentry duties. "There is another task we've yet to discuss," he says, and the words reverberate into the high ceilings of the throne room.

The mixed males and females fall quiet, turning expectantly toward him.

Ryon breathes deeply. *Let them see reason.* He thinks. "We've sought our own freedom from Vasteel's court and won. It is time we aided his other prisoners."

There is a pause, confusion, and then, "The human slaves?" asks Adrik. "They are free to come and go as they please, of course." He has turned away again before the sentence is through.

"I am not speaking of the prisoners here in Glacia," Ryon counters. "I speak of the Ledge."

There is silence, taut with conflict. Each face wears a variance of bemusement, even outrage. And then, the quiet breaks, and each voice collides with the next.

"They are not our responsibility, Ryon."

"What of our own kin in the Colony?"

"So, we doom them there for all eternity?"

"If we do not move them, we must provide for them."

"Surely this is an argument for another time?"

"There is no other time," Ryon cuts in, his own voice squashing the rest. "Humans were not made to survive this mountain. If we ignore them, then we condemn them. Whether or not it is fair, the Ledge is now our responsibility." Ryon scans his audience. Some of the faces before him are wary, indignant even. But some… some are contemplative.

"Those who can, should fly them into Terrsaw," Tasheem interjects, nodding her head. "Not to do so would be a cruelty."

Another Council member, Veritt, scoffs. "And you think those Queens would allow us to enter their territory? They'd fire their arrows upon us."

"They needn't know," Ryon argues. "They will be none the wiser in their palace. We will take the humans to the other side of the Boulder Gate and no further."

"I see no sense in leaving them there, beyond that Chasm," Rivdan says, his voice low and thoughtful. "We'd only be saddling ourselves with their lives. More mouths to feed. Better to bring them back to the valley."

Ryon nods to Rivdan, a silent gesture of thanks, and he nods back.

"And what will happen, deshun, when we descend on the Ledge, to whisk its people away?" Adrik asks.

The question lingers and Ryon does not answer it, because in truth it is an obstacle he is yet to see around.

Adrik continues. "The people on the Ledge only know enough to fear us. And if Dawsyn Sabar is any indication, they are a violent people, very capable of defending themselves."

Ryon seethes quietly at the mention of her name, somehow wrong on Adrik's tongue.

"They will not understand, deshun, and they will not go quietly."

Ryon squares his shoulders. "Dawsyn will go with us, and she will help to explain that we mean to help." He meets the eyes of the other Council members in turn. "It will not be an easy endeavour, but their lives have fallen to us. If we need to attempt their liberation several times over, then we should do so."

"You would risk our lives then, to save theirs?" Brennick asks now, a man Ryon considers a friend.

"It would hardly be a risk to your life, Bren. You can put those wings to use, if need be. The humans can only throw their weapons so far."

Brennick smiles wanly, tiredly.

"Dawsyn Sabar risked her own life to help our kind be free from Vasteel," Ryon says now, scanning the faces of the other Council members one by one. "She almost died to a cause not her own, in the hopes that it may one day lead to the liberation of her own people – people who were thrown into the pool season after season. There is no doubt that their sacrifice has spared our kind the robbing of many souls. If not for their existence, we would be nothing but breeding stock, herded into the pool. We owe Dawsyn and her people this much," Ryon concludes, eyeing the pool, filled with the souls of the Ledge. "They have earnt the freedom we now relish." This last is directed to Adrik, who has certainly indulged in all of freedom's comforts.

"Let us vote, then," Adrik says now. "Shall we free the people on the Ledge, or leave this matter for another moon? Those in favour of going to the Ledge this very day?"

Ryon raises his hand, his heart sinking.

Tasheem raises hers, high and sure.

Then Rivdan, his eyes on Ryon.

Then, surprisingly, Brennick.

But it isn't enough.

"Those in favour of reconsidering in the future."

The remaining nine, Adrik included, raise their hands.

And it is decided.

CHAPTER TWENTY-SIX

Dawsyn was not permitted to attend the Council meeting. Neither were Baltisse and Ruby, a development that leaves a bitter taste on her tongue. She supposes bitterness is all she is comprised of now.

They had been given luxurious rooms within the palace to wait, rooms with vast beds and stone wash basins big enough to fit entire bodies – even winged ones. Dawsyn retreated into her chamber alone, pacing impatiently, her heart in her throat.

Dawsyn's room hosts a large mirror, one that has been skied upon the wall to reflect her entire body. She stands before it now, having never seen herself in such a way.

She lifts one foot and watches as the woman in the mirror does the same. She wonders why a Glacian would need it, or is this a mere trophy, stolen from elsewhere? Perhaps it was taken from Terrsaw, while her own ancestors reigned.

Slowly, she lifts her hands to remove her furs, letting them fall to the ground. She takes off her leather boots and throws them aside, relief spreading fiercely through to her toes.

Her body is… sharp, she thinks. Shoulders that cut right angles, prominent cheek bones. She is somehow… disappointed. She looks as she feels. Unforgiving, inflexible.

Frustrated, she lifts the hem of her tunic, throwing it aside, and does the same with her pants, and then her shifts.

And like this, without clothing to hide her, she is softer. Not gentle, exactly, but more pliant. Her hips do not simply slope to the beginnings of her thighs, and there are too many scars for her skin to be considered smooth. The muscle beneath is evident, but she does not blanch to see any of it. She is supple. Strong.

She lets her fingers trace along her thighs and over her hips. She watches them dip in at her waist and then outline the curve of her breasts. She unties her hair from its knot and lets it fall to her back and over her shoulders. She takes herself in.

She wonders if one day, she can will herself to change. She wonders if she has it within her to be more than just bitterness.

Hours have passed, and she has heard nothing. She had considered leaving the room in search of Ryon herself, but she was loath to find herself lost within the palace. Instead, she fills the bath and steps into it, lowering her body into its tepidness. Taking more care than she normally would, she removes the grime in her nail beds, douses her hair and scrubs her scalp until it stings. She finds a comb beside the basin and drags it through her hair over and over again until it no longer snags. Still, no one comes.

Night has fallen; the narrow window reveals it. Clothed once more in a shift, she tries to find sleep on the grand bed. She has never slept on anything like it. The mattress is so soft, she feels cradled by it. Experimentally, she stretches her limbs as wide as she can, and they still do not reach the edges of the bed.

Her body automatically wants to recoil. It only knows small spaces in which to find sleep, tucking onto narrow cots, curling in for warmth. The thought of sleeping the night on a bed so unending makes her wary. She feels defenceless there on the mattress. She does not trust this room, this palace. It is smeared by the image of Vasteel, and she cannot separate the two.

Dawsyn tries to comfort herself in the knowledge that the King has fled. He was chased from this kingdom by those he sought to repress. But even in his absence, a wicked tang sticks to her throat. In the space Vasteel once presided, another seems to have taken the mantle.

She does not trust Adrik.

She had been wary of the mixed-blood upon their first meeting, and the sentiment remains. Dawsyn's skin had crawled to see him perched in a king's chair, lording over his admirers while his councilmen presumedly laboured elsewhere, restructuring a kingdom for the people they freed. Ryon had nearly died in Terrsaw, and yet Adrik – his mentor, a man who had supposedly given him purpose – had acted with dispassion upon his return.

She had watched Ryon carefully in that receiving room. She could see the confusion, and then the understanding blossom in him as he watched Adrik's comrades jest and drink. He had seen Adrik's truest form in that moment, just as she had, she was sure of it.

Ryon. *Where is he?* Though to see the hybrid is to bring discomfort upon herself, she wants nothing more than to speak with him. She needs to know what he knows.

Would the Council fly the Chasm to the Ledge? Had Ryon convinced them to liberate her people?

The longer she waits, the more her stomach tangles into knots, her nerves feeding the iskra within. The magic is there, unfurling, seeking… something.

She cannot stay upon the bed a second longer. She cannot wait alone in this room.

Standing, she goes to the window, placing her hands along the cold wooden frame. So high above ground, her eyes can reach the peaks of the Pure Village and its steepled rooftops. She looks past them. Beyond is the Colony, where the lean-tos bend with the wind. The moon does not shine here, where the fog is a cloying blanket, meant only to smother its light. Yet light can still be found there on the outskirts, where the mixed-bloods light their wax and burn wood to stave off the dark. The Colony glows with dull obstinacy through the mist, making ghosts of the squalls that twist through crooked lanes.

Her stomach rolls, lurching in the direction of those small beacons.

She dons her fur cloak, pulls on her boots, and turns for the door.

Wary of the maze that is the palace, Dawsyn does not stray from the known path she walked earlier. She follows it back down a stairwell, out into a wide corridor.

It is, perhaps, foolish to be wandering alone – particularly here, in a place she does not know and where she has little in the way of friends. She ought to wait in that infernal room until Ryon comes with his answers.

He should have come by now, though.

Dawsyn guesses that the night is at its peak. The palace is quiet, save for an errant Izgoi here and there, stumbling drunkenly.

She is restless, and it grows worse the longer she wanders without finding what she seeks. She turns a corner to yet another hallway and finds someone she recognises. Finally. A man with auburn hair and beard, one she recognises as a member of the Council. He turns at the sounds of her approach, eyes widening at the sight of her walking the Palace of Glacians, hair in disarray, cloak unfastened.

"Miss Sabar? Are you well?"

"I need to find Ryon… Mesrich," she adds. "Is he within the palace?"

Though as she says it, she knows, without question, what the answer will be.

And how can that be?

"He left, prishmyr," the man says. She does not understand the word. "I'm not certain where."

Dawsyn, however, somehow *is*. "Thank you," she tells him, before continuing.

"He seemed… taxed. If you are searching for him, I'd let it wait this night. Ryon seeks solitude before company when his mind is occupied. I have prodded his temper often enough myself to know."

To her surprise, it does not annoy Dawsyn to have the man assume to instruct her. "I have prodded his temper often enough too," she grins. "His bite is not so terrible."

"Then he must be more taken with you than even *I* believed, prishmyr. Ryon Mesrich's bite is well known in the Colony." His smile was small, but sincere.

Dawsyn hesitates for a moment. She knows very little about propriety, even less about mixed custom, but despite herself, she feels obliged to say, "I don't know your name."

She means only to inquire, but the words come hard and closed, like she merely sought to air the statement. "I mean," she says, breathing deeply, willing her shoulders to relax. "What is your name?"

Lines appear at the corners of his eyes as his smile deepens. "Rivdan, miss."

She nods, unsure of what next to say. Instead, she looks past Rivdan, to the flickering light of the sconces that will guide her to a tunnel, if she is not mistaken.

She hears Rivdan sigh. "Can I accompany you, at least?"

"No," Dawsyn answers immediately, and then adds, "Thank you."

"I thought not. Take care on the ice."

But Dawsyn is already walking on, an inexplicable drive propelling her forward.

Once outside of the tunnel, the wind is not so tempered. It chills the skin on her cheeks, and she has to bury her hands inside her cloak, but the cold is not ravenous this night. It is slower, lazy in its grasp, and Dawsyn's body remains warm enough as she hastens through the Pure Village, knowing only the vague direction of the Colony, keeping the looming palace at her back.

The distinction between the Pure Village and the Colony is painfully apparent. There is an empty channel of space between the last building and the first makeshift shelter, where the wind disturbs the fresh powder unobstructed. It might as well be a chasm.

Dawsyn slows as she passes the Colony homes, weaving amongst them in the dark. Ahead, the outline of a post appears, its top exceeding the height of the tents and shanties. Confused, she walks toward it, rounding shelters, her feet hardly heard upon the powder.

Finally, she comes to a break in the maze. The shelters leave an open space, leaning away from the wooden instruments in the centre, as though recoiling from them.

A tendril of wariness caresses Dawsyn's neck. At first, she thinks it is the ominous quality of a place such as this, so quiet and empty. It automatically brings about a sense of threat. There are stocks, chains, a tree trunk long since cut and stripped and erected here, Mother knows what for.

The awareness licks at her again, raising the hairs along her arms, and it is only then that she sees him.

In the dark, Ryon sits at the base of the wooden post.

Dawsyn freezes at the sight of him. She notices, though she is remiss to, the settling of her restlessness. The fist within her chest that had stayed clenched and unyielding evaporates as she takes him in.

He looks straight at her, perplexed, as though unsure of whether she might be a trick of the dark. His wings are vanished. His boots are spread apart, knees drawn up slightly where he rests his forearms. His shoulders rise and fall heavily. He looks away from her, his head shaking somewhat.

Dawsyn approaches, stopping as soon as she can be sure he will hear her above the gentle wind. "I was looking for you," she says. "You did not come back after you met with the Council."

Ryon raises his head and meets her eye, his jaw ticking as it does when he is agitated, his eyes unfathomably tired. It makes her want to go to him. It makes her want to comfort him. An urge altogether unsavoury.

"I'm surprised you would come so far to seek me," he says absently. "I apologise. I should have come to find you earlier."

He appears spent, enough to already be asleep, and Dawsyn wonders why he would come here, to this dismal place, so very far away from the palace. "Why didn't you?"

His gaze clouds with something like dread. Dread for *her*, she realises. He dreads her reaction to whatever it is he must say.

"The Council won't agree to fly to the Ledge, Dawsyn," he tells her, voice carried swiftly away.

Dawsyn's gut hollows and falls away. Yet, it is what she'd expected. Adrik solidified the answer almost as soon as they'd arrived. What she hadn't expected was that the weight of this burden might rest as heavily with Ryon as it does her.

He looks how she feels. Powerless. Depleted.

All this way. They had come this far.

Dawsyn looks around at the Colony and understands now why Ryon came here: he wanted to spare her these feelings a little longer.

"What is this place?" She does not need to know where they are, really. She does not exactly *care* to know, either. She wants to push Ryon to recount every word uttered in that Council meeting. She wants to rage about the injustice of it. She wants to demand that Ryon fly her across the Chasm tonight, right now. But she can't.

She can't even raise her voice to him. She can't watch him blanch there where he sits, awaiting her wrath, as though he is responsible for those on the Ledge.

Instead, she says anything else. She keeps her voice even, rather than worsen his guilt.

Once more, a feeling wholly unsavoury… unfamiliar. And indeed, Ryon looks confused by her reaction. It takes him a moment to answer. "The Kyph."

"A Glacian word?"

Ryon nods absently. "Means 'hell'."

"Ah," Dawsyn says, trying to ensure her tone is measured, not sharp. "What do the mixed do here?"

"Mostly they whipped me," Ryon answers. "Or cut, or burned, or whatever cruelty they were ordered to enact. If not me, then there were others."

Dawsyn's eyes trail up the post at his admission, finding the marks and scorches that adorn the wood, and seeing them with new understanding. She remembers Ryon describing the way the brutes would order him punished, and demand that the mixed administer it. A useless bid to create animosity between him and his kind. Her teeth grind. The etch marks start low to the ground and then rise in increments, stopping where she imagines Ryon reached his full height.

"Only you?" she asks. Her voice more controlled than she feels.

"No," he shakes his head. "As I said, others were found guilty of some crime from time to time."

"But mostly you," Dawsyn finishes for him.

"Mostly me," he agrees.

For a long time, Dawsyn stands, Ryon sits, and neither says a word. Dawsyn cannot turn and leave, and Ryon does not seem inclined to either. He only stares and stares into a depthless nothing.

Eventually, he looks back to her and says, "Did you know you are the only one I've ever… cared for?" he confesses, stumbling over the words. "Truly cared for, I mean. Worried for. Longed for. I thought of you… endlessly."

Dawsyn knows a little of this same madness. It hurts to hear it voiced.

"I failed you," he tells her, though Dawsyn gets the

impression that he doesn't say it *for* her. He says it for himself, to vent his thoughts, release some sort of inner haunting. "I found you," he murmurs. "Finally, I found you. Someone just like me. And then I failed you." He lifts a hand to his face and scrubs it, eyes pained, tortured. He looks like a man crumbling under the pressure of the world. "Tonight, I failed you again."

With no mind to do so, Dawsyn moves. Her feet carry her across the snow and onto the dais, and she sinks down to Ryon's level. Her arms go around him, her chest to his, and as though he were waiting for her, had expected her, his arms slide instantly into her cloak, over her shift. "You're hardly wearing enough," he says into her hair, voice muffled. "You'll freeze." He tightens his hold around her waist, pulling her closer.

She says nothing in return. Dawsyn isn't entirely sure she wants his hands on her, but she wants hers on him. She wants someone to bring him solace. She is made of opposing forces pulling her in opposite directions.

His face buries into her neck, breathing warmth to the skin beneath her ear, and one half of her wavers. She wonders if it would be so bad to stay here, small and bound with the illusion of safety… even if she cannot trust the binder. She feels the pain in his grasp. The quiet remorse. Dawsyn feels the cuts to her soul that he rendered and knows that he feels their ache as she does.

"Please," he whispers to her, and it is just barely discernible above the beating of her heart. "Find a way not to hate me."

She lets her lips glance over his shoulder, just once, and pulls back, standing once again, lest she begin making vows that won't keep.

Chapter Twenty-Seven

When the wind begins to pick up, Dawsyn and Ryon make their way back. He does not reach for her hand, and Dawsyn is grateful. There is careful distance between them instead. They are in a state of imbalance, and it is clear to them both. Dawsyn does not know a great many things, but she knows the two of them are not fixed. There can be no reparations.

Dawsyn steals glances at him as they traipse toward the palace, eyes lurking on his stubble, his eye lashes, the curve of his cheek bones. A small, irrepressible part of her wishes she could be careless and stupid and forget every misdeed, every secret, and let them both fall back into their places of old, where the world did not seem like one vast deadly trap. But they are not children in the throes of play fights, and the frays between adults are rarely resolved with one embrace.

However, Dawsyn muses, *the embrace ought not be repeated.*

It would be best if Ryon remained in Glacia, Dawsyn has already concluded. Their attempt to free the Ledge, for now, has failed, and though she knows Ryon thinks he holds a stake in this quest, the truth is that his own quest has already come and gone. Glacia has been conquered. Ryon has delivered freedom to the Colony. He has earnt his rest.

They could let this be the inevitable conclusion to a sad story, one of unlikely allies who dallied in the prospects of love, and learnt they were destined for war. He needn't follow her all over this mountain in a bid to win back her favour.

A shiver courses down her spine. She readies herself to say what she must. "I will return to the Ledge," she says, hollowed and sure. "If you'll fly me there."

Ryon halts. Lines appear in his furrow. His mouth opens, aghast. "What?"

"I cannot return to Terrsaw, Ryon," she continues calmly, her reasoning already prepared. "I cannot look over my shoulder every second of the day, wondering when the Queens will come for me, and I do not want to." She expects him to argue with her, to claim that she belongs in the valley, in the sun. But perhaps he sees the danger she sees, becoming an outlaw, a vagrant in a place where she knows very few.

She can see him reaching desperately for an alternative. "Stay here," he bids.

Dawsyn shakes her head. "I cannot."

"You can. Help me to change the minds of the Council. We can make them reconsider."

"Adrik will not even let me attend a meeting, Ryon."

"*Fuck* Adrik!" Ryon spits. "He is not the only one with influence."

"No," Dawsyn says, "there is *you* as well." She takes a deep breath, preparing herself to ask. "*You* can change their minds. It might take some time – years, even. But you, perhaps even Tasheem, can sway them eventually."

Ryon growls, turning his face to the sky. "And you?" he asks. "What of you?"

"I will live on the Ledge, free from the threat of Glacians. There will be no Selections. I will try to teach the others the truth," she lets her eyes delve into his. "I will tell them that one day, a Glacian such as they have never seen before will fly over the Chasm, and he will not come to steal us away. He will come to free us all." Dawsyn almost goes toward him. Almost.

"I will prepare them for the day we will be saved by your kind. And on that day, they will go willingly."

Ryon closes his eyes for a moment, and Dawsyn knows that he sees the sense in it. It is, at this moment, all they can do. They can bide their time. Try again.

Pain returns to his features – lethally sharp. "And if you die before then? From sickness? Hunger?"

She cannot bring herself to be flippant. "All I know," she says, "is how not to die."

If there are truer words within her, she is yet to know them.

"Dawsyn," Ryon says softly, the word seeming to escape him unbidden. "I... Please stay."

But she won't. She does not want to. Dawsyn cannot fall into him again, as she did before, and forget herself. She doesn't want to lose the knowledge that *she* is all that she needs. To wake up, to continue.

She desperately does not want to return to the Ledge, where she knows every tree and rock and cabin. She does not want to fight the mountain each day, staying the frost. She cannot stand to watch the Chasm. But Dawsyn and Ryon both have rarely been handed what they wished. There is no other way. No other place.

"If you tell me you want to go, I won't believe you," he says.

Dawsyn turns her face to the ice, to look at anything but him now. "Not a person living or dead could ever *want* to go."

"Then–"

"No," she says, louder than she intended. "I can't stay here for you."

She hears him breathe in and out, and it sounds like it isn't without effort. Still, she does not look up.

"With all that was done to us," Ryon says, and it sounds like begging. "And all that we did... I do not think we were meant to part."

Dawsyn gives a pained smile to the night, the iskra tries valiantly to claw her apart, and she softens the words as she says them, as though it could lessen the wound. "We were never meant to be together," she says. And then she walks onward, alone. As she was made to.

In the palace, Dawsyn enters the bed chamber once more and shuts the door behind her. She sighs deeply, feels weariness leak into her limbs, and leans back against the wooden bedhead.

Her chest hurts.

Dawsyn had thought she was familiar with most pains of the body. Aches of arms and legs were easily recognised and remedied. Pain in the back or the neck took longer. Pain in the head, or in the heart were the worst, she knew. She had learnt as much when her Grandmother had breathed her last and has known it several more times since.

This pain, though, is different. It is constricting. She thinks of Ryon and it cinches tighter. She feels a strange urge to break into her own ribcage and slice it free, this thing that steals her breath.

She shakes her head. Banishes her thoughts.

On the window adjacent, a mark remains from where she had rested her forehead earlier. The view beyond the glass has changed since then. The first fingers of day reach to caress the dark. The bleak grey that precedes dawn dulls the white of the snow. There are no more candles burning in the Colony. The world sleeps.

Dawsyn lays her body down on the bed, the cloak billowing out around her. She lets her muscles melt into the absurd comfort of the downy quilt and tries to relish in it. Soon, she will return to the shelf she not long ago escaped, where nothing is soft, and comfort is scarce.

She wonders what she will find when she is reunited with her den of girls, her family's cabin. Who will have occupied it in her absence? She is not fool enough to think that someone hasn't taken what she left behind. She has never known a cabin on the Ledge to remain empty. She only hopes that whoever claims it now is alone, and that they are smart enough to leave.

Only the stupid need die, her grandmother would say.

How wrong she was.

She will freely return to the monotonous tasks of her former life. She will take up the war against impending death, the fight against the mountain for food and wood and warmth. But this time, she will know of lands below where people turn their faces away from the mountain, forgetting its existence entirely.

Not yet, though. For now, she will sleep and sleep. She will rest her body and accept the comfort and try to commit the feel of it to memory. On nights when the frost creeps beneath her clothes and the hearth can't help her, she will draw on thoughts of luxurious beds and impenetrable walls.

The sound of the door creaking open has her sitting upright in a flash.

"Dawsyn?" comes Ruby's voice through the crack.

Dawsyn relaxes, sighs. "Yes, I'm here."

"May I come in?"

How she wishes she could say no, but Ruby peeks her head around the frame of the door, and it is clear she has not slept. There are deep shadows beneath her eyes, tendrils of deep brown hair hang limp around her face, having escaped the tight knot she keeps at the back of her head. It seems she has been as anxious to learn of the Council's decision as Dawsyn had been.

Dawsyn slides her body to the edge of the bed. She cannot bring herself to send the captain away. "Come in," she says.

Ruby closes the door behind her, then twists her hands together. "Have you heard anything? Will the Council help us free the Ledge people?"

Dawsyn appraises her before answering. She sees the red rawness of her eyes, the set of her jaw, the tension she holds in her clasped fingers. She looks older than she should this way.

A woman untravelled. An easy target in such a hostile place. A woman of some standing with an honourable position in her Queen's court. It would have been so much easier for her to remain in Terrsaw.

"You actually care about them, don't you?" Dawsyn asks.

A line appears between Ruby's eyes. She appears confused. "I've told you as much."

"It is odd of you to do so," Dawsyn comments. "They are no responsibility of yours. You don't know any of them. You cannot claim to *like* them."

"And do *you* like them?" Ruby replies. "I can't imagine you admiring anyone at all."

Dawsyn's lips quirk at their corner. "There are some I am fond of… and some I am not."

"And will you forsake the ones you find unlikeable?"

Dawsyn shakes her head, more to herself than to the captain. She has, it seems, come to admire Ruby, despite knowing the danger of it, for Queen Alvira is not witless. Her captain could still prove an enemy.

But Dawsyn watches Ruby pace impatiently and finds it improbable.

"I'm afraid all of them will be forsaken," Dawsyn says finally, making Ruby halt in her tracks. "The Council voted. They will not lend us any of the mixed to help free them."

The captain's chest deflates. "But… why?" she asks. "You said they were unlike the pure-blooded."

"Yes." Dawsyn nods. "But I've found that humans and Glacians alike do not willingly take responsibility for lives that are not their own, the exception being yourself."

"And Ryon?"

Dawsyn feels her chest cinch tighter. "Yes… and Ryon."

Ruby lets out an indignant sound, resuming her pacing. "Is that it, then? Is there nothing to be done?"

"There is much to be done," Dawsyn corrects. "But the only thing that *you* must do, is return to Terrsaw."

CHASM

The captain's head whips around. "What?"

"Ryon will take you off the mountain," Dawsyn explains. "I have already arranged it with him."

"In case you were slow on the uptake, Sabar, I committed high treason to come here."

"Which the Queens needn't know," Dawsyn argues. "Tell them we held you hostage, and you escaped. Tell them you killed me, if you'd prefer. Her highness may even throw a parade for you."

Ruby gives a huff of derision. "I will be stoned to death in the street by the townsfolk, and you know it."

"This is not your battle, Captain. You should return home."

"And you?" she demands, her anger evident. Ruby's voice shakes, her face flushes.

"I'm going home too," Dawsyn replies, and in saying it, she feels ill. "Back to the Ledge."

There is a silence, as Dawsyn knew there would be. She looks back to the window, where the sky grows lighter. She hears Ruby breathing unevenly behind her, and then a voice speaks that Dawsyn does not expect.

"You tend toward theatrics, Dawsyn Sabar. Did you know? Return to the Ledge, indeed. Stupidest thing I've ever heard, and I've listened to Esra speak on the subject of wigs for over an hour."

Baltisse stands in the open door, her hand still grasping the handle.

"Mother above, must you slink around like that, Baltisse?"

"If one wants to hear more than what was intended for them, then yes." The mage enters the room with casual arrogance, sitting upon the bed with a grace any woman would envy, if the woman gave a care for such things. Baltisse crosses her legs beneath her skirts and looks expectantly at Dawsyn, and for one who claims to have overheard bad news, she appears decidedly unrattled.

"The Council voted," Dawsyn says carefully.

"I know," says the mage, rolling her eyes.

Dawsyn frowns. "And yet you do not seem concerned."

Baltisse shifts her long hair over her shoulder. "I am merely unsurprised. Were we not expecting some resistance? I believe it more important to know *why* they resist. Or, more specifically, why does that troll, *Adrik*, resist?"

"It seems he thinks of himself as Glacia's new king," Dawsyn answers, crossing her arms. "I assume he has no interest in offering the Izgoi to help a village of humans if it does not benefit him."

"I'd wager," Baltisse retorts, her eyes burning brightly, "that you've only scratched the surface there, sweet."

Dawsyn frowns at the mage. Ruby's head whips back and forth between the two. There is a pause, and then Dawsyn asks, "What do you know?"

"Not enough," Baltisse says. "Not yet."

"You heard Adrik's mind, though, didn't you? In the receiving room? What was he thinking?"

"I only heard small murmurings, I'm afraid. As you know, I only hear thoughts projected toward me, which is why I need your help, Dawsyn Sabar."

Dawsyn sighs. "I'm regretting it already."

"In the receiving room, Adrik did not speak with me, or even acknowledge me, and there was therefore no clear path into his mind."

"A path?" Ruby murmurs.

"Yes, child, a *path*," Baltisse quips, as though the concept should be an obvious thing. "Before Dawsyn skips off over the Ledge to prove her honour and what have you, I need her to *create* a path, between Adrik-the-troll's mind, and mine."

"And how shall I do that?" Dawsyn asks.

"We will speak with him again," Baltisse says easily. "And you will direct the conversation toward me. Say my name to divert his attention. In fact, tell him I'm a mage. Tell him I want to uncover the secrets of Glacia. Often times the ones who hand me the most useful of their thoughts are the ones trying to hide them. Let us find out what dear Adrik's true intentions are." Her tone deepens. "Ryon seems to hold him in high esteem, but if that troll means him any harm... I will relieve him of his skin and wear it like a robe."

Ruby grimaces with open disgust. "Lovely."

A word Dawsyn would hardly use to describe the mage's nature, but if Adrik's mind reveals any plans to betray the mixed, Dawsyn will help her peel.

"And should you find your way into Adrik's mind," Dawsyn says. "What, exactly, do you expect to find?"

The mage's eyes twinkle in response.

The mixed of Glacia have awoken by the time the women leave Dawsyn's chamber. The Palace echoes with the activities of those within.

Down a wide hall, Tasheem turns a corner and spies them. She already holds a large crate of tools, sweat beading across her forehead.

"Good day," she tells them, setting the crate down. "Why do I get the impression you three are off to burn bridges and torch castles?"

"Where can we find Adrik?" asks Dawsyn.

"Ah," Tasheem nods. "Straight to the heart of it, then. Good for you. May I join?"

"Only if you lead us to him," Dawsyn allows. She does not claim to know Tasheem well, but she suspects the female did not cast her vote against Ryon's. Baltisse looks to Dawsyn warily. *Relax,* Dawsyn thinks at her.

"Tasheem? May I ask a favour?" Dawsyn asks as they walk.

Tasheem looks over to her, her head titled with curiosity. "Of course."

"Will you fly me to the Ledge, this day?"

Tasheem does not halt, merely lowers her head, as though

ashamed. "I can't imagine why you would want me to, but if you truly wish it, it's the least anyone of us can do."

Tasheem leads them to the throne room, where many of the Izgoi sit to break their fast or converge in groups. It seems most have inhabited the palace in favour of the Pure Village. Amongst them, before the vacant throne, is the Pool of Iskra, churning with sluggish obligation, and surrounded by a makeshift fence of what appears to be iron gates. Dawsyn wonders briefly what doorways in the palace they took them from.

She does not get a moment to take in more, for at the entrance stands Ryon.

Her eyes find his as he turns, and the pair still momentarily.

Why must her mind stutter when he is near?

Ryon tears his eyes away from hers, and they fall on the rest of their group. Dawsyn watches him grow curious, and then wary. "Dawsyn," he asks, looking at her again. "What do you plan?"

"What makes you think we plan?"

He frowns. "A hunch."

She looks to the place where Adrik stands amongst a group of Izgoi, deep in discussion. "Some of us have come to speak with Adrik one last time, others have come only to listen," she says, nodding to the mage. "And then Baltisse and Ruby will need to be flown back to Terrsaw. Tasheem will take me to the Ledge."

Ryon's eyes flit to Tasheem and harden. "Tasheem?" He murmurs, before facing Dawsyn again. "No."

"It is not for you to decide."

But Ryon steps forward. "I will see that you are safe."

"Tasheem is perfectly capable," Dawsyn argues. "She will take me home."

Ryon comes close. Too close, his hand hovering dangerously over hers. "That place… is not your *home*," he murmurs, his breath a little too rough, his voice a little too quiet.

She breathes in his scent, feels the cold radiate from his skin, heady and threatening. She hears what he wants to say and is grateful that he doesn't voice it.

He is not her home anymore either.

She walks onward, and leaves him once more in her wake.

Adrik sees Dawsyn and the others approach, despite all the activity in the room. He steps away from his fellows, and approaches them, arms wide in welcome.

"Miss Sabar! I must apologise the vote did not fall in your favour. I assume Ryon has told you already."

"He has," she says, as Baltisse comes to stand beside her.

"There is much to rebuild, here in Glacia," Adrik says. "We can reconsider at a later date, to be sure."

"And while my people on the Ledge await your consideration," Dawsyn mutters, irritation licking its way into her mouth, "will you ensure they are supplied, as your predecessor did?

"Predecessor? I am hardly a king, miss," he says, chuckling lightly. "But of course, we will continue to provide for them. I do not, of course, wish them to suffer."

"More than they already will." Dawsyn nods, and watches the barb strike, watches Adrik's eyes harden. "How generous."

"You are welcome to stay in Glacia, Miss Sabar. We are indebted to you, after all."

Dawsyn smiles, though she is sure it does not fool him. "Kind of you. I wondered if you might agree to host my friends as well. Baltisse," Dawsyn says, turning to gesture to the mage, who has her eyes pinned to Adrik's, "is a mage. She is vastly interested in the Pool of Iskra."

And just like that, the pathway opens. Dawsyn watches as Adrik's eyes widen in disbelief, turning toward Baltisse. She sees the male's expression become closed and careful. She watches his body shift infinitesimally to conceal the pool behind him, as though he would shield it.

"Of course," he says tightly. "Though, I'll insist you stay in the village. There is much work to be done in the palace."

"Thank you," Baltisse says. "I would ask, however, that you allow me to view the pool from time to time. I'm very curious of its power."

"I'm afraid it is unsafe," Adrik says, his words casual, but his gaze sharp. "You should all keep your distance from the pool while in Glacia," he says to all of them. "Ryon, will you find this lot some lodgings? And you might explain to them the importance of refraining from that infernal pool."

"We wouldn't want anyone getting too close," Baltisse says, her eyes growing eerily still.

"No," Adrik agrees, and then, looking uncharacteristically off balance, he nods and turns away.

But Dawsyn is more intent on the mage, and she watches the fire in her eyes darken to ash. Her glare turns to Dawsyn.

And Dawsyn sees... death.

Her blood turns cold.

"Can you find us some privacy?" Baltisse asks of Tasheem.

In silence, their strange clan leaves the throne room, following Tasheem around a corner, down a vast corridor. The fall of their boots echoes off the walls and gives sound to their tension. Their steps are hurried, anxious. Each of their number seems to move with the understanding of necessary haste, even before a word has been uttered.

But the mage vibrates, practically quaking with whatever information travelled the path from Adrik's mind to hers, and her wrath leaks to the rest, washing them in dread.

In this moment before disaster strikes, while her skin pricks with the first signs of fear, Dawsyn's eyes drift to Ryon, and it hurts her anew. The familiarity. The brilliance of his stare brings acute pain and comfort both, and she is too filled with quiet terror to wonder why this is the face she seeks when control lapses.

As their heels clack down the hall, she feels Ryon appraise her, his worry apparent. While the others hurry ahead, he lets the tips of his fingers graze over hers.

And she feels warmer.

CHAPTER TWENTY-EIGHT

Tasheem leads them into a room with walls that soar endlessly upward and hold shelf after shelf of what appear to be... bones.

"I loathe this room," says Tasheem, wrinkling her nose with distaste. "But at least we won't be interrupted."

Ryon's face has become strained. His wrist flicks restlessly, as though he would draw a weapon.

"What is this place?" Dawsyn murmurs, mouth gaping.

"The remains of any who sought to defy the King," Ryon answers acidly.

Dawsyn's eyebrows hitch. The bones are displayed from floor to ceiling, the collection staggering. "So many?"

Ryon grimaces. "Eventually he proclaimed it impractical to mount the bones of every enemy and so opted to toss them into the Chasm instead."

Dawsyn notices that his eyes do not quite meet the shelves and their trophies. "Vasteel wanted your wings to be cut from your back before we were pushed into the Chasm," Dawsyn says.

"Did he?" Ryon asks, distracted.

"Would they have ended up here?"

He shrugs. "Maybe."

Baltisse is pacing. Dawsyn has never seen her pace, and it serves to draw her attention away from this hideous room and it hideous contents, and reminds her that there are worse things to learn than the practices of a vanished king.

"Baltisse?" Dawsyn calls to her, and the mage stops. She looks from Dawsyn to Ryon, and her jaw moves, as though in restraint, her teeth grinding at the effort.

Ryon frowns, disturbed. "Are you truly without words, Baltisse?"

She narrows her eyes. "I want to be sure my words won't ignite a war the second I say them."

"I spent years waiting to strike when the time was nigh, and now you doubt my control?"

"Not yours," Baltisse says. "*Hers.*"

All eyes fall to Dawsyn.

The mage observes her with shrewd calculation.

"You're concerned for my control?"

The mage sighs. "Your lack thereof."

Dawsyn does not wish to waste time in idle debate. She does not bother to quip and argue, because if it is *Dawsyn's* control she fears, then surely what she means to reveal pertains to the Ledge, and the people on it.

And what could be worse than what they already know? What could be more dire than leaving them stranded?

Dawsyn's breath stops.

The mage grimaces.

Ryon curses.

And Dawsyn has her fears realised in Baltisse's expression. She sees it when the mage reads her thoughts and confirms them in her lack of denial.

"Would someone fill me in?" Tasheem asks, and the question echoes around Dawsyn's skull, for she is already gone, her mind skipping ahead to where she will go and what she will do.

"Adrik," Baltisse says aloud, "has been drinking from the pool, and he plans to continue. In fact, he has gathered a band of fellows, who seek to do the same."

"Drink from the Pool of Iskra?" Ruby asks, her head turning to Dawsyn. "But, why?"

"Power," Ryon answers, and his voice is an awakened creature of another realm. "Control."

"Immortality," Tasheem concludes, her breaths short.

Adrik, sitting in the place of the king, feeding his chosen few all the food and drink and luxury they could possibly want. Dawsyn bites her tongue and tastes blood.

"But... he would need human souls," Ruby says.

He would. He does.

"Stop her!" Baltisse shouts.

Ryon's hand reaches for her.

And Baltisse's magic wraps Dawsyn in a vice.

But Dawsyn's own magic has not merely awoken, but exploded, and with an almighty flash of brilliant light, the bindings Baltisse meant to stop her fall away, and Dawsyn is running, running, running.

For Adrik, the newest king of Glacia, *will* need human souls, and there is a herd of them across the Chasm, ripe for the picking.

Somewhere behind her, Ryon curses again, and calls, "Get Rivdan, if you can!" and he falls into pursuit close behind.

Dawsyn runs past doors and halls through the Glacian palace, past Izgoi who watch curiously as she passes. The iskra within her rejoices with each step, urging her onward, toward her ax, toward retribution.

She reaches her room, the door slamming into the wall before she can touch it, the chamber darkening as she steps within. Her ax glints from beneath a pillow and it seems to slide into her hand before she can truly grasp it.

But a hand stops her. Large fingers grip her wrist, and she wrenches her hand out of its grasp. She turns on Ryon, skirting around him for the door, and almost reaches it, but then his arms are around her, pulling her backward.

"Dawsyn, *listen!*"

But what possible reason could there be to listen.

No, she thinks. *I've heard enough!*

And perhaps she says it aloud, because he turns her around, one hand on her forearm, keeping the ax from reaching his person, and he crowds her to the wall, pressing into her firmly, his face pleading.

"Please stop! You will be killed."

"AND SO WILL HE!" she bellows.

But he doesn't flinch.

He does not cower.

"I cannot let you," he says, and it sounds like an apology as much as an assurance. "Think. Just *think!* It is not just your life and Adrik's. Ruby, Baltisse, even Tasheem… they will all die defending you. And so will I." His breath finds her cheek, her neck, and she shivers, despite the burning anger. The hot panic.

His thigh is pressed between hers, his hands pinning her arms to the wall. He uses his whole body to still hers. So very unbearably close.

"I will take you to the Ledge," he says, voice low, desperate. "I'll kill Adrik myself if you tell me to. But please. Don't do this. Not yet."

Those damnable eyes, so strangely deep, pierce hers. They bind her more thoroughly than his entire frame pressed to hers can. For a moment, it is just her heavy breaths, combining with his, her mind churning wildly with Adrik's face, Tasheem's, Ruby's, Baltisse's.

And then the people of the Ledge. The ones she had believed they would save.

All that she and Ryon did…

All that they have done, has been for nothing.

Dawsyn's eyes swim, and then close.

She feels him release one of her arms, and then his fingertips are on her cheek. By degrees, her forehead lowers, and lowers, until it touches Ryon's shoulder, skin radiating cold beneath his shirt.

She feels the iskra concede its pursuit and shrink away.

Silent tears fall down her cheeks, and her body becomes slack. Ryon becomes the thing to hold her up, rather than to hold her back, and he drops her other arm. There is a clang as her ax falls to the floor, but neither of them reacts to the sound.

Ryon wraps his arms around her. "I'll go to the Ledge with you," he vows. "We will save as many as we can." But they both know it is not enough, and maybe that's why he says again, "If you want me to kill Adrik, now, this day, I will do it."

She does. She wants Adrik and any other who would follow his lead to die. She wants him to suffer for the way he manipulated Ryon, for the way he used them both to fight his battles and win his court. For the way he replaced a king who had intended no better.

But Ryon would die too. The Izgoi would not stop to listen to reason, and there would be no fighting their way out of a palace crawling with them. More bloodshed, more killing for the sake of yet another tyrant.

"Not yet," she whispers.

Those words transport her, for a mere moment, back to the mouth of the cave where the waves crashed against rock below and the horizon beckoned them. *Not yet,* she had told him then, as she tells him now.

She lifts her head to see him. "We go to the Ledge," she says. "Now."

CHAPTER TWENTY-NINE

It takes moments for Dawsyn to collect her possessions, minutes for them to traverse a path through the palace to find the others, to explain their next course, to allow them time to bow out.

But none do.

Baltisse rolls her eyes. Ruby simply looks back to the door of the bone room, and shudders, "I'll go anywhere but here."

And then come Tasheem and two other mixed, both male, and one who Dawsyn recognises as Rivdan.

"What is this, Ryon?" the unfamiliar one asks, his voice showing casual curiosity, though his brow furrows and the corners of his lips curve downward at the sight of the present company. "A mutiny, I presume?"

"Not a mutiny, Brennick." Ryon says. "A rescue."

The man named Brennick lets his mouth hang open, and then he laughs, short and humourless. "Come now, Mesrich," he huffs. "You cannot possibly mean the Ledge? It is noble, brother, but we will need many more alongside us. Four sets of wings are not enough. You must know that."

"I do," he says. "But I must ask it anyway."

"And why," Rivdan adds, appearing to brace himself, "must you ask it?" Unlike the one named Brennick, Rivdan does not seem merely suspicious, but expectant.

Ryon exhales in a gust, before saying, "Adrik intends to take the king's seat. He wants the Pool of Iskra."

Brennick's and Rivdan's eyes go round, and they wait for something further. They look to Tasheem, who nods.

Brennick laughs again, a hint of desperation marring its casualness. "No... Ryon he only drank from it to unlock the portcullises. That is all."

"That is not all," says Dawsyn.

Brennick eyes her cautiously. "How could you possibly know?"

"Because I read his mind," Baltisse says lazily. "And it is as filthy and insidious as that nest atop your head. Holy mother above, Glacian, do you never *bathe?*"

Brennick turns to Ryon, "Who the fuck is she?"

"A mage," Ryon answers. "We haven't time for this."

"She's a witch?"

"Don't call her that."

"Why?" And then he goes down, curling in on his stomach as pain overcomes him.

It is a sight to behold, but Baltisse looks almost bored of it. Before Brennick can shout or scream, his body releases, the pain that gripped him suddenly gone.

"That's why," Ryon mutters. He stoops to help Brennick to his feet, and then claps the man's shoulders with both hands. "Adrik will have us selecting humans on the Ledge to feed the pool before long. I must ask you both to defy him. If you refuse, I only ask you to say nothing. Do nothing. Let us be on our way."

Rivdan and Brennick look at each other, and then back to Ryon.

"I've known you both since we were infants," Ryon says. "We grew together. I wouldn't ask if I was not sure I could trust you."

Ryon steps away. With a gust, his wings are summoned, and he looks to the passage behind his comrades. "Make your decision. We leave now."

Before either can answer, the sound of approaching footsteps echoes down the corridor. Ryon vanishes his wings again, and Rivdan and Brennick turn expectantly. Tasheem affects an unconvincing casual position by leaning against the wall, and Dawsyn reaches for her ax.

But it is Gerrot who turns the corner.

The man, his trousers belted around his severely thin waist, walks resolutely into their midst. His cheeks are sunken, no doubt a consequence of the tongue that was cut from his mouth by the brutes. He looks, from all angles, as though a gust of wind might fell him – except for his eyes, which are alight with a ferocious kind of determination.

"Gerrot," Dawsyn says, and the old man's eyes find her. Without further preamble, without a word of question from the others, Gerrot very purposefully points to himself, his finger to his chest, and then points to a window high above, where the daylight offers a lighter shade of grey.

Every set of eyes turn to the window in question.

"What can he mean?" Tasheem asks.

Gerrot's jaw flexes. He points to himself once more, and this time, he points straight at Dawsyn.

Dawsyn frowns, "Wh–"

"He wishes to journey with us," Baltisse interrupts, her shoulders slumping. "To the Ledge."

Dawsyn does not know how Gerrot has come to learn of their plans in such a short space of time, but she suspects that the man is far quieter and less noticeable than even his frame would suggest. She eyes him. "It will be dangerous."

Gerrot does not react to her words. Instead, he lifts his chin, and allows his stare to bear down on her.

She remembers the way he'd hurried away from Adrik and his admirers in the King's rooms, a tray in hand. She remembers the wordless sound that had escaped his lips on the day his wife had died. The thoughts pass through her mind fleetingly, her decision made by the time they dissipate. Yes.

He shall be returned to Terrsaw as well. He should not stay in this place a moment longer. "Very well," she says.

Ryon looks briefly at the resolve in her expression and nods. "Then," he says, turning back to Rivdan and Brennick, "it seems you are the only two left to declare yourselves."

Rivdan steps forward first, his expression steely. "I'll follow."

But Brennick shakes his head. "No," he says. "I cannot." And he is already backing away, already separating himself.

Ryon calls to him. "Brennick! Please listen. Adrik–"

"Adrik would not fall to such temptation."

"Bren, I would never cast such an accusation if I wasn't *sure*."

But Brennick is turning away, shaking his head. "I cannot, Ryon. I... I can't."

"Then say nothing," Ryon asks. "Please, brother."

But Brennick is already hurrying back the way he came. He does not look at Ryon again.

"Fuck," Tasheem spits.

"We go," Ryon proclaims. "Right now."

They must run. Down the stairwell, through the tunnels, beyond the portcullises. The ice beneath their feet is not particularly slick, but Ruby stumbles often anyway, unused to the terrain. They will not have time to tend to her skull if it cracks.

Tasheem wraps her arm around Ruby's back and half carries her toward the Chasm, its impossible width growing, stretching further with each step. Rivdan lifts Gerrot over his shoulder, the old man unable to keep pace as they hasten.

"Ready yourselves," Ryon calls as they get closer.

Tasheem takes hold of Baltisse, Ryon moves toward Dawsyn.

The Chasm is a monstrous void, swallowing the world, and they tear across the ice toward it. She hears Ruby utter a small cry of fear. She hears Baltisse pant out a curse.

There is no slowing.

"Stop!" Ruby yells, "STOP!"

But Tasheem lifts both her and Baltisse from the ground, as Rivdan does Gerrot. Dawsyn turns at the exact moment that Ryon reaches for her, and then they are flying.

CHAPTER THIRTY

The people of the Ledge tell stories of how the Chasm came to be.

How could a mountain so mighty find itself cleaved in two? The Ridge is named for its vastness. From the valley, the mountain looks to be one giant mass, scaling unendingly skyward. There is only one interruption, and it is that of the divide between the people on the Ledge and the rest of the world. It is reasonable for the people there to assume that the mountain had, in one fragment of history, been whole.

Valma Sabar had told the story of the Chasm often, and as Dawsyn grew, she suspected the woman had likely spun the tale herself.

Dawsyn's younger sister would shout, "Grandma! Tell the Yerdos story." And Dawsyn, who had heard it a hundred times more often than Maya, would groan.

"Hush, Dawsyn. Let her pick."

"When is it that she does *not* pick?" Dawsyn muttered.

Valma allowed Maya to climb onto her lap, and the old woman groaned. Each day, Maya grew heavier, and their grandmother grew weaker. The coughing had started. It would continue for another year before it would overcome her.

"Yerdos was a creature of the mountain–"

"Not a Glacian," Maya cut in.

"No, not a Glacian," Valma agreed. "Yerdos was a hawk, as large as a human. For thousands of years, she soared over the mountain, guarding all the living things upon it. It was a simple task. The Mother had given her a lush, green mountain, and she only had to ensure that none came to threaten it. Yerdos swooped at those who tried to lay claim to it, she scared away the humans that came to climb it. She succeeded. Her bird's call was a clamour that could be heard all the way to the ocean, her beak was as sharp as a sword and just as unbreakable. No human nor beast dared to take her mountain.

"But then, one day, a creature came that was unlike any other. A creature with no talons or weapons, but that of fierce breath."

"Moroz," Maya inserts, her eyes expectant.

"Do you want to tell the story, child?"

"No," Maya answered, rolling her eyes.

"Moroz crept onto the mountain so slowly, that at first, Yerdos did not notice. Moroz came in small scatterings of fine white powder, in mists and fogs. The creature crept higher and higher, and by the time Yerdos realised that her mountain was under siege, the animals had already begun to suffer. They dug below ground or left the mountain altogether. The plants were shrivelling. Soon, they were inundated with blankets of snow, and Yerdos couldn't find them at all.

"Nothing Yerdos did worked. Her beak did nothing to Moroz, who was everywhere and nowhere. No matter how much Yerdos called, it was no match for the wind. Moroz would snatch Yerdos's cries up and carry them away.

"Yerdos was distraught. Her mountain had been taken by something cold, unyielding. For the first time since she was granted the mountain, she left, soaring high into the clouds to consult the Mother, who perched at the very peak of the summit – a place no other could reach.

"The great hawk begged Mother for help. She told her of Moroz, and the death and destruction it had brought upon the mountain, and Mother laughed at her. 'Dear Yerdos,' the Mother said. 'All seasons must come to a close.'

"Yerdos was furious. She screamed into the wind all the way down from the mountain peak. She plummeted down, her blessed beak as indestructible as ever. When she saw the mountain below, covered in snow, desolate and cold, she did not stop her descent. Instead, she collided with it. Her beak struck through the stone, and the ungodly sound of the rock splitting apart silenced all else. The mountain quaked as a crack spread the length of it, splitting trees and boulders, and inch by inch, the mountain separated at the point where Yerdos's beak had pierced it.

"Yerdos still lives there, in the bottomless Chasm, nursing her rage. She collects the fallen, protects them, and curses Moroz for continuing to kill and destroy. Her hawk's call, the one she once used to warn away her enemies, is still trapped in the wind of Moroz. It howls and screams, not to warn away her enemies, but to warn away any who might fall prey to the terrible cold that still grasps her mountain."

Dawsyn was already approaching sleep, her eyelids giving way. But before she settled properly on her cot and turned her face toward the hearth, she heard Maya say, "Maybe one day Moroz's season will end as well."

"Perhaps."

"And we will fight Moroz until then."

Their grandmother chuckled. Not in a way a grandmother should, with crinkled eyes and tenderness, but with a dark knowing. An insatiable bitterness.

"No, child," she said. "There is nothing to fight. The cold is not alive."

Chapter Thirty-One

There might come a day when Dawsyn does not fear the sensation of her stomach disintegrating as her feet leave the earth, but it is not this day. They glide over the black depths of the Chasm, flying within reach of its grasp. Dawsyn knows they must remain low to escape notice from the palace but hates it even so. So, too, should they keep their approach concealed from the people of the Ledge, who might see them and assume that they have come to select.

The lip of the Chasm comes before them, the treeline beyond it. The ice angles upward, away from the cliff edge, glistening threateningly. Suddenly, Ryon is holding her aloft. He descends gently, letting her feet settle on the snow.

And she is back.

The pine grove looms ahead, swaying precariously in the wind. The branches creak ominously as they bend beyond their scope, and it echoes down to them. Wind howls through the trunks, wailing its ancient sinister song. *Moroz*, Dawsyn thinks.

A great hollowness seizes her. Her mouth turns dry. As though commanded, her very being adjusts. Her toes curl inward, as though they would grip the earth. She leans away from the Chasm, she listens for the sounds of anyone approaching, so intently that at the swoop of wings and boots, she jumps.

The others land.

Baltisse unfurls herself from Tasheem with no small amount of distaste, her nose wrinkled. "Even the wind hurts here," she calls, and makes to step forward.

Dawsyn grasps her elbow before she can, making the mage grunt indignantly. She turns to look past her furred hood, glaring at Dawsyn.

"Ice," Dawsyn says simply, and with the toe of her boot, she nudges the thin layer of powder aside to reveal the clean pane below. They are too close to the lip. Mere feet. Plenty have slipped into the Chasm from a distance far greater. "Careful," Dawsyn calls to them all.

Ruby, however, awed by the towering mountain face and ghostly pine wood, gives no sign at having heard. Her mouth agape, she curses lowly, eyes wide, stepping forward.

And she does not tilt to the Face, the way a person of the Ledge would. She does not spear her toe into the ice to find safer purchase. Instead, her boot hits the deception of powder, the ice waiting below it, the ravenous chasm behind, and she slips.

"No!" Dawsyn shouts.

Ruby's hands hit the ground before her, and she slides, and slides, her face stricken with terror, scrambling to slow.

And the Chasm awaits, insatiable, impatient.

Dawsyn dives, one hand outstretched toward Ruby, the ice carrying them both to the edge. Dawsyn lifts her ax and throws it with as much force as she can into the frozen ground, and her fingers graze the captain's as the woman's body falls over the lip – first her feet, and then her waist, and then the rest.

Ruby falls.

But Ryon follows.

Dawsyn looks over her shoulder in horror as Ruby's fingertips vanish into the white, and a great dark mass of wings follows her, diving down into the Chasm. It is only a moment.

One moment of consuming terror as Ruby's scream splits the air in two, and Dawsyn shouts Ryon's name.

And then relief.

Ryon suddenly rises over the lip, Ruby in his arms. This time, he gives the ice a fair breadth, only putting Ruby on her feet when they reach the treeline.

Dawsyn drops her forehead onto the ice, ignoring the sting of the cold, her gasps slowing. *Thank the Mother.*

Rivdan bends to her hand on the ax, grasping her wrist carefully. "Come on, prishmyr," he says softly. "Careful now." Rivdan's talons pierce the ice, and she uses him like an anchor to heave herself toward him, only bending to retrieve her ax once she has regained her footing.

"Quite hysterical," Baltisse remarks casually. "The diving, I mean. Almost as though there weren't a clutch of winged persons on hand to save the dear captain."

Dawsyn, for once, says nothing. She feels her blood heat at the collar, lifts her hood back over her head. Embarrassment overcomes her, a feeling altogether unfamiliar.

It was an overreaction. That was all. She has seen too many people slip toward the Chasm. An instinctive response. Many would do the same.

"Weird of you to yell out *Ryon's* name, of the two, though. Wouldn't you say? Almost like it was an unconscious th–"

"We have more important matters before us," Dawsyn says loudly, spearing the mage with a foreboding glare. Dawsyn's skin prickles with discomfort. "Do watch your feet, witch. I wouldn't want you to slip away."

"At least I know there's someone nearby who will dive to my rescue. Not *you*, of course, Dawsyn. I'd likely opt for one of these hulking louts with the means to fly."

Tasheem chortles, and Dawsyn's glare falls to her too. She immediately sobers.

"Just watch the fucking Chasm," Dawsyn grumbles, and moves off with careful strides, digging the toe of her boot into the ground with each step until the powder thickens, and her feet sink with ease. She doesn't look back to note if the others follow.

Before they reach the treeline, Baltisse, persistent as ever, appears at her shoulder. "When will you admit it, Dawsyn Sabar?"

Dawsyn groans internally. At this rate, she may just push the witch over the edge herself. "Admit what?"

She chuckles darkly. "You called his name to the wind like you were possessed. You care for him still." The superiority in her smile is almost too much.

Dawsyn grits her teeth. "An ailment I aim to be rid of, I assure you."

"It is hardly up to you, sweet," she tsks.

Ryon is ahead, watching Dawsyn approach, his eyes steadfast on her feet.

"You called his name because love forfeits sense."

"*Fear* forfeits sense," Dawsyn says between her teeth. "I need his help. The people here need his help."

"And he will give it," Baltisse says bitingly. "He will do anything you ask him to do, Dawsyn, without question, without hesitation. As I said, love forfeits sense."

It isn't love, Dawsyn thinks, but it comes automatically – a useless reflex.

Baltisse sighs, presumedly having heard her. "It certainly isn't *sense*. And I can read it clearly in his mind. He is desperate to atone. So, I will grant you the favour of fair warning, Sabar. If you *use* him, if you take advantage of his remorse for the sake of a quest you know will fail, you will make me into an enemy."

Without another word, the mage steps away.

Dawsyn watches the back of her hood move ahead and bites her tongue. Her first instinct is indignation. Does Baltisse truly believe that she would use Ryon, and then discard him?

But is that not exactly what she intends to do?

Dawsyn's chest aches uncomfortably, but she pushes the feeling aside. This is what must be done. She has very few options. Ryon can make his own decisions. He can choose to bow out whenever it pleases him.

But he won't. Dawsyn knows it, just as Baltisse does.

And if he, or any other should die in this improbable quest, it will be because she allowed it. The fault will be hers.

"My apologies," Ruby says as the party reaches her and Ryon. "I was careless."

"That is the next one," Dawsyn answers.

"The next what?"

"The next lesson," Dawsyn clarifies. "Watch the Chasm. Many who were born here have slipped before you. Are you all right?"

"Yes," the captain answers. "Thank you, Dawsyn."

"For what?"

"For bothering to try and save me."

Dawsyn resists the urge to deny the fact. Instead, she nods, then strides through the space between Ruby and Ryon, without making eye contact with either. She takes to the pine grove, shrugging away the swirl of impeding thoughts that only serve to distract her from the task ahead.

She walks upon the ground of her first home with company of dubious loyalty: a half-Glacian she cannot allow herself to trust, his friends of whom she knows very little, the Queens' most honoured guard, and a mage who threatened retribution not moments before. Together, they make the most tenuous of factions.

And there is the kingdom of Glacia behind them, who might intervene at any moment.

There is little choice. She is always with so little choice. She ploughs on through the snow, with no plan to achieve what must be achieved. Nothing ahead but the pine, the snow, the Face, and of course, those she means to save, should they only allow themselves to be.

Through the trees comes a familiar sound: rising voices, a cacophony of shouting, discord, and unrest.

"What is that?" Tasheem asks, her wings twitching at the hint of danger. "What is that noise?"

"That," Dawsyn says, tramping onward through the wood, "is the sound of my people."

CHAPTER THIRTY-TWO

"What are they doing?" Ryon asks, his eyes ahead to where the trees thin.

Dawsyn sighs. "Fighting."

The others fall silent, possibly awaiting her elaboration. The sounds of tumult continue, building and then ebbing.

"Fighting over what?" Ruby asks when Dawsyn fails to explain.

Dawsyn shrugs. "It cannot be the Drop," she surmises, eyes flitting to the sky. They would have seen the Izgoi flying overhead. "My guess is food."

"Why food?" Rivdan asks.

"When was the last time a Drop was made?" She does not look over her shoulder to see his expression, but when no answer comes, it is answer enough. Dawsyn closes her eyes momentarily.

It has happened many times before. The Glacians neglected to bring their scraps and rations to the Ledge. There was no rhyme or reason. No cause to be discerned. The time between Drops would lag, and the people on the Ledge would grow slowly hungrier. There is only so long one can stretch their food stores. There's an infinitesimal amount of game to be hunted on the Ledge. The ground does not yield enough to farm much other than turnips. After the Chasm and the cold, the most deadly thing on the Ledge is hunger, and the way it possesses the mind.

And now she must throw herself into the fray and ask that they lend an ear.

Impossible, she thinks, and yet she must try. Perhaps... perhaps the hunger will make them desperate enough to risk giving themselves to the mixed-blooded Glacians she has led here.

The raucous echoes heighten, and a pained shout rings through the air.

Perhaps not.

"We should stop them," the captain says impatiently, staggering forward.

"Have you a sword, Ruby?" Dawsyn asks.

The captain pauses. "Yes?"

"Good. Get it out."

Dawsyn takes the lead once more, stalking purposefully toward the cause of the noise, jaw set and stomach churning. She speaks without lowering her voice, for it will not be heard above the sounds of discord. "Ready your wits," she says to them all. "And stay quiet. I will speak for us."

"And if they do not listen?" Ryon asks from behind. He has stayed much closer than she thought.

"Then we take to the skies," she tells him. "And pray we are fast enough."

Through the trees she emerges. Dawsyn alone, holding her ax at her side. "Stay back," she says to the rest, and steps from the shadows.

She takes in the familiar scene before her. Amidst the cabins, a circle of her people jostles and jeers at the spectacle within. Two men wrestle upon the snow, their faces imperceptible. One, in fact, is so bloodied and bruised Dawsyn assumes he fights blind.

Not food, then. Pine.

Only the claim of trees brings two people into a match such as this. When the tree in question cannot be identified as belonging to one person or another, a fight to surrender – or more often, to death – is the decider.

The man with his back to the ground suddenly throws his quarry off and struggles to regain his feet. One of his legs drags, quite obviously broken. Still, he manages to land his opponent with a blow to the head as he straightens, sending him back to the snow once more.

The victor drags his wasted leg to circle the man, readying to deliver a death blow. And Dawsyn sees his face clearly.

Hector.

It is as though she'd shouted it. The same moment she recognises her friend, he lifts his weary head, and his eyes find hers over the crowd.

She sees her own name form on his lips, his eyes wide and disbelieving, and then he disappears. The bodies of the spectators conceal him as he falls, his competitor rising to stand over him, and Dawsyn's breath stops. *No!*

She begins to run.

The man leers down, lifting his fist to strike again.

Dawsyn shoves two onlookers aside, half falling into the circle, where the snow has turned pink and slick. She lifts her ax, an ax so obviously not hewn and crafted on the Ledge, and regrips it at the neck, swinging the handle wide until it contacts Hector's opponent, the wood making a sickening thunk as it collides with the back of his head.

The man falls, though Dawsyn doubts it will be with any permanency, and the crowd, taken aback, falls quiet.

Dawsyn spins the ax in her hand and holds the blade aloft. "Stay back!" she warns, for she knows the shock will soon turn to violence.

Silence. The crowd does not number more than twenty, but the silence is deafening.

"Dawsyn Sabar?" one mutters. And then another. The men and women back away, drawing their weapons from their waistbands, pockets, sleeves.

"But she was *selected.*"

"How…?"

"Dawsyn?" Hector gasps, rising before her. He blinks, as though she might dissolve in an instant. His eyes run slowly from her boots to her crown, and they remain wide. His mouth hangs open.

There is a cut on his forehead. It leaks blood through his eyebrow and down his nose. Beneath the faint bruises beginning to blossom, he appears gaunt. Sallow. But his hair is the same shade of brown-blonde and the curls still hang in his blue eyes with obstinacy. He still stands as tall, his shoulders hunched just so.

She is immeasurably relieved to see him alive.

A man Dawsyn knows as Des Polson steps forward, a crude knife outstretched. He is advanced in years, with a beard that reaches his chest. But Dawsyn does not mistake him as slow. She once watched the man fell a bird at twenty feet with that blade. "Well, well," he says hoarsely. "And just *how*, pray tell, did you manage to find your way across that fucking Chasm, girl?"

The rest can do little more then watch on, their bodies tight with tension, eyes wide, ears keen.

This is her chance. The only one she will get.

And there is so much to tell.

So, she sticks with the most pertinent, the most practical, and hopes it is enough.

"I come with good news, in fact," Dawsyn begins, her voice uneven, her ax still raised. "The Glacian King… he has fallen… and you may be free."

If the silence was loud before, it is now just as thick. It stretches across the Ledge, brings curious onlookers to their cabin stoops, all beholding the Sabar girl, the selected, the first one of their kind to be taken and returned.

And then they laugh.

It starts with Polson, who lifts his chin to the sky and lets out a bark that reverberates through the rest, and then it spreads. They laugh at her – with disbelief, with distrust.

"Get your things, lads and ladies. Let us hop over the Chasm, then, and see this freedom!"

Dawsyn's eyes slide to each of them in turn, their faces a mixture of wariness, mirth, bitterness. Already, they have stopped listening. "I was there when Glacia was conquered!" she shouts, attempting to drown the sounds of their disregard. "And I learnt much that we could never have guessed. I've been to the valley, to Terrsaw!" her mind stutters. "I've... I've learnt the *truth!*"

"Have you now?" Polson asks. "And just how did you find your way back?"

She is losing them. Some have even turned their backs on her. She can think of only one thing that might give them pause, if her presence is not proof enough.

Baltisse, Dawsyn thinks. *Tell them to come.*

"I was carried over the Chasm," Dawsyn answers. "By a half-Glacian."

"Were you indeed?" Polson smirks.

"She was," calls a voice, from a distance none too great.

From the grove steps Ryon, his footing strangely sure on the drifts. Behind him come Tasheem, Rivdan, Ruby, Gerrot and Baltisse. So many strangers to the Ledge, whose people have not seen an unfamiliar human in fifty years.

With deliberate slowness, Ryon summons his wings, and they stretch wide and sure. Undoubtedly Glacian.

Fear, sudden and suffocating, grips the Ledge at the sight of those wings. Wings that signal an immediate knowledge in the people here. Wings that have snatched and stolen their sisters and brothers and parents. Their lovers and children. Wings that command the wind and the clouds, whose sound lives in each of them, for it has always preceded destruction, death, grief.

But the people on the Ledge are also well versed in their meaning. And so, at the unfurling of those wings, even black ones such as these, the humans stand still. They do not run, but remain frozen, save for the wind that stirs their clothes. For when the Glacians come to the Ledge, they come to select their prey.

And the prey that runs is always hunted.

Dawsyn moves, coming to stand between her allies and her people, turning her back on Ryon and the rest, a show of trust.

Hector is the only other one to move, raising a hand as though he might stop her, viscerally reacting to the sight of her so vulnerable to the Glacian at her back.

"Not all Glacians are alike," Dawsyn begins, trying in earnest to make her voice louder than the squalls. But a storm comes, she can smell it, feel it on the back of her neck. The wind is growing stronger. "You need not fear these. The white beasts who flew over the Chasm each season have been defeated! These are mixed-blooded Glacians, more human than not, and they suffered similar torment at the hands of the pure-blooded who ruled us."

"Their skin…" a woman mutters in awe, her voice quickly swallowed by a gust.

"Human skin," Dawsyn implores, turning to gesture to the others. "But wings that might free you from here. They will take you to the valley, away from this mountain, should you wish it. *You will be safe there!*" Though this last part, Dawsyn knows, cannot possibly be guaranteed.

"Allow them to take us?" Polson asks, eyes unable to leave the sight of those wings.

"Yes." Dawsyn nods. "You will be free. You will not be harmed!"

A great pause ensues, and all hold their breath. The people of the Ledge watch with quiet panic as the Glacian-like creature before them bides his time, not swooping to attack, not sinking his talons into the shoulders of the selected. Dawsyn begins to hope. Perhaps it is enough that the Glacians she brought here are different. Perhaps it is enough that they do not attack and take as they undoubtedly could. Perhaps…

"*Lies!*" Polson calls, and his voice, tremulous with his conviction, seems to only heighten the fear. "All of it!"

"I do not–"

"It is not enough that we stand prone before our stoops each season, willing to sacrifice ourselves to these beasts? Now they come to take us all at once!"

"No."

The people stir at his accusation, and the wind grows wild.

"They will have us go with them willingly, so they might consume us as they please."

"Stop," Dawsyn begs, feeling the shift in the undercurrent.

"And Dawsyn Sabar will be spared, it seems, so long as she helps them–"

"If you stay here," Dawsyn interjects. "You will *starve*. A new king sits on the throne, and he will come. He will take as many of you as he can."

The wind grows fierce. Howling now. Moroz awakened.

"So, the danger has not passed then, as you said," Polson says.

Dawsyn realises the mistake too late.

"As I thought," he sneered. "The freedom you spoke of was a *lie*."

Dawsyn closes her eyes. Prepares to beg if she must. "Please. Listen to me. If you stay, you will starve. You will be taken!"

"We have always starved."

"You needn't–"

"And we have always been taken."

"You're a fool."

"And you are a *traitor*, of the worst kind!"

"I want to *save* you!"

"Perhaps most here have forgotten what the Sabar name means," Polson says acidly stalking toward her. "But I, girl, have not. And I answer to no damned royalty, neither here, nor in that fucking Glacian kingd–"

But the man can say no more, for Dawsyn holds up her ax, the bit aligned between the man's eyes. The slightest movement will see him split in two.

Dawsyn shakes, her entire being trembling with pure, desperate rage. She feels the iskra, snaking a leisurely path up her torso and down the arm that holds the ax. The magic walks freely, unlocked and unchallenged. It surfaces through her palms and over her fingers, along the ax handle. She welcomes it.

Polson's eyes turn from enraged to panicked as the magic creeps toward him, bridged between its host and him by way of the ax.

"If you remain," Dawsyn says, her voice barely heard as the wind whips the powder into a frenzy, their legs and bodies and faces sliced by the fierce squall. "You will die."

But Polson does not take heed. Instead, in that moment, he raises his blade to Dawsyn's abdomen, meaning to shunt it into her stomach.

And she almost doesn't catch it. *Almost.*

She screams, the sound exploding from her lungs with a ferocity to rival the mountain itself.

The magic in her expands, and then breaks.

The light at her hand detonates, sending Polson soaring. There is a sickening crack as his head hits the ice, and then he lies still and unseeing.

Dawsyn does not see the way Polson's blood courses a river along the ice. She does not see how the people run from her, or from the storm that threatens to drag them down this tilted shelf. She only feels her body convulse and thrash. Something inside grips her, squeezing her lungs. The iskra strains within, tearing her apart.

She feels Hector grasp her shoulders, his voice yelling to her, though she hears nothing. And then there are strong arms encasing her, encasing Hector and her both, and they are leaving the ground. Leaving the Ledge. It grows impossibly smaller below them.

Then there is nothing at all. No pain and no light. Just a numbing blackness, with a voice, slick and familiar, that whispers incessantly.

If only, it says, *you would release me.*

CHAPTER THIRTY-THREE

Ryon's wings strain against the wind as he ascends, the task made all the more difficult by the weight of Dawsyn, and the other – particularly the other, who pushes against him, wrestling in an absurd attempt to break free.

They are already over the Chasm, already headed for the ridge. If he falls now, he'll meet a swift death. "Stop fighting!"

The man curses and grunts, trying to head butt and kick and peel Ryon's forearm from his torso. "Let me go!"

Ryon considers it. His other arm is wrapped tightly around Dawsyn's ribs, crushingly so. She is slumped, a dead weight. There will be bruises when she awakens. If this man would stop *fighting*...

"LET GO OF ME!"

He'd never meant to take him too, but the people of the Ledge were panicking, Dawsyn had lost control of herself, and they had to go. He had to get them away. And the man had been there, his arms wrapped around Dawsyn. To protect her.

Friend or not, he is proving a nuisance now.

The force of the gale drags him lower, his wings overexerting from the added burden. If they can get to the ridge, the mountain will offer a buffer from the storm. The recently repaired hole in his chest is straining with increasing intensity. One wing trembles and retracts an inch, and they dip threateningly. The man squirms again, and Ryon curses loudly.

He looks to either side. Tasheem carries Baltisse and Gerrot both. Rivdan with Ruby. The man is flying against the wind with more ease than the rest, and he meets Ryon's eye. Rivdan must see the struggle Ryon is enduring, must see the plead in his eyes, even from a distance, because he moves lower, taking a position beneath.

Together, they soar.

Unevenly, gracelessly, their wings find ways to cut through the wind, and the ridge grows ever closer, promising respite. The mountain is bowled out on its side. They will fly low until they reach the Boulder Gate.

"Fucking Glacian SCUM!" the man shouts, throwing an elbow into Ryon's jaw.

Ryon grunts in pain, the ridge passing beneath them, and he plummets over the rock face, the wind stilling almost immediately.

"UNHAND ME!"

"Very well," Ryon murmurs darkly, and without warning, he releases the human from his grip, watching as he falls, his scream of terror frightening the ravens from the treetops below, and then Rivdan's arm encases him.

Ryon adjusts Dawsyn against his chest, his arms aching. She turns her face to him. Her eyes are still shut, but her breaths are even.

He will take her to safety. To Salem's inn. She will rest and eat, and she will be well. He comforts himself with the thought.

But what of her mind, when she wakes to learn that they have saved only one other?

Ryon sees again the desperation on her face as she tried to reason with those humans. Humans with missing teeth and cracked lips. Humans garbed in layer upon layer of clothing most would consider rags. Humans with eyes full of hatred. Full of fear. Full of their own battle-weary desperation.

Ryon had known instantly that they would not believe her, the second he'd summoned his wings, and he'd seen their eyes turn from dark suspicion to fear. To loathing.

They would not go.

He looks down at Dawsyn once more, unable to stop himself. The truth was her magic had frightened him. She'd frightened everyone.

They had gone to the Ledge with the bleak hope of offering salvation, and she had killed a man instead. Unpredictable as she is, Ryon does not know what she will do when she awakens and learns the scope of their failure.

They set down just over the Boulder Gate, and Dawsyn still does not wake.

Tasheem lands last and releases Gerrot from her grasp, the old man sporting a sickly pallor. But Baltisse is not with her.

Panic grips Ryon. "Where is–"

"She *vanished*," Tasheem sneers, groaning as she stretches her arms. "One moment she was complaining about the wind, the next she'd disappeared."

"It was the better option, to be sure," comes a voice from further off, and suddenly Baltisse is stalking toward them from a copse of trees. "You would have dropped me."

"I had a firm hold before you started whining."

"You certainly had a firm hold of *something*," Baltisse snaps, reaching their group.

"What does it matter what I grabbed, so long as I grabbed you? Would you have preferred to stay on the Ledge–" Tasheem suddenly keels over, her back hitting the ground in an almighty thump. She groans loudly, her hands clasping her head.

Baltisse only smiles, her eyes flaming.

"Fine company you keep, Mesrich," Tasheem grumbles from the ground.

"Sounds as though you deserved it," Ryon comments, his eyes roaming over the mage. Her frame is straight and tall, and her gait is steady. But the distance she folded was vast. He is surprised to find her upright.

"I am *fine*," the mage sniffs, throwing her fair hair over her shoulder. "Practice builds endurance."

Ryon notes her cheeks are without any colour at all, and her hands give away a slight tremble. As the thought comes, he watches Baltisse tuck them into her cloak.

"Put me down, hybrid," says a smaller voice, one much closer to his ear. Dawsyn jostles in his hold and he feels a breath of relief leave him at the sight of her awake. He sets her down carefully.

She, too, looks drawn, pale. Her usual sleek hair hangs limp, and without thinking, he wipes it away from her eyes.

She pushes his hand away instantly.

How mighty the pain of such a small reproach. His hand, tingling, falls to his side.

"Dawsyn?" comes the quiet voice of their newest party member – the man of the Ledge. He staggers before Rivdan and Gerrot, appearing as windswept as the rest, but unlike them, he also sports a bloodied face and a prominent limp, tokens from his fighting match.

The man is quite clearly shaken. He looks, indeed, like he might collapse at any moment.

"Hector," Dawsyn gasps, stepping toward him.

The name is familiar to Ryon.

"They…" He thrusts a finger at Ryon. "We flew… and then…"

"Are you all right?" Dawsyn asks.

"I… I do not know. I–" Hector struggles, then falls forward, catching himself awkwardly. Even as he does so, his eyes wheel wildly at the sights surrounding him. "Where are we?"

"Easy," Dawsyn says, kneeling before him. "This is Terrsaw. The valley."

Hector groans suddenly, rolling onto his back.

"His leg," Dawsyn says, distracted. "Baltisse. Can you–?"

Baltisse is already approaching the man on the ground, already placing her hands to his calf. Hector hisses, and grasps the mage's wrist.

"Easy, boy," Baltisse murmurs. "Close your eyes."

Ryon turns his face away as light bursts from Baltisse's palm. There is a keen ringing in his ears, one Ryon has come to associate with the mage, who has helped to heal his own maladies on more than one occasion.

When the ringing fades, Ryon turns to find Hector breathing in great, rasping heaves. Dawsyn helps him to stand, and the boy does so with little difficulty. He tests the ground beneath his feet, lifting them from the soft soil and regarding the muddy print his boot leaves in its wake. He blinks up at the sun, obscured by cloud but still bright. "I... It is warm."

Dawsyn, for all her unyielding sternness, gives a bark of laughter, the sound escaping despite herself, it seems. "Yes." She nods, smiling tiredly. "It is."

Ryon can't help but notice Baltisse, who is yet to rise from the ground. Her face is hidden, but it seems she is... regrouping, galvanising. Clearly, she is much less than fine.

"Dawsyn?" Ruby broaches. "What happened up there? What happened... to your hands? That light?"

Dawsyn's eyes glaze, all vestiges of humour dissolving. She looks to the mountain, looming above. Ryon can only watch on as she appears to recall the events that transpired on the Ledge.

All await her answer, falling perfectly silent. They watch as her expression becomes intense with something akin to pain, and then flattens, evening to nothing but an impassive stare. Unreadable. Whatever emotion swept through her is visibly squashed. It seems she will not answer.

"Iskra," Baltisse says from the ground. "It resides in her, still."

"From the pool?" Ruby questions uncertainly, eyes widening.

"It's a rather long story. One that will need to wait," Ryon says. "For now, we must find shelter. There is an inn; it is not so far. We will be safe there."

Baltisse's head whips around. "Surely you don't mean to burden Salem with–"

"*Surely,* I have no choice." Ryon bites. "Let us go, before we are discovered. And vanish your wings... *now,*" he adds to those bearing them.

Ruby takes pity on Hector and guides him away from the mud puddle that has stunned him into a stupor.

Before Ryon leads their party away, he approaches Dawsyn in a manner that can only be considered cautious, like a man readying himself for punishment. "Can you... walk?" he asks, already cringing at the response he is sure to receive.

And she does not disappoint. Dawsyn turns to him, several feet shorter, but fierce all the same, and gives him her most contemptuous glare. "If I fall behind, you can always use that magic ring of yours to track me down."

He ought not to respond, he knows. He wishes to ease the tension between them, not stoke it. But instead, he lets his juvenile mouth have its way. "You protest, but you are yet to remove its sister. I can see it around your neck."

Idiotic. Masochistic, even.

Do her hands glow, or does the light deceive him?

She deliberately steps on his foot as she passes, taking the lead into the forest.

And still, Ryon notes, the necklace remains.

CHAPTER THIRTY-FOUR

"Dawsyn? Wait… Dawsyn!"

It feels as though it's all she has heard since waking. It is a ringing that grows ever louder. She squints her eyes, tries to escape it.

"*Dawsyn!*" Hector calls in earnest, reaching her side.

Hector. Her friend. Here in Terrsaw. She should speak with him. He must be afraid.

This morning he woke on the Ledge, as he has done each day of his life, and tonight he will lay his head down in the valley. She should be elated to see him. She owes him that much.

"I'm glad to see you alive," Dawsyn manages, slowing to accommodate him. It isn't a lie, but her mind is a churning current. It is hard to muster friendliness amongst the tossing waves. He quickens to keep pace alongside her, lifting his feet high, as one would in the snow. His steps are comically exaggerated. She remembers how hard it was to break the same habit.

"And you," he says, and indeed he seems stunned by the very sight of her. He stumbles over trailing thickets, unable to remove his gaze.

And she stares back. He is familiar, and not.

"You look… new," he says, failing to duck beneath a broken branch. "Like a different person."

She smiles tightly. If only he knew.

"What happened to you?" he asks now. "After your Selection?"

She sighs. It feels like an eternity ago and yesterday, all at once. Either way, the days between then and now have been so altering that she doesn't know where to begin, and doesn't much want to. "It is a long story," she tells him, and sees the way his eyes glaze with irritation. "And I owe you its tale, I know. But not now. For now, all you need know is that those with us are allies," she says, hoping it is the truth. "They will not harm us. We are safer here in Terrsaw, but there are still threats."

"What threats?" asks Hector, immediately searching the forest. "Who threatens us?"

"I will explain everything to you, I promise. Unlike others, I don't hold a penchant for gate-keeping certain facts," she says rather loudly, and rather on purpose.

"I would never accuse you of such," Hector huffs, eyeing her warily.

"I assure you, you are better off here. What I said to Polson was true."

Hector nods. "I've never known you to tell tales, Dawsyn. I believe you."

Dawsyn smiles ruefully. "I am sorry we could not save your mother," she says, for she knows how closely Hector had always guarded her. It must pain him now, to have been wrenched away from her.

"She… she is dead."

Dawsyn stops on the path, eyes on her friend. Hector pauses alongside her, but neglects to meet her eye. He fails to hide the sorrow. He has always been inept at concealing his feelings.

She rests a careful hand on his shoulder, squeezing it. "I am sorry, Hector," she says, knowing nothing better to say. There is nothing that could quench such an acute ache.

He shrugs – a useless attempt at bravado – but pats the hand that rests on his shoulder. Dawsyn wonders how long he has gone without any form of comfort.

"How?"

"Some illness," he says. "I had never seen it before. It took her quickly."

Dawsyn nods lamely. Some sickness bred by the cold, perhaps, or the food from the Drop.

Dawsyn pats Hector's shoulder once more. "We should keep going," she tells him, nudging him. "We must find shelter."

"How far will we travel?" he queries, his face reddening with the heat. He still wears his many layers, and like Dawsyn, his body is unused to the warm temperature. The fertile season is reaching its peak. Neither of them has ever felt air so stifling, still and humid. Air that clings to their skin.

The mixed seem to struggle as well. Ahead, Ryon adjusts his shirt, wiping sweat from the back of his neck. Tasheem outright curses the sun every few minutes. The only one who seems unfazed by the temperature is the captain.

She walks with her many layers and weapons, finally at ease on ground she knows, one that doesn't shift or change beneath her. "The Fallen Village is ahead," she says casually, her breath steady while the others pant, taxed and irritable.

"What is the Fallen Village?" Hector questions as they clear the forest, rounding the bend in the path to see rolling green hills.

"Where our people lived, before they were taken," Dawsyn tells him, nodding to the first sight of a ruin – a crumbling home, its roof long ago caved in.

The party traverses the Fallen Village slower than they ought to, but some sights are not to be ignored. Even the mixed tread lightly over the household items that have been left in their places and reclaimed by the wilderness. Their eyes do not stray from the sights of homes, black with ash, wagons crushed and splintered, now tangled in covetous vine and weed.

Dawsyn looks over her shoulder and finds that Gerrot has stopped.

The man stands before a ruined cottage, its door missing, the stone chimney strewn along the ground. There is a great hole in its thatched roof, where a tree now grows clean through, rising toward the sun.

Dawsyn sees the man's eyes become wet, his hands clenching and unclenching at his sides.

She doubles back, allowing the rest to walk on. "Gerrot?" she calls softly.

The man – widower to a medicine woman, prisoner of the Ledge, slave to the Glacian King – does not turn to acknowledge her. He swallows convulsively, eyes shining, and only blinks when a tear escapes, tracing the many lines of his face.

Dawsyn looks to the ruins before them. "This was your home?"

For several seconds he does not respond, and then, a small nod.

"When you were a boy?"

Another nod.

She thinks of the journey this one man was forced to endure. First the raid of his childhood village, then the Ledge, and finally Glacia. This one human, who lived and survived all kingdoms and their callous rulers, now back at his beginning.

And despite the tree and debris that impedes what once was his, it is undeniably *right* that he is here. Alive.

He is home.

Dawsyn grasps his hand, and for a moment the young and the old stand together in a Fallen Village amongst the ghosts and wreckage of their shared people.

"You made it back," she tells him, and is awarded the pleasure of seeing him smile. Gerrot takes his free hand and places it on her cheek, and then taps a finger on her chin.

You as well.

* * *

Hector trails behind the rest. Dawsyn cannot tell if it is the mixed Glacians or the fatigue that shortens his steps. Indeed, his cheeks redden further with each minute, but his eyes, squinted against a sun brighter than he has ever seen, tend to drift to the backs of Ryon, Tasheem, and Rivdan with wary contemplation.

Dawsyn does not slow to join him again. She tracks him, glances often, but cannot, for reasons yet to dawn to her, bring herself to talk with him anymore than she already has. Seeing him here, sun bleaching his hair to a true shade of blonde, boots muddied, furs slung over his shoulder, is inconceivable. Each time she remembers his presence, the incredulity strikes her anew. The sight of him, the sound of him, is tied to a place she considers an enemy. She finds that she cannot simply untangle the two.

She opts instead to trail behind Ryon and Baltisse, who know the path to Salem's better than any other.

In the distance, white smoke curls above the treetops, snaking toward the clouds.

"The inn is ahead," Ryon calls, his eyes skirting quickly to Baltisse, with what Dawsyn knows is unease.

"Stop concerning yourself, Ry," the mage mumbles. "I am merely tired."

"I am not concerned."

"Your mind," she sneers, "begs to differ."

"And *your* mind has recently taken up a proclivity for heroics," Ryon says quietly. "Risks be damned."

"You'd be wise to mind your thoughts."

"And *you'd* be wise to redirect your energies," he snarls. "You are no help at all if you're dead."

The mage narrows her eyes, but, shockingly, falls quiet. It strikes Dawsyn as the first time she has heard Baltisse concede an argument. A telling omittance.

The mage shudders then. Not the shudder of cold bones, but the kind that signals awareness.

She halts so suddenly that the rest halt with her, an eerie silence befalling the forest. No one dares to break it. They wait, eyes to the back of her unnaturally still form, slowly absorbing the sure presence of dread.

The mage inhales, pulling the air from the forest, the sky, the very earth it seems. Dawsyn has the unsettling sensation of oxygen being pulled from her lungs. It is as though the mage has claimed the air. Tastes it. Then, she expels her breath, and the feeling is gone.

"Danger comes?" Ryon asks, expression darkening.

"No," the mage answers, her voice, for once, shallow. Afraid. "The danger has already been."

Suddenly, the mage is running, her eyes to the smoke that has thickened with their proximity. A plume of grey, ascending in volumes, so obviously not that of a chimney. They race down the well-worn trail, where ash litters the path. The closer they come, the more cloying the air.

There is a difference between the smell of wood burnt in the hearth, and that of a home set alight. The latter is noxious, a deadly blend of all that once comprised someone's existence, now melted, charred.

Their feet pound the trail around the last bend, but their haste is for nothing, of course. The smoke is weak in colour, having already consumed all it could. The forest is blackened with debris.

They break free from the forest path. Ryon, Baltisse, and Dawsyn stop first, all three within inches of each other, and at the same time.

None speak. There is too much shock to speak.

There is only breath.

In tandem.

In, out.

In, out.

"Mother above," Tasheem exhales behind them, coming clear of the trees. "What happened here?"

Before them is what remains of a building – the wasted, blackened skeleton left to slowly smoulder. The top floor has crumbled inward, smothering what once lay below. The pigs and chickens lie dead in their pens.

"Salem's inn," Ryon finally answers. His voice quavers, his eyes are wild. He stalks forward, unbalanced, the hide of his boots singeing on the burning rubble.

"Ryon!" Dawsyn calls out, but the hybrid continues on. Glass shatters beneath his weight. "*Ryon!*" she calls again.

The wreckage of Salem's inn still burns, and she knows it is not safe to touch. Even as she thinks it, Ryon stumbles trying to climb the heap. His hands catch his fall.

"*Fuck,*" he grunts, palms likely searing.

Dawsyn lurches forward. "*Ryon!* Get down–"

But a sound reaches them, stilling them all. It is distant. Smothered.

Baltisse's eyes go round, and Dawsyn almost doesn't hear her say it. The pounding of her own blood behind her eardrums nearly drowns it out, but she sees it. The mage's lips form the word, *Esra*, and it is followed by another far-away cry.

"Esra?" Ryon says, eyes falling to the pile of smoking rubble. "ESRA?" he roars. It is a sound to awaken beasts. Nearby birds take flight in flocks, if not jolted from the sound, then startled by the charge in the air. Dawsyn's skin shows the static of it.

At once, Ryon rips the swords from his back and throws them aside. He takes the vest of hide from his chest and wraps his hands in a frenzy. "*Help me!*" He calls to the rest and begins lifting away the debris.

Dawsyn takes her gloves from her waistband and dons them as she leaps over a crate, a window frame, a banister. Ryon growls as he tries to dislodge a stair railing from the heap, and Dawsyn brings her ax to the point where the frame traps it, cutting it in two. Ryon hurls it away.

They all dig and pull and break, the sounds of snapping

timber echoing between the surrounding trees, and all the
while a keen screaming arises from the depths of the rubble,
growing less and less distant the further they dig.

But the digging is so achingly slow. The pile is too high. The
smoke and ash are clinging to her tongue, her throat. Keeping
her eyes open is painful, sucking at the air is painful, and it
seems they come no closer to the voice that cries and breaks
somewhere beneath the mound.

She coughs, her chest heaving, and someone grabs the back
of her coat, pulling her away.

It is Baltisse, eyes churning like tempests.

"Damn the mother. Step aside!" She calls, and the others have
a mere second to leap away before the ground beneath their
feet begins to quake. Baltisse stares with fierce determination
at the place where the screams come from, face screwed tightly,
morphing into a creature of a different realm.

Dawsyn feels the iskra pricking at her fingertips and wills it
to be still.

The ground beneath them quakes. The rubble begins to lift.
The mound rises from its middle first, as though it might erupt,
lifting higher, higher. And then Baltisse groans the words of a
language Dawsyn has never heard, and it breaks. The broken
pieces of Salem's home fall away like waves, leaving a hole in
its middle.

The crying stops.

"Esra?" Ryon calls. There is no answer. The smoke born
from the disruption makes it difficult to see. Ryon glances at
Dawsyn, and together they begin clambering back over Salem's
burnt and broken inn.

Where Baltisse cleaved the burning debris away, there
lies a trapdoor. Dawsyn recognises it immediately, though its
wood is burnt and blackened like everything else. The handle
is the same. When Ryon grasps it to wrench the door open,
she can hear it sizzle against his skin. He ignores it. He heaves
upward.

Time slows. Sound is muted. Her eyes water incessantly, but not enough to blind her to what lies beneath, in the cellar that Salem dug out himself.

A cellar that she crawled into with the hybrid.

The smoke swirls in the air, and Ryon shouts something to her but she can't make sense of it. He jumps into the hole.

Dawsyn's eyes are glued to the man in the depths of the cellar, the man Ryon lifts into his arms.

A scorched body. A dress melted and blackened, catching on the splintered wood, its lace ripping away.

Esra.

"*Dawsyn!*" Ryon shouts. "Dawsyn, help me, *please!*"

But there is no help to give. There is nothing to be done.

"Dawsyn, get Salem. *Get Salem, now!*"

Salem?

Someone slides down the rubble beside her. Rivdan. He takes Esra's body from Ryon and summons his wings. He is gone a second later.

Ruby and Tasheem are suddenly there, huddling around the open trapdoor as Ryon reappears a moment later, his arms flexing, teeth gritted as he hauls another body upward.

Ruby and Tasheem grab Ryon, hauling him out, and with him comes Salem.

Salem's body, though slack, is not blackened or bloody. His eyes are closed, his limbs hang like that of the dead. There is soot around his mouth and nose, but a sound comes from him. Small gasps, a ragged pull through his lips. He is alive.

Dawsyn stumbles. *Alive,* she thinks.

One lives, she thinks.

Not both, but one, she thinks.

Not as bad, she thinks, her mind stroking and hushing the pieces of her threatening to break away, cooing lies to quell its imminent collapse.

It isn't enough. She can feel her chest cleaving by inches.

Before she can convince herself to move, to do something, Tasheem takes flight with Salem.

Ryon comes to Dawsyn. He pulls her to his chest, wraps an arm roughly around her back, and his wings appear.

He takes her out of the fire and smoke.

And there is nothing to do but hold on.

CHAPTER THIRTY-FIVE

On the Ledge, the people wait outside at the beginning of each season.

No one is exempt. Babies are layered and carried to the stoop, the sick are propped up between members of their houses, or if none remain, they prop themselves in their doorframes.

One, and only one, need venture further than the stoop, out onto the Ledge, idle game.

Every so often, there is a household that fails to leave their cabin, sometimes out of necessity, but more often out of defiance. One such household was that of the Polson's, which stood close enough to the Sabar den that Dawsyn could see the roof through weak fog.

At the close of the hostile season in Dawsyn's thirteenth year, her grandmother took the place at the head of the family and her kin watched on from the stoop. The sky above was still, undisturbed. It would not remain that way for long. The Glacians would come.

Dawsyn looked over to Hector's family, his father stood ahead of him and his mother. She nodded to him, and he to her. Her eyes skirted further then, along the Face, coming to the Polsons' cabin.

"No one has come from the Polsons'," she mused aloud, brow furrowed.

"What?" Briar asked.

"The Polsons have not come out," Dawsyn repeated, pointing to the cabin, where no one graced the threshold. Not Helena Polson, or her daughter, June. Not Des Polson, who should have taken his place beneath the sky, praying not to be reaped, like everyone else.

Above, the cloud swirled into a vortex. The first sight of white wing appeared, dipping below the cloud, followed quickly by another.

They were here. The Selection was starting, and not one Polson stood where they ought to.

"*Fuck*," Briar said openly, her breath misting heavily before her. "Maya. Talk to Dawsyn for a moment."

"But–"

"Sing to me that song you learnt," Dawsyn said quickly, her eyes wheeling from the sky, where the Glacians were circling in full view, to the Polsons' empty stoop, back to Maya, who was blessedly distracted.

"What song?"

"The song Grandma taught you – the... the one of the nymphs."

"I hate that song."

"*Then sing another*," Dawsyn insisted, spittle flying, her voice far harsher than casualness warranted.

Maya picked a song she made up herself. Dawsyn does not remember it now, only that it was accompanied by the sounds of wreckage as the Glacians dived, tearing the Polsons' roof apart, collapsing its frame.

There were shouts across the Ledge as the unlucky were pulled from the snow and hauled into the sky, and by the time Maya had finished her song, the Selection was over.

Their grandmother remained, and Dawsyn did not bother to feel guilty as she silently thanked the Polsons for so blatantly drawing attention to themselves.

Then another clamour came, echoing off the Face and

bouncing to where Dawsyn stood with her family. Des Polson, bursting from his cabin, blood running down his cheek from a gash on his forehead. He fell to the snow, and even from their vantage, they could hear his retching.

While her grandmother took Maya inside, Briar and Dawsyn traipsed carefully to the Polson cabin. Hector and his father joined them, and like hares approaching a likely trap, they came nearer to the man in the snow, weeping soundly, his blood colouring the powder.

Behind him, his cabin sagged inward, the roof destroyed.

"Des?" Briar said softly. "You cannot remain on the ground."

He nodded and the crying softened to weak, uneven breaths. "Just one," he mumbled to himself. "Just one."

"What is he saying?" said Hector's father, leaning to help pull Des up from the snow.

Dawsyn heard a noise then; they all did. They looked toward the broken cabin, where the door hung open. In its frame stood a young girl.

June Polson.

"They only took one," Des mumbled, a keening sound escaping thereafter. "Not as bad." He shook uncontrollably. "Not as bad." But as they shuffled him out of the cold, his eyes closed tightly, and the sounds of his sorrow continued to escape unbidden. He muttered those lies to himself, as though they might rally him to face what lay ahead.

CHAPTER THIRTY-SIX

Ryon lands at the forest edge and places Dawsyn on her feet. She is vacant. While he… he is fracturing.

Away from the haze of smoke, he sees Esra and Salem clearly.

They have been laid down on the forest floor, the inn still smoking behind them. Baltisse already has her hands on Salem's chest, determined.

"Close your eyes!" Ryon calls abruptly and snaps his own shut. He does not know if the others take his advice, but from the painful, burning light that shines beyond his eyelids, he imagines they have little choice.

The light dissipates, and Ryon opens his eyes again, leaning immediately to take Salem's hand.

The older man's mouth is no longer covered in ash. His eyes are open, blinking in rapid succession, scowling when they come to Baltisse, who remains hovering over his body.

"Salem," she breathes.

"The guards…" he mutters. "The guards came."

Baltisse doesn't pause to reply. She is already crawling to the blackened heap of Esra, and Ryon moves with her.

"Is he dead?"

"I don't know," Baltisse hisses.

"Can you–"

"*I don't know, Ryon,*" she bites, pulling Esra's head into her lap.

Ryon's heart beats rapidly enough to burst. "Try. *Now!*"

"SHUT UP!" Baltisse yells and places her hands on Esra's chest.

But Ryon sees how her hands shake, how ashen her cheeks have become. She's expended so much power, too much power already.

And Esra looks… gone. Ryon barely recognises him. His face is burnt and mottled, his flesh gleaming pink in places and bleeding. There are terrible wounds to his body. Places where the fabric of his clothes has melted to his skin.

Esra. Never dull, dreary, or punishing. Never devoid of exuberance or colour. Consistent. Loyal. Everything the world around him so often isn't.

Save him, he thinks desperately at the mage. *Please.*

He feels Dawsyn at his side, sees her hand reach out to take Esra's.

Her fingers, dirtied and calloused, intertwine with his, palm against palm.

Baltisse draws breath the way the moon draws the tide, and there is another blinding eruption of light.

Ryon's eyes slam shut, but he hears the mage's moans as she stretches whatever power remains to its thinnest extent. If she should stretch it too far, it will be Ryon who lives with the guilt of it. He is the one who has pushed Baltisse, after chastising her for pushing herself.

If she should die to save Esra, it will be no better.

Baltisse's light burns on, harsher, hotter, and she is growling, shouting in spells, urging her power onward, onward, to its peak, and it sounds desperate, tenuous.

And it won't work.

Esra won't be saved.

Baltisse will die.

Ryon reaches blindly, his eyes unwilling to pry open. He

means to shout for her to stop, but suddenly, impossibly, the light doubles.

He feels the force of it knock him onto his backside, hears the curses of Rivdan, perhaps Hector, too. But the light is scolding, prying through the slits of his lids, burying into his sockets. He cradles his face on the ground.

"BALTISSE!" he yells, sure that she will not, cannot, hear him. "STOP!"

And then the light is gone. The presence of magic lifts, and all that remains of it is distorted sight as Ryon blinks away the brightness. He hastens back to where Esra ought to be, crawling blindly. "Baltisse?"

One or both? His mind demands. *One or both?*

For it cannot be neither.

The glare blanketing his sight dulls in painful increments, but even after all becomes clear, it takes a while longer to understand what he sees.

Esra's body lies still.

Baltisse slumps over his head, her hair obscuring him, shoulders trembling.

And upon Esra's chest, stacked and still prickling with light, are the mage's hands. And Dawsyn's.

"Ryon?" Comes a weak voice.

Ryon's pulse thrums.

Baltisse startles and straightens. They look down and see the dark-eyed stare of Esra looking back. "Ask me how much I'd have wagered that I'd wake up between Baltisse's tits."

Something unravels in his chest. He has to place both hands to the dirt for balance. He breathes once. Twice. "How much?"

"Not a dime," he intones, his voice coarse and cracked.

Esra, he thinks. And then to Baltisse. *Thank you.*

"Thank *her,*" the mage replies aloud.

Ryon looks to Dawsyn, who is staring at her palms as though their lines have been redrawn.

Ryon stares too, his mouth hanging open.

"Did I at least save the old man?" Esra croaks.

Salem has already crawled to his side, and he comes closer now. "I told yeh them holes in the ground would be useful, now, didn't I?"

"Just my fucking luck," Esra splutters, a cough wracking him. "He lives."

"Aye," says Salem, a sad smile stretching the width of his wide face. "Yer a bleedin' hero, now, Esra."

Ryon thinks Esra's broken voice might be the most resounding thing he has ever heard. "I'll have to remedy that," his friend says.

As Esra fades back into unconsciousness, Ryon meets Dawsyn's eyes. Eyes that flash with uncertainty, with fear, hands still alight with a magic neither of them know.

While Tasheem and Rivdan scout the immediate area, Baltisse and Dawsyn continue to hover over Esra.

Salem has stumbled away from the others, seemingly needing to collect himself. Ryon leaves the rest of the group to loom uselessly over in a cluster, not knowing what to do next. He instead goes toward Salem, where he sits slumped on the ground alone. Ryon suspects it is not ailment that grounds him. It is something else entirely. He watches the plumes of smoke churn in the breeze.

"What happened, Salem?" Ryon asks when it is clear Salem will not send Ryon away again to leave him to his solitude.

Salem's eyes follow the swirls and whorls of smoke as he speaks. His voice is distant. Detached. "Shoulda known they would come," he says. "Couldn't bring meself to leave, though. Had to stand me ground like a fuckin' hero. Ha!" he huffs weakly. "What a lotta good it did."

Ryon grimaces. "You said the Queen's guards came?"

"Aye. Whole contingent of 'em. In the dead o' night, mind yeh. Tried to torch us while we slept." Salem looks over to Esra's sleeping form across the way. "Threw their torches through the windows an' stood there a while, watchin' it all burn." The man's colour rises with the words, great red splotches climbing his neck. "I were a fool, Ry. I tried to save it from goin' up in flames. It were no use o' course. Last thing I remember, Esra was draggin' me into the cellar. Everythin' collapsin'... blockin' the doors. The smoke... it was suffocatin'." Salem swallows thickly, and he looks again to the languid smoke rising to join the clouds. "I knew they'd come eventually, what after stickin' me nose out the way I did at Dawsyn's hangin'."

Ryon flinches.

"Didn't think they'd come an' reap it all though," he spits. "Gutless... *godless*–"

This is the precise moment that Ruby, adorned from head to toe in Terrsaw regalia, steps into view, heedlessly placing herself between Salem and Ryon.

"Ryon," she interjects. "We cannot remain here long, have you any suggestions on w–"

But whatever she means to say is cut short by a grunt of outrage.

Salem stands abruptly, his eyes locked on the captain's. His face resembles something pustular – red and shiny and prone to bursting. "*You!*" he accuses. "Yeh... *you* are here? Now?"

Ruby takes measure of his aggressive stance, the violence laced in his tone, and she squares herself to him. "Salem," she says slowly, carefully, as though not to provoke him.

"Yeh came to me inn, askin' us to trust yeh," he says. "An' then yeh order yer guard to burn it to the *ground?*"

Ruby's shakes her head avidly. "What? No, sir. No, of course I didn't."

"Yeh the captain of the fuckin' guard, ain't yeh?"

"I would *never* order the burning of one's home," Ruby implores.

"*But yeh did nothin' to stop it!*" Salem shouts, lips trembling.

Ryon comes between them. He puts a hand to his shoulder.

"She couldn't have known, Salem. She abandoned the guardianship, her title along with it, when she helped me escape. It is not she who did this to you, my friend."

"Just the army she raised then!" Salem says darkly, piercing Ruby with an accusatory stare. "Just the comrades she trained. Did yeh teach 'em to torch homes by night, Captain? While the unwitting slept in their beds?"

Ruby looks to her feet as she answers, true shame entrenched in her words. "I… I cannot imagine your suffering–"

"Ain't no need for imaginin's," Salem sneers. "I got plenty of sufferin' to impart."

"*Enough!*" Ryon says, moving his hand to the man's chest, staying him. "Salem. You have every cause in the world to be angry, but Ruby is not your target. She would not be standing here alive if I thought she was to blame."

"She's one of them, Ry!" Salem says, incensed. "She still bears their emblem."

"She is with us, Salem. I assure you."

Salem trembles with ill-suppressed rage for a moment. Then, turning, he curses loudly. He stomps in the direction of the flattened inn, but not before turning back to point a meaty finger in Ruby's direction. "Keep her the fuck away from me!" he rasps.

They watch him go.

Ruby sighs tiredly. "I apologise," she tells Ryon. "I should not have interrupted the way I did. I thought he had already noticed me amongst the rest."

"Evidently not," Ryon intones. "But you have nothing to apologise for," he assures her, laying a hand briefly on her shoulder.

She dips her chin down, letting the dark fringe of her eyelashes conceal her feelings. "Someone should," she says, then turns away.

* * *

They cannot go to the Mecca. To be sure, Queen Alvira will have them stoned, hung, maybe even beheaded, should she feel inspired. Certainly, they cannot remain beside the blackened ruins of Salem's Inn, where its owner picks over its fragments, searching for the salvageable. His big hands come up empty. He stoops to turn over part of a tapestry, a brass knocker, a shard of stained glass, and a noise escapes him. A sob that he strangles before it can give him away. He finds the sows covered in ash lying trapped in their pens, and he wipes his face, turning away from the rest, scrubbing grief from his eyes.

Ryon watches his friend's face contort and slacken over and over in a useless attempt to appear like a man without feeling until he can stand it no longer. He goes to him, places a hand on the older man's shoulder, and grips tighter when Salem tries to shrug him off.

"Only a heap o' rubbish," Salem mutters, his words unsteady. "Not worth more'n a few coins."

But it was a place that was his own. A place he pieced away and let others own too.

Ryon says nothing. There is no peace for Salem to find in his words, and Ryon often has very few. Instead, he stands with his friend in the pain. In the loss. He waits as long as he must for the gentle shudder of the older man's frame to ease. He waits for Salem to drop the fragment of stained glass back onto the ground, and then guides him away.

They cannot stay, so they go.

Esra must be carried by Rivdan. Though miraculously alive, he is not wholly healed. One side of his face remains scorched, the flesh a dreadful shade of red. His right eye, once big and round, appears ruined. Wounds glisten along his legs, and their odour makes Ryon think of his time in the Kyph, where the brutes were so fond of the way his skin melted under burning iron.

Esra whimpers as Rivdan lifts him, and then falls back into

his pain-addled slumber, trembling, and smaller than Ryon has ever seen him.

Baltisse is grey with fatigue, but she slaps Ryon away when she tries to aid her, and Dawsyn is… Ryon does not know what Dawsyn is.

Withdrawn. Spooked, perhaps.

As an assemblage, they are all battered, fractured. Still, they must make haste, lest the guards who burnt Salem's inn to the ground come back to admire their work. No one speaks. They do what they must.

They journey for a time with rudimentary aim and no target, other than to steer away from the mountain, and away from the Mecca. They walk the tenuous line between the two.

"We could take them to my cabin," Baltisse says eventually, her feet dragging. Ryon is surprised she walks at all. "The surrounds are protected by my enchantments. We won't be found."

He nods, and they begin to steer their party in the direction of the river. But moments later, Baltisse is stumbling, her legs give way. Esra is crying out with pain more frequently, and the rest are weary. The heat in the forest is oppressive, and it has been an age since they all slept. Ryon knows they must stop.

He can hear the river in the distance, not so far that they can't retrieve fresh water. The tree cover is dense, the ground dry, and they have come as far as they ought to.

"We should camp here for the night," he says to the group, who all show visible signs of relief.

All except Dawsyn.

As the others find comfort on the ground, against trees, or flat on their backs, Dawsyn hesitates. She looks down at her hands, which, Ryon now notices, shake. Coupled with the soot smeared over her cheek, her eyebrow, and the disarray of her hair, Ryon would almost call her… frazzled. She looks over her shoulder, back into the labyrinth of the forest. Then, in silent retreat, she slinks away.

Ryon watches her slip between the trees and tells himself not to follow. She has made it clear, after all, that he should leave her be, and he wants to listen. He wants to do what she has asked of him.

The last of her disappears into the forest and he runs his hand over his tired face.

Then he follows.

Chapter Thirty-Seven

Dawsyn is fairly adept at skinning animals. Granted, Maya was always better, but Dawsyn still knows intimately the way the knife carves a path between skin and tissue, and she has the undeniable urge to do away with her own. She is a stranger to herself.

She walks through the forest, unable to sit still in her body. She has a desire to flee the parts of her she does not recognise, but it is no use. She walks and walks, but everywhere she goes, there she is.

She comes to a fallen tree and sits upon it. The ax on her back digs into her and she tries to adjust it, but she is too uncomfortable, itchy, aching, insatiably restless. With a cry she hurls it away, burying the blade into the soft ground with a dull thunk.

Her hands, cracked and blackened by soot, wring together. She drops her head into them. *Fuck.*

Her fingers tremble. They haven't stopped since she placed them on Esra and allowed that strange power to find passage through her palms. A feeling unlike any other had washed through her, light and willing. It had filled her with warmth and wonder. It was something so contradictory to the way she had erupted on the Ledge, the iskra exploding from her palms. Even now, she feels those two disparities: the extraordinary glow and that darker matter. Is it as simple as the parts of the iskra that want to obey, and the parts that do not? Is it the difference between healing those she loves, and extinguishing those she loathes? Perhaps it is not the iskra that had killed Des Polson, but her own pitiful, destructive animosity.

She wonders if they'd left his body in the snow drift.

"Dawsyn?"

She turns at his voice and sees him standing a short distance behind her. She doesn't bother to stand or move away. She is too tired. Despite herself, she can't seem to find the pretence of dispassion.

When she says nothing to send him away, he comes closer. Instead of finding a place on the fallen tree, he rounds it, his heavy footfalls surrounding her. He squats down in front of her, leaving a large space between them.

For a moment they only stare.

She wishes she didn't still want to go to him.

His fathomless stare implores her. "Tell me," he bids, a whisper. It feels the same as his breath on her throat, his fingers on her back.

She closes her eyes, lets all that has transpired win the war in her mind. There is so much she could unleash. Adrik's betrayal, the fire, the magic… Des Polson. A man she'd tried to rescue, and killed instead. Killing is what she is good for. Not saving. Not heroics. Of all the times she's been betrayed these past months, the knife that runs deepest is her own, when she vowed to herself that she would do good in this world.

So much she could spill, but she condenses it to this one thing, one incessant thought that corrodes her slowly, consumes her. A thought with claws pierced so deeply into her flesh that it cannot simply be pulled out. It is the only one she can convey. The only one to be untangled from the rest.

"I can't free them," she says aloud, and a tear escapes. She feels it course along the curve of her nose. Then a hand is there, cupping her cheek, wiping the tear away.

She doesn't want to see the way he looks at her, so she keeps her eyes shut, but it does nothing to mute his voice, and the way the deep timbre reverberates inside her own chest.

"It isn't your duty to free them, malishka."

She shakes her head. "I meant to save them, and I killed one instead."

"You did not mean to," he answers immediately, his other hand coming to her face.

"Salem's home is gone. Esra is hurt, because of me."

"Because of *them*."

"Because of *me*," Dawsyn repeats, her eyes opening and delving into his. "And I have done... *so* much worse in my life."

"You had little choice."

But there were times when she had choices. Times when she could have weighed another's life more than her own and she didn't. Perhaps she thought that freeing the people on the Ledge would balance her deeds.

She has failed. The Queens will raze homes in search of her, a new king will drink from the pool in Glacia, and the people on the Ledge will remain. All will be unchanged.

She will resume her pursuit to stay alive, continuing her life's work even beyond the Ledge, and know that she could do nothing to stop it.

"You saved Gerrot and Hector," Ryon says gently. "You saved Esra. That ought to count for something."

Dawsyn sighs. "And they will be doomed to a life of hiding."

Ryon hesitates before speaking, a crease appearing between his brows. "I don't recognise you, malishka."

"Don't call me that."

"It isn't like you to feel sorry for yourself."

She sighs, twisting her face out of his hands. "I know what you are doing."

"And what's that?"

"Goading me into fighting with you."

He grins just slightly, but it disappears when he sees that she won't be goaded. She won't be poked and pulled out of herself.

He takes her hands in his and lowers his forehead until it meets hers. For a moment he waits there, perhaps expecting her to push him back. But she is entranced by the closeness of him, the warmth of his skin, and all she wants to do is to forget... to stay.

"Tell me what you want, and I will do it," he says.

And there are so many things that she desires. Retribution for the Queens, and all that they've done, freedom for the Ledge and the destruction of the Pool of Iskra. The resurrection of her family. The death of Adrik. The healing of Esra's wounds. Escape. Safety.

Safety, above all else.

If she asks it, he will die to achieve it, she knows. It is perhaps the most dangerous imbalance between them. Baltisse had said as much to confirm it. For all he did to endanger her, she does not wish to use him, to take advantage of his remorse.

So, she tells Ryon nothing. Instead, she presses her lips against his, starved for his comfort. Desperate for diversion.

Ryon's hand grasps her chin, and he holds her there.

It's like breath, this kiss. It fills her. She moves against his mouth and even this slow friction is intoxicating. She is nothing but her spent mind and dormant desire. Her body inches closer to him, her hands gripping his neck, her thighs sliding off the fallen tree so that her chest and stomach can find him where he kneels before her. She wants to feel his arms wrap around her and pull her in tightly. She wants to be small and disappear within him, let him obliterate her.

His lips pull away just enough. Enough that her whole body reaches for him, frustrated, but not enough that she doesn't hear the words that skate over her face.

"I love you."

She stills. Her eyes open. It is not passion that comes to engulf her, or tenderness. It is, of all things, terror.

Dawsyn has faced predators, starvation, imprisonment, poison, near-drowning, and felt terror with each. Now here, in a forest with no threat in sight, it floods her again.

His face, so close to hers, is pained. His eyes are closed, his head bowed, awaiting a rebuff. There is a pause wherein her body slowly shrinks away, and he grips a little tighter, trying to stop it.

She swallows but doesn't speak and hopes he will follow suit.

"I love you," he says again, softer this time.

Damn him.

She shakes her head. "No." It is cold. Final.

Ryon sighs, leaning away from her and dropping his hands. "My apologies. I know… I know you do not wish to hear it."

Dawsyn presses her palms into her eyes, wanting to wipe the words from her memory. "You do not love me."

Ryon stills. She can practically hear his mind whirring. "You deny me my feelings?"

"I deny your assignment of them," she says, shaking her head. "It is not love that you feel."

Ryon's tone turns acidic. "What other name should I give this torment?"

Dawsyn does not have an answer. She merely knows that she is not one to love. Not with all that has happened. Not with all that she has done. All that she is.

Ryon's chest rumbles with some unspoken frustration. "The only woman I've professed myself to," he mumbles to himself. "And she contradicts me."

Dawsyn scowls at him. "Would it truly be kinder to entertain false notions of love?"

"They are not *false*, Dawsyn."

"They certainly cannot be *true*."

"I love you," he says again.

"You cannot."

"And *you* love me."

A bark of laughter escapes her. She shakes her head at him, shocked. "I don't."

He raises an eyebrow, and the gesture is so offhand, so out of place in the climate of their tension, that it aggravates her.

"I *don't*," she repeats.

He watches her until she needs to look away, and she hates that she must cede this small war as well.

He speaks gently. "I heard your voice after Alvira ran me through with that sword."

Her breath leaves her.

"I heard you call my name over and over, but I couldn't see you. I was so sure they would kill you next."

She cannot help but turn back to look at him. He is staring at her, unblinking. "You think yourself wicked?" he asks. "My last thought was how grateful I was that they killed me first, so that I would not be made to watch you die."

Her throat closes around something. Something painful and urgent, but she swallows it. She can't bear to have it known.

Ryon huffs his frustration and rises, turning to retrieve her ax from the dirt. He pulls it from the earth and turns it over, inspecting the carvings on its handle, the double-edged blade. He smiles wanly at it and then walks it back to her, proffering it in his palm.

"Why are you smiling like that?" Dawsyn asks, her voice quieter than she'd like.

He considers her for a moment, his eyes tired and sad, despite the smirk. "I've been plagued by the thought that you may never forgive me, that you may never see the truth. All of my loyalty, every last bit, lies with you," he professes. "The thought that I might be doomed to a life trailing in your wake has... disturbed me. Now I need not be plagued. It's fear that distances you," he states, and it is gentle, kind. "Not anger."

For the first time since their paths intertwined, she has no quick words to wield, and it is unbearably exposing. Instead, she says, "Leave me be."

"Not a chance." He takes her hand and lifts her from the fallen tree. "I need to go back and ensure Esra is well, and you will come with me."

"I will?"

"You will," he says, allowing her to slide her hand out of his grasp. "I know everything seems irretrievable, but you will see, this is the part of the story where the heroes rise from the dust and renew their energies to the task ahead."

They walk back to the others in silence, though Ryon seems to buzz with an unnameable energy. His strides are surer, his head higher.

Their party lies dazed and broken in the clearing between trees, some human, some only in part. "Not a likely group of heroes," Dawsyn remarks.

Ryon looks to Hector, who bunches his body against the base of a tree, watching the mixed-Glacians with weary vigilance, then to Baltisse who sleeps between Salem and Esra, the latter grimacing with pain. He sees Rivdan and Tasheem, red-faced and panting in the heat, and Gerrot, apparently awed by the leafy canopy above. Last, he looks to Ruby, still adorned in her captain's uniform and resolutely ignoring Salem's livid stare.

"No," Ryon allows. "Though, *you* are entirely unlikely in as many ways as one can be considered. So perhaps you're to blame."

Dawsyn sinks to the ground on a dry patch of dirt and weeds. "Perhaps," she mutters, looking up to the dappled light, and wondering if while she sleeps her skin will leak the feeling of futility into the soil, and she'll wake knowing what next there is to do.

Chapter Thirty-Eight

Dawsyn does not sleep for long. In fact, the entire camp was awakened in the night when Esra rolled onto his side and screamed with renewed pain. Then a second time, and a third.

The fourth time Esra's cries pierce the air, it is quickly followed by the sounds of Salem staggering to his feet, storming at Ruby with a maddened, "Yeh-motherless-wench-I'll-wring-your-fuckin'-neck-for-what-you-did!"

And so, not only awakened but now on their feet, the entire party – save Esra – hastens to stop Salem from doing as he promises.

Ryon lies flat on his back with a twisting, writhing Salem captured atop him, trapped in the cage of his arms and legs. It would be comical, if not for the burst blood vessels in Salem's eyes and his obscenely purple complexion.

"Stop, Salem! She's here to aid us!"

"Don't fuckin' care why she's 'ere. She ain't stayin'!"

Dawsyn does not flinch at the venom in his tone. She remains between where he wrestles Ryon and where Ruby stands huddled amongst Rivdan and Tasheem.

"She played no part in the fire, Salem," Dawsyn adds.

"She wears the same fuckin' garb as those bastards tha' came to me inn and torched it! Look at Esra!"

"And *they* will pay for it, Salem. But Ruby did nothing. She hasn't earnt your anger."

"I'LL KILL THE WHOLE LOTTA 'EM!"

"Good god, Salem. You sound like a blithering idiot," Baltisse comments. "Let go of Ryon's ear, before he drops you in the river."

"They took everythin'. EVERYTHIN'!"

"The entire continent heard you, Salem. You're being a child. The captain didn't take your toys."

Salem turns a frightening shade of deep puce and Baltisse huffs her impatience. "Can't I just put him to sleep?" she asks, raising an eyebrow at Ryon who dodges a stray elbow that Salem throws back, barely managing to keep hold of him.

"*Fuck!* Salem, give up, man! Don't you *dare*, Baltisse. Give him a minute."

"I'm sorry, sir," comes a voice. Ruby has stepped forward, an ill-advised choice considering Salem's renewed energies to reach her. "Truly."

"They set it alight while we slept! While we SLEPT! We nearly died! An' all because I dared to put a roof o'er their heads!" he cries, gesturing to Dawsyn. "All because yer fuckin' Queen wants this daughter of a Sabar wiped from the earth! That's the *demon* yeh serve!" he roars, his voice cracking, eyes streaming. "Esra's face won't never look like it should! He covered my body with his! He saved my sorry life! The poor lad's been threatened an' beaten enough in his life. He don't deserve what they did!"

Salem finally slackens then, his face crumbling. His body shakes, and Ryon heaves a sigh of relief, loosening the arm against Salem's throat to pat him roughly. "It's all right, you old codger," he says, panting heavily. "Let it out."

Baltisse merely wrinkles her nose at Salem, but Ruby leans to the ground beside him so that her eyes are level with his, and says, "I cannot help your friend." She looks over to the place where Esra lays prone and unconscious once more. "But I can promise you this: the Queen wears a ring on her right hand with the Terrsaw Emblem. They say it was taken from King Sabar's body the night he died. One day I will cut that ring from her finger, and it will sit on the mantle in your new home."

They all watch warily, lest Salem decide to take liberties with the shortened distance between he and his target. But he only looks keenly into her eyes in a way Dawsyn recognises as his custom, and seems to find no duplicity in them.

"I'll hold yeh to it," he puffs.

Ryon rolls him over, releasing him, and both men sit panting on the forest floor.

"Why didn't yeh spells work, Baltisse?" Salem laments, his face turned to Esra. "They ain't never failed before."

Baltisse blanches, and all look back to poor Esra whose right ear, eye and cheek are shocking shades of black and red. He will bear the scars for the rest of his life. Whatever Baltisse and Dawsyn did to him, it was merely enough to save his life but not his flesh, and his wounds may foul yet.

"I assure you, I expended all the power I could, but my stores were already low after lifting an entire house off you. If it weren't for Dawsyn aiding me, he and I would likely be dead."

All eyes now turn to Dawsyn, who shifts uncomfortably. "I don't know if *aiding* you is what I did."

"It is," the mage says with finality.

"Dawsyn?" Salem asks. "But how, lass?"

"How indeed," the mage mutters.

Dawsyn frowns. "The iskra, obviously. Of which I have very little control."

"And yet you mastered it to save Esra," Baltisse muses.

"I–" Dawsyn starts, but she has no response, which seems to be happening with increasing frequency of late. Instead, she looks around at them all, her self-consciousness swelling with each second they insist on staring at her. Eventually she turns on them all and stalks away.

"Peculiar," Tasheem mutters to Rivdan.

To which Baltisse replies. "Quite."

To which Dawsyn replies over her shoulder, "Shut up." And she sinks back into her place on the forest floor, intending to feign sleep for as long as necessary.

When they wake next, morning is breaking and the smell of cooked food lures them from their various nests.

Gerrot sits before a fire, a large stick with several skewered fish in his hand. He rotates it slowly in the flames and the smell makes Dawsyn salivate.

They race to reach him first, and Gerrot points to a large stone with several more fish laid out neatly, ready to cook.

Tasheem groans with satisfaction, then bends to kiss Gerrot's hollow cheek. "I knew I loved you, old man."

Gerrot only smiles in his serene way, and offers her the first fish.

"Thank you, Gerrot," Ryon says, resting his hand on Gerrot's shoulder. "You must have woken long before you ought to for such a haul. Luck sided with you this day."

But the river doesn't sound so far away, and there is a glimmer in the old man's eye as the others claim their share of food. Dawsyn suspects that he needed no luck at all.

She chooses a spot on the ground beside him and helps him stoke the flames, watching him smile gently at all he sees – the lick of the flames, the looks of satisfaction, even the sight of Dawsyn. He pats her leg now and then, for no reason at all, and Dawsyn does nothing but smile back. Such pure, simplistic joy is hard to turn away from.

Dawsyn tries to look at the woods around them and see what he sees. She tries to absorb the filtered sun, the warm breeze, the sound of racing water, the smell of cooked meat and be fulfilled. She wants to see her surroundings and be repaired, contented, but all she sees is what was taken and what ought to be returned.

Perhaps she helped to bring him here, Hector too. She only wishes it was enough to let her slide away into the world, to find her corner of it and live out her days unburdened by the rest of them up there on the Ledge. And why shouldn't she do just that? The very people who plague her conscience are the same ones who didn't believe her, couldn't trust her.

Can she not be content knowing she tried?

Ryon has taken food to Esra, and she waits, like a coward, until he leaves Esra's side before approaching herself.

She lowers her body next to the man. He lays on a pallet of furs and coats from the others in attempt to keep the worst of his burns from the ground, but Dawsyn worries it will do very little. On the Ledge, burns were easier to treat with snowpacks, but these burns are like none Dawsyn has ever seen.

"I know its unsightly, dearling," Esra murmurs. "But I'll sooner die if you stare at me like I'm not the best-looking gent you've ever seen. I couldn't bear it." His voice is slow and hoarse, and seems to pain him. He gazes at her through his uninjured eye. The other is mottled into something unrecognisable.

"As luck would have it, there is little competition amongst this lot," Dawsyn grins.

"Liar." He winces. "Though I can hardly blame you. Ryon has always made quite the impression, all dark and dangerous. The first time I met him, I threw my pants at his feet and offered him my virginity."

"No, you didn't."

"No, I didn't," he sniffs. "I'm afraid my chastity was long ago misplaced."

She smirks and silently thanks the Mother for the blessing of Esra. "Do you need anything?"

"Mother above, no," he groans. "Baltisse has been feeding me the most ghastly concoction all through the night. Salem hovers. Ryon has brought me more food and water than I can bear. I asked him for a hand bath, but he declined–"

"If you ask me to take you to the Mecca, to find a healer," she interrupts. "I'll do it."

He smiles. It isn't without effort. "I know you would. But no healer in the Mecca or in between would dare afford their care to me, Dawsyn, even if the Queen's wrath weren't hovering over them; they find me rather unsavoury."

"We all find you rather unsavoury," Dawsyn quips.

"Yes, though it has naught to do with my choices in fashion."

Dawsyn's eyes narrow. "Your proclivities offend them?"

"Often. Though I do much enjoy offending," he says wryly. "So, you could say I invite their disregard."

"I'd much rather have their disregard than their favour if something so trivial should signify."

"Oh, I *relish* their disregard, love. It's why I make a point of doing away with clothes altogether on the solstice. I dangle my dangles all through the Mecca just to see how close I might come to the palace before the guards are called."

"*You* are the solstice braggart?" comes Ruby's voice. A chunk of fish slips from her fingers as she stares, mouth open.

"A braggart, you say?" Esra asks, turning his face slowly. "You see, Dawsyn? Perhaps they will not lend me their attentions when I am wounded, but they most certainly know that my naked form is something to be bragged about, and in that, I have their attention."

Dawsyn laughs, her head thrown back and eyes cinched shut, and some of the others laugh along. She falls onto her backside and has to brace herself to keep from tipping further. She doesn't calm until her eyes are wet. When she opens them, they find Ryon's, watching her with some unknowable emotion flitting across his face.

"I took Baltisse to her cabin," Ryon says when the laughter dies. "She is brewing you some kind of remedy, Esra. I can take you there when you feel ready."

Esra blanches. "I must decline, I'm afraid. I feel simply dreadful."

"Don't be a child, Es," says Salem. "Go and take whatever potion the witch makes."

"Ugh, they taste like all my sins coming back for repentance," he moans.

"She don't got a cauldron big enough for that, lad," Salem says gently, his eyes skittering over Esra's frame with deeply etched concern. "Off yeh go, now."

After much arguing, Esra eventually allows Ryon to take him gingerly into his arms. Seeing Ryon encase him gently, the care he takes to ensure Esra's comfort... it forces Dawsyn to swallow thickly, to avert her eyes.

They will need to cross the river to find Baltisse's cabin somewhere beyond, but Ryon will otherwise keep to travelling on foot to escape the notice of anyone nearby who might look to the sky.

The rest prepare themselves to follow. They will not all be accommodated within Baltisse's small house, but they will at least find themselves better equipped. They can only hope that they will be far enough from the roads and paths that no one will come upon their camp.

Hector stamps out the fire while Rivdan and Tasheem don their shoes. The heat of the valley still challenges them, and Tasheem grimaces as she slides her weapon sheaths into place.

"Did Gerrot go to relieve himself?" Dawsyn wonders aloud, noticing his absence. The man is so very unassuming.

"I didn't see him leave," Ruby answers.

"Nor did I," Hector adds. "He didn't mention it."

"How could he, yer dunderhead? Hard to say 'I'm off fer a piss' when yeh ain't got a tongue."

Several minutes pass, and Gerrot doesn't return.

"I'll look around," Dawsyn says to the group at large. "Don't leave until we've returned." She holds her ax by the throat but lets its blade dangle toward the ground. She sees the fish bones littered on the ground as she passes the still-smoking ashes and pauses. She turns her head to the sound of the river, the water scurrying to sea. She looks down at the bones one last time and then alters her course.

The river takes mere moments to reach. The ground grows thick with moss the closer she comes. Ahead, muddied prints lead to the man who sits upon the bank, dangling his feet into the quieter waters below.

"Gerrot?" Dawsyn calls, coming closer. "We are making ready to leave."

Gerrot doesn't respond. When she comes closer, she sees his eyes are shut, the picture of peace. His boots sit alongside him, bare feet disturbing the mud in the shallow water.

Seeing him so content, she finds it difficult to disturb him. Instead, she sits down next to him, and is rewarded by his answering smile, another soft pat on the knee. He moves his feet back and forth in the water, and sighs deeply, lifting his face to the sun.

Dawsyn contemplates. Though she does not have a favourable history with this river, it does, by all accounts, seem inviting today. She takes off her boots too, placing them alongside Gerrot's. Then she eyes the water shrewdly. The last time she offered herself to it, it nearly drowned her. That water had been freezing then. She pulls up her pant legs and slowly lets the tips of her toes kiss the water.

It is cool, but alluringly so. She sinks her feet to the ankles and feels immediately soothed. She is abruptly overcome with the desire to submerge her entire body, despite the danger of the rapids. She has slowly broiled beneath all of her layers since the sun rose. "Thank the Chasm, that's good," she groans.

Gerrot grins at her but shakes his head. *Not the Chasm*, he seems to say. *The Chasm is not to thank.*

Dawsyn has not uttered those words in an age. On the Ledge, a person's death would be considered fortunate if it escaped the clutches of the Glacians. A swift descent into the Chasm, illness, frost, starvation, and the people would bow their heads and thank the Chasm, not the Mother above. The people promptly forgot the spirit of the Mother when she failed to save them in their plight.

"I've never felt such simple relief," Dawsyn says lightly, watching the water grow murky with the swish of her feet.

Gerrot sighs, his shoulders rising and falling easily.

"They will never know it, you know," she says now. She finds it... easy to speak in his presence. "The children up there. Their parents, too. They will never know what it's like to sit where we sit."

The old man only watches her as she speaks. He does not appear saddened, as she expected. He is, of all things, hopeful. His lips purse, one shoulder lifts.

Perhaps one day they might.

Dawsyn frowns. "No," she says. "I know now... they can't be brought over the Chasm. Nothing will convince them to leave."

His hope, she knows, is in vain.

Gerrot looks her in the eye, his confidence unflinching, and sends a pointed finger right to the centre of her chest. *You can.*

She shakes her head, looking down to the water once more. At the idleness of her feet the water has returned to its beautiful clarity, the dirt settled. Gerrot points to her toes, and Dawsyn sees a small fish meandering around her ankles.

Standing in the water, Gerrot reaches for Dawsyn's hands. With his fingers around her wrists, he slowly guides them into the river. They wait, Dawsyn's heartbeat accelerating, until the fish swims ignorantly between her waiting palms.

She slams her hands together, the slick tail of the fish escaping her clutches.

"*Damn!*" she hisses, pulling her hands out, feeling the spot on her thumb where the fish's scales nicked her.

But Gerrot only pats her arm. He lifts a hand, signalling her to hold until the sediment falls. *Wait for the water to settle.*

When the fish reappears, still dallying in the shallows, he

guides her hands into the water once more. He nods down to it. *Try again.*

She holds her hands steady, refusing to flinch when the fish brushes against her fingertips, and when it slides between her palms, she grabs hold of it.

"Ha!" she cries, holding it aloft. "I caught it!" The fish wriggles frantically, trying its hardest to return to the river.

Gerrot smiles widely, nodding. He points to the fish and juts his thumb at the river. *Throw it back.*

"Why?" Dawsyn asks. "I caught it."

Gerrot's shoulders shake with his amusement, and he takes the fish from her grasp. He throws it over the boulders that trap the water in these shallow parts, and it soars out and into the rapids. Back to where it belongs.

For a moment they both stare at the place where the fish disappeared, and Dawsyn hears familiar words in her head. *All things find a way back home.*

Gerrot smacks a withered hand to her shoulder, grasping it tightly, and then juts his chin up the river, to the colossal mountain that rises in the north.

Dawsyn looks too. It looks perfectly unclimbable, disappearing into permeating cloud. Stealing the sun and its wonder from all that live there. A fate no human was made to suffer. A fate none should ignore.

"I do not know if there's enough left in me to try again," Dawsyn admits.

Gerrot does not hear her. He is already returning to camp, boots in hand.

Chapter Thirty-Nine

There is notable distance between Salem and Ruby on the short journey to Baltisse's cabin, and yet it doesn't stop him from glaring back at her from the head of the party.

"Salem?"

"What?" he barks.

Dawsyn frowns. "Eyes forward before you lead us in the wrong direction. You're the only one who knows the way."

"Aye, though it might serve me to lose one of our number."

Dawsyn sighs. "She's given up everything to side with us, Salem."

"And if she decides to go runnin' back to the Queens, we'll find ourselves in a mound o' pig shit."

Dawsyn has considered as much, but the thought never seems to hold any weight. The captain has done nothing but follow Dawsyn into impossible situations at her own risk. In fact, she feels a strange, improbable kinship to the woman. "Ruby had no hand in the fire," she says firmly. "You're laying blame where it doesn't belong."

"Aye. Well, you'd be one to speak on the topic, wouldn't yeh, Dawsyn?"

They scowl at each other a moment before Dawsyn gives in. "I've no idea what you mean."

"Yeh blame Ryon for the Queen's deception, no?" he says.

"Yer punishin' him for some lie the Queen told yeh to get yeh riled up and spittin' mad."

"I do not *punish* him," Dawsyn bites.

"I've known that boy fer years," Salem tells her. "Nary a moment I've seen him as wounded as yeh make him now, Dawsyn. I know yer tough. Yer tougher than anyone ought to be," he says. "An' it ain't yer fault. It's what that mountain needed yeh to be. But yeh needn't be so tough on someone who accepts you anyway, ax an' all," Salem grins dryly. "He was doin' his best, in the most difficult of circumstances. Surely yeh see that?"

"You might come to the same conclusion about the captain, then," Dawsyn remarks, though his words have niggled into a pocket of her brain she normally shields.

"Perhaps," Salem allows. "He helped me, yeh know?"

Dawsyn looks back at him. "Who? Ryon?"

"Of course, bloody *Ryon;* who else?" Salem shakes his head at her. "The day we met, I was being dragged from me own inn by a few men who'd shoved a sack over me head. Ryon happened to be travellin' by and he saved me."

"Do I dare ask?"

"I may have gotten meself into a spot of debt," he says furtively. "Yeh see, I'd developed a little problem with gamblin' and the like. The inn's a lonely place most nights. Me older brother was supposed to run it but he'd long since passed. His death was somethin' I've never gotten over," Salem admits, his stare drifting away for a moment.

"I'm afraid I got meself mixed up in the head. I had no more coin to me name. I hadn't paid the bill with the liquor man and so the bar was emptyin'. I was lookin' at closin' it down fer good." He shakes his head at the memory. "Then the bookie's men came. Slugged me over the back o' me head and started carryin' me out the door. I didn't even bother to fight 'em off. I'd given up, see? I surrendered meself to whatever end they had planned fer me." Here, Salem pauses. Lost in his thoughts.

Dawsyn wonders how alone he must have felt, how defeated, to have given up the way he did. She wonders if Briar Sabar had once felt that exact excruciation.

"Now, I couldn't see well, what with that stinkin' sack on me face," Salem continues. "But suddenly I hear this boomin' voice, yeh know? The type of voice that makes yeh quiet, and then Ryon says, 'If that's the inn owner, I'll have to ask yer pardon fer whatever he's done. I need a bed, and I'm far too tired to walk on.'" Salem grins widely, the first true smile she has seen since he awoke before the ruins of his inn.

"They told him to fuck off, as yeh can imagine. A few moments later, I was sprawled out on the ground. Them boys were walkin' away, fists full of coins, and Ryon was helpin' me up and sayin' that he had no more money for a room, but that he was gonna take one anyway. Boy has been fleecin' me ever since," Salem chuckles.

"He was the one who brought Esra into our lives 'n' all. He was the only liquor man left in Terrsaw that'd dare trade with the likes o' me. I was blacklisted with the rest.

"When Ryon showed me what he really was..." Salem's eyes go wide with the memory of it. "There was always somethin' 'bout that boy that didn't fit right. Noticed it from the beginnin'. Still, nearly soiled meself when he brought them wings out. I'm not too proud to admit it, Dawsyn. I was right scared o' him then.

"He told me that he'd let me hang if I ran meself into mischief again. I didn't dare go against his good faith. I kept meself straight and narrow after tha'." Salem tugs the waistband of his pants up, as though demonstrating his resurrection from rock-bottom.

"Esra helped, o' course. He's a right handful, and he took it upon himself to outstay his welcome whenever he could. A mighty distraction from one's own troubles, if ever there were one." His smile weakens at the mention of Esra, whose pained whimpers echoed back to their camp earlier as Ryon had carried him away.

"My point being that Ryon Mesrich is a good man. A half-man, perhaps, but a man willing to look by yer past deeds, yer exterior, and consider the soul beneath."

Dawsyn feels it again, that wheedling in her brain, telling her that she has it all wrong. That it is not Ryon who should repent. It is not he who is of little worth.

"I don't suppose I know you half as well as I'd like to, Dawsyn. But I'd guess you've got quite a few misdeeds under yer belt too."

A gross under-estimation.

"How could yeh not? I can't imagine yeh made it to Terrsaw twice now without gettin' yer hands dirty. Ryon is possessed of that rare quality that looks by it all. He'd take yeh, no matter yer faults, because he sees yeh clearly. And I think," – Salem sighs – "he deserves someone who'd do the same fer him."

Dawsyn swallows. She remains quiet as they come to a bend in the trail. Ahead is the cursive of smoke rising into the treetops. Baltisse's cabin is near.

"I'm sorry for your brother," Dawsyn finally says, her throat tighter than she wants it to be, her words raspy and weak. It is the only part of his tale that she can safely speak on. She feels a strange unfolding, layer by layer with each piece of Ryon she comes to learn.

"Aye, me as well. Poor lad."

"What happened to him?" Dawsyn asks. Anything to keep the conversation from Ryon and all his good qualities.

"Warner was his name. He insulted a nobleman, I'm sorry to say. Fell in love with a pompous man's daughter. Next thing he knew, the lass was pregnant, and she ran to her father before she bothered to tell Warner. If there's one thin' our mother told us more'n once, it was 'no fraternisin' with the proper folk,'" Salem says in a high-pitched voice. "People o' our class don't take those liberties, yeh know? But my brother, well, he had a mind fer women and not much else, and this girl was at our inn more nights than not. I warned 'im, too! 'Call it off,' I said. Next thin' we know, the guards were at our door with that nobleman leadin' 'em. They took Warner away and I never saw him again."

"They hung him?" Dawsyn asks, shocked.

"Aye. Those arrogant folk up there in the court," Salem nods, his voice becoming gruff. "They don't much care about what happens to us, yeh know? It ain't ever been about what's good for all. Only what's good fer a few."

This, at least, they can agree on.

Dawsyn is lost in thoughts of Salem until Baltisse's cabin appears. They all come to a stop.

Rivdan drops his weapons and Tasheem helps Gerrot inside. Hector begins collecting sticks and kindling, and Dawsyn looks at her surroundings. There are times when she feels she has lived in two different realms, and this is one of them. In this one, Glacians give everything to help strangers, and humans kill for petty matters.

Hector and Gerrot will live out their remaining days hiding their true identity, lest any good folk learn that they come from the Ledge. Rivdan, Tasheem, and Ryon will be attacked if found by humans and now likely Adrik, too, should he be inspired to descend from his perch. Salem, Esra, and Baltisse will continue on as they have, hiding on the fringe of society.

And Dawsyn, she supposes, will need to do something about it.

She is many bad things, she knows. Malevolent and spiteful and more than a little arrogant. She is not gracious like Gerrot, or self-sacrificing like Ruby. She isn't determinedly optimistic like Esra is, or as generous as Salem. She is not like Ryon, who gives pieces of himself away to those in need of him.

But she can be willing. She can be brave. She can repay the lives she's taken with lives that should be saved. Before she dies, she can nod toward the reinstated good and say 'See? I saved more than I took. Are we not even? Am I not made of many shades?'

She can keep fighting. She can do this much.

Ryon, Baltisse, and Tasheem come out of the small home. Dawsyn imagines that Esra and Gerrot will occupy most of the space now. Esra needs a comfortable place to rest, and Gerrot is the weakest of their lot. The others find places on the ground to sit, talking quietly amongst one another as Hector lights a small fire.

Dawsyn clears her throat. It is awkward and forced but it gets their attention, and they turn to her.

"I think," Dawsyn says, swallowing hard. "We must try again."

There is a small pause while the rest look around at each other, their glances questioning. Tasheem says, "Well, of course." And they all go about their conversations once more, ignorant to the warmth that floods Dawsyn's chest.

CHAPTER FORTY

For days, Dawsyn camps with the rest and speaks when spoken to, but her mind is consumed by the task ahead. How does one rescue a hundred humans from the Ledge with three sets of wings and a mage?

The answer is simpler than it should be: one would need more sets of wings. Or more Mages. Moreover, where would they put a hundred people? Certainly not in Terrsaw, where the Queens will view them as a threat. And if not here, then where else?

The thought of the Queens often brings the magic right to the tips of Dawsyn's fingers. She watches it warily each time. Anger lures it out. Fear, too. But while she can lure it into her palms, she still cannot command it, and it is quickly becoming a source of diverting frustration.

But she had commanded it at least once, had she not? The day Ryon dragged Esra from the burning rubble of Salem's home, she had laid her hands to Baltisse's and bid whatever power she had to rise. She begged it to help. In the moments before, she had seen a world where one such as Esra didn't exist and found it intolerable. Dawsyn doesn't remember deciding to add her magic to Baltisse's; she just knows that she did. It hadn't felt searingly cold or sharp. It hadn't been reluctant or explosive. It was warm. It was pliant.

It worked.

And how can that be?

These are the thoughts that trouble her most as she goes for water, as she sleeps on a pallet beneath the stars, as she sits alongside Salem, or Hector, or Tasheem, and pretends to listen to what they say.

"It still feels so peculiar to rest my ass on the ground," Hector says.

Dawsyn and he have found a quiet spot in the forest away from the others. They sit with their backs to a towering tree trunk, its bark caked in soft, damp moss. It cools them in the relentless heat.

"Hm."

"Truly. I still await the snow to soak through to my nether regions, and yet they remain blissfully untouched."

Dawsyn only nods slowly, her eyes distant.

"Dawsyn?"

"What?" she asks, finally looking at him.

"Are you listening?"

"No... sorry."

"I was speaking of my nether regions."

"Then I'm not sorry."

"Are you well?" Hector asks. Hector himself seems challenged by the heat. Since first setting foot in the valley, his cheeks have been flushed and his forehead damp.

"I am," Dawsyn tells him. "I'm... I'm thinking."

"About how to be saviour of the Ledge?"

Dawsyn narrows her eyes. "Do you mock me?"

"No," Hector mutters, subtly shifting further from her. "It's not mockery, it's concern."

"For whom?"

"You. Us. Going back there." Hector hesitates. "I can't help but think it's exactly what we should be avoiding."

"And so we should leave the rest of them there?" Dawsyn asks, and not with malice, but with a genuine need to hear another's reasoning. "To be selected? To freeze and starve?"

"No," Hector allows. "But you must see what I see?"

"And what is that?"

"That you are likely to fail once more."

Hot ire climbs her spine. She feels the iskra crawl into her palms.

Hector sighs. "I only mean to say that I don't want you to *die*, Dawsyn. We made it here, alive. We deserve to spend the rest of our lives trying to feel safe." He rolls his eyes at her, as though he finds her exasperating. "I'm not trying to insult you. Unclench your fists."

"I'm deciding whether I should put one in your face."

He chuckles. "The last time you tried, we were twelve, and I shoved a handful of snow down your shirt for it."

"Well, there's no snow here, Hector. And you wouldn't dare stick your hand down my shirt now."

Hector thinks for a moment, wiping his forehead. "No, I suppose not. I get the impression that large Glacian would bite my head off."

Dawsyn says nothing, but her stomach tightens at the mention of Ryon. She picks a leaf from the ground and begins pulling it apart.

"Ah," Hector murmurs, watching her. "So, I am right. You two are lovers?"

"We are lots of things. Lovers is no longer one of them."

Hector grins. "And you loathe complexity."

How nice it is to be so easily understood. "I do."

"Yet, you're one of the most complex people I know."

Dawsyn's head whips around. "How so?"

"You're impenetrably stern, yet you care more than most."

Care is not what she does. "I–"

"You're fierce and confident... but scared."

She bristles. "I'm–"

"You crave safety, and yet you see any offer of protection as a threat."

"It usually *is* a threat," she argues.

"I would have married you," Hector says now. "I told you enough times. We could have helped each other on the Ledge. Did you think me a threat?"

Dawsyn hesitates a beat too long. "Of course not."

"But you didn't marry me. You wouldn't sleep in my cabin. I could have offered myself for Selection in your place as well as my mother's. You're too practical to pass up an offer like that out of pride, so I can only assume it was fear that stopped you."

"You can't honestly believe I fear you," Dawsyn scoffs, knocking her shoulder into his. "I once pinned you down by the throat until you admitted to stealing my sword."

"It was a miniature wooden sword."

"It was *my* wooden sword."

"Regardless, no. I don't believe you fear me, or anyone else," Hector continues. "But I think you fear anyone knowing you well. I think you fear becoming predictable to another. You see safety in distance."

Dawsyn only stares at her friend, her face blank and impassive. She has always considered him to be a source of comfort. He was familiar. Indeed, he knew her better than anyone else on the Ledge. He has watched her grow from a girl to a woman, watched her traverse the loss of her family members, one at a time. If anyone could define her in the scope of words, it would be him.

If only he weren't so probing. So unsparing. Some things ought not to be brought out and inspected. Some stones should remain unturned.

So that you can continue to run from yourself? some invasive thought asks. And there it is once more, this slowly expanding awareness in some forgotten crevice, deep in her mind. A place not yet explored. A corner that was squashed and sealed to make room for far more vital occupations, like hunger, defence, survival. But now, away from the Ledge, where it isn't so difficult to keep her heart beating, those new, niggling thoughts begin to flourish from their roots, creeping outward like vine, finally forcing her to look inward, to dissect herself.

"You're not going to pin me down again, are you?" Hector asks.

Dawsyn grins wanly. "I might."

At that moment, the sound of footfalls on the leaf-strewn path interrupts them and they look up to see Ryon and Rivdan passing with pails full of water. Rivdan nods to Dawsyn and Hector in his genial way, but Ryon doesn't offer any pleasantries. He stares at the two of them as he passes, his eyes flitting back and forth, growing darker. His knuckles around the handles become strained, and for a moment there is a glimpse of his wings. He diverts his stare, placing his attention purposefully on the back of Rivdan's head. Dawsyn feels the necklace on her chest grow cool again as he leaves.

Hector pokes Dawsyn's hand. It is curled into a tight ball on top of her knee, her nails biting into the flesh of her palm. "Of all the people for you to fall for, I would never have guessed it would be a Glacian."

"*Half*-Glacian. And I did not *fall*–"

"Your cheeks are flushed, Dawsyn, and you're wound so tightly I fear you'll burst."

Dawsyn shakes out her fingers, realising too late that her breaths are coming rather fast for one sitting so idle.

"I assume from the glowering that he knows about… our past?"

"He does," Dawsyn murmurs.

"And is he aware that there is no romance between us?"

Dawsyn rolls her eyes. "I told him as much."

"Good. Perhaps he won't kill me in my sleep."

Dawsyn chortles. "He might if I ask him to." Another barb to the brain. Another enigma to turn over relentlessly.

"Do you love him?"

Dawsyn shifts uncomfortably. Her mind shouts competing answers to her, and she thinks how right Hector was when he said that she hated complexity. She *hates* this. "I don't know," she says finally, covering her eyes with the palms of her hands and pressing them tight. It is, at least, a more honest answer than she allowed herself until now.

"And you can look past… all the bad? You can look past his nature?"

"He isn't one of *them*, Hector," she rushes to explain. "He never came to the Ledge to take our people and drink their souls. It's not his *Glacian* heritage I question. Not anymore."

Hector frowns. "So then you question his motives?"

"Of course I do!" she exasperates.

"Do you believe he would take Glacia for himself?"

"No, I don't think that," she says, pressing her fingers to her temples, where a steady pounding has begun. "He seeks freedom, not power."

"Then what *do* you question?"

How to explain the unexplainable? That she was lashed to her core and she cannot let the wound simply heal, as though it had never been there at all. That she needs to keep the gash open as a reminder to herself. As a punishment. That the mere thought of giving someone the power to afflict her again is intolerable. "I question his motives with me."

"But why?"

"*Mother above.* Because *look* at me, Hector!" she says, holdings out her arm. "What could he see in me? I'm not nice or gentle. I'm not Glacian like him, and I hardly belong here in Terrsaw either. I'm good at being alone. I'm good at minding myself. I'm good at fending off anything that sticks its nose my way. I cannot simply shed that skin and adopt something softer."

Hector frowns at her a moment. Deliberating. "You're right," he says finally. "You're not nice or gentle. You're not good at relying on anyone else."

"That's what I just said." Dawsyn sighs.

"But you *listen*," Hector implores. "You're clever. You have wit. You're steadfastly loyal to people who would not necessarily return the favour. You're kind to those who've likely not known much kindness in their lives. You empathise. You're the bravest of us all, and it doesn't hurt that you're easy on the eyes." Hector smirks when Dawsyn looks away. "He sees what we all see."

Dawsyn shifts awkwardly, thinking that she attributes each of those words to Ryon herself, when she forgets to hate him. Finally, she meets Hector's eyes. He is still a boy to her. A boy in a man's body. "I think you're my dearest friend."

"I'm glad to hear it, because you're my *only* friend." Hector takes her hand and hauls her to her feet. "I haven't got a single hope of making it here without you. Where you go, I go."

"Out of necessity?"

"Certainly," he says. "Not all can be as brave and loyal as you."

Dawsyn rolls her eyes as they stride through the forest aimlessly. If she were to close her eyes, she could conjure the sights and smells of the Ledge, the bite of the frost on their cheeks. It could be the pine grove they walked through as children, shoving each other into snowbanks and arguing meaninglessly. They are different now, and yet so much the same.

"If you ever reclaim that castle in Terrsaw," Hector muses. "Will you let me have one of the rooms?"

"No." She smiles.

Hector laughs. "And may I ask how you intend to save everyone on the Ledge?"

"I haven't found the means yet," she mumbles.

"Well, if anyone shall succeed, it will be you."

"And why is that?"

Hector winks at her. "You've always had something others don't."

Dawsyn muses that, while it was not necessarily true before, it seems that it is true now.

CHAPTER FORTY-ONE

The days that follow become monotonous tedium. Most of the others are lethargic from the heat but busy themselves around the camp rather than remaining still. They are a sombre bunch without Esra to taunt and tantalise them. He remains within Baltisse's cabin, making slow improvement with the persuasion of the mage's odd remedies. She seems put out that she cannot conjure the power to heal him fully and redirects her energies by making salves for his skin and tonics for the pain. It is Gerrot who becomes Baltisse's right-hand man in nursing Esra. He helps to lift him, clean his wounds, collect herbs, and it makes Dawsyn think of his late wife, Mavah, a medicine woman of the Ledge. She wonders if he once assisted her up on the mountain before he was selected.

Baltisse, shockingly, allows his interference. Perhaps it is his inability to speak that appeals to her. The two remain sequestered in the cabin with Esra, watching over him without respite. By the third day in their new settlement, Esra's cries of agony begin to cease. He is finally healing.

Salem nurses his rage quietly, and there is not one amongst their party who dare chastise him for his self-pity. Every so often, Dawsyn sees his glare divert back to Ruby, but he makes no more effort to confront her.

Ruby makes attempts to appease the others. She offers to

collect water, to cook, to clean Esra's bandages, and it serves to slowly thaw Salem's hostility toward her. Eventually, he makes peace with the captain's obvious remorse.

Hector asks incessant questions to whoever will answer. He is intrigued by the mixed and their way of life, by Terrsaw, by all that he sees. Dawsyn remembers feeling the same when she first set foot in this strange valley, though she was radically less annoying about it. Tasheem grows tired of the man quickly, threatening to dump him back on the Ledge if he continues. Hector, who has spent his life fearing the Glacians, heeds the warning immediately.

Dawsyn, who is unused to being in close quarters with so many, opts to slip away as often as possible. She is made uncomfortable by more than one internal struggle, and it makes present company and the lack of any activity all the more unbearable.

She wanders the woods under the guise of surveillance and stalks the perimeter of the camp at a wide radius. She listens for the sounds of an unfamiliar approach, perhaps from a Terrsaw guard or a wayward traveller, but the bulk of her thought is ensnared with the Ledge.

All the others are relying on her to coin a plan, and she is abundantly aware of it. They have followed her whims thus far. They are willing to follow her back to the Ledge once more, and she cannot fail them all again.

Dawsyn remembers that her grandmother once called Briar a 'reluctant servant.' A woman who took the place of Dawsyn's mother when Harlow Sabar died of the cold. A woman who became the head of their family. A woman who slept with a knife beside their door, lest someone unwelcome breach its threshold.

Briar never asked to be a heroine, Valma had said. *But our blood decides, Dawsyn. She is our hero, no matter how reluctant.*

That is the truth Dawsyn accepts now. She, too, is the reluctant servant. The unwilling saviour. She is well aware that not a single soul has asked her to shoulder this burden. Not one person has requested it, and yet she feels the responsibility rest with her anyway.

She will fulfil it, because if not her, then who else?

Dawsyn's hide boots crush the dried leaves beneath her. It is a satisfying feeling, far more so than the crunch of ice or snow. She walks and walks and tries to conjure the answers she needs.

Flowers are wilting on their stems all around. It reminds her of the blossoms that Baltisse lured into her palms. The mage has such influence over her own power, despite its current depletion. If Dawsyn had the same abilities, the quest ahead might be that much easier.

Tentatively, Dawsyn slows. She stops at the sight of a primrose bush. The petals droop, suffocating in the heat of the fertile season. She understands how they feel.

With grim determination, she reaches toward one of the delicate yellow blossoms. It might be a trick of the eye, but Dawsyn thinks she sees it lift a little as her fingertips come closer, reaching toward her, magnetised.

Bolstered, Dawsyn searches within herself as Baltisse had once bade her to. She tries to recall what the mage had said.

If you demand it, force it, it will bite. If you want the magic to rise at your will, then you will find the ways to coax it out.

Dawsyn finds the iskra dormant and waiting.

You may come, she thinks. *It is safe.*

She feels it stir – that strange, heavy entity. It uncoils, uncertain.

I'll lay the path, she vows. She tries to make her limbs pliant, welcoming. *Come.*

It remains. *Release me,* it says in return.

Dawsyn grits her teeth. She tries to supress her irritation, her frustration. *Show me how.*

But it ignores her, curling back into itself, unwilling or unable to rise from her depths.

STACEY MCEWAN   291

Dawsyn growls, ripping the primrose blossoms from their stems. *"Fuck!"* she shouts.

The path is not clear, the iskra murmurs, an echo that repeats over and over. *The path is not clear.*

"Prishmyr?"

Dawsyn startles at the voice, turning to find the speaker.

Rivdan approaches, his flaming hair and long beard gleaming where the sun finds it. He is mere feet from her, and that alone is disturbing. Dawsyn is unaccustomed to being taken by surprise.

This magic confounds her.

"Are you all right?" he asks. His eyes track down her arm, and Dawsyn follows his stare, finding where the veins have become prominent, the muscles strained, the flowers crushed in her fist.

She promptly releases them.

"Fine," she says mildly, though she feels anything but. "I was finding some plants for Baltisse and her concoctions."

Primrose could be poisonous, for all she knows. It likely is.

"I don't mean to disturb you," he defers. "I heard your shout as I was passing."

Dawsyn nods, discomfort prickling her skin.

"You need not be so harsh with yourself," Rivdan says then, and he sounds hesitant. "I hope I don't speak out of turn. We do not know each other well. But I *do* know Ryon. Known him since he was a wayward urchin running about the Colony. He would not follow someone he did not believe in."

Dawsyn does not answer. The truth is, she has wondered whether Ryon, whether *all* of them for that matter, were merely delusional for following her.

"I'll leave you be, prishmyr." He turns to leave, his size casting shadows over the forest around him.

"Rivdan?" Dawsyn calls.

He pauses. "Yes?"

"What does prishmyr mean?" she asks. Dawsyn has only heard the man use that name with her.

Rivdan smiles. "It means 'princess.'"

If it were another, Dawsyn would assume it an insult, a sneer. But Rivdan, with his quiet manner and gentle temperament, seems incapable.

"I'm no princess," she says quietly, not wishing to scold him.

Rivdan only shakes his head. "I've never seen another princess in the flesh," he admits. "But I imagine they'd pale in comparison."

Dawsyn feels that same discomfort once more, making her skin feel too small for her. "May I ask something else?

"Of course."

Dawsyn sighs slightly and meets his curious gaze. It is a kind face. It invites others in. Dawsyn notices the green flecks in his eyes and struggles to imagine him as an Izgoi warrior. He does not seem at all menacing if you can look past his bulk.

"Why did you agree to come with us?" she asks bluntly. "Flying over the Chasm was… hasty, at best. Dangerous. Why would you wish to join such a cause?"

Rivdan's lips quirk, his beard with it. "I would have thought the answer obvious."

"Not to me."

Rivdan sighs. "Well, the first part of my answer is that I did not agree with the Council majority vote. It seemed a very great cruelty to leave people trapped on the Ledge, where they were no longer needed for Vasteel's fodder. It sat quite badly with me," he murmurs darkly. "Pitting our own existence above theirs. It felt similar to the ideals of the brutes, when we had fought so hard and long to dispel notions of status in the Colony. For years we had preached about equal opportunity. And then when we had what we wanted, the entire slogan was set aside at the mention of the Ledge," Rivdan shakes his head. "A people just as oppressed as us – more so. I reassured myself that at least they would not be stolen from their side of the Chasm and stripped of their iskra. It was the only thing that made leaving them there tolerable. A passive kind of cruelty, at least." Rivdan gives her an apologetic shrug. "But Adrik snatched even that much away. After Ryon revealed it, it felt as though all other choices were lost. I didn't think so much about my options, prishmyr," he says. "There only seemed to be one. I won't live under the rule of another tyrant."

Dawsyn purses her lips. "I think there *was* another choice," she says. "Though, you, perhaps, are too noble to venture it."

Rivdan bows his head at the compliment. "I'm yet to prove myself, prishmyr," he says. "But if you lead the way, I will try to live up to such a compliment." With that, he leaves her on the path, his frame disappearing around a bend.

Dawsyn is left with his voice ringing in her head, right next to the waning echo of the iskra, and the stain of primrose on her palm.

"Mage? I need you to teach me how to use this godforsaken magic."

Dawsyn stands in the open doorway with her ax in hand. The door, which she'd opened without announcing her arrival, had given such a loud crack against the wall that Esra shouted something that sounded like "holy mother of dick."

Esra sits naked in Baltisse's wash tub, his knees extended from the water. At Dawsyn's entrance, he sloshes water over the side, narrowly missing Baltisse, who in turn curses and glares viciously at them both.

"Dawsyn! I'm nude!"

"I see that," Dawsyn says, pacing further into Baltisse's home without further preamble. She lets her eyes sweep over Esra's body under the water. "You look improved."

Much to Dawsyn's surprise, Esra blushes. "Eyes on mine, woman. This isn't a show."

Dawsyn frowns. "You can't honestly claim to be modest now, Es."

"I'm not looking my best," he says coyly. "And Baltisse treats me like a child."

"An impertinent one," the mage agrees, running a sponge gingerly over Esra's back. The scars on his body are prominent, but with Baltisse's healing, there are no longer patches of red and raw flesh marring his skin. The wounds are blistered over, new skin is forming quickly. Half of his face is mottled with fresh scarring and one eye remains shut, but the other is just as sharp as ever, glinting brightly. "It's all very demeaning," he says, lips turned down.

Baltisse tsks. "I swear, if I could be sure I'd never hear your whining again I'd lay down and die," she snaps. "But I fear your thoughts would follow me to the afterlife. Now, hold still."

"Allow me to relieve you both," Dawsyn says. "I need your help, Baltisse."

The mage eyes her warily, but continues her ministrations. "Yes, you said. And what exactly do you intend to do with your magic? I assume a grand plan has dawned on you."

Dawsyn looks at her head on. It is not a grand plan, but it's not nothing. It isn't wandering uselessly in the woods willing a grand plan to fall from the sky. "I want you to teach me to fold."

Baltisse finally stills, the sponge in her hand dripping over Esra's shoulder. Her irises swirl, and though her tone is grave, Dawsyn senses something like excitement exuding from her. "Folding is for mages," she says.

"So is healing," Dawsyn counters, looking over to Esra. "But I managed that."

"I do not know if you have the capability," Baltisse adds.

"But you think I might," Dawsyn nods. "And if I can, then it will be another way to transport people off the Ledge."

"So you *do* have a plan?"

"Not... entirely," Dawsyn says. "But I will."

Baltisse grins, then looks back to Esra. "Will you need my help getting dressed?"

"Leave me here, girls. And do me a favour? Leave the door open as you leave. Maybe convince that handsome Ledge boy to walk by."

"Hector?" Dawsyn asks.

"He has eyes like the ocean, does he not?"

Dawsyn grins. She is, and not for the first time, immensely grateful that he lived. "Perhaps he could help you dress?"

"A fine idea."

"Don't humour him," Baltisse says, walking by her. "Come with me."

Baltisse takes her to a clearing. The sun shines unimpeded to the earth and Dawsyn feels her face heat almost instantly as they step into its glare.

"Must we do this in the sun?"

"You'll grow used to its bite," Baltisse says. "It is not as sharp as yours."

Baltisse rounds on her when they reach the clearing's centre and gestures for Dawsyn to hold out her hands. The mage takes Dawsyn's palms into her own, examining them closely. "Does the iskra continue to seep out?"

"When I'm... bothered."

"And when you're not?"

Dawsyn deliberates for a moment. "It is dormant. I feel it hiding away, as though it... cowers."

The mage grimaces. "I don't know if it's possible for you to fold, Dawsyn Sabar. But if you are to have a chance, you will need to have control of yourself. Your thoughts. Do you understand?"

"That's why I'm here."

The mage backs away several paces, creating a sizeable distance between them. "Close your eyes," she says.

Dawsyn laughs. "No."

"Just do it, sweet. I promise I won't steal your silly ax."

Dawsyn narrows them instead, and finally closes them reluctantly. It is… uncomfortable to do so.

"Can you find the iskra? Do you feel where it lies?"

She feels it, lurking in its dark hideaway. "Yes."

"Good. I want you to ignore it."

"What?" Dawsyn blurts, her eyes opening. She was ready to lure it out, as she had been shown before.

"Just once in your life, Dawsyn, resist the urge to debate everything."

Dawsyn almost grins. The mage sounds so very like her grandmother. She closes her eyes once more. She studiously ignores the oily glow of the iskra, sulking within.

"Do not call to the iskra. Look for something else instead. It is in the mind, not in the blood – a spark. It will feel warm and pleasant and light as air, right behind your eyes. Do you feel it?"

"No," Dawsyn says, frowning.

Baltisse huffs. "Think of something nice, then."

Dawsyn wants to roll her eyes. "*Nice?*"

"Stay focussed. Think of a time you were happy. Content."

Quite a feat for one such as Dawsyn. There is only one time she can recall in recent years, and she is reticent to think of it at all. Her mind reaches back further for something else, anything else, but she knows that there is nothing more contenting that this: her head against Ryon's bare chest, the rise and fall of his breath, the warmth of the fire. The quiet, the stillness, the restfulness of it. The feeling of… safety. She could try to match it with thoughts of her childhood, but nothing will feel as warm as this.

So, she draws the memory out. She views it as if she were hovering above, looking down at the two on the grimy cabin floor, their skin illuminated by the tongues of flame in the hearth. She watches as the man sleeps, his arm around her waist, his hand on her hip. She sees his face turned into her hair, as though it comforts him. She watches the woman inch her naked body closer and softly smile.

And even with her eyes closed, it's as though a light makes the memory brighter. She feels that elusive spark Baltisse spoke of, one Dawsyn now attributes to the zeal of joy, the blissful jolt of rightness when all minute cosmic interferences align.

"I feel it," she tells Baltisse.

"Good. Now offer it a place in your hands, and it will go there."

"How–?"

"It won't be forced, Dawsyn. You must simply lead it."

There is no time to feel stupid or inept. She worries that if she loses that small speck of light in her mind, she won't find it again. She opens her palms before her, she gives every inch of her focus to it and thinks, as she has before, *Come.*

Dawsyn feels it move instantly, as though it had waited. She feels her body leading that light down her neck, over her shoulder and along the length of her arm. She feels it settle in her palm.

"When you are ready," the mage says quietly, closer than Dawsyn expected her to be. "Think, *igniss.*"

"Igniss?"

"Fire," Baltisse answers.

With the light beneath the surface of Dawsyn's hand, warm and welcoming, she thinks *igniss* and waits.

But nothing happens.

"Open your eyes now, Sabar."

Dawsyn sighs. She opens them. She expects to see Baltisse frowning. Instead, a flickering catches her eye. In her palm is a small flame, no bigger than that of a candle, moving languidly in the still air.

A stuttered breath leaves her. The flame is hot but doesn't burn. It came from her. It *is* her. She looks back to Baltisse, who smiles knowingly.

"Dawsyn?" comes a voice.

Into the clearing steps Ryon, his eyes wide.

For a moment, Dawsyn and Ryon only stare at one another. Ryon's eyes shift between her hand and her face, and when their eyes meet, Dawsyn can't help but smile widely. Awed. Triumphant. *Look,* she wants to say. *Look what I made.*

Ryon's eyes soften. A grin creeps into his cheeks. His laughter is a soft huff of astonishment.

Dawsyn's hand trembles, but it isn't the fire. The magic beneath her palm isn't a cause of strain or discomfort. What makes her shake is the man ahead of her, who looks at her with that unflinching wonder, despite all she's done.

It only lasts a moment, that glowing pride. That wonderful weightlessness.

A breeze tumbles through the clearing and the flame sways and flickers wearily.

Then Dawsyn yells, collapses, and the flame extinguishes altogether.

As though a hand had gripped her stomach, there is an almighty pull within her, and she goes down. Her shoulder hits the earth first and her breath is forced from her. Something is crushing her organs from within. Something is squeezing, twisting, and she cries out with each pull.

"Dawsyn!" she hears.

Ryon, she thinks.

CHAPTER FORTY-TWO

"*Dawsyn?*" Ryon calls again, his hands on her shoulders. But Dawsyn only writhes on the ground, her face the picture of pain, her body curled into a ball.

"*Baltisse!*" he shouts, but the mage is already there, already kneeling over Dawsyn's form. "What's wrong with her?" he demands.

"The iskra."

"FIX IT!"

"I *can't!*" Baltisse's eyes beseech him, just as desperate as he is. In his panic, he wants to demand that she try something. He wants to find the iskra inside of her and cut it out. Dawsyn cries out again and he almost does it. Her face turns slowly redder, and he cannot just sit here, he can't just watch her twist and scream and do nothing.

His blood cools and his wings appear. He'll carry her somewhere, anywhere. He has no plan in mind, just the desperate need to do something. But just as he's about to collect her from the ground, she stills. As though something had her in its clutches, she is released. She goes limp. Her eyes open, a lighter brown here in the sun, and her breaths drag through her teeth a little slower.

Ryon feels his wings sag as relief sets in. "Dawsyn?"

She only breathes in rattling gasps. Sweat dampens her

brow, her hair, but she nods her head. She can hear him.

Ryon pushes the strands of loose hair back behind her ear and lowers his forehead to her side for a moment, calming himself. He takes one breath, then another.

She's all right, he thinks, soothing the race of his pulse.

It is Baltisse who continues to look on with dread. Her eyes, always so tumultuous, are now morbidly still, and she looks upon Dawsyn as though she were facing the gallows. As though death hung over her head.

Just as quick, Ryon's panic returns. *What is it?* he thinks, knowing the mage will hear.

Baltisse doesn't look at him, doesn't deign to answer him. For a moment, she only watches Dawsyn. The mage's jaw works back and forth, her teeth grinding with the storm of her thoughts. Finally, she turns to Ryon.

"Help me bring her back to camp," Baltisse says calmly. "She'll need to rest a while."

Dawsyn shakes her head, lifting it from the ground. "I didn't force it this time," Dawsyn rasps, her voice uneven. "I didn't… force the iskra. I swear." Dawsyn seems to be waiting for an answer, an explanation.

Baltisse doesn't give it. She averts her eyes, rises, her dress falling to brush the ground. She turns away from Dawsyn, away from them both, away from the questions that Ryon's mind shouts to her, and hurries from the clearing before he can say anything more.

Ryon looks back to Dawsyn, who still works to slow her breathing. He watches her colour return to normal, and wonders what the mage could possibly know to stare at Dawsyn as though she were condemned.

Exhausted, Dawsyn sleeps as Ryon carries her back to camp. It is one of the only times Ryon can recall when she hasn't shown reluctance at being reduced to fit in his arms. She rests the side of her face against his shoulder, her hands cradled together and shoved between their chests.

It's a difficult thing to know someone loves you before they know it themselves. He must reconcile with it all the same. It would be worse to have her realise she loves him and disregard it anyway. Every day he worries that it has already happened, that she has deemed their differences too vast, insurmountable. If that's the case, then he is doomed to spend the rest of his life thinking she's wrong, and there will be no way of showing her.

Ryon doesn't waste any time getting back to camp. If he were smarter, he'd lengthen the trip and delay the moment where he must distance himself again. But there are more pressing things he must deal with. He must find Baltisse and force her to explain everything he saw in that clearing.

The fact that Dawsyn's iskra seems to surpass his expectations is something he has mused over more than once. His own magic, long since dried up, was mostly an inactive entity, nothing but a strange burning in his stomach and palms if he became too animated. It lasted little longer than it took to save his life.

Dawsyn's is different. Perhaps it's that she is human and the iskra is incompatible. Perhaps she was overcome, there in the clearing, by magic meant for a beast.

But she healed Esra, where Ryon knows he couldn't. She conjured fire, a thing not done by any Glacian magic he's ever seen.

Despite his own confoundment, it seems that there is *someone* who knows exactly what is happening to Dawsyn Sabar.

Dawsyn opens her eyes and asks to walk as Baltisse's cabin comes into view.

"Can you?"

"Of course," she mumbles, already untangling herself from him. He sets her down, and watches warily as her legs shake.

"I wish you'd let me help you," he says, unwilling to let go of her wrist.

"I know," she says, surprising him. She looks up and smiles weakly. "I'm working on it."

Ryon's heart stutters, a flood of warmth spreads within his chest.

But for now, headstrong as ever, Dawsyn pulls her hand free and walks off in the direction of the camp.

He sighs deeply, grits his teeth at what will come next, and heads to Baltisse's cabin.

Within, Esra sits on a stool, spooning broth awkwardly into his mouth. "Ryon, my love!" he says. "Come and speak with me."

"Soon," Ryon answers. "I need to speak with Baltisse first."

Baltisse stands over a shallow basin, washing her hands with the utmost attention.

"Baltisse?"

She doesn't answer, doesn't look up. The mage keeps her back turned from both men and acts as though they weren't there at all.

"What's the matter with her?" Esra muses. "Baltisse? Are you and Ryon amid a quarrel? If so, don't mind me. Speak freely. Tell him how you hate the way he struts about. *Pigeon-chested*, you called him. She says it all the time, Ryon. But if you ask me, she's envious that her own chest doesn't command quite the same atten–"

"Shut up, Es!" Ryon and Baltisse say at the same time.

Esra looks at the two of them, noticing for the first time the intensity of the tension passing between them. "What's going on?"

"Are you feeling improved, Es?" Ryon asks.

"Well… mostly."

"Some fresh air will help," Baltisse proclaims, and suddenly the door flings open.

Esra eyes her warily. "I suppose I don't have a choice."

"You never do." The mage takes the spoon from his hand as she passes him.

Esra gives a long-suffering sigh. "Help me stand then, Ry, before you cast me out."

Ryon takes his hands and helps him to stand, and as soon as he is beyond the stoop, Baltisse closes the door behind him.

"Baltisse?" Ryon starts, but the mage still won't face him. She remains with her hand on the doorknob, reluctance showing in every part of her frame. It scares Ryon. In the time he has known the mage, he has never before seen her shy away from him, or anyone else for that matter.

"What were the two of you doing out there, in the clearing?" It's surely an easier question than the one he wants to ask, and it works. Baltisse turns and leans against the door, her hands behind her.

Ryon has never seen her so… human.

"She wants to learn to control the magic. She thinks it will help when it comes time to return to the Ledge."

Ryon had presumed as much. "And can she?" Ryon presses. "Can it be controlled?"

Baltisse contemplates Ryon, rather than answers, but he waits. He won't be diverted. Eventually, Baltisse mutters, "It is not a simple answer," and then says no more.

Ryon closes his eyes. He supresses his frustration. "You will answer it anyway."

"I will not be *commanded* by–"

"*Enough!*" Ryon yells, drowning the mage's voice. He can feel the might of her power permeating the room. He knows how readily she could have him flat on the floor and begging for her pardon and it still does not stop him. "You've kept your secrets from her. You've forced me to keep them, too. You've compromised me in that regard, and I did it out of loyalty. But you will not begin keeping secrets from *me*, Baltisse."

"And who's to say you have a right to know what I do?"

"If it concerns Dawsyn, then I should know."

"Because you love her?"

"Love is a *trace* of what I feel," he snarls.

Both pause in the echo of his voice. After several moments, when the beating of the half-Glacian's heart has slowed, the mage's eyes finally rise, and they are benevolent. "I warned you. I told you to let her go."

She had. In Salem's inn, when it still stood, and Dawsyn had yet to learn who she was. It feels like a lifetime ago. "I no longer believe I was meant to."

Baltisse grimaces. "Unfortunately, nor do I."

"So, tell me," Ryon says. "So that I might have some warning if… I'm to lose her."

The mage doesn't balk at his words. She doesn't rush to correct him, and he is flooded with fear.

The mage nods again in a way that reminds Ryon of how truly old and weary she is. "I'll tell it to her directly," she says. "It would be unfair to do otherwise."

"All of it?" Ryon frowns.

Baltisse moves to the basin once more and declines to answer. "Fetch her," she says tiredly, her head bowed. "She should be the one to decide if you can hear it all, too."

CHAPTER FORTY-THREE

Dawsyn enters the cabin wearily. Her bones feel weighted and unamenable, but Ryon ushers her intently, the determination clear in his expression.

Baltisse waits by the tiny bench top, her hip pressed to its side, her sights set on something out the window. She does not turn when Dawsyn slumps into one of her chairs.

"What is it?" Dawsyn asks, eyes flitting between the two of them. She feels the obvious strain in the room. The mage and Ryon fighting some silent battle.

Dawsyn sighs. "Perhaps this is a conversation for tomorrow, if it is so difficult to say," she suggests. Truly, her body wishes for nothing more than respite.

"No," Ryon says immediately. "We should speak now."

Dawsyn presses her hands to her eyes. "Surely, whatever needs to be said will grow no more dire come night."

Ryon groans. "*Baltisse*," he beseeches. "Do not delay any further."

"Delay *what?*" Dawsyn asks, dark suspicion finally setting in.

Baltisse draws her gaze from the window for the first time since Dawsyn entered. "I believe I have uncovered the… the curiosities of your magic," the mage confesses. "As well as your afflictions."

Dawsyn stills. She feels her pulse jump into her throat, the hairs on her neck rise. "You know why it rejects me?"

Baltisse nods, but her hesitancy is clear. Whatever she means to reveal, Dawsyn doubts it will bode well for her. "I have suspected for a time, though I couldn't be sure. There is very little about magic that is sure." Baltisse bites at her lip. "I asked you to perform a very particular piece of magic today, in that clearing, for a reason. It was a risk, I'll admit. I knew it may very well inflame that war that ensues inside you. But it gave me the answer I needed, despite the detriment."

"Speak plainly," Dawsyn says, her stomach churning.

Baltisse lifts her chin, galvanising herself. "The last reigning monarch in your family was a man named King Launce Sabar," she begins. And Dawsyn is taken aback. What should *this* have to do with the iskra?

"Patience," Baltisse bids, hearing her thoughts. "It is important you know it all. King Launce married a woman who was murdered shortly after birthing his only child: Valmanere. This woman – the *Queen* – was killed by a group of zealots that fancied themselves witch hunters. They hadn't taken too kindly to the King marrying a *mage*, of all things."

Dawsyn's heart jolts. She forgets to breathe.

"Your great-grandmother, Melares Sabar, was mage-born, Dawsyn. Not a widely known fact, and the King had every single one of those witch hunters captured and hung, lest they go about wagging their tongues and inciting more hatred. The mages left in this valley are few, but we remember. I remember." She pauses, watches Dawsyn closely, likely noticing the gooseflesh that has riddled her skin, the small shudder of her frame. "There has always been something elusive about you, Dawsyn. I felt it the first time I saw you. I can smell another mage a mile away, but *you* were harder to grasp. Do you remember the day we first met?"

Dawsyn remembers. Salem's inn was still standing, and Dawsyn stood before the mage, who perused her bare body. *I cannot decide what you are,* she had said.

"It wasn't until you were imbued with iskra that it

awakened that other magic inside of you. Only then did I start to believe there was something else. Something that lay dormant in your grandmother's blood. Likely in your mother's as well. It doesn't always catch, you see? But in you, I believe it did. Today, in the clearing, I found proof."

"Dawsyn is a mage," Ryon says, his voice barely above a whisper.

"Or something like it," Baltisse returns.

Dawsyn swallows, tastes bile. Waves of questions compete for attention, crashing all at once. It is difficult to put them in order. She sits on her hands to still their incessant quaking. "What do you mean, 'or something like it'?"

"I mean that there is mage blood in your ancestry," Baltisse answers. "Albeit a few generations removed. Still, Melares Sabar was a force to be reckoned with. It is unsurprising that her power lingered, however meagrely."

"The... *spark?*" Dawsyn says. "The one you asked me to find in my mind?"

Baltisse nods. "I first saw it when you healed Esra. I wondered if I was mistaken."

Dawsyn turns away, hands scrubbing her face.

"It felt different to you, did it not Dawsyn? When you healed him? Or when you conjured that flame in your palm? I imagine it feels unlike the iskra does."

Dawsyn addresses the wall rather than Baltisse's open curiosity or Ryon's shock. "It feels warm."

"And the iskra?"

She shudders. "So cold that it burns."

"Yes," Baltisse mutters. "Light and dark."

Ryon scrubs his face with both hands. "Two different magic sources in one body," he says, shaking his head, disbelieving. "Have you ever heard of such a thing?"

"No," Baltisse says. "The two are kept apart for a reason."

"And what reason is that?" Dawsyn asks. And here is where they will come to it, Dawsyn knows – this thing that curls

Baltisse's toes where she stands and bunches her shoulders. The deep, dark thing she has come to know.

"Light and dark – two opposite ends of the spectrum. They are not meant to meet. Not made to share pathways. I don't believe that any one person could sustain them both."

Dawsyn can feel them now, that dark compressed energy, curling away from the impeding light. *Release me.*

"And what happens to the person who tries?" Dawsyn asks, shutting her eyes to mask her fear.

The mage falls silent for far longer than she should, long enough that it becomes a cruelty.

"Baltisse?" Ryon presses, voice strained. "What will happen to Dawsyn?"

Baltisse breathes deeply beyond Dawsyn's closed eyes. Once, then again.

"I'm afraid, Dawsyn... that you will not sustain this for long. Sooner or later... you will be overcome."

"And then?" Dawsyn pushes. She needs to hear the mage say it aloud.

"It will kill you," Baltisse says quietly, and a great, heavy silence befalls the cabin. Befalls Dawsyn. Befalls the rattling in her head that has ailed her for months.

It will kill her.

"I believe the mage magic sees the iskra as a contaminant," Baltisse continues. "It is fighting hard to annihilate it altogether."

"And what if it succeeds?" Ryon asks.

"It cannot succeed," Baltisse answers. "Magic cannot be destroyed, no matter its source. If Dawsyn had but *drunk* the iskra it would simply be spent after a time. But the iskra is within her now. It cannot be felled."

Ryon turns away from them both, his neck and shoulders a landscape of tension. He heaves one great breath, and it shudders through him. Through Dawsyn, too.

"What if I learnt to... manage them?" Dawsyn asks quietly. There is little hope in her voice.

"I..." Baltisse stumbles. "We will try."

"But you believe I will fail." It is not a question. The mage has never looked at Dawsyn with pity before; she would not be doing so now if her fate were not sealed.

"I believe that you have astounded me before," Baltisse says softly. "You may stave off that war inside you a little longer yet."

Ryon spins, his face a myriad of taut lines. "What should we do?" he asks. "Tell me what to do!"

"Nothing, Ryon," Baltisse says ruefully. "We do nothing."

"*Nothing?*"

"No," she says. "What happened in the clearing today... it will grow worse. We must try to slow its progression. We keep Dawsyn calm, keep the two sides of her magic away from each other. If the iskra does not rear its head, the mage magic should not have a reason to strangle it."

"And if it does?" Dawsyn asks. And even now she feels the iskra creep into her palms, unbidden, attaching itself to the chaos of her thoughts, her emotions.

They all watch as it quietly spreads, lighting her hands with a cold, ethereal glint.

"Then it may strangle you with it," Baltisse breathes.

CHAPTER FORTY-FOUR

Dawsyn leaves the cabin with limbs that do not feel her own, in skin she does not fit. Her mind is... heavy. So unbearably heavy. That, at least, is familiar.

She hears Ryon follow her out into the lingering afternoon light, but the last thing she wants is to turn and read in his eyes every revelation they heard inside that cabin.

The campsite is full. Hector, Ruby, Esra, Salem, Rivdan. She does not wish to face them either.

She turns to the forest.

"Dawsyn?" Ryon calls.

"I am all right," she says hastily, continuing into the trees. "I need a moment."

The highest branches are filled with birdsong, the nearby creek adding its lazy tinkling to the ensemble, completely at odds with the reckoning occurring inside her as she passes through.

She walks in carefully measured steps – not so fast as to cause alarm. She fastens her thoughts to the sounds and smells around her, rather than the sensations within – impending collapse, looming catastrophe. Panic-driven desperation. Dawsyn has felt her fair share of existential dread, but now she must squash it. She must temper it, and then mould it into something softer, lest it provoke these *entities* that seem to awaken when she is most disquieted.

She thinks of them as monsters she ought not disturb.

Dawsyn screws her eyes tightly shut. *Breathe,* she bids her lungs. *Be calm,* she bids her blood.

She walks despite her fatigue – it may even make it easier. The tiredness seems to keep the magic at bay. Her body is too spent now to host that battle. She sorts through her musings with care, trying not to let them dictate her emotions, her reactions.

She tries and fails to reconcile with the idea that she is... contaminated. Taken hostage by opposing powers that will try to extinguish each other, and her along with them.

But though this thought tumbles to the forefront again and again, it does not take precedence over one matter that concerns her more:

She cannot use these powers to liberate the Ledge.

And lastly, she may not live long enough to liberate it at all.

Dawsyn stumbles her way back to camp when darkness threatens her sense of direction. She finds the site blissfully filled with sleeping bodies. She sets herself down in the space between Hector and Salem. Hector tosses fretfully, pulling his tunic away from his neck and chest as it tries to cling to his sweat-slick skin. Salem snores ceaselessly, one arm thrown across his eyes.

Between them, Dawsyn takes an age to settle. She has surpassed her body's tolerance for wakefulness. Adrenaline keeps her conscious now. Her muscles ache at the memory of the pain, twisting and squeezing and crushing her. Is that truly the way she will die? Strangled from within?

With these thoughts tumbling together and self-destruction simmering under the surface, she eventually falls into the gap between awareness and dreams. Her mind turns to things of comfort, rather than pain.

In the years she spent alone on the Ledge, her consciousness could stave off the madness born from fear with pleasant things. In sleep, her mind would replay the sounds and smells of food, of family, of games and songs and embraces. While awake, she sought safety in solitude, but in her dreams, she was never alone. Sleep would bring her what she lacked: comfort, companionship. It reached into the crevices of her memory until it found a sanctuary in which she could rest.

This is why, though she isn't aware of doing so, she rises, her eyes blinking drowsily, and stumbles to the far side of the camp, where the bulk of a thin blanket covers a person beneath. Dawsyn's body finds the ground beside his, her eyes already shut. Somewhere outside of herself, she feels the weight of scratchy wool settle over her. Her hand reaches forward of its own accord, searching along the dirt. Searching until her fingers are taken, cradled with gentle devotion.

Dawsyn sleeps soundly, and when she wakes the next morning, watching Ryon's back as he slinks away, she notes her change in setting. Notes it, but allows it no further thought.

It does not take long for Ryon to seek her out. It is likely too much to ask that he forget all that Baltisse had revealed, condemning her to probable death, though she could ask that he not spread the news to the rest of their party. The thought of tolerating their looks of pity makes her cringe.

"Dawsyn, we should speak," he says in an aside. Dawsyn is carving wood, trying her hand at etching a mountain cat out of a broken branch – albeit, not particularly well. It is a previous pastime of hers from the Ledge. It seems a placid enough activity, tedious enough to temper the magic within, until she makes the mistake of glancing up at Ryon, where he hovers over her.

He wears the face of a tortured man. It is clear that sleep eluded him. The beard on his jaw is thickening, growing scraggly and unkempt. Coupled with the deep shadows beneath his eyes, the creases that line his forehead, one might guess that it was Ryon himself nearing his demise.

Dawsyn nods reluctantly. She watches him be seated on the ground beside her, both of them looking out at the campsite, where the others mill.

He speaks lowly. "I know you will tell me you are not afraid–"

"I *am* afraid," she says immediately. There is little point in lying. She digs the tip of a knife into the hind leg of the wooden figurine.

Ryon looks up from the ground, contemplating her. "As am I."

Dawsyn resists the temptation to lean into him, let her side rest against his.

"I will speak with Baltisse again," Ryon says now. He nods to himself, his hands pressing tightly together. The muscles along his arms strain in response. "We will think of a plan."

Dawsyn's hands pause. She takes a steadying breath and looks out at the others, oblivious to their conversation. "Can I ask that this... *business*, does not reach the rest?"

Ryon simply nods, gets to his feet, and breathes rather heavily through his nose. "Of course."

She smiles wanly at him, by way of thanks, and resumes her attentions to the carving.

"Is there something... some way I can..." Ryon stammers. Dawsyn sees his eyes sweep to the heavens and back. "Give me *something* to do," he begs. "Please."

Dawsyn regards him, notes how tightly wound he is.

Love, he'd call it. Perhaps it is true.

Dawsyn places her hand on his arm, feeling the coiling tension there. She meets his dark eyes and tries to take some of the panic from them. "You can try not to vex me," she says, a grin appearing. "Lest I become too excitable. You heard Baltisse."

Ryon takes her hand in both of his, cradling it as though it were a life source. He brings it to his lips, lets his breath warm her fingers. "There is not enough distance in this valley to keep that from happening," he grumbles.

Dawsyn finds Gerrot sitting by the campfire. Surely, of their party, Gerrot is of the most calming persuasion. The wood carving has only led her thoughts to the Ledge, and that will not do. She needs restful distraction.

Dawsyn joins him, and after a few moments, the man wordlessly collects twigs from the ground and offers some to her.

The pair spend an hour sitting opposite each other, playing a game typical of Ledge children. Gerrot holds three twigs in his hand, Dawsyn four. She is losing. Gerrot taps Dawsyn's free hand with his twigs, and she narrows her eyes. "Just get me out, old man. Don't toy with me."

Gerrot only grins, his remaining teeth showing. Dawsyn bends to pick up three more twigs from their stash. She taps Gerrot's hand, and he collects three twigs, before bringing both of his own down on Dawsyn's, defeating her.

"All that to beat me on both hands, Gerrot? Really?"

Gerrot gives a husky breath of laughter and then bows his head in mock humility.

"Save it," Dawsyn says, thinking Gerrot is likely as obnoxious as the rest, without the advantage of having a tongue.

"Where is that damned mage?" Ryon appears suddenly, stalking amid the camp. His wings unfurl at the sound of his urgency. His arms are marked with shallow scratches, as though he'd blundered through the forest without regard for low-hanging branches.

"Easy there, Ry," Salem calls. "She's only gone to the Mecca." He squats before the fire, roasting pheasant on a poker.

Ryon, far from placated, rounds on him. "What?"

"She went early this morn," Salem adds, eyeing the hulking

man warily. "What's wrong with yeh, Ry? Put them fuckin' wings away."

"The Mecca?" Dawsyn says, standing. "Is that not dangerous?"

"In case yeh hadn't noticed, love, she can disguise herself bloody well."

"Salem, what has she gone to fetch?" Ryon presses, his voice darkening.

Salem shrugs. "I dunno, do I? Eggs, pork, a new pair o' boots? How in the blasted–"

"You didn't *ask* her?" Ryon growls.

"I don't ask tha' woman much of anythin', only that she don't turn me into a toad, thank yeh very much."

Ryon curses, turning back the way he came.

"I'm sure she'll return jus' as fast as she left, mother help us," Salem calls to his back, but Ryon only radiates frustration, leaving their camp with nothing more than a string of curses muttered to the breeze.

It is four days before Baltisse returns, and when she does, it's to find their band in various states of panic and disarray.

Dawsyn continues the tedious work of keeping herself occupied and diverted, as well as calm. She feels the iskra sleeping in its corner and sees that it remains unaroused.

It has been days since they made camp, here in the mage's wood, and the lack of activity is growing tiresome for many of them.

Tasheem, a vigorous creature by nature, paces the camp with increasing levels of annoyance through the afternoon.

"Fuck it!" Tasheem barks suddenly, breaking everyone out of their lethargic reveries. They watch her with varying degrees of shock as she marches to the mage's cabin and kicks in the door, quite unnecessarily.

The group looks at one another in confusion, all except

Ryon and Rivdan, who roll their eyes and grimace expectantly.

A clamour comes from within the cabin, and then Tasheem appears once again in its doorway, her arms wrapped around a dozen bottles of what appears to be wine. "I'm not sitting here idle another night unless I'm completely pickled."

"Tash," Rivdan starts. "I am not sure it is such a good–"

"A *brilliant* idea from the winged lady, I say!" Esra pipes up.

"Yeh tellin' me the mage's been hidin' me wine here all along?" Salem hollers.

Esra takes one from Tasheem's arms. "Hector, sweet boy! Come here and try some wine. I think you'll find it quite pleasing."

"*Esra*," Dawsyn warns. She remembers the effects liquor had on her not so many months before.

Hector approaches with something like benign curiosity, a lamb to slaughter.

"That drink will muddle you, Hector," Dawsyn calls to him, but it's too late. He takes the bottle that Esra uncorks and within moments, a third of the wine is gone.

Hector splutters, his nose wrinkled in disgust. A blush rises up his neck. "It is awful," he proclaims.

Tasheem laughs first, the sound muffled as she tries to hide it. Then Esra starts, his face a picture of shock. Slowly, the rest begin to chuckle as Hector gags, the cacophony growing.

At that moment, Ruby steps out of the brush with her arms full of kindling. She looks around at them all, confused, and then sees Hector. "Why does your face resemble an arse boil?" she asks dryly, and the rest fall into fits of unbridled laughter.

By the time the sun sets and the air cools, Esra has found a mandolin inside the cabin and brings it to the camp to play. Hector and Tasheem have their arms linked and are skipping circles around each other, and Gerrot is leading Ruby in some kind of folk dance. Rivdan has had two entire bottles of wine to himself and has fallen into a drunken sleep without drawing any attention to himself at all.

Esra passes the instrument to Salem, who plays with surprising skill and sings a hearty ballad about a woman who stole his shoes but won his heart. It makes Dawsyn throw her head back and laugh.

Esra spins Hector around the fire for a while, both as drunk as the other, but when Esra sees Dawsyn sitting alone he breaks away to coax her up. She has had her fair share of the wine and finds herself feeling pleasantly light – just the thing for a woman primed to combust. The liquor adles her, as it did months before in some godforsaken tavern. It loosens her limbs, makes each movement languid and unhurried.

With a bottle in one hand, Dawsyn allows Esra to lead her into a strange skip around the circle, following the silent instruction of Gerrot.

The more wine Dawsyn sips, the more frenetic the night becomes – a tangle of laughter and firelight and fast music. Her entire body hums. Not with magic or rage or lust, but with something else. Her cheeks hurt from grinning too widely, her belly from laughter, her feet from dancing, and yet none seem to pain her at all.

Ryon, who at first refused the offer of wine, eventually fell to the lure of its numbing bliss. He now offers his hand to Esra and leads him into a clumsy but exuberant turn about the fire while the rest clap out of time. Esra spins out of Ryon's arms, and both men pull another partner into the circle. On and on it goes, and Dawsyn finds herself pulled in to dance with Hector, with Ruby, and then, inevitably, with Ryon.

How he glows.

He takes up her hand and the small of her back and pulls her into a gallop, following the others around and around. Dawsyn has to grip him tightly to avoid losing her footing, and she does so without reserve, without inhibition. The wine has taken away her fear. All that's left is the blur of orange light as it whizzes by, the vastness of him surrounding her. His smell, his voice, the gentle way his hand clasps hers, and she thinks she'll never find another man, half-human or not, who will make her ache half as much as this.

"Did you say something?" Ryon asks her suddenly. But he is whisked away, pulled into the arms of Tasheem, while Dawsyn is spun into the clutches of Esra, and the dance continues.

They carry on for hours. Dawsyn dances with Ryon several more times, and with each turn she relaxes further, holds herself closer.

Eventually, the wine gone, Tasheem and Esra stumble away to collapse on softer ground. Hector throws up his share of the wine somewhere nearby in the forest. With a weary Gerrot alongside him, Salem begins to play a slower, sadder melody. Ruby continues to dance alone with a surprising amount of grace, despite her unfocussed stare.

It leaves Dawsyn to steal away under the cover of night, out to the forest, silver and beckoning. She trips and feels nothing but giddiness. A pleasant tilting of her vision.

"Dawsyn."

Ryon. Always Ryon. "I am all right."

"Where are you going? You'll become lost."

"Even better."

A curse, and then footfalls behind her, or perhaps beside her. It is difficult to tell. She continues on.

They trip over tree roots and become entangled in brambles. Ryon saves her from walking headfirst into a wide tree trunk, and it sends him into a stream of expletives while she chuckles.

"You lose all sense of preservation when you drink, girl."

"You seem preserved enough."

"Only because I can hold my own drink with more dignity."

Dawsyn looks up at him and tries to narrow her eyes. She has no idea whether it is effective. "I accept your challenge."

Ryon shakes his head. "I offered no challenge."

"I accept the inference of your challenge."

"I *inferred* no cha–"

"We will duel!" Dawsyn calls out, arms raised. "The winner will be forever deemed more dignified than the other."

"Well, the other will be dead," Ryon intones. "Not exactly a fair proclamation."

"Two will fight, only one will survive."

"And what of *weapons?* We have none."

"We'll use what nature gave us, hybrid. Our bare hands."

"Mother save me."

"Take your stance."

"I decline."

Dawsyn squares her feet. "Ready?"

"*No.*"

"Mind your mark."

"*Dawsyn,*" Ryon warns, exasperated.

"Fight!" With that, she lunges forward, her fist jutting out, caught easily by his hand.

"Dawsyn! Stop it."

But Dawsyn only strikes again, and again, each one blocked by Ryon who slowly works his way backward until his shoulders slam into the trunk of a willow. "Ow. *Fuck it!*"

Dawsyn swings a wayward fist again, but Ryon only pushes it wide, catching her as she spins and falls with her back to his front, where he binds her tightly with his arms. "Ha! Where to now, girl?"

She struggles, her mind too foggy to recall what move to make, what place to strike. She only writhes in his hold, a hysterical chuckle rumbling in her chest.

There's a smile in Ryon's voice too. It curls into her ear, so close. "I win."

"I'm not dead yet," Dawsyn reminds him.

"If it's all the same to you, I still win."

She laughs again, and ceases her pointless struggle. "Fine."

"A trick? If I let you go, will you pounce at me again?"

"The price you pay when you fight with honour, I'm afraid."

Ryon laughs and releases her, but only enough to allow her

to turn. Only enough that his arms might hold her, but not restrain.

Dawsyn looks up at him. She winds her fingers into his shirt. She rests her head against his chest to still the spinning in her head, but says nothing.

The silence is pregnant. Tangible.

"You love me," Ryon tells her. She wonders if she imagines it.

She sighs, the effects of the wine beginning to lessen, but not enough to silence her. Not enough to ice her over. "I'm afraid of you, too."

His hands tense against her back. "Because of what I am?"

"Because of what you could do to me." Dawsyn squeezes her eyes shut. The uncertainty is returning, the weight of mistrust.

With his mouth pressed to the top of her head, he exhales deeply, and the breath touches every follicle, sending shivers down her neck. "One day you won't be afraid, malishka. I'll await that day."

And before her sense returns, before she can remember why she shouldn't, she turns her face up to his, already so close that she can see the dark freckles beneath his eyes. She reaches her hand to the back of his neck and pulls his lips down to hers. When they touch, she feels drunk once more.

It is short, this kiss. She lays her hands on either side of his throat and lets the feel of his lips wash over her. With Ryon adoring her, revering her, it is hard to think of anything else. How simple it would be, to be lost in him.

He doesn't stop her from pulling away. He just watches her go with his jaw tense and his eyes ardent. She is already too far away when he turns and throws a fist into the tree trunk. She doesn't see it. She only hears its echo and the grunt that follows, reverberating through the woods, cutting her like a knife.

She thinks Ryon might be right. There is not enough distance in this valley to keep them from colliding.

CHAPTER FORTY-FIVE

At dawn, the camp is awoken by shouts.

Dawsyn hasn't slept. Instead, she spent the night contemplating the days ahead, wondering where the mage was, and when she would bother to return. She therefore has the pleasure of watching the entire spectacle unfold from a stump by the snuffed fire.

Hector, who was asleep and quite firmly entangled with Esra, stirs, his head rising from Esra's chest. He blinks wildly, eyes bloodshot, and when he spies his own limbs wrapped tightly around Esra's body, he jolts.

Hector lurches away, landing himself squarely in Salem's lap.

Salem howls, pushing Hector to the ground and curling in on himself, hands to his crotch. Hector mumbles an apology and tries to stand, but treads instead on Tasheem's hand. The female shrieks and suddenly there are wings unfurling, Rivdan is drawing a knife, Salem is still cursing from the ground, and Hector is in the middle, hands up in surrender.

The camp is full of panting, staggering, as all try to take stock of their surroundings. All except Dawsyn, who shakes her head at the lot of them, and Ryon, who never returned to camp after Dawsyn kissed him in the woods.

Other than the intermediate grunts of, "Me tackle!" from

Salem, everyone falls awkwardly quiet. Dawsyn has had the advantage of sobering through the night, drinking water, eating something, but the rest look as though a stiff wind might thwart them. Tasheem is shading her eyes with her hand, though the sun has only risen enough to bruise the sky purple. Ruby is cradling her head in her hands and moaning about needing pork grease. Gerrot wears the look of a man who has no idea of his surroundings, and Esra takes one bleary-eyed look around, and then retreats to unconsciousness again.

"Good day, everyone," says Dawsyn, smirking.

"Shut up," says Tasheem, her wings collapsing into her spine, her form sinking to the ground again.

"Sorry," Hector says to no one, to everyone.

Tasheem sniffs. "You shut up, too."

Dawsyn smiles, watching them return to their various states of uselessness.

"Where is Ryon?" Rivdan asks aloud, running a hand through his wild hair.

No one answers, not even Dawsyn. She imagines that he is just simply staying away from her. Perhaps he's grown tired of waiting for her to set her mind straight, to decide whether she'll deny them both forever, or give in.

With her current afflictions, something so trivial should hardly matter to her.

"Dawsyn?" Ruby asks, hauling herself upright. "Is there any water left?"

Dawsyn passes her a half-drained cup she'd meant for herself, and Ruby swallows it as though near death with thirst. "Is there any more?"

Dawsyn grins. "No. I'll fetch some."

"I'll come with you."

"You won't collapse?"

"I might," Ruby yawns. "But it will serve me right. I'll never trust Tasheem or Esra again."

"You and me both."

Dawsyn takes a barrel and leads Ruby away from the camp. There is a creek not far from Baltisse's home, and they'll hardly need to filter the water before it is ready to drink.

"I've rarely felt more sorry for myself. Mother above, my head is pounding."

Dawsyn's lips lift. "You're quite the dancer."

"I am?"

"I've never seen someone tumble over fire before."

"That explains the singed hair, then," Ruby remarks, running the ends of her braid through her fingers. "I learnt long ago not to drink like that, but it's hard to remember why when there's no example to set."

"You never drank with the other guards?" asks Dawsyn.

"No," Ruby admits, brushing aside branches. "I was their captain. And it wasn't worth the wrath of Their Majesties if they caught me without my wits."

This gives Dawsyn pause. "What was it like?" she asks now, her curiosity sincere. "To be at their service?"

Ruby seems to weigh her words for a moment before answering. "At first it was an honour, a privilege, even. I was raised on the fringe of the Mecca and my family had very little money, as you know. You also know they were devout to the monarchy. Here I was, their first-born, earning more than we'd ever seen, and regarded by the Queens themselves." The set of Ruby's mouth is grim. "I was proud. The Queen had proclaimed that I'd do great things and I was quickly promoted in rank. Before long I was the captain of an army, four hundred strong, and the men amongst them hated me for it."

"I do not doubt it," Dawsyn murmurs darkly.

"It was the Queens who set them straight," Ruby continues. "They imprisoned two men who tried to beat me to a pulp the night I was promoted. By the time they were released, the rogues were... well, they were no longer fit to fulfil their duties," Ruby mumbles. "After that I was merely the source of resentment, and they began to listen to me out of fear. In time, they came to respect me, but it was hard earnt, let me tell you. There were many I had to put on their backs to prove I was a worthy captain."

Dawsyn smirks. Men could be baser beings, only ceding to a show of dominance. "Good."

"I imagine you did much the same on the Ledge?"

Dawsyn shrugs. "I had no need for respect. I mostly just killed them, but it amounts to the same."

Ruby gives her a look that clearly says she does *not* think it amounts to the same at all. But Ruby has never lived on the Ledge. Death, and the threat of it, pervaded every breath they took.

"I revered the Queens. I didn't know then what I know now, of course. To me, they were regal, unshakeable, dauntless, the very picture of the woman I wanted to be. If they asked me to strike, I struck."

"But something changed?" Dawsyn asks, watching the former captain closely.

"Slowly, perhaps," she says. "So slowly, I barely noticed."

"We would all be cooked in slow-boiled water."

"Indeed," Ruby nods. "The first time I saw it, Queen Alvira ordered that I arrest any in the Mecca who grew their own produce without a permit to farm. I disagreed, of course. Debated with them. I thought of the families I knew on the fringe who relied on their tiny vegetable patches to supplement their pantries. But in the end, I walked out of the palace chambers with my head hanging, ready to order the guards to search every courtyard in the Mecca. I found myself doing things I was ashamed to admit to my mother and father when I would call on them. When I tried to reason with Queen Alvira, she somehow always managed to turn the conversation in her favour."

"She's manipulative," Dawsyn says.

"Masterfully so. It took a long time for me to see it."

They walk on silently for a few moments more. Dawsyn is

deep in thought, imagining what it must have taken to leave it all behind. The strength to start anew on the other side. "You may be one of the bravest souls I know," Dawsyn tells her.

It isn't soft when she says it. Dawsyn doesn't mean to comfort her with flattery. The words come out flat and unremarkable – a statement of fact.

But Ruby only shakes her head. "I merely seek penance. I hope I can balance some of the wrongs I've taken part in."

Dawsyn nods. "I know the feeling."

"Is that why you are so intent on saving your people?" Ruby asks. "To right your wrongs?"

Dawsyn deliberates. She has long wrestled with it. "It is... part of it," she says. "The other part is something less shallow. Something nobler. Or, at least, that is what I hope."

Ruby tilts her head. "And do you have a plan yet? To free the Ledge?"

Dawsyn sighs. What little idea she had has now been abolished. She cannot imagine returning to the Ledge without it descending into bedlam. And how will *she* fare in such a heightened state, with iskra that heeds the call of chaos and her mage blood waiting to choke it?

Perhaps it matters not. Perhaps she must go anyway, consequences be damned. "Not quite," she finally answers. "But it is not as simple as gaining their trust. After they've been carried from the Ledge, it still leaves the conundrum of finding a place to put them. A place where they won't be recaptured by the Queens." Dawsyn looks around, contemplative. "The woods here are our only option, but how long could they possibly go unnoticed?"

Ruby frowns, severe in her musings. "A good while, perhaps. But you're right. Eventually the Queens will get wind of it. We might continue to escape notice with our current small number, but a hundred or more?" Ruby shakes her head. "It cannot be kept secret for long."

"And then they'll come," Dawsyn says. "Or Adrik will."

"Have you considered bringing them into the Mecca?" Ruby asks then.

Dawsyn halts. The creek is ahead, still a few feet away. It is confusion that brings her up short. "*Into* the Mecca?" she repeats. "I might as well shepherd them to the gallows."

Ruby turns to Dawsyn. "Think about it. The people in the Mecca recognise you now. They know you escaped the Ledge and there has already been unrest. If you paraded into town with a hundred survivors, there'd be no way for the Queens to seize them all without causing a riot. Terrsaw would revolt."

"Would they?" Dawsyn asks dubiously. She imagines many would be too afraid.

Ruby smiles wryly. "You've still not had a chance to learn much of Terrsaw, Dawsyn," she says. "After the razing of the Fallen Village, when Terrsaw learnt about the Queen's bargain, people despaired. Some wanted to go to war with Alvira, but she was persuasive when she confronted them. She convinced the people that the damage was done, and now all could heal. My father always said he could feel the surrender amongst them. They relented. Not *immediately*, but they did. They fell under Alvira's rule, too frightened by the Glacians to do anything else, but that doesn't mean they didn't feel the burden of *guilt*." Ruby's eyes are alight. Dawsyn sees that this is a strength of hers. The art of strategy. "There is nary a citizen of Terrsaw who goes to sleep each night without shame in their heart. Perhaps they did nothing to stop her then, but they'll stop her now. I know it."

With that, Ruby walks onward, bending at the creek bed to cup water in her hands. She washes her face, then her arms, pushing back the sleeves of her guard's tunic, now stained and limp.

Dawsyn thinks over her words, wonders if there's some merit to them. She hasn't forgotten the sounds of unrest that seeped through the cracks of the castle walls and into her cell. She remembers how quickly they pushed back against the guards who sought to execute her.

"What of your soldiers?" Dawsyn asks, coming to stand beside Ruby on the bank. "What will they do when they see an escaped prisoner like me stroll through their city with an army of my people behind me?"

Ruby stands, her glossy skin dripping, and turns a menacing smile on Dawsyn. "Some will seek to capture you," she says simply. "But it will be nothing you can't handle. Besides, most are just like me Miss Sabar."

"And what are you?"

"Crippled by the blood debt of our Queen, and unwilling to pay the same dues twice." Ruby takes the barrel from Dawsyn and turns its lip to the water, filling it.

"You wouldn't be attempting to lead me straight into the dragon's lair, would you?"

Ruby straightens, her water sloshing heavily.

"Of course I am," is her reply. "How else are we to slay it?"

Dawsyn raises her eyebrows at her. "So, you wish to *slay* your Queen now? You're committed to the purest act of treason?"

Ruby sighs, turning away. She takes a moment to answer, her gaze distant, and Dawsyn thinks she detects a sliver of fear in her frown. A flicker of distress. "I fear there is no other end to all this," she says.

Dawsyn feels the heaviness of it – her betrayal to her Queens, the risk she poses to herself and her family.

Dawsyn takes up the other side of the barrel so they might carry it back to camp between them. "The word 'brave' doesn't do its duty in describing you," Dawsyn says simply, and then says no more.

They walk back slowly, the weight of the water dragging at their arms. The sweat running down Ruby's throat and the slump of her frame show the lingering effects of last night's liquor, and Dawsyn can't claim that she's any better off.

She hasn't slept. Her mind races. There is a restlessness in her chest she can only attribute to the plan Ruby has put before her. Try as she might, she cannot deny its cunning. The

Queens will never accept those on the Ledge, but could she force them to?

There's a thread of hope that weaves its way through her. A path opening in her mind. She can see Alvira's face, that wretched smile stretching reluctantly as her people rejoice. She can see the fear sliding down their throats as they swallow the orders they can no longer give, not with the Ledge people in their city, safe and revered. Not with all of Terrsaw celebrating their miraculous return. What are the Queens to do, alone in their contempt?

Dawsyn smiles to think of it – the satisfaction, the justice. Her hands tingle with iskra, the matter travelling along the thrill in her blood. Her hands grow cold.

Before she can act on it, tamp it down and hide it away, the glow in her mind expands, becomes a striking serpent.

As quickly as the iskra comes, it is thwarted.

The barrel falls heavily, overturning and flooding the dirt. Ruby shouts. Muddied water finds its way into Dawsyn's nose, her mouth; it sullies her hair, dampens her clothes. She feels none of it. All sight and sound and smell are overwhelmed by the grip of pain – a hand that tries to squeeze the air from her lungs, the food from her stomach, the blood from her veins. It clenches, tighter and tighter. Constricting.

She struggles to isolate them – the iskra and the mage magic, the light and the dark. One wraps so tightly around the other they coalesce. They burn in tandem.

Somewhere above there are voices shouting, calling her name, touching her. She recognises only one.

A hand sweeps over her forehead – ice cold. It is the only thing that her mind can grasp amid the heat of pain. It is a snowpack on burnt skin. A cold compress to quell an aching head. Even down here, in the depths of her agony, she can recognise this sweet relief.

Release me, the dark gasps.

Release us both, she thinks alongside it.

Suddenly, the pain disappears, as quickly as it came. The fist in her stomach relinquishes, and she feels her body wilt against the earth, just as it did in the clearing.

"Open your eyes, malishka."

Are they not already open? She swears she can see him, hovering over her, each inch of his face in vivid detail. She blinks, and the vision blurs, replaced by the harsh sunlight, the distortion of faces.

But she can smell him. She can feel his cool hand now warming against her neck. And when she shuts her eyes again, it is with the fatigue-hazed thought that she can sleep safely.

He'll not let her come to harm.

CHAPTER FORTY-SIX

Ryon hovers around Dawsyn.

Ruby has offered to relieve him, but he is busy wrestling with a snare of wild thought, and it won't let him think of rest or sustenance.

Dawsyn sleeps on Baltisse's mattress. Ryon has pulled a chair to her side, where he has remained since setting her down more than a few hours ago. Her eyelids don't flutter, her fingers don't give a single twitch. A dead sleep.

This iskra, this thing that contaminates her body, was not meant to be absorbed, and he should have known it. He should have considered it before leading Dawsyn on a quest into that fucking pool. He wishes he could see inside of her, find the magic defiling her and wrench it free. She's suffered enough.

She's suffered enough.

He swore he wouldn't see her suffer more.

His mind is a tempest, berating him. Condemning him. Suspicions roll together, catastrophising more and more the longer she sleeps. *Where is Baltisse? Why is she hiding? This will kill her, won't it?*

He can feel it. This will eventually kill the woman he loves. The only person who might help her has disappeared. But the worst of his suspicions, the niggling thought that troubles him most, is that Baltisse disappeared knowing that she cannot help at all.

The door to the cabin shudders as it is pushed inward, and Rivdan ducks through the opening.

"Rivdan?"

"Sorry to disturb you," he says in his quiet way. He must remain stooped to fit inside the cabin. Ryon imagines it's a source of vexation for someone so reticent to take up space.

"What is it?"

"I brought you some stew," he says, holding a tin cup aloft. "Has she woken? I can fetch more for her if–"

"No," Ryon mutters, taking the stew and turning back to Dawsyn. "Thank you."

Ryon says nothing more, expecting the man to leave, but if there is anyone who could tolerate silence, it is Rivdan.

"You are very fond of her," he remarks.

Ryon sighs. It is perhaps the most benign way to describe what he is. "I ought to be."

"Then you needn't worry for her, Mesrich."

"Why is that?"

Rivdan chuckles softly. "When we were young, you and Tash would hustle the rest of us out of our suppers. Do you remember?"

Ryon scoffs. "There was no hustling. You were foolish enough to bet against us."

"Yes. I remember when you placed your hand on the ground and bet that a dropped knife would fall between your fingers, and it wouldn't pierce your skin. I dropped that knife myself, and sure enough, it struck the space between your knuckles. You ate my broth right in front of me."

Ryon can't help but grin. "A fair victory."

"One of hundreds." Rivdan nods. "You always had a way of willing things to happen, Ryon. We used to call you *Gervalti*, do you remember?"

"Fortune from misfortune," Ryon murmurs, the meaning returning to him. "Yes, I remember."

"For such an unlucky hand dealt to you, you've always found luck where you looked, Mesrich. Your girl, Dawsyn, she will be all right if you wish it. I am sure."

Rivdan turns to leave, but before he can close the door behind him, Ryon speaks. "You're only recalling when the knife missed me, Rivdan," Ryon murmurs. "You've forgotten all the cuts my hand bore to begin with." Ryon rubs his eyes. He wishes everything were as simple as his will and the strength with which he compelled it. "It didn't always hit the ground."

Rivdan hesitates in the doorway but says nothing to argue. He isn't the type to offer false encouragement. Instead, he clicks the door shut, and Ryon hears his boots on the rough path, leaving him in peace.

A strand of Dawsyn's hair falls over her forehead and Ryon reaches to brush it away. There is a scar along her hairline. Another near her ear. A woman who shouldn't be alive, but has been too busy fighting to die.

Ryon cannot name what it is in her that ties him here – her wit, or her stubbornness, or her temper. The shape of her eyes, the feel of her skin. The way it feels when she looks at him. He suspects it's not one, but all of them. Mother knows, it would be easier for them both if they weren't so tethered.

Dawsyn's chest rises and falls evenly. Ryon frowns as the iskra creeps into her palms and then disappears, over and over. He drinks his watery stew, plays out a thousand different scenarios in his head, all doomed. He promises himself that if the mage does not return soon, he will find her.

He will find a way through this challenge. They all will.

When her hand frosts over again with the pool's magic, Ryon takes her palm in his. He studies her hand, smaller than his own. And when he interlocks their fingers, he expels a heavy breath.

"Stay the frost, malishka," he tells her softly.

Ryon does not leave the cabin until early the next morning when the call of nature makes it impossible for him to stay. He leaves the cabin to relieve himself. He finds water and boils it. The sun has only just begun to tinge the sky from ink blue to purple. Birds call across the valley, the sky beckoning them to take flight, and he feels that shared yearning along his spine and shoulders. His wings long to take him away from the fears he faces on the ground.

The shapes of sleeping bodies lie around the camp. The nights have been almost unbearably hot for the mixed-bloods amongst them, and it shows. Rivdan sleeps half naked and Tasheem is splayed out as though she's been drawn for quartering. Hector and Esra sleep alongside one another, the latter snoring soundly. Hector seems to have thrown one leg over Esra's lap, at which Ryon smiles.

He looks around for the rest, Salem, Ruby, and Gerrot, but they aren't here. Ryon has been the first to rise each morning since they made camp here, but perhaps the heat got the better of the others. They have likely taken to one stream or another to wash.

A few moments later, while Ryon stokes the flames of a weak fire, there is a faraway cry.

Swallows take flight all around, the sound of their wings replacing birdsong.

Ryon stands, his ears pricked. It was distant, the sound. He can't be sure it wasn't an animal. If it was one of their party, he isn't certain it was a call of distress. He waits, his muscles coiling with a deep, dark dread. The forest is eerily silent, and then...

Another cry.

Ryon runs. At the sound of his haste, some of the others wake, call to him.

He sprints in the direction of the sound, striding clear of gnarled roots and thickets. As he gains distance, other noises reach him. The sounds of steel, the panicked whinnying of a horse, more shouts, more voices. Salem's.

Ryon quickens.

Ahead is a wagon path. He can see the gravel through the gaps between trees. It is where the sound of the fray comes from. He can see the silver flash of steel colliding, hear the grunts of exertion.

His wings unfurl. In one heave, he swoops them down with enough force to strip the nearby branches of their leaves, and tears into the sky.

Below, on the road, Salem holds off two uniformed men – guards. Swords drawn, they slash and strike at Salem, who holds only a barrel between him and them, deflecting their blows and staggering backward. Gerrot lingers behind, hands empty. Not a single weapon between them.

Ryon plunges. He comes down on the guard who lingers behind – a coward, allowing his comrade to take the lead with two men and a barrel. His boots land on the guard's shoulders before he has the sense to look skyward. Ryon crushes him into the gravel, his full Glacian weight breaking the man instantly.

Ryon rights himself atop the dead soldier to see the remaining Terrsaw guard wrap his arm around Gerrot's neck. Gerrot claws at the guard's arm, but his fingers slip from the polished armour. The guard's sword presses tightly across Gerrot's torso.

"Ryon," Salem pants, swaying as he drops the barrel. "Thank the fuckin' Mother."

But the guard is shuffling backward with Gerrot. Ryon can see blood blooming beneath the old man's tunic as the guard stumbles. Beneath the helm, the stranger's eyes shine with terror. "Stay back!" the man spits, panting heavily.

"Who sent you?" Ryon demands, advancing slowly.

"H-Her Majesty," he says. "The Queen. *Stay back, I say!*"

Gerrot lets out a strangled whimper, and Ryon halts, holding his hands up. Gerrot's watery eyes plead with Ryon. Beg of him. How many times did he pass by this human in the Glacian palace, unable to help him? "Let the man go."

"Leave, beast!" the guard shouts. "Now!"

"Let my friend go," Ryon bids carefully, watching as the blood drips from Gerrot's shirt. "And you can go back to your Queen. You can tell her you found yourself a Glacian in the woods."

The guard retreats further, pulling Gerrot with him. "Y-you'll kill me."

"I won't," Ryon says firmly. "You have my word."

Hesitation. But a Terrsaw guard will never take the word of a Glacian. "It is *him* that I want," he says, nodding to Salem. "He is a wanted man."

Ryon gives the soldier some credit for his boldness, but there will be no negotiation, and Ryon does not take his eyes off him. "Do you have a family, soldier? Someone you love?"

A flicker of contempt. "A woman."

"A good woman you'll never see again if you act rashly today," Ryon tells him slowly. "You can go back home to her tonight. Tell her the tale of how you escaped a Glacian today. Give your knowledge to your Queen. Let her hail you a hero."

Gerrot whimpers again, his wide eyes imploring Ryon. Eyes that have seen each version of this world and still manage to be gentle.

"Let him go," Ryon begs. "And I'll let *you* go in kind."

The guard errs. His sword eases an inch, though his grip on Gerrot's neck remains. "How can I be sure?"

"You can't. I can only swear that I have no desire to kill you now." Ryon marks the guard's feet angling away, desperate to flee. "But if you kill this man, I will hunt you to the darkest corners of this world and rip you apart."

The guard hesitates again, his armour clanking awkwardly. He looks away, down the road, and then back to Ryon. "Get me my horse."

"Salem?" Ryon calls.

Salem makes a noise of assent, his stare not leaving the guard's. He walks slowly to the side of the road, where a horse trots restlessly in place, its reins ensnared in the bushes.

"You'll have your horse," Ryon addresses the guard. "You'll release our friend and be on your way."

"You won't follow?" the guard asks, and Ryon hears the immaturity in his voice. He wonders if the guard is any more than a boy.

"I'll have no need," Ryon says placatingly. "Unless you give me one."

The guard hesitates a moment longer, then, blissfully, mercifully, he nods, just once. His grip on Gerrot relaxes by degrees.

A clamour from the woods. Tasheem, Rivdan, and Dawsyn come hurtling onto the road, the Glacians with wings extended.

The Terrsaw guard shouts.

Dawsyn lifts her ax.

The horse bucks.

And the sword against Gerrot's belly plunges.

Gerrot topples.

"*No!*" Ryon shouts, already running.

The ax flies end over end, swooping through the air, racing Ryon to the guard. Ryon catches the ax handle mid-air as it passes in front of him. Then, he lunges.

When Ryon collides with the guard, he wedges the ax deeply into his exposed neck. The other hand is mashed against the Terrsaw steel, splitting the skin of his palm.

The guard chokes, his mouth seeping with blood so dark it looks like tar. "R... r–" he stutters, so softly that Ryon can only make out the shape of the word.

"Ru... by," he mouths, the name a silent call into the ether. "Ruby."

The guard's body becomes slack in Ryon's hold, staring unblinkingly into the sun.

"Fuck," Ryon whispers down at him. "*Fuck!*"

But there is another sound brewing, and it drags his attention away from the blood on his hands, the body beneath him. The sound of wind, of a great inhaling. As though the oxygen were being pulled from the trees and lungs and the very pores of the earth.

Ryon turns quickly to see Dawsyn, standing over Gerrot's still form.

And she is a vision of cold, endless wrath.

Chapter Forty-Seven

Gerrot is dead.

A man taken from his home and returned, only to die, here on this road, at the hands of his own kingdom.

His lined face, still kind even in death, is eternally still, his soul now in the hands of the Mother. Finally free of a world that did all it could to grind him down.

Unhinged, unfettered rage. She can't dispel it. It seeps from her heart and into every fibre of her. The iskra imbues it, solidifies it. She knows her hands glow without needing to look at them. She takes a breath and feels the way her lungs fill with air from every corner of this world, and the worlds beyond.

And when the breath in her lungs and the heat in her head will no longer be contained, she screws up her eyes, obliterates the image of Gerrot splayed on the dirt, and lets everything out.

Her wrath and hate and shock.

Her love.

Her weaknesses.

Her exhaustion.

She releases it back to the earth, the sky. She lets her knees fall to the ground, and braces her hands against the gravel, her own unbroken bellow ringing in her ears.

The ground around her goes cold, the magic finding its way into the dirt and seeping outward. It doesn't retreat until her lungs are empty, her throat desiccated. She pants as it crawls back into her hands, back through her blood.

When Ryon's hands grip her shoulders, she feels their trembling. His voice shakes too, calling her name and coaxing her to look at him.

She opens her eyes. The planes of his face are a reprieve. A place to rest.

"Dawsyn!"

"I can hear you," she pants, surprised to hear how much her voice wavers, how raspy she sounds.

"We need to go. Now. There could be more coming."

She nods. "Yes."

"What was that?" Ryon asks, piercing her with his stare. It is all she sees.

"What was…?"

"What did you do?" Ryon says again, pulling her to her feet carefully.

"I…" Dawsyn starts. But she doesn't know how to go on. She suddenly remembers the Ledge, and the way her outburst had killed Des Polson. "Did I hurt–?"

"No. No one is hurt," Ryon tells her, huddling her closer to him as he strides her away. "You only scared the Holy Mother out of us all."

Dawsyn's sense finally returns at his words, her chest tightening. As Ryon tries to hurry her off the road, she looks back over her shoulder.

On the ground before Gerrot is a web of white, frozen earth, spreading like veins from the spot where she must have knelt. The trees on either side of the road look as though they were bent by ungodly winds, their branches stripped of foliage and near breaking.

Did she do that?

"Gerrot…" she begins, but doesn't know how to finish.

Ryon sweeps her back through the woods, the others running alongside them, all wearing looks of shock and confusion.

"Ryon... the magic–"

"No," Ryon says sharply. "No more of this." And though it is low, Dawsyn thinks she hears him mutter Baltisse's name, along with a string of threats.

Her body feels empty, and she wants to rest. But the magic has not debilitated her. The mage blood did not rise, provoked by the upsurgence of the iskra. Her muscles are sore, but they can keep going. She feels tired, but not spent. She is muddled, but not buckled and bent by the after-effects of using opposing magics that should not be able to coexist.

It makes no sense.

"Has anyone seen the captain?" Ryon calls over his shoulder, his feet pounding over the soil.

"No!" Tasheem calls. "She wasn't at camp. We expected to find her with you."

Ryon's head turns. "Salem?" he asks.

"She weren't with us," he replies, hurrying to keep pace.

Dawsyn's head spins. Nothing makes sense.

She'd awoken in the cabin with cold hands and knew that Ryon must be gone. The absence of his warmth is what stirred her. Then there were the sounds of commotion – something dropped, Ryon's name, the sound of boots hurrying away, more following.

She'd rolled off the mattress, found her ax on Baltisse's wooden table, and thrown herself out into the morning air.

And then the guard...

And then Gerrot...

"There they are!" Hector calls as they thrash their way back into camp. There's a circle in the dirt where he and Esra have paced.

"Is Ruby here?" Ryon asks at once. Rivdan doesn't await an answer. He strides around camp, looking to the ground for tracks. The ground here is too dry; it will not reveal Ruby's whereabouts to them.

"She might've wandered off to the creek," Salem mutters. "Why the sudden concern?"

An excellent question. Dawsyn turns to Ryon. "You think–"

"I don't know what I think yet," Ryon cuts in. There is a warning in his eyes.

"Fuck me, Salem darling," Esra interjects. "You're looking a touch worse for the wear. Though it seems to be your vintage."

"He was just attacked by Terrsaw guards, Esra. You'll forgive him this once," Ryon states.

A beat of silence, and then. "MOTHER OF ALL FUCKING–"

"Wait, Esra," Hector says, gripping him by the shoulder. He seems to have noticed what Esra has failed to. "Where is Gerrot?"

The silence that follows this most awful of inquiries is hollow. Deadening. Rivdan's head drops to his chest. Tasheem shuffles uncomfortably.

Dawsyn looks Hector in the eye. She watches him find the answer himself. "Dead," she voices finally. "He's dead."

Minutes stretch and no one speaks. Dawsyn is thankful for it. Tasheem seems on the cusp of saying something consoling but stops herself. Instead, they each remain suspended in a state of disbelief.

Dawsyn doesn't want sorrow and grief. She wants anger. She wants action. She wants someone to pay.

Ryon is the only body not frozen in the upheaval. He paces in small circuits, the muscles beneath his clothes bunching with agitation. "What were those guards doing on the road? So near?"

"They were hidin' behind the treeline," Salem says. "On the far side. Gerrot and I woke early. Thought we'd go foragin'. We stepped out onto the road, and they…"

Ryon curses. "As though they were waiting for someone. Any one of us."

"But how did they know where to be?" Dawsyn asks. "Baltisse said that–"

"That this part of the wood is protected from outsiders," comes an unexpected voice. "Yes. I did say that."

Dawsyn turns.

There stands Baltisse where before she had not. She looks haggard, her long, normally lustrous hair tangled. Her posture slumps.

No one says a word at first, and then–

"Are you well, mage?" Ryon asks. Fair words, bridling with outrage. Dawsyn sees the way his hands tremble.

Baltisse cracks her neck, groaning at the relief. "Hush, Ryon. Your mind is gratingly loud," she says. "I've been better, to be honest. But I'll live."

"I'm much relieved." Ryon sneers. "Now will you deign to tell us where the fuck you've been?"

"Watch your tone."

"Baltisse, I *promise you*–"

"*Enough!*" Dawsyn hisses. Placing a hand on Ryon's chest as he advances. "We have matters more pressing."

"I seem to have missed quite a lot," Baltisse says slowly, her eyes piercing Ryon's. Whatever Ryon shows her, it makes her pale.

"Yes," Ryon says icily. "You have."

The pregnant silence that follows stretches until it is interrupted by Esra, who says, "Baltisse? When you have a moment, I have a very peculiar rash that I need tending–"

"Gerrot is gone?" Baltisse asks, her stare on Dawsyn, who nods.

"The Terrsaw guards," Baltisse says, eyes distant. "They seem to be all over the valley, crawling into every hole they can find, searching. The forests included. It's likely a coincidence that you came across two."

Ryon scrubs his face wearily. "I doubt it."

"Where is Ruby? Surely she may shed some light–"

"The captain is missing," Ryon says loudly. "And I think I know where she has gone."

Dawsyn blanches. Her fingers turn cold. "No."

"The Queens," Ryon states, his voice firm and sure.

"What?" Tasheem blurts.

Salem scowls. "Yeh think she's bolted?"

"When was it that any of us last saw her?" Ryon asks, turning to Tasheem and Rivdan, to Salem, Esra, and Hector.

For a moment, they all stand uselessly, staring back at one another.

"I don't remember seein' her las' night," Salem mentions. "Though she tends to sleep away from me. I though' she were with yeh, Ryon."

"I was with Dawsyn in the cabin as she recovered," Ryon says. "She wasn't there."

At the mention of Dawsyn's recovery, Baltisse pales.

"Ruby ate supper with us," Hector says. "I think she went into the forest to wash while there was still light in the day."

"And she didn't return?"

"I fell asleep," Hector shrugs. "I think we all did."

"Plenty of time to find her way back to the Mecca. Especially if she ran into a friend," Baltisse says, her tone black.

Tasheem curses. "You think she turned traitor? She sent those guards out here to find us?"

"No," Dawsyn says again, though she is the only one.

"The guard on the road," Ryon starts, his eyes on Dawsyn. "The one that killed Gerrot. He said Ruby's name."

Dawsyn feels suddenly and painfully empty, as though a hand reached inside her and scraped a well in her stomach, hollowing her out. She remembers holding her ax to Ruby's throat, remembers warring with indecision. She had been sure it would be a mistake to trust her. But Dawsyn had come to know her better, come to think of her as a friend. Dawsyn had even thought her noble, brave, if a little lost... like herself.

More likely, it was only what she had led Dawsyn to believe, to quell Dawsyn's concern that the woman might be exactly what she appeared.

"After all of it," Dawsyn says, so quietly that Ryon comes closer to hear her. "She was a fucking traitor anyway?"

How stupidly obvious. So very insultingly plain.

"I heard nothing traitorous on her mind," Baltisse argues, shaking her head.

"That trick has holes, Baltisse, and Ruby knew of them," Ryon mutters.

But Dawsyn shakes her head. "No."

"Dawsyn..." Ryon begins, his tone placating.

"No," Dawsyn says, firmer this time. "No. If she ran back to her Queens, there would be an army here to hunt us. Not a pair of guards and their horse."

"Where has she gone, then? If not back to the Mecca?" Esra asks.

Dawsyn approaches the mage. "You said that the entire guard was searching the valley?"

"Like cockroaches." Baltisse nods. "They're everywhere."

Dawsyn chews on her tongue. She cannot swallow the idea of Ruby as a spy. She helped Dawsyn escape. Ryon, too. She could have left in a thousand different moments before now. It makes no sense. "She may have been found last night when she left camp. Detained."

"She's a Terrsaw fucking captain!" Tasheem spits, hurling a stone into the woods in her frustration. "We should have dropped her into the Chasm."

"No," Dawsyn says once more. "She hasn't betrayed us."

"Lass is fuckin' smart, I'll give her tha'," Salem groans. "Convincin' like. Even *I* had begun to believe her."

"*She hasn't betrayed us,*" Dawsyn repeats again.

Rivdan's voice is even, stern. "What matters," he says, "is whether we are still safe here, with dead guards on the road nearby, and an entire army searching."

"How could they know we're in the valley?" Dawsyn mutters, her gaze distant.

Ryon catches her eye. He says silently what the rest are clearly convinced of: *Ruby.*

But Dawsyn shakes her head. She won't believe it so easily. She can't.

"The spells I cast around this clearing merely obscure us in shadow," Baltisse says. "Shadows are easy to walk through. We are not in plain sight, and there won't be any clues to lead the guards here, but we can quite easily be stumbled upon if they look hard enough."

"So then, time is against us," Ryon proclaims.

Tasheem's wings extend, vibrating with agitation. "If you've got a plan to save your Ledge people, Dawsyn, you'd best share it now. It'll be awful hard to save them wearing chains."

Baltisse clicks her tongue. "If you think the Queens will let us live, you have more faith than you ought to. If we're caught, it means death."

Dawsyn laughs at that. It is without a trace of humour, just cold, dead certainty. It roots everyone in their place. It calls their attention, sends a shiver scuttling across their skin. "Kill us? Mixed-bloods? Ledge prisoners? A mage?" Blood pounds behind her eyes. "*If* they catch us," she says, eyes glinting. "Death will be *theirs.*"

CHAPTER FORTY-EIGHT

The road beneath the wagon becomes more forgiving with time. Still, Ruby winces at each bump. If she had to guess – and she must, for the wagon bed is enclosed and the slats press too tightly to see through – she'd guess they were passing through the fringe of the Mecca. The wagon bounces precariously over potholes, but this part of the road is well travelled, smoother. A welcome relief.

The captain's mind clangs against her skull incessantly. She hadn't realised the distance between Baltisse's patch of forest and the Mecca, but it has been hours in this wagon that smells like urine and horse shit. She is tired. Desperate to arrive and be done with the indignity.

Soon after, the horses are called to halt. They whinny and clip their hooves on the cobblestones. There are shouts, orders given by voices she recognises. The clanging of iron keys, and then brilliant sunlight. She raises her hands to shade her eyes.

Ruby scoots her much-abused backside to the opening of the wagon hold, cursing the Mother for the damage to her tailbone and the cramping in her legs. Hands take hold of her forearms. They bring her to standing.

"Good morrow, Captain," says a voice. And when Ruby finally manages to blink the white light from her eyes, she sees the Queens, Alvira and Cressida, before her. They stand on the palace steps in their royal garb, despite the lack of spectators.

"Your Majesties," she answers, bowing. They appear delighted, jubilant even.

"But where are your weapons, Captain? Your armour?"

"It's been an unusually hot season," Ruby answers. "And I couldn't tell you where my sword is."

"Well," says Queen Alvira, descending the steps to Ruby's level. "I'm glad to see you." Her smile is brilliant. Promising.

Ruby smiles back, the bleakness of these circumstances notwithstanding. "I'm afraid, Your Grace, I cannot say the same."

Alvira gives a small huff of laughter and taps the irons on Ruby's wrists once. "To the keep, if you please," she says to the guards at her shoulders, and then to Ruby, "I'm sure you recall how these things go."

The lump on Ruby's temple continues to drum its obstinate beat, but despite it, Ruby keeps a straight spine. She will not squat on the floor of this stone cell with defeat in her posture. She was once their captain, after all.

Two guards stand at the keep entrance, guarding the gate. She must look unrecognisable to them. Her dark hair is matted in places. She smells of sweat and smoke. Without her armour, she looks like a peasant.

The discomfort of her wardens is obvious. She trained them when there was no hair on their chests or chins. Now they avert their gaze. They say nothing to one another. When Ruby asks them for water they flinch, hesitate.

Scared. Ruby thinks. *This whole kingdom runs on fear.*

She leaves them be. Her grievance is not with them.

When she was seventeen, Ruby guarded this keep while a cell full of drunken louts bleated and bellowed about corruption in the palace. They'd fumbled a half-cocked plan to storm the castle after spending what little coin they had on whiskey. Their army of a dozen hadn't even breached the gate.

That night had dragged endlessly. The insults were constant. But past the anger, there were accusations.

Took me only son! Me only son, a soldier at thirteen!

Doubled the taxes? As if they weren't high enough!

Sabar would turn in his grave, rest his soul.

A permit for a tomato bushel and some potatoes? A fucking permit, they ask of us!

It was difficult to hear under the name-calling, the slurs, the cursing. The noise of hatred always dilutes injustice, makes it too easy to disregard, but she still heard it.

It might bring her some small relief to shriek the way those drunken aggressors had. She could bellow about fear and all the ways it bends integrity, and the two poor lads at the gate would be forced to listen. They might even believe her, sympathise with her. But then they'd wake up tomorrow, don their uniforms and carry out their scheduled duties, chained to the commands of their Queen whether they sympathise or not.

Footsteps echo down into the dungeon, glancing off the stone walls. Someone is descending the stairs. The guards straighten.

The sound disappears, and then a voice rings out. "Leave us."

"But... Your Grace–"

"*Now*, if you please," the voice says.

"She might be dangerous, Your Grace."

"Who? Young Ruby?" it says, coming closer to the keep entrance. Queen Cressida suddenly strides from between the guards and through the open gate, making the men jump to the side to avoid touching her, such would be their bad luck. Cressida comes down the row of cells to the very last, where Ruby is caged. "She wouldn't dream of harming one of her Queens, would you, Captain?"

Her instinct is to nod her head, to lower her gaze. But she thinks of Dawsyn sitting in this very cell, undaunted, and lifts her chin instead. For the first time, she lets her eyes sweep the length of Cressida, lingering over her silver hair, the jewels resting on her bosom. "I doubt I'll get the opportunity," she says icily.

Cressida's head snaps to the guards. "I said, *leave!*"

The men shuffle away at once, the clatter of their armour dissolving slowly. And when it is silent once more, Cressida turns her glare back on Ruby.

Cressida, the largely disliked Queen of Terrsaw with a stare more cutting than a carving knife. *Too bitter for a Glacian to eat*, the people say, and her scrunched nose often gives weight to it. Her lips press together as though an unpleasant taste lingers there, and so a perimeter of deep lines encircle her mouth. Ruby knows that Alvira rarely allows her to leave the palace. Cressida is, and always has been, harmful to the palace's image.

Ruby, however, is not so easily fooled by a scowl. The woman has far more wit and perception than most.

"My dear wife will join us shortly," Cressida says now. "I wanted the chance to speak with you myself first."

Ruby only waits. She knows what lies before her, and it isn't mere conversation. Torture, then starvation, then the gallows.

Torture is the most efficient way to find answers. Starvation is effective, but not as swift; best to test a prisoner's grit first. Death is salvation, in the end. Ruby should know, she's seen it enough times.

"Why did you do it?" Cressida demands. "Why did you run away with that half-breed and the Sabar girl?"

It's not the question Ruby is expecting. She deflects it. "How did you find out what became of me?" she asks in kind.

"Ah." Cressida nods. "You are *very* clever. Those guards chased their sorry tails right back to the Mecca, heaving and hailing about how you'd been taken, which we all believed, of course."

"And yet here I am."

"Here you are," Cressida agrees. Her frown deepens.

"Fortunately, we are acquainted with a new friend in Glacia. I believe his name is Adrik."

Ruby's stomach tightens painfully.

"He got word to us that you'd paid him a visit. We're working toward a new truce agreement, you see. It was a show of good faith. He mentioned you had all taken your leave rather unexpectedly."

Ruby's fingers flex and clench restlessly, but she remains silent.

"I answered your question," Cressida says, her tone darker now. Gone is the lilting titter, that infuriating tenor of superiority. In its place is a voice that Ruby has rarely heard her use. Careful, quiet. "You'll answer mine."

Ruby does not allow her eyes to trail away from the older woman's. "You ask me why I followed a girl up a mountain, like the thought is impossible, but that's not what I did," she says, her upper lip curling into a sneer. "First, I looked around the kingdom and saw its monuments and shrines. Then I heard the voices of its people, crying and begging for the mercy of just one of their own. I followed the last living Sabar to the Ledge, and I saw for myself its people, *our* people," Ruby impresses, "and the hell we have condemned them to. I went to find those we trapped like animals across the Chasm, and you ask me why?" The captain laughs bitterly, acidly. "What queen sees a bid for her people's salvation and asks *why?*"

Cressida says nothing. Those lines etched around her mouth deepen.

"Only a self-serving one," Ruby answers for her. "A cruel one."

For a moment Cressida is still and quiet, her jaw tensing. "You wish to free the Ledge too, Captain?"

"It is well past time that we do," Ruby replies.

"And the Glacians? What of them?"

"I've met a few on my journey. Most are not a threat to us."

"And those that are?"

Ruby laughs again. "You fucking coward."

Cressida shows no outward reaction to her mockery. "So you'd start a war with them, Ruby? A brave soldier and her guards against the wings and talons of a Glacian horde. How many of ours would die, do you suppose?"

Ruby's head falls back as she sighs. Weariness suddenly overwhelms her. She is so tired of speaking in circles with those who don't want to listen. "Admit your truest concern, Cressida. We both know you care very little for the lives lost in war. There are plenty of boys and girls who will sleep tonight and wake up as men and women in the morning, as so deemed by your wife. A guard's role is easily replenished, but... so is a *Queen's*." Here, Ruby stops. Watches. "That's the true fear within you, isn't it? How long have you carried it around? Quite a burden that crown must be, knowing it might be snatched away just as easily as it was won. I didn't always see that. I didn't always see the fear you guard. It must make one considerably bitter."

Cressida's eyes flash. "Quite," she says. Her mouth is so taut Ruby wonders how the word finds its way out.

A stretch of silence follows, and Ruby is determined not to fill it. She wants to hear Cressida speak the words, admit her purest intentions.

Instead, the Queen turns away, eyes suddenly distant. The volume of her skirts whispers against the grate. "I didn't seek it, Captain."

Ruby frowns, stares at Cressida's back. "Seek what?"

"Power," she returns, not bothering to face her. "I had very little interest in it when I was young."

Ruby hesitates, guessing that Her Majesty must be lying, though something about her posture, the deadened quality of her voice, seems... genuine. "Then what–"

"I worshipped *her*," Cressida says, her breath suddenly, unexpectedly uneven. "I would have followed Alvira anywhere. But there's a strange curse that comes with power."

She sighs. "The one who has it becomes nothing without it."
Slowly, the woman turns just enough to glance back over her
shoulder, meeting Ruby's glare.

An old woman who'd never sought power and won it.

A young woman who'd earnt hers and thrown it away.

"Her Majesty is determined to find Dawsyn Sabar and her
gang of sycophants. If you were practical, you'd part with
names and whereabouts swiftly."

"If I were *practical*, I would have made myself deaf and dumb
a long time ago," Ruby mutters.

Cressida's eyes become piercing. "Two guards were killed
yesterday, on a wagon trail to the North. I'd imagine your new
friends aren't far away."

Ruby freezes in the act of turning, but her pulse races on.

"Young Leeson. Such a pity to lose him. And I believe you
knew the other boy quite well also…"

Ruby swallows.

"Brockner was his name. Will Brockner."

For a moment, Ruby remains rigid, the name sliding through
her like frigid water. It puts a tremor in her hands, shrivels her
lungs, makes it difficult to draw breath.

"I'm told you were quite fond of him."

"Fuck you," Ruby spits, but the words are breathy, weak.

The Queen sighs again. World-weary. Tired. "She'll kill you,
Captain," she says, and her tone is neither bitter nor glad.

Of course, she will. Ruby is no fool. "I am sure she'll do
quite a bit more besides."

CHAPTER FORTY-NINE

"Where are you going?" Ryon says suddenly.

Dawsyn turns. She was making her way back into the forest. She cannot leave Gerrot on the road. She wants to go back for the body herself. She expects Ryon's eyes to be bearing down on her, but he isn't addressing her at all. He looks instead to Baltisse, her body turned in the opposite direction.

"To fetch something." The mage sneers.

"No," Ryon says abruptly. "Not a fucking chance."

The mage's eyes become bottled storms. Unspoken words pass between them. Whatever is said, it causes a tick to jump along Ryon's stubbled jaw.

Baltisse grits her teeth. "*Soon*, Glacian."

"No," Ryon says again, this time with finality. "Now." He strides across the camp to her with all the intent of a wild predator.

"Ryon? What do yeh think yer doin?" Salem asks. But Ryon ignores him, taking Baltisse by the wrist and pulling her back.

"Are you crazy?" Esra gasps. "Unhand her, Ryon! Baltisse! Blow up this man's arse!"

"Leave it, Es," Baltisse mutters in a bored voice, but she does wrench her hand free. "*All right, Ryon.* All right. Calm yourself."

Dawsyn frowns at them, Ryon leading Baltisse to her cabin, ushering her inside.

Dawsyn shrugs. She turns on her heel, making to leave.

"You too, Dawsyn," Ryon says, all but pushing the mage into her own home. "Come."

Dawsyn narrows her eyes.

"*Please*," he says emphatically, his fist clenching with barely suppressed rage. He makes a particularly derisive sweeping gesture, as though she were a queen being welcomed.

Within the cabin, Baltisse divests herself of her travelling cloak, letting the material pool on the table. She sits with a deep, expectant exhale, and lifts her chin to Ryon. "Well," she says to him. "You may as well say what's on your mind and get it out of the way, Ryon. If you wish to whine at me, it will be much more relieving to do it aloud. Then perhaps we can move on to all the important things."

Dawsyn feels like an outsider, a mere audience to their dispute. She crosses her arms and waits.

"Where have you been, Baltisse?" Ryon's tone is quiet, but something wild stirs beneath the façade of calm. Dawsyn is not surprised to hear it. Blood still mats the hair on his arms. His face is speckled with it.

"Do you really have such a poor opinion of me, Ryon, after everything?" is the mage's only reply.

"Two more attacks since you left, Baltisse. *Two*."

Me. Dawsyn thinks. *They're speaking of me.*

"She's getting worse. I – We watched her drop like a stone, screaming, shaking..." His voice tapers off a little. He regains his composure. "You are the only one who could help her, and you *disappeared*. Took a trip to the Mecca? Where the fuck were you?"

"Well, Ryon, despite your assumptions, I did in fact leave with Dawsyn's predicament in mind."

"*Predicament?*"

"Hush," Baltisse says sharply. Dawsyn watches as she leisurely crosses her legs at the knee, much more at ease than the last time the three of them stood in this cabin, speaking of Dawsyn's imminent death. "I went for *help*, Ryon. There's a... woman of magic. She might be able to help us understand Dawsyn. Help her overcome the resistance she experiences."

"And this took you days to accomplish?" Ryon sneers. "Finding this woman?"

"Finding her wasn't so difficult, though she *was* well hidden. Convincing her to follow me here, however, was another matter entirely. It took more time than I'd hoped."

Ryon walks in a circle, the air thick with his irritation. He mutters to himself, hits the door with his fists, and then abruptly turns to face them, his finger pointed at the mage. "You will tell her now," he says. "I've given you enough chances to do so."

Dread slides down Dawsyn's spine, all the way to her heels.

A secret, of course.

A secret she is not party to. One that Ryon has kept from her. Again.

"Tell me what?" Dawsyn asks darkly.

"Don't throw your anger at me just yet," Ryon tells her, voice hoarse. "It was not my story to tell."

"A story?" Dawsyn repeats, her teeth gritted. She turns toward Baltisse. "How nice. Do tell it, witch."

"And leave our guest out in the forest, waiting to be introduced?" Baltisse asks, and Dawsyn notices the shift in the mage's expression, the evasiveness of her tone.

Her suspicions darken further. "Why the delay, mage?" she asks, the words pinning the woman in place. "Surely this secret is not more terrible than the ones you've already revealed."

"I believe she delays," Ryon offers, a thread of dark, deadly warning in his tone, "to avoid your... reaction."

The mage's chin lifts, and she looks directly to Dawsyn, ignoring Ryon altogether. "Fine," she relents. "The story first, then. Though I'd have preferred to live another century never telling it again."

Dawsyn sits. An unnameable weight is settling on her,

threatening the bone and muscle and will that she is made of. "If I must know it," she says, "then your preference is no fucking concern of mine."

Baltisse's shoulders curve inward, as though she feels the weight too, and then, "Have you ever wondered where the Pool of Iskra came from?"

Dawsyn does not respond. Of course she has wondered. She waits for Baltisse to continue, growing impatient.

"Centuries ago, long before histories were written, the King of this valley was an ordinary man… his name was Vasteel."

Dawsyn blanches. Her head swings to Ryon. "That can't be," she asks of him, but Ryon is nodding.

"It was," Baltisse remarks. "Vasteel was rather different to the monarchs who preceded him – kings who admonished anything that threatened their power, namely, the existence of mages." Here Baltisse's eyes whirl viciously. "But Vasteel saw the way mage power could become useful to him. Far from having us hunted, he welcomed us into the fold of his advisors, and treated us like nobility. Me, two others by the names of Roznier and Grigori, and my mother, Indriss." Baltisse pauses, as though the name brings with it a bad taste. Dawsyn recalls the last time the mage spoke of her mother, this *Indriss*. Her demeanour had lacked tenderness then as well.

"Vasteel wanted small things from us at first, and we gladly gave it. Good weather. Healthy crops. Quite a task for just one mage, but there were four of us and we were strong. We practised our magic daily, free from the aspersions of the public. We grew stronger. We became cocky, I think. We thought ourselves indestructible. But the laws of magic have always been the same: you do not ask for more than what nature will readily give, or you will invite destruction.

"But we were free, you see? For the first time in our lives, we could wield the kind of power we'd been forced to hide. It was… intoxicating." Baltisse's lips turn down. "So intoxicating that when King Vasteel asked for more, we barely thought it through before we complied. Perhaps just to find out if we *could* do it, if we could achieve such sorcery, such *control*. My mother was fixated. She began to think of magic as something to be leashed and unleashed. To be bidden and unbidden. But magic has never behaved that way. It is intuitive. It has its own will. It knows its own bounds.

"Vasteel was fascinated with the life span of a mage. We are not *immortal*, of course. But we barely age. So when he bade us to make him immortal, I was unsurprised. What else could a man want when he already has power, wealth, an adoring populace?" Baltisse scoffs weakly. "There is nothing else, but *more* of it – an endless, bottomless supply. Vasteel asked for an eternity."

Dawsyn's teeth clamp so tightly they ache. She has begun to piece together the finer details of this story, the path that leads to its end.

"It is the ultimate act of sorcery, harnessing nature itself. My mother, Roznier, and Grigori were drunk with the idea of that kind of power, a feat so large. And I'm sorry to say, I was too. It took years. Years of honing the craft, of theorising and trial. But almost a decade after Vasteel had asked for immortality, we gave it to him in the form of a pool."

"You..." Dawsyn can't finish the sentence. The words sit on her tongue, but nothing is said. She feels the iskra rearing its head and tries to ease the sickness unfurling inside her. Tries to sequester it again.

"We believed ourselves the cleverest beings to have ever lived, of course," Baltisse continues, and there is shame in her voice. "But magic gives and takes in equal share, and we realised *what* it would take before one could be given immortality.

"Human souls," Dawsyn says blankly.

The mage nods, watching her closely. "A life for a life. When we explained the magic to Vasteel, he said, 'their spark.' Eventually, he coined it with a word from the old forgotten language: 'Iskra.'

"At first, Vasteel refused the magic he'd asked us to conjure. 'I cannot take another's iskra,' he told us. And for a time, he put the entire idea of eternity aside.

"It was my mother who convinced him otherwise," Baltisse says icily. "The dungeons were overflowing at the time – anarchists who believed that we mages were corrupting the palace. They were rioting. Vasteel had them locked away until they saw sense. It was a useless endeavour, of course. It is difficult to dispel hate. But suddenly my mother had a fine solution. 'Give them to the pool,' she told Vasteel, 'and rid the world of their prejudice.' It took some persuasion, but eventually, the King did just that.

"At first it was only the criminals that went into the pool. They were meant for the gallows anyway. Violent men and women – best to put their iskra to better use. Put that spark in a man who knows how to serve his populace. That's what he told himself. It's what *we* told him.

"King Vasteel was teeming with life. The iskra healed any sickness or injury that ailed him. Soon, he began to allow his most esteemed noblemen and women to reap the benefits of the pool too. A select few who he believed would bring Terrsaw to a better future. It was the highest of honours to be let in on the secret, to be granted life. But the more Vasteel shared the pool, the drier it ran. Those who drink iskra must do so frequently before mortality sets back in. The dungeons were empty of thugs, and suddenly Vasteel was naming lowly crimes punishable by death. First it was petty theft, evading taxes, brawling. Terrsaw was the most law-abiding city you'd ever seen. The wrong insult said too loudly would have you arrested. And still, it wasn't enough to keep the pool filled.

"The King was changing at the same time. His skin was pale and cold. He was strong and virile, but he resembled a statue more so than a human. His hair turned an astonishing shade of white. He had become addicted to the iskra, and so had many of his inner circle.

"Years went by, and after a time, they barely looked for reasons to take people from the street and throw them to the pool. When they ran out of bad people, they made do with the good. They took orphans, beggars, widows, and the sick. Those who lived on the fringe were the most vulnerable. Vasteel was evolving before our eyes. A benevolent king became a callous one. A threat to his people.

"That was when I began to regret it all. Not *sooner*, mind you," the mage admits stiffly. "No, I'm no saint – far from it. But I could see how bending nature had produced something unnatural. Something that ought not exist.

"There were rumours abounding. Some thought the land had been cursed, but others questioned the King's unnatural pallor, his apparent good health despite his age. They wondered if he'd been possessed. They guessed correctly that he was using the people of Terrsaw for his own ends.

"When the speculation came too close to the truth, Vasteel became paranoid. He was sure that all in Terrsaw would try to take the pool if they knew of it. He ordered his mages to move it."

"Move it?" Dawsyn repeats, her confusion apparent.

"Yes." Baltisse nods. "Or the magic *inside* it, anyway. Another feat that has never been duplicated."

"How could it be moved?"

"We absorbed it back into ourselves and–"

"What?"

"Yes," Baltisse says simply. "The pool's magic – that voice that calls to your soul when you're within its grasp – it came from us. A piece of our own power. We carried it inside us and brought it to a place of Vasteel's choosing; high up on the mountain, where no one would dare go."

"Glacia," Dawsyn says.

"Or what it was before it became a kingdom. Vasteel had a palace built around the pool eventually, but before that it was simply a place where he and his noblemen could go with their victims, drink their iskra and stay a while before we mages folded them back into Terrsaw.

"But in the valley, a revolution was beginning to stir. The people had long since prayed for a new monarch. King Vasteel had sired no heirs and he was mysteriously alive and well after far too many years. He was cold, cruel, often absent. The land around him was being laid to waste. And he did nothing to stop it.

"I wanted to find a way out of the mess I'd helped create. I met a man in a tavern who was heading the resistance aiming to bring about Vasteel's downfall. The man's name was Cazriel Sabar. He would soon become the very first sovereign of the Sabar reign."

The name reverberates in Dawsyn's mind. She needs to remember it, but before she can test it on her lips, Baltisse continues.

"He was a good man. An honest one. He came from the fringe, and he'd made it his life's mission to care for the poor. He could speak well, too. He was rallying people for the usurping of the palace with impressive speed. There was not one self-serving corner in his mind when I heard it. So, I told him when and where we mages would fold Vasteel and his noblemen back into Terrsaw. Cazriel Sabar was to be there waiting with his battalion of rebels, ready to kill their King who had become more creature than human." Baltisse pauses a moment. Dawsyn watches the colour of her eyes shift infinitesimally darker, more foreboding.

"Indriss, my mother, was the one to foil the plan," Baltisse intones, her voice deadened. "She could listen to minds, as I can, and I hadn't been careful enough. Of course, I never supposed she might become so intent on protecting Vasteel. By then, I'd tried to make the other mages see the harm we had done, the destruction of nature's ways. I was sick with guilt, and I could feel that same sickness in the minds of Grigori and Roznier. Gone was the vengeance against a race who had hunted us, burned us. There was only shame left. But my mother, she felt nothing but pure obsession. Like Vasteel, all of her was tied to power, and the need for more.

"So, my mother informed Vasteel of the ambush, and I folded off that fucking mountain within an inch of his sword. I found Cazriel Sabar and told him to prepare for battle. Grigori, Roznier, and I went to the base of the mountain and put our hands to the ground. We pulled every scrap of our magic to our fingertips and lured colossal rocks from the earth to form the Boulder Gate. We hoped it would be enough. And then we waited."

Dawsyn reels. She pictures the Boulder Gate, towering above her. She cannot imagine the measure of power it had taken to conjure such a thing.

"It took seven days and nights for Vasteel and his merry men to descend the mountain. Cazriel's band of rebels fired arrows at them before they could find a way through the Boulder Gate, and they quickly retreated. All except Vasteel. The former king only smiled. He was a ghost now. White as snow. He closed his eyes, and we watched in horror as wings unfolded from his back. The first Glacian.

"Vasteel flew over the Boulder Gate, and we could do very little but watch in terror. He plucked a rebel from our battalion and flew him skyward, talons buried in the man's shoulders. 'Tell them their King will be back!' he called out. 'And I will take as many as I might carry.' He flew away, back to his mountaintop, and the battle was both won and lost. Cazriel Sabar led Terrsaw from that day until his death, and he did all he could to protect his people from the Glacians, as we came to call them. Those cold, winged men and women who would swoop into the valley every so often and steal its citizens away. They couldn't be stopped, couldn't be conquered, and the people of Terrsaw had one righteous place to turn their blame, their wrath."

"Mages," Dawsyn says. She remembers once asking

Baltisse if she hated the people of Terrsaw for the vilifying of her kind. *No,* she had said. *I do not hate Terrsaw.* And now Dawsyn understands the shame she'd sensed from her then. She senses it tenfold now. The mage is permeated with it. Made of remorse.

Baltisse's glassy stare won't meet Dawsyn's. Instead, she looks to the tabletop, her finger following the circular grain of the wood. For the first time in Dawsyn's recollection, she appears... old.

"And so, there it is, Dawsyn Sabar. A very good reason to cut off my hands, weight my feet, and sink me to the bottom of the ocean. And you'd be right to do it. I only ask that you let me undo some of the wrongs I was party to beforehand. In the meantime, you can trust that I've had many lifetimes to soak in the worst of my sins. I've laid still while the guilt has peeled each layer of skin from my body. Every morning, I rise knowing I was born for destruction, but I continue now to choose a different course," Baltisse presses her lips together. She looks at Dawsyn, and her eyes reveal every ounce of remorse, of self-contempt. "You are not like me, Dawsyn Sabar. You were born as Cazriel Sabar was born, and I see his unflinching mind in your own. You were not born for destruction, or for the Ledge. You were born for Terrsaw."

Dawsyn feels her fingers aching with cold. She feels the iskra stirring darkly while the light in her mind grows warm in response. She is too filled with revelation, too filled with inherited duty. Dawsyn feels she could combust. A million pieces of Sabar and Ledge and Terrsaw and iskra and mage and Dawsyn, spreading farther and wider while divided than she ever could whole.

A hand comes over her shoulder, encasing it completely. It is warm and firm, attached to someone who knows all the sides of her. Perhaps the only living soul who does. It helps her to remember herself.

"You are wrong," she says to Baltisse, ignoring the roiling

within, the pull in so many directions. "I am Ledge-born."

Baltisse first looks wary, but then she hears Dawsyn's thoughts – the tenor of forgiveness. "And I *am* like you. I will rise each day and choose my own course."

CHAPTER FIFTY

Ryon's hand remains on Dawsyn's shoulder as they all await the heavy silence to unburden them. His palm grows steadily cooler with his mounting tension.

"Baltisse?" he finally says, unable to delay it a moment longer. "We must make a plan. Dawsyn has only worsened in your absence and–"

"Yes," Baltisse nods. "I have thought much about it these past days. About the balance of the two magics, and their coexistence alongside one another." Her eyes travel to the window, as though the forest beyond might provide her the answers.

"Enlighten me," Dawsyn says, her tone even, though beneath Ryon's hand, her body tenses.

"The Pool of Iskra's magic is dark," Baltisse tells them. "Cursed, in a way. We mages traded much of ourselves to procure it. Blood, bone, and more insidious things. It is, in its essence, the worst of us. Your mage power, however, is light. It is of the place it came: nature. Pure and unadulterated life. These opposites, they are not compatible in one body. I believe they battle within you, the iskra alternating between hiding away, or seeking freedom, and the mage magic trying valiantly to trounce the iskra when it feels threatened."

"*Release me,*" Dawsyn whispers. It is so quiet Ryon can't be sure he hears it correctly. "But neither can win," Dawsyn says quietly. "Neither can lose."

"*You* can lose, Dawsyn. If you cannot guide it, teach it to live peacefully inside of you, it will shred you to pieces. Sooner rather than later."

Ryon closes his eyes. His stomach turns.

And what will he do then? What will he become in the aftermath of her nonexistence?

"And if I can?" Dawsyn asks. "Teach it, I mean?"

Baltisse gives a small smile. A shadow of something eager and wistful. "Then you will be a most powerful being indeed."

Ryon returns, though his expression is deeply clouded, wrecked with fright. "This person you've brought with you. The woman of magic. Can she cure Dawsyn?"

"Magic isn't something to be *cured*, Ryon. Only endured," Baltisse corrects. "But she offers an insight I do not have."

"And what is that?" Ryon bites, the tension getting the better of his control.

"*Glacian magic*," Baltisse smiles. "They call her the iskra witch."

Both Dawsyn and Ryon freeze in their places.

"Dawsyn, I'm sorry to tell you that you were not exactly the *very* first person to escape the Ledge. There *was* just one other before you." With that, Baltisse walks to the door, and pulls it open. "Come with me," she says, pointing out into the bright daylight.

They allow Baltisse to lead them into the forest, rounding scraggly roots and shrubs as they go. A short distance from the cabin, Baltisse ducks behind a copse, and reappears a moment later, a taller woman in her wake.

"Yennes," Baltisse says to her. "This is Dawsyn Sabar of the Ledge and Ryon Mesrich of Glacia."

The woman is statuesque. Ryon would put her at age fifty

or more. She wears her tightly curled hair high on her head, tied with a scarf. Layers of thin shawls cover her frame, draped elegantly over her shoulders, around her hips. She stares at them, her interest plain. Her eyes sweep over Dawsyn first, and then they find Ryon and stick there.

Ryon's jaw flexes. "I don't bite," he says lowly. His impatience is clear.

The woman's eyebrows rise. And then, despite Ryon's surliness, a smile appears on the woman's face, small and soft.

"Yennes?" Ryon asks. It is a word from the old language. A word still used in Glacia. "Survivor?"

The woman speaks. "It is what they called me," she says, and her voice is as soft as her smile.

"They?"

Yennes does not answer. She only continues to stare at Dawsyn and Ryon both in equal measure.

"Baltisse says that you escaped the Ledge," Dawsyn offers, unsure whether it could be true. "Can you tell us how?"

Yennes nods a little, her fingers twisting together in a gesture that gives away her nerves. "I don't speak of it often."

"Perhaps today warrants it?" Dawsyn's tone is uncharacteristically soft. "We can trade tales."

Yennes stares at her a moment more, then sighs, resigned. "Let's take some warmth?"

"It is already stifling," Ryon says, confused. But the words make Dawsyn smile.

"She means tea," Dawsyn translates, and Ryon understands that these are words of the Ledge. "Let's make some tea."

When they are settled around Baltisse's table, a lethargic flame licking the sides of a pewter kettle in the hearth, Yennes begins.

"I was selected and taken to Glacia when I was little more than a girl," she says shakily. "It was terrifying. It still wakes me in the night to dream of it. That place..." Her eyes go distant for a moment, then she shakes her head as if to clear it.

"When I was pulled before the pool, before the King, I...

I knew I couldn't let that magic have me. I had seen what it would do. Perhaps, though, it would have been wiser to let it take my soul after all. I still wonder sometimes..." She trails off again, her fingers tumbling over each other. "I went into the pool, and when it tried to lure me to sleep, I did the opposite. I fought. I panicked. I tried to breathe. When those Glacians scooped me out, I was still me," she smiles a little, lips twitching. "I suppose everything that happened after was worth it, just to know that. To know they couldn't best me."

Ryon narrows his eyes. "And how did you come to find yourself in Terrsaw afterward? Quite the accomplishment, I must say. Even more so than Dawsyn's, to escape Glacia unaided." Ryon himself has never heard of her – a woman other than Dawsyn who escaped Vasteel's grasp? How is it that her story never reached him?

"I did not say I was unaided," Yennes replies quietly. "And the rest of the tale... is something I'd rather not recall."

He can't imagine it, how this woman came to find the slopes. How she managed to traverse them, assisted or not. She is curious, but there are other matters to tend to while he has Yennes's attention. There is a sense of flight in this most strange woman.

"So, you have the iskra magic inside you still?" Ryon asks instead. "You've lived with it all this time?"

"Yes," she assents. "It was resistant at first. Though my struggle with it was nothing like yours. Baltisse told me of your mage blood. She hopes I can guide you to use the iskra, while she helps you with the other."

"And will you?" Dawsyn asks. It seems she knows it is past time to deny help from anyone who offers it.

Yennes scrutinises her for a moment, her fingers burrowing beneath the table, likely to hide their frenetic jittering. "I will try to show you what I know of iskra, but as for convincing the light and dark to share?" Yennes says. "You will have to uncover that knowing on your own."

The vice that has gripped Ryon's heart loosens an inch. Whoever this woman might be, perhaps she can offer a glimmer of possibility.

Dawsyn turns her face to his, sharing with him a look of fragile, vulnerable hope. It is a face that has morphed slowly since he first saw it. It is wearier now, less sure. It shows each and every one of her burdens.

Beneath it all is the memory of a girl hiding in a warren, her teeth gritted and eyes wild. A girl who moved across the snow like she was made from it, lifting her face to the sun and becoming aglow with its light. Smiling so rarely that each one wrenched his heart out. A person who doesn't recognise her own softness for all the hard things endured. Sharp and impenetrable and unyielding… except to him.

It is not often, and it is not without effort, but these small moments when he earns her gentleness is better than drinking the sweetest elixir.

Mother above, help the ones who try to take it away.

CHAPTER FIFTY-ONE

There's blood in her mouth. Her jaw is locked so tightly, she wouldn't be surprised to find her tongue bitten off.

"Focus, Dawsyn. It can only hurt you for as long as you fail to stop it."

But she can't. There is only the horrible, suffocating pain and the will not to scream.

"Dawsyn, breathe."

She can't.

"You can. Call to the magic. Make it listen," comes Baltisse's voice.

Dawsyn wants to succumb to the pain instead. It is blinding. Its squeezes and squeezes, the light wrapped around the dark in her chest, refusing to let go. But there's that other part of her that hasn't completely relented. It can hear the voices outside of her.

"Call it back, Dawsyn. It won't be forced, but you can guide it. The pain will be gone."

Just try, she thinks.

Release me, the iskra hisses.

You must try. And there it is. There is this task, or there is failure, and nothing else.

It is only pain, she thinks. *We know pain.*

Dawsyn summons every lingering tendril of her awareness.

She pinpoints the light, trapping the iskra in its grasp, and thinks, *Stop.*

"No," says Baltisse. "The magic will only do what it believes it needs to, Dawsyn. You must convince it."

How?

"Show it that the iskra is not a threat."

But she can't.

"You must!"

STOP! She screams within herself and feels the horrible sensation of being twisted. The light is winning.

"Dawsyn, go easy!"

But the pain is unbearable, her awareness is trickling. She can feel the black corners of consciousness coming to swallow her. To rescue her.

"Get back!" shouts a voice.

"STOP!" Dawsyn screams. But the word is too big to remain inside her chest and it passes her lips. It fills the room. And with the reverberations of her roar, the light in her chest erupts. The iskra expands, races to her fingertips and out.

Dawsyn feels the burning frost of the iskra as it explodes from her. She sees the brilliant light through her closed eyelids, and she feels the receding glow of the mage magic returning to her mind, raw and defeated.

She wants to sleep. Those black corners in her mind lurk, ready to drag her into their recesses. She is so... so very tired. But Baltisse is shouting, her voice edged with concern, and Dawsyn forces her eyelids to open.

"Yennes? *Yennes!*"

Dawsyn sees the ceiling of Baltisse's cabin first. When she turns her head, she sees the wreckage. Baltisse's table and chairs, the hanging herbs and plants, a basin, cutlery, a kettle, all of it is upturned and lying in a heap against the far wall, as though a gust of wind had come through.

Baltisse lifts a chair out of the mess. "Yennes?"

Yennes. Is she hurt?

"Come, Yennes. I'll help you stand," Baltisse says, leaning down to a crumpled form.

Dawsyn rolls to her side and feels sick. Fighting nausea, she pushes her head from the floor in time to see Ryon barrel through the door.

"Dawsyn?" He bends down to her form on the floor.

"I'm fine," Dawsyn whispers. "... Yennes."

"I'm well," comes Yennes's voice. There is some clamour as she finds her feet amongst the heap. "Just a knock on the head."

"What happened?" asks Ryon.

"A minor thing," Baltisse says. "Did I not ask you to stay away while we work, Ryon?"

"I came to–"

"See if your beloved was hurt? Yes, I know. As you can see, she is not. Now get out."

Ryon scowls at Baltisse but doesn't argue. He storms out of the cabin without a backward glance, slamming the door behind him.

"Do not pay him any attention. His mind is a storm and he's exceptionally nosey. He can barely stand not being involved." Baltisse helps Yennes to a chair, and then begins to right the rest of her discarded furniture. "Well, Dawsyn. You both succeeded and failed. Congratulations."

Dawsyn sits upright, her stomach rolling in sickening waves. "Is there any chance all of that," – Dawsyn points lethargically to the mess – "wasn't me?"

"None."

"What was it? That... explosion? It happened on the Ledge, and on the wagon road. It killed a person."

"The iskra," Yennes answers, her fingers pushing gingerly at a spot on the back of her head. "Anger, anxiety, fear. All of it gives the iskra a pathway. I had several *incidents* myself at first, when I was pushed to my limits. It is not your fault."

"Instead of stopping the mage magic, you lit a fuse for the iskra," Baltisse adds. "Effective, but dangerous."

"I tried to call it off," Dawsyn says.

"I told you. You must *convince* it that the iskra poses no threat."

"How?"

"Show it."

"*How?*"

"Can you call both to your palms again?" Baltisse asks.

Dawsyn laughs at that. Her voice shallow and weak. "No."

When Yennes and Baltisse had suggested it the first time, she'd thought it a joke. Calling both powers to the surface that way? Asking them both to dance? It was sure to incite a battle. A minute later she was on the wooden floor, writhing and gasping.

"Rest a moment, Dawsyn," Baltisse says ruefully. "When your strength returns, we will try it again."

"To what end?"

"The one that ends with both sides of power learning to cooperate."

Dawsyn rubs her face. "Perhaps it is not possible."

Baltisse looks down at her with an expression that says she fears the same.

"I think it is," Yennes interjects quietly. "After all, we are each filled with darkness and light. We must always learn to balance the two."

Dawsyn lets her eyelids drift shut. "Poetic," she mutters.

The two women leave her be for a few minutes more, but when she opens her eyes again, they are still watching, still waiting. Dawsyn nods her head.

She stands and guides both the light and the dark, the warm and the cold to the surface, without a clue of how to combine them.

It continues for days. While the others are cast outside and forbidden to enter, Dawsyn, Baltisse, and the woman called Yennes remain inside. Dawsyn invites the magic of Glacians and mages to the battlefield and asks them not to fight. The only progress made is in managing to untangle the two when they come to blows. Despite her exhaustion, Dawsyn is learning to push the pain aside for long enough to scold the tussling masses like a harried mother. The more frustrated Dawsyn becomes, the easier it is. The iskra wins, sending that warm, white light back into the safety of her mind, and the pain dissipates. Baltisse's furniture takes further loss.

Yennes watches the progress with grim disapproval. "Allowing anger to dispel the pain won't be enough in the end," she says. Dawsyn can't help but find that prophetic. Alas, she is hopeful.

"I'm separating them faster," Dawsyn tells Yennes and the mage. "At least there's that."

"It isn't enough," Baltisse says. "So long as they are at odds, you will be vulnerable. The iskra may wait until you are exhausted, injured, sick. There will be a time when you are not strong enough to break them apart."

It is the middle of the night, and Dawsyn has had very little to eat. She already feels that exhaustion the mage speaks of.

"Perhaps the combined magic could be used for different means," Yennes mumbles, pacing around the cabin, eyes far away. "A common... purpose?"

"What is she saying?" Dawsyn asks wearily. She has learnt over the last few days that Yennes prefers to confer with herself, rather than the room at large. *A lone woman's occupation*, she had said by way of apology.

Yennes turns back to her in her hesitant manner, eyes flitting to Dawsyn and away. "I wonder if perhaps the two sources would work together, if you gave them common ground," she says softly.

Baltisse's eyes roll. "Ah," she breathes.

"And what exactly would constitute common ground?" Dawsyn asks.

"You," answers Baltisse. "Both sides of the magic share the

same objective, and that is *survival*. The most common rule of nature. All things do what they must to survive."

"And to survive," Yennes continues, "both sides of the magic need *you*."

"So, what? Try to kill me, and maybe the iskra and the mage magic will work together to save my life?"

"Maybe," Baltisse answers. "But we need not resort to that. All we really need is the *fear* of dying."

"Oh," Dawsyn drawls. "Wonderful."

"My sweet Dawsyn," Baltisse simpers. "What thing scares you to death?"

"My sweet witch, you can go fuck yourself."

A ghost of a smile crosses Yennes's lips. "Fear is a powerful motivator, Dawsyn. It may be helpful."

"Yes, dearling," Baltisse grins. "Tell Yennes and Baltisse. What is a thing most scary to you?"

Dawsyn scoffs tiredly. "I don't know, mage. Why don't you rattle around inside my head and find something yourself?"

Baltisse's smile only widens. Her eyes turn volatile–

"Wait! Mother above. *Fine!* Give me a moment, for the love of–"

The door to the cabin opens a fragment. Hector's face appears through the crack.

The mage mutters a curse. "Hector! Did I not ask you to–"

But Hector cuts in with a finger to his lips. It is then that Dawsyn hears it. Outside, footfalls can be heard. Many of them. Close by in the forest.

Guards, Hector mouths to them, and then steps back, leaving the doorway open.

Heart in her throat, Dawsyn grabs her ax and follows immediately, Baltisse and Yennes close behind. Under the light of a half-moon, Hector creeps back toward the rest, all standing in various poses of stillness around the dwindling fire, weapons in hand.

Ryon has his hand on Salem's shoulder, closest to the edge of their camp. His eyes find Dawsyn's as soon as her feet leave the stoop. In them she sees reflected her own alarm, for the forest around them echoes the sounds of an approaching battalion, voices muted and cautious. A horde. All of them searching.

"Don't move," Baltisse murmurs, and somehow, they all hear it.

Will they be able to see us? Dawsyn thinks toward the mage.

Her lips are bloodless. They barely move when she answers. "Only if they come close enough."

Together they wait. Each pulse in Dawsyn's throat feels more painful, more threatening than the last. The desire to hide, to do anything other than stand here in the open is tangible amongst them.

Baltisse's spell will obscure this place, Dawsyn tells herself, eyes darting when she hears a rustle nearby. *They will walk right by us.*

Suddenly, a whistle, short and sharp, cuts through the night air. It could have been a bird, except for the abrupt halt of marching feet, the nickering of horses.

"Split apart," comes a man's voice in the distance, low and abrupt.

Feet scuttle fallen leaves, hooves tread on the ground, branches scrape against Terrsaw armour. It comes from more than one angle, ever closer.

Ever closer.

Dawsyn watches from behind as Ryon's wings unfold. Slowly they appear. He holds them carefully upright at first, not daring to extend them where they might scrape the low hanging branches. Tasheem and Rivdan do the same. She sees their outlines, trembling with the urge to take flight.

From the near darkness comes a voice. *"Shit."*

A grunt. Then the clang of metal.

A guard appears. He stumbles through the woods nearby, the moon glinting off his armour as he weaves between trees. So close. Too close.

Dawsyn's fists clench. Her stomach turns over as the guard's gaze lifts, slowly higher, and straight into the eyes of Esra, not five feet from him.

But the guard's eyes slide away again quickly. It's as if Esra were part of the woods, perfectly blended with his surroundings.

"Tawny, man. You stray too far alone, son. If you come across those mountain beasts, they'll rip you to shreds." A voice from the north now, tone urgent but muted. "What are you doing?"

"I thought I saw firelight," the guard named Tawny mutters, staring straight at the fire in question. Flames dance in his eyes. A piece of burning wood tumbles from the smouldering heap and rolls across the ground. Tawny only shakes his head and looks away. "These woods trick the eye at night."

"They do," says the other man, coming closer.

The newest guard treads a path around the outskirts of their camp, and his quarry holds a collective breath nearby – nearby, but still unnoticeable somehow. So long as these guards come no closer. If that fine line between them is not crossed…

And it seems they won't. The guards murmur quietly to one another, looking away, back through the trees.

Then, in a procession of cruel coincidence, several things happen at once, all with aching, serendipitous precision.

Salem steps backward, his bare foot hovering cautiously for a moment and then coming down, straight on top of that stray smouldering timber. He gasps in surprise, the sizzle of his skin heard from where Dawsyn stands.

The guards spin, swords drawn, eyes on the place where Salem hunches in pain.

Ryon immediately steps to the side, his wings shielding Salem. He trembles behind Ryon, eyes streaming, a fist between his teeth.

"Did you hear that?" Tawny murmurs, his eyes still skirting to every corner of the clearing and acknowledging nothing.

"Of course I fucking heard it," says the other.

They shift forward, eyes darting around the camp, searching

but finding nothing. The tips of their swords are only several paces away, pointed directly at Ryon's chest.

Move! Dawsyn thinks. But he won't and she knows it. He won't risk the clamour and leave the rest of them behind. She feels the words she wants to shout to him and can't. Fear seeps in. Its wicked hand claws up her stomach and behind her ribcage, into her throat.

The sword tips come ever closer. Ryon is forced to shift backward, his feet whispering.

The guards follow. And then suddenly freeze.

Dawsyn could draw that invisible line in the dirt, the one between Baltisse's magic and the rest of the wood. The guards' eyes turn wide and round as they cross it. Where before they wandered, they now stick to the form of winged man before them.

"What in the…"

"Fuck," Ryon hisses, and whirls.

The hilt of Ryon's short sword cracks against the temple of the guard named Tawny. The man's eyes close before he hits the ground, unconscious, but not before the second guard lifts his own sword, swinging it toward Ryon's neck.

The rest of the camp is a wild flurry of useless motion. Tasheem and Rivdan rush in. Salem reaches upward. Baltisse shouts. Esra cries Ryon's name.

Dawsyn raises her ax.

They will all be too slow, of course. The horror, the fierce gravity of it fills her. The ax leaves her palm, flying eye-over-handle toward the guard.

But it won't land before this other sword can.

It won't save Ryon, and she will lose him.

Again.

No, she thinks.

And it is not a shout into the void. It is a simple refusal. Every cell in her body remembers the anguish of old grief. She remembers the misery of absolute aloneness on the Ledge.

With perfect clarity she recalls the weeks in a stone room with flaking, dried blood, a dead rat, and the enduring pain. It is a simple acceptance of her inability to endure it again.

Heat and ice fill her, coalesce and burst.

Light and dark combined.

And the very air explodes.

CHAPTER FIFTY-TWO

First, the air rushes into Dawsyn, all at once, and everything stills. The ax halts in its path through the air. The guard's sword perches on the very precipice of Ryon's throat but doesn't enter. The rest are frozen in their movement.

Dawsyn sees it all, in that singular microcosmic moment – time, and the way she can stretch it before it resumes its shape; space, and how it might be folded. She is full of glowing light, radiating dark, all-encompassing fear, and when she nods to the guard, the magic understands. She releases time from her grasp, lets go of the air that she stole from the world, and lets it detonate.

The guard is hurled away, his sword with him. The titanic gust forces his feet from the forest floor, and he is thrown away until his back meets a tree trunk. A crack rings out as it crushes his spine, and then the wind is gone.

The guard slumps into the leaves and dirt.

A collective breath is taken. A release of tension amongst them all. As one, they turn their faces to her, a corpus of shock and confusion.

Beads of blood collect along a shallow line at Ryon's neck, and Dawsyn can hardly look at anything else.

"Thank the Chasm," she says. She breathes the words, sheets of relief billowing from her lungs, the fear ebbing away with it. She closes her eyes against the moisture gathering in them.

She breathes, and breathes, and with each exhale she feels the dark and the light recede back to their respective territories.

Baltisse speaks before the rest can. Before the remarks and questions can begin to fly. "We must leave," she says quietly. "Now."

Already, the footfalls of the battalion sound more frenetic, closer. Too much disturbance in a forest so quiet. Too many guards to hold back. They are coming.

Ryon's hand trembles and his eyes are still stuck on Dawsyn's, but he nods. He goes to Salem and helps him limp to Tasheem. "Take him."

Rivdan grabs hold of Esra and Hector. Ryon goes to Dawsyn, wiping her cheeks roughly with his thumbs. "Where?" he says to Baltisse, hurried and quiet.

It is Yennes who answers, stepping further into the camp, her hands uncharacteristically clenched into fists. "I know a place," she says. "I can lead you."

There is no room for argument. The boots of a hundred guards inch closer.

"Go with Baltisse," Ryon tells Dawsyn, clasping her arm and pulling her to the mage. "Yennes, with me."

"You know where to fold?" Yennes asks Baltisse, who nods, taking Dawsyn's forearm in her hand.

Ryon lifts Yennes into his arms and his wings swoop down. The sound of armour and boots is drowned by the sounds of Glacian wings.

"Brace yourself," Baltisse warns, and then Dawsyn is being compressed, her blood and bones grinding inward until she isn't there at all.

When Dawsyn begins to feel her body unspool, she remembers to bend her knees. This time, she can feel the delicate way the collapsed space opens, one piece after another. She can identify the slow unleashing of time and space.

And suddenly, her feet are against solid ground.

"Not even a twinge," Baltisse remarks smugly, as though to herself.

The smell of brine finds Dawsyn first, then the mist of wind-carried spray against her face. She opens her eyes to it: the boundless expanse of inky sea beneath the half-moon. Sluggish waves churning onto a sand and stone shore.

The same sea she once stood before with Ryon, resolving to turn her back on it and the escape it offered. The same sea, but from an unfamiliar perspective. A sea cast in shadow. Cliffs do not line the shore as they did the last time. The long grass that sways between her legs undulates to the sand's edge.

It's the colossal shadow that looms over the water that makes her turn. She traces the shadow along the shore, watching it stretch to the east, the water tunnelling into a channel.

A channel that cuts the land in two, right to the opening of mountainous rock.

Dawsyn staggers backward. Behind her, shallow forest is eclipsed by the endlessly rising obsidian rock face.

The mountain, just another side of it.

The sound of wings turns her gaze. The mixed appear in the distant sky, growing ever nearer, their wings unfathomably wide. A few moments later, Ryon lands and sets a drawn-looking Yennes on the ground. Her hands wring together immediately.

Tasheem comes next, balancing Salem gingerly on his uninjured foot, and then Rivdan, his burden heavier than the others. Windswept and panting, they turn their heads from the sea to the mountain.

"Is this – are we still in Terrsaw?" Hector asks, eyes wider than the rest as they take in the sight of the ocean for the first time.

Yennes answers hesitantly. "On the edge of it," she says, and then with a nod, she directs their eyes to a chimney between the low treetops.

"You live here?" Dawsyn asks.

Yennes nods. "Dawsyn, can I speak with y–"

"Fucking Queens coming after us again! *Again!*" Esra whirls about, finding a stone on the ground and hurling it into the water. "Mark me, Baltisse, your cabin will be burning rubble by now."

Salem groans. "Quit yer howlin', Es."

"*You* quit it, old man!"

"Come 'ere. I can still kick with me good foot."

Baltisse twitches her hand, and Esra and Salem fall suspiciously quiet, their lips tightly pressed. "Mother above, you imbeciles. Stop it."

"To the… east?" Ryon murmurs.

"Yes," Yennes answers.

"What is that?" Tasheem asks, pointing to the channel of water that disappears into the gap of the mountain.

Yennes's hands flitter together before her. "I wanted to show Dawsyn–"

"The Boulder Gate does not reach this far around the mountain's base," Tasheem remarks, her voice far louder than the older woman's. "Though there would be no need for one here, I'd suppose. No human could possibly climb this face."

"Are we safe from the guard, here?" Ryon asks, his eyes shifting between the mage and Yennes.

Baltisse nods. "Even if they knew where we were, we would be difficult to reach. There is no bridge over the river to the west."

Rivdan speaks next. "Can we find Salem a place to rest in your home, Yennes? His foot should be bandaged."

"Bandaged?" Salem splutters. "The mage can bloody well heal me. The amount o' wine she's swiped from me stores these pas' years."

"Small compensation for the absolute drivel I've been

subjected to while drinking it. And that's when you're sober."

Ryon groans tiredly. "*Fucking idiots*. Baltisse, be useful and mend Salem's foot here, would you? Save us the trouble of carrying him."

"I'll carry him," Esra murmurs darkly.

"Get the fuck away from me, Es," Salem warns. "I told yeh I would *cut* those wandering hands off if they groped me arse again."

"I wasn't so much planning on groping as I was murdering. I am saving any future groping for backsides far more favourable." Esra winks toward Hector, who blushes.

The arguments continue, irritation flaring amongst them, but Dawsyn barely notices. Her attention, instead, is given wholly to that channel – the place where the mountain is cut in two. She watches the water flow in and out of the wide gap, lapping up the rock face.

Dawsyn's feet take her toward it, away from the others. Several strides along the shoreline, the bickering behind her becomes faint. She stares.

She feels it when Yennes comes to join her, though the woman keeps a careful distance, always uncertain. Always unsure.

"Is that...?" Dawsyn asks, though the name hitches her tongue. She swallows it instead.

"The Chasm," Yennes finishes, and it feels like a foot against Dawsyn's throat. "It's the Chasm's end."

Dawsyn is stunned to stillness. *The Chasm is unending*, said Briar, said Valma, said the people of the Ledge. *Bottomless*.

As though she is possessed of the same mind tricks as the mage, Yennes shakes her head gently. "It is not endless," she says. "Everything must end, Dawsyn. I rather think it suitable that the Chasm end here."

Dawsyn thinks of the questions Yennes avoided, the admissions that seemed unlikely. King Vasteel had once told

Dawsyn that not a single selected human had taken to the slopes and reached the bottom.

"This is how you escaped," Dawsyn murmurs, her voice skittled by wind and ocean mist. "You walked through the chasm, all the way to its end."

When she turns to look at Yennes, the woman's fingers are a blur of disquiet. Her eyes watch them intertwine and untangle but see something else entirely. "There was no walking," she says woodenly. "Only running."

Chapter Fifty-Three

Dawsyn watches the water rush through the Chasm's opening and recede, pulling in and out of a mountain split in two. A side for the Ledge, a side for Glacia.

And a path between the two.

"There is much I'd like to tell you, Dawsyn Sabar," Yennes says, finally bridging the gulf between them. She places a timid hand on Dawsyn's arm. "But this night has drained much from us, and... I would ask for a few hours more to gather what I will say. I am not so accustomed to speaking with others. Not anymore."

Dawsyn nods. Behind them, the agitation is swelling. This night has revealed much more that it ought have. There are other things more pressing. Always other things more pressing.

"Upon morning," Dawsyn says to the woman named Yennes, the second returned prisoner to the first.

Yennes nods, the shawls over her head and shoulders sliding back. "Upon morning," she vows, though her eyes do not meet Dawsyn's for long.

All of them cluster within the cabin, somehow finding space in a place meant for one. Salem stands on two feet, his injury now healed by Baltisse, but not without her uttering threats. "If you make me come so near your feet again, I'll replace them with stumps, old man. How can feet so small smell so abominable?"

"They ain't *small!*"

"They *are* rather small," Esra had added. "I'd never noticed."

"Aye, come here, Es. I'll boot one up yer arse!"

"It would certainly fit, now, wouldn't it? Best boot them both, Salem, if you mean to make an impression on me."

"Fuckin' smart-mouthed, loose-legged, empty-headed..."

It had occurred to Dawsyn that Esra and Salem would be something of a hindrance in their ploy to liberate the Ledge. They had neither wings, nor magic. They possessed nothing in the way of skill to be used in battle. Even Hector, who was without any ethereal aptitude, could fight well. There was simply that of their need to be *somewhere,* and with someone who might heal their injuries. But there was this: on a night that saw them killing and fleeing, that saw Dawsyn stripped and remade, they still managed to make them all grin. A certain magic the rest sorely lacked.

Yennes's cabin is a replica of one found on the Ledge, and it sends a strange slither of familiarity through Dawsyn. The hearth is clean, a waiting stack of wood at its side, neatly sorted. A cot rests on short stilts along one wall, a bench and basin along the other. The floor, which is covered in soft animal skins, does not creak underfoot. The makeshift insulation muffles one's feet. One small, solitary window beside the door, so the inhabitants might see who approaches. Through it, there is a scattering of salt-crusted wisps of trees, their anaemic foliage blowing haphazardly between the sea and the mountain, back and forth, as though in warning. Then the ocean itself, turned black in the night, rolling like oil onto the waiting sand. She can hear the soft sound of it, the rush and whisper as it unfolds. Farther away is a sound more violent – the water colliding and collapsing against rocks as it funnels through the Chasm.

"Garjum has not given up yet," Dawsyn whispers to herself, listening intently to the ebb and flow.

"Garjum?" Esra asks loudly. He stands closest to Dawsyn and draws every face toward her.

"Nothing," Dawsyn mutters, shaking her head.

"Garjum?" Yennes repeats, the word falling hesitantly. "The sea monster?"

Dawsyn's lips part, but no answer comes. Her grandmother's stories – she had not thought them known outside of her den of girls. "You… know the tale?"

Yennes nods. "I know it."

For a moment, Dawsyn and Yennes stare at one other, forgoing the others. Dawsyn has looked at this person these past days as a reclusive woman of magic. A woman of Terrsaw, living as Baltisse does – on the edges. It is only now, standing in this familiar cabin with the knowing look in Yennes's eyes, that Dawsyn sees it. She sees it in the lines that crease her face, the scars on her fingers that work and worry constantly. This is a woman of the Ledge, as tried and true as Dawsyn.

"I don't know it," Hector yawns, his back sliding down the wall until he finds the floor. His eyes already closing.

"Well, don't hold us in suspense," Esra prompts, sitting as Hector does alongside him. Dawsyn watches as Hector leans instinctively toward him, his head falling to Esra's shoulder. "Tell us the story, dear Dawsyn."

Dawsyn wants to decline, but the others are drooping toward whatever surface they can find, eyes expectant. And when she finds Ryon's, the protest sticks to her throat. His dark gaze is so attached to hers, so hungry for this piece of her, that she finds herself expelling the tale, her grandmother's voice passing through her.

She tells them of how Garjum was pulled from the valley and into the ocean, of how he looms in its depths as a prisoner. She tells them of the endless cycle for his freedom, clawing for the shore and pulling the tide with him. When she's finished, all are asleep but for Yennes, Baltisse, and Ryon.

"All things find a way back home," Ryon repeats quietly, his stare still holding Dawsyn's.

"I always thought it was nonsense," Dawsyn says.

"And yet you've proven it true."

Dawsyn nods to Yennes. "It appears I am not the only one."

Yennes smiles thinly, but lines of worry etch her forehead.

"I must say, I am surprised to see you still standing, Dawsyn," Baltisse interrupts. The mage's eyes swirl slowly. She looks tired, though the grin she wears shows there is something she has been waiting to say.

Dawsyn thinks of the rush of iskra and mage magic that came together and burst from her earlier. She remembers the guard she set that magic upon with a mere thought. Such a display should have reduced to her to water.

"Yes." Baltisse nods, intruding on Dawsyn's thoughts again. "Quite the display, indeed."

Ryon groans. "Have the conversation *out loud*, if you are to have it."

Baltisse's grin widens. "Well, Ryon, as it happens, you are the *focal point* of this conversation."

He narrows his eyes at the mage. "How so?"

"It's the funniest thing," she begins. "You see, we've been trying to find a way to persuade both the iskra and the mage magic to merge. Not a thing ever done before, I assure you. But Yennes and I wondered if there was some... *compromise* that could be reached. We thought maybe the two powers would work together if shown that their main objective was the same."

Ryon waits, but the mage only smirks toward Dawsyn, who merely stands there, growing increasingly uncomfortable.

Ryon growls impatiently. "What was the main objective?"

"I'm so glad you asked." Baltisse sneers. "Dawsyn's survival, of course. We thought about pushing her into the river–"

"You *wha*–"

"But coincidentally," the mage continues smugly, "something

else came along and provided the perfect threat. And it worked. Dawsyn's magic combined, and because of it, you're alive to hear the tale, Ryon." Baltisse smiles darkly, but doesn't allow either Dawsyn or Ryon to interrupt. "I know what you're thinking, Ryon, and not just because I've divined it. You're thinking that it must have been that foolish *guard* that scared the wits out of Dawsyn, that she feared for her own life, and it conjured the coupling of her powers. But I'm afraid you would be wrong." Baltisse's eyes spear Dawsyn now, daring her to interrupt. "You see, it was not her *own* life she feared losing, but *yours.*"

Dawsyn curses inwardly, her heart throbbing painfully against her ribs.

"Happily, Dawsyn-the-unfeeling was able to recognise how deeply she cared for you," Baltisse continues. Unbearably. Intolerably. "She seems to find your demise as a precursor to her own. That is to say, she cannot *survive* without you. Romantic, isn't it? Only took a sword in regretful proximity to your throat for her to admit it to herself... but there it is."

In the far corner, Yennes smiles at the floor with studious concentration.

Ryon and Dawsyn, however, stand at opposite ends of the small room, amongst the sleeping bodies piled on the floor, Baltisse between them, looking exactly like the demonic hag she proclaims not to be.

Dawsyn's teeth are clamped so tightly shut that she is in danger of reducing them to dust. "Are you finished?" Dawsyn says, the words thick and poisonous.

Baltisse sighs cheerfully and finds a spot on the floor. "I am." She sighs. "Ugh. It feels good to get that off my chest."

"Thank the fucking Chasm," Dawsyn grits out, and in her mind, she lists a hundred threats and hopes she hears them.

Ryon waits, his patience returned. He raises his eyebrows at Dawsyn. She can't be certain, but she thinks she sees his lips twitch, as though fighting a smile. Somehow, he manages to maintain a look of passiveness.

If only the ocean would rise and swallow her now, pull her to the bottom with Garjum. Her hands tremble. She has a strange urge to draw her ax. She wants to break eye contact with Ryon, but she can't. She fears it might signal defeat. Instead, she crosses her ankles, preparing to lower herself to the ground. Perhaps he'll just let her go to sleep. They can allow this moment to slide by.

But as she begins her descent, Ryon's gaze becomes a frown. It renders her incapable of ignoring him. He shakes his head once. *Not a chance*, he seems to say.

You will rue this day, mage. Dawsyn thinks.

As one, both Ryon and Dawsyn turn for the door, making their footsteps light as they step over torsos and limbs.

Mother help me, Dawsyn thinks, opening the door to the warm sea air. *Garjum save me.*

CHAPTER FIFTY-FOUR

Dawsyn walks ahead of Ryon back to the water. It is most important that she lead *him*. She isn't certain why, only that she needs the upper hand somehow. Along the way her mind is a distortion of thought, running wildly between outlandish accusations to bald-faced denial. Her hands flit from her stomach to her hair to her throat to her hip and she wonders where the iskra is now. Where is the mage magic? Why does it sleep quietly when what she wants, more than anything, is some kind of protection?

From what? she asks herself. *Ryon?*

No. She isn't afraid.

"This will do, malishka. Unless you plan on walking into the ocean and letting it carry you away."

Malishka. That word does something to her. She cannot identify if its touch is withering or wonderful. "Don't call me that," she says, finally stopping where the sea licks the tips of her boots. She doesn't turn around immediately. Instead, she waits to hear his feet against the rock and sand. She determines how far away he stands, the distance between them, whether it is safe. And then, gathering her wits, she turns.

If not for his height, the cut of his jaw, the width of his shoulders, Ryon could just be a man standing in weak moonlight, his skin and eyes and hair made impossibly more beautiful by its silvery glow.

"Tell me why I shouldn't," he demands.

Dawsyn groans, and then begins pacing the waterline. "You must be so fucking pleased with yourself. Knowing you won."

Ryon only grins. "What did I win? You?"

"I–" Dawsyn stutters. "I… No! I don't belong to you, hybrid."

"Never said you did."

"*Malishka*," Dawsyn sneers. "As though I'm a thing, a treasure to possess."

"Ah. Well, I'm afraid I'll have to treasure you in secret then, girl."

But Dawsyn barely hears him. "I didn't mean to do it," she says, pacing back the way she came, eyes on the stars.

"Save me?"

"Love you," Dawsyn spits, kicking a rock into the water. "Before we took back Glacia. Before the Queens captured us. I didn't mean to love you."

"No," Ryon muses. "Nor I. Though I no longer believe it was something that could have been helped."

"And then I hated you." Dawsyn whirls, her jaw aching. "I hated you."

Ryon nods. "But you don't anymore."

"I do."

"You don't," Ryon says, coming to block Dawsyn's path. The water slips over his boots, but he doesn't seem to notice. He doesn't touch her, doesn't impose himself upon her, but still, he commands her attention. "It's a very convincing lie you've told yourself since Alvira slid that sword through me, but it doesn't sound true anymore. Does it, malishka?"

Dawsyn's eyes narrow. Her hand comes over her shoulder, toward her ax.

Ryon tracks her movements as she wrenches it free with less finesse than usual. They both watch her hand raise it slowly until the bit is aligned with the space between his eyes.

"Do it," he says evenly. There is not a trace of fear in his voice. "Prove me wrong. Throw your ax and tell me you hate me."

The ax trembles in her hand. Inside her, tightly bound tension is unravelling – days and nights spent tied in knots, the ends fraying each time his voice slid through her, each time their stare held too long.

With a sharp gasp she steps away and hurls her ax into the sand bank beside them. Her breaths are short and ragged, her chest splitting wide open and then caving in on itself with each one. She turns to face him once more. Finds him waiting for her. Quietly expecting her.

"Are you done now, malishka?"

It seems she is. She is tired of denying herself. Tired of fearing this tether between them. Her heart, her core, they scream for her to relent.

And Ryon's expression says the same. "Please," he begs her, his chest rising and falling heavily. His hands tremble.

Dawsyn shakes her head at him, and then she moves, she walks right into the circle of his arms. She presses her face into the wall of his chest. She breathes.

Ryon's hands come to the back of her neck. They tilt her face up to his.

His forehead comes to hers, his breath so close and sweet, Dawsyn finds it hard to care who wins and loses. "I can say it for you," he tells her, uttering nothing more for a moment. "You love me," he says, the words travelling over her mouth. "And I, you."

Dawsyn is the one to press her lips into his, relishing the shape of his mouth, the taste of him. Her entire body thrums with the need for closeness. She's staved that desire away for too long, tempted it more than she ever should have. When his hands move over her back and down to her waist, when she feels his lips spreading into a victorious smile beneath hers, she presses closer.

And then he is pulling away. Just as her tongue begins to trace the seam of his lips, he gently untangles himself from her grasp. His mouth leaves hers, his hands gently unwind her arms from his body, and he steps back, shaking his head.

"That's enough for now," he says hoarsely.

A laugh, exasperated and breathless, escapes her. "*Enough?*"

Ryon grins again, and it is so radiant, so filled with love – for *her* – that she almost ignores him. To hell with his protests.

"I'm not going to let you forget this when the sun rises, Dawsyn. I won't listen to you when you claim that you never admitted to loving me."

"I *didn't.*"

"You did," he laughs. "I know you too well by now, malishka. I won't have you try to pretend this is nothing more than desire."

Dawsyn steps toward him, only for him to take a step back. He shakes his head. "Not until you tell me that this is what you want. Not just tonight, but from now on."

Dawsyn tilts her head. She is easily lured into a test of wills. Her favourite game with him. She remembers those moments on the slopes when it was her against him, before it was them against the rest. She remembers the baiting, the taunting. She remembers undressing in front of him, and the way he'd swiftly folded.

She looks out to the sea then down, out to the warm water curling over her feet, and then rolls her shoulders back.

First, she rids herself of the holster on her back, and then her boots. Ryon watches, frowning uncertainly. But the more she devests of her outer layers, the tighter his jaw becomes. Stoically, he tries to give off passiveness, as though he is unaffected. But when she stands with only a long tunic covering her to her thighs, his eyes darken. "Don't," he says simply.

"You could always turn your back," Dawsyn says.

He doesn't.

She doesn't bother hiding her smile as she lifts the hem, pulling it higher and higher over her body. She pulls it free of her hair, dropping it to the ground, and looks up to see Ryon alight with desire.

Dawsyn faces the water. She wades in.

"You can't swim, Dawsyn," he growls.

She clicks her tongue. "I have every faith in your ability to rescue me."

She smiles at the horizon, where golden light is just starting to spread at the divide. The tepid water reaches her hips, and then her waist, and just as it skims the underside of her breasts, she hears an exasperated laugh from the beach.

Moments later, she hears the thrashing of water displaced as Ryon follows her out. And she can hardly wait.

"It's beneath you to force my hand."

"You needn't touch me," Dawsyn answers without turning.

But she hears him exhale, and then hands go around her waist. Slowly skimming her skin until they meet at her diaphragm. "Fine," Ryon rumbles, his mouth at her ear. "You win."

He moves his lips to her neck and presses them softly under her jaw. He hovers there a moment longer, taking in the scent of her skin, pulling her into the hard wall of his body. No clothes between them. No battle to distract them. The light too dim for any to find them here. Just the two of them, the ocean, and the horizon ahead.

Dawsyn turns. In that moment, she becomes imbued with something new, a sense of conviction, of rightness. A certainty that there isn't anywhere else he or she should be, but here.

"I fear I may love you," she tells him, her smile gone, finality in its place. And what she means is, *I couldn't stop.*

"Ah," Ryon says, cradling her body in his beneath the water, pulling her legs around his waist. "Then we both win."

Their lips find each other's, their fervency increasing with each lazy lap of the ocean. It's as though Dawsyn's body is attuned to his. It remembers the curve between his neck and his shoulder, the shallow dips of his stomach, the jut of his hips. His mouth moves over her throat, rediscovering all the parts of her as well. He grips her thighs tighter, and then his lips trace her collarbone, then lower.

Dawsyn sucks a breath between her teeth as the warmth of his mouth comes over her breast. His tongue flicks over her, and she squeezes her thighs around him in response. The more his mouth torments her, the more persistent her hips become, finding the hard length of him. She rocks back and forth impatiently, gasping as her pace quickens. It draws a dark rumble from him. She needs him more desperately than she's ever needed another person before, and she doesn't bother to conceal that desire, finally unbound. She lets him see it.

"Please," Dawsyn whispers, the word carried away on the wind. "Please."

Ryon presses his forehead back to hers, wrapping her tightly in his inescapable embrace. This close, she can see the flecks in his irises, the water droplets on his lashes. "Anything you want," he says, lowering her onto himself. She gasps at the shock if it, being so filled with him. "I've been waiting for you," he says, softly kissing her again. "I'm yours."

And then she is consumed with him, with them, with the feel of their bodies combined and moving together. And she follows the feeling of ecstasy into oblivion.

CHAPTER FIFTY-FIVE

As the sun bleaches the sky, Dawsyn and Ryon leave the shoreline behind them, damp but dressed. They walk back to the cabin with deliberate slowness. It brings to mind the nights Ryon spent in the Colony, loitering where he ought not be until the night leached away and he had to return to whatever bed, in whatever lean-to he then resided, with whatever kind soul he then burdened. He would drag his feet and kick at the ice and opt for the longest path, weaving his way back, step after reluctant step, wringing out every last second of solitude.

Ryon keeps his hands to himself for little more than a moment before he lays a palm to the back of her neck, slipping his fingers into her wet hair.

"Do you think the others will have noticed our absence?" she asks, tucking into the space at his side, pacing her steps in time with his. Close enough for him to feel her chilled skin.

He wraps his arm around her. "I can't bring myself to give a damn."

A smile. Slight, but true. Her eyes change when she smiles. They widen. Soften. The lines from years spent peering into the wind are replaced with something gentler. He cannot name which form of her he favours, the calm or the storm. Any. All.

"Why do you smirk?" Dawsyn asks abruptly. The wind carries ropes of her raven-black hair across her nose.

Ryon breaks from his reverie. "I'm thinking about how insufferable Baltisse will be."

A small pause. Dawsyn considers it. "We could always weight her feet and drown her."

"I'm afraid I'd have to protest. There are more than a few outstanding debts I've yet to repay her."

Dawsyn sets her eyes on the cabin, smoke beginning to unfurl from its chimney. "As do I," she says.

Ryon breathes a sigh of deep contentment. Beneath his skin, where Dawsyn cannot see, there are knots – entire nests of them – becoming free. A slow release of tendon and nerve, brought by the dawning of relief. A correction made to his dangerously teetering world. Restraints that steadfastly held him at a distance are gently released. He can reach for her once more. He can touch the line between her brows, follow the pathways of her palm. He can weave whispers into her ear until her eyelids droop and she falls asleep. All of it… returned to him.

"We shouldn't be for each other, you know," Dawsyn says slowly, gaze unwavering and open, searching. Tender.

Ryon understands what she means. It is a weak, surface-level truth. Humans don't belong with Glacians. "I know," he says.

"I've asked myself why I didn't try harder to ignore it at first. Ignore *you*." Her brows bunch and release. What he wouldn't do to hear her mind.

"And what answer did you give?"

Dawsyn brings them to a stop outside the cabin. They can stretch the journey no longer.

She observes him before responding, mapping his features. She is delving into him, seeing each dark, fetid corner of him and remaining undeterred. "I think we were unavoidable, you and I. Do you feel it?"

He thinks of waking in a dungeon with his chest burning and his blood singing for her. He remembers the shock of black hair against the stark snow and the way it had made him want to pray, give thanks, because he'd found her. He thinks of the hundreds, the thousands of moments his hands have ached for Dawsyn, when he could do nothing but watch, keep his distance, be patient and hopeful. Knowing all the while how helplessly tangled his existence was with hers, whether she came back to him or not.

So, he nods, gently brushes his fingertips along her jaw. He releases the smile he's been dulling and lets her see the full extent of his wonder. "I feel it," he says.

The others are in various stages of waking within the cabin. Yennes has lit a fire. She deftly chops stored root vegetables while the others grunt and scrub their faces. As predicted, Baltisse oozes smugness. She says nothing as Ryon and Dawsyn sit beside each other on upturned buckets, but her grin is serpentine and her eyes churn with superiority. Ryon glares back, and it seems to dissuade her from offering any remark, at least.

Dawsyn, however, pays Baltisse and the others no mind. Instead, she tirelessly tracks Yennes's movements. Ryon passes her a bowl of soup, and she thanks him, but her gaze doesn't leave the woman before the hearth, busying herself with serving their party a heartier meal than any they've had in weeks. Amongst the clamour and flurry of many bodies in a small space, Dawsyn's stare is unbroken.

The others eventually venture outside, seeking relief from the oppressive heat of a cabin made for colder climates, but Dawsyn doesn't follow. And when it is only her, Yennes, and Ryon left, Dawsyn wastes no more time.

"Will you tell me now how you did it?" Dawsyn says to Yennes's back. "How you escaped from Glacia?" The timbre of her voice fills the ceiling and walls and empty spaces between. It isn't to be ignored.

Yennes turns with a wet rag, winding it manically around her hands. Her eyes skit between Dawsyn and Ryon and away. She seems even more furtive than usual. "Of course," she says. "I... will try."

The woman's voice, the very sight of her, daunts him. Ryon cannot explain it in his mind. Perhaps it is only the risk of a stranger in their midst, the knowledge of power lurking beneath her skin. No matter how harmless she appears on the outside, Ryon can't help the faint wariness that arises at the sight of this human. Some keen sense within tells him to ready himself.

When it seems she cannot pluck free the words to start, Dawsyn clears her throat. "You were selected from the Ledge?" she asks, letting the words linger.

"Yes," sighs Yennes, her breath trembling. "It was... horrific. Worse than I ever feared. It will be... quite difficult for you both to believe, but I was not always the shaky leaf you see before you. I was once quite... fierce, I suppose. Callous, as one must be, up there. Meekness is the swiftest path to death on the Ledge."

A pause, one that draws out. "It is," Dawsyn answers. "Go on."

"I'd imagined my own Selection many times. I thought about the talons that would dig into my shoulders, and I reasoned away the likelihood of pain. I'd once cracked my cheekbone on the ice and split it open. Misha Lochmore had once jammed a pick through my foot when I tried to steal her cabbage harvest. Talons couldn't be worse than that. Being devoured would be, if nothing else, quick; at least, that is how I comforted myself." Yennes shrugs awkwardly.

"At the start of the season, my father took ill and was confined to his bed. He tried to rise to his place before our family but collapsed instead. Lung sickness already had hold of him, and I couldn't bear to bring him outside. It had already taken my mother. I stood outside the cabin, at the head of my family for the very first time, and gritted my teeth. I reassured myself that it wouldn't be me. I wouldn't be taken. And then I was.

"It was… unimaginably painful, the journey over the Chasm. And when it was over, they didn't even have the decency to kill us. They chained us, beat us, imprisoned us, and made us wait. If there is something worse than slaughter, it is waiting for its arrival."

Ryon feels sick at her words. He remembers all the people, lying cold and broken on the floor of the Glacian dungeons.

"But death did not come. That King – Vasteel. He said his piece. I am sure you don't need me to reiterate. We saw those ghost people. The ones who were selected and reduced to their shells. I resolved myself to become the same." Yennes pauses. Her eyes turn filmy and far away. Some internal battle wages within. Something haunting.

"You went into the pool?" Dawsyn asks when it seems Yennes may not speak again.

Yennes blinks. Twists her hands. "I did. It… spoke to me. As I'm sure it did you both. It was difficult to ignore. Despite it, my wits somehow held. I listened to the pool's magic, warning me not to breathe. And I breathed anyway. As I said, I was more oppositional back then.

"When they fished me from the pool, my soul was intact. I was filled with foreign iskra, that sentient substance of the pool. I made my stare as dead as those poor fools who had been pulled out before me. I was taken to the Chasm, led right to its edge, and my… my arrogance left me. I shook. Frost coated my hands. I whimpered like a child." Yennes shakes her head as she remembers. Clenching her hands together to stay their incessant turning. "It was a Glacian who saved me," she says, looking to Ryon. Their eyes hold for a moment, before she looks away, as though the memory is one she'd rather not revisit. "I still don't know why he did it."

"A Glacian?" Ryon asks, taken aback. "Who?"

"I do not know the name."

"And this Glacian, he flew you to the bottom of the Chasm?" Dawsyn asks. "He told you to find its end?"

Yennes nods slowly, her teeth grinding. "Only two paths. Both are filled," she mutters, spoken with her tongue but with the echo of someone else's. Her sight is elsewhere again. Ryon wonders if she meant to utter the words at all. It seems the woman is often in conversation with herself.

"Two paths?" Dawsyn repeats, her voice slipping into thought.

But Ryon has already put it together. He can see the ends of those paths, the opportunity in them. "The one that leads to Terrsaw," he says. "And the one that leads away."

Dawsyn gasps. Frost begins to creep over her fingers.

"You took the path that led you back to Terrsaw," Ryon says. "To this cove. But had you walked in the other direction…?"

"I do not know what I would have found," Yennes says gently, apologetically.

"Ryon," Dawsyn says. "Did any Glacian ever speak of it? What lies on the other side of the mountain?"

But Ryon is already shaking his head, his mind keeping pace with hers. "The mixed could not leave the Colony, malishka."

"But the Chasm must end somewhere," Dawsyn answers. "It must lead to a place on the other side."

"Or, it could just end," Yennes offers. "I'm sorry, Dawsyn. I cannot promise another side. I do not know if one exists."

"Someone must know," Dawsyn presses. "A species of winged creatures surely can't exist without *one* of them exploring the other side of this fucking mountain."

"Dyavnon," Ryon says, the name slipping free without his consent.

Dawsyn turns to him. Waits. "Dyavnon?" she repeats. "What does it mean?"

Ryon shrugs. "It's a Glacian myth. I hadn't remembered before now. You said you don't believe Glacians would have neglected to explore the other side of this mountain, but they had a reason to avoid it." At the look of painful impatience on Dawsyn's face he gives her a stiff grin, holds up his hands. "I could explain, but I'll let Rivdan tell you instead."

"Why Rivdan?" Dawsyn asks.

Ryon's grin widens as he goes for the door. "In Glacia, Rivdan went by two names," he says. "Rivdan and the Storyteller."

Chapter Fifty-Six

Dawsyn stands as Ryon leads Rivdan into the cabin, the latter with arms laden with cut wood. He nods to Yennes. "For you, miss," he says, and adds it to her existing pile beside the hearth.

Ryon clears his throat. "Riv? We need your stories, brother."

The man's eyes narrow, but he asks no questions. Dawsyn notes how he studies them all. He seems to take note of the edge in the room. He is a calculating man. "Which?" he asks.

"Dyavnon."

Rivdan blanches. He gives Ryon a withering look.

Strange, Dawsyn thinks.

Ryon hardens his stare. "Please?"

"It is not a story still told, Ryon. Bad luck."

"Ha," Ryon puffs. "Brother, if more bad luck finds us, we'll merely add it to the pile."

Rivdan seems to hesitate, his jaw clenching.

"It is superstition, Riv. Nothing more."

"All stories are born from seeds of truth," he mutters petulantly. He is reluctant, that much is clear. But eventually Rivdan sighs and nods. "Very well," he begins. "When the sun was first born into the sky, no hill or mountain lay upon the land. Any creature could easily walk from shore to shore. It was, therefore, vulnerable to Dyavnon."

Dawsyn understands now why Rivdan was named *Storyteller*. His voice is oddly hypnotic.

"Dyavnon, a creature of the underworld, rose from the earth and wreaked havoc on all that lived on the land. She would break a creature with a mere thought, until the bones showed through their flesh, for she needed them. Each bone she took helped to remake her. She longed to be a living thing once more, to untie herself from the dark earth. She was tethered to the surface, you see. She could roam across it, but her feet made from stolen bones could not leave the ground. Only winged creatures could survive her. Glacians could take flight and avoid her grasp."

"But Vasteel was the first Glacian," Dawsyn interrupts. "And the ground was not flat when he changed."

"It's a myth, Dawsyn," Ryon says. "But it's an important one. Go on, Riv."

"The Glacians could not remain in flight forever. They used their power to raise a mountain from the earth, for they knew that Dyavnon would not be able to climb something so steep – it would bring her too close to the sun, too close to the Mother who had banished her to the underworld long ago. No, she would have to remain in the mountain's shadow, where she was closest to the underworld.

"But the Glacians were merciful. They saw no need to forsake the other creatures who shared the earth. So their mountain kept Dyavnon on one side, blocking her path to the other, where animals and man could keep on living. Dyavnon was doomed to wander her side of the mountain forever, lusting for bones to complete her transformation, and awaiting the time a foolish Glacian sought what lay beyond the Ridge, so that she might snap them in two, and harvest their skeletons."

Rivdan's deep timbre lingers moments after the tale is told, and Dawsyn can't help but be affected, despite the gaping holes in the story.

A pause, and then Dawsyn says. "I've heard many myths, but never one so full of shit."

"And can you guess who would have concocted a tale so blatantly dishonest?" Ryon asks her. "One that painted Glacians in the light of heroes? One that bid Glacians never to travel to the other side of the mountain? A myth told to infants, designed to scare them into compliance."

Dawsyn grimaces. "All stories are designed to scare children into compliance."

"Not all," Rivdan corrects softly. "Just the ones told by wicked kings."

"Vasteel." Dawsyn sighs, and notes the way Yennes blanches at the name.

"I think we can be sure of where Vasteel now lurks," Ryon says darkly. "I've wondered what hole he may have crawled into. What better place than one Glacians have long been conditioned to fear?"

"The other side of the mountain," Dawsyn says. "You think there's something there?"

"I do," he replies, his dark eyes flashing.

"That does not mean the Chasm will lead you to it, Ryon," Yennes says.

"Perhaps not," Dawsyn answers. "But we will soon learn."

Rivdan frowns. Ryon grins. Yennes shrivels.

"That is how we will save the people of the Ledge," Dawsyn says with finality, for it is the only way. The only path that leads away from both Glacia and Terrsaw. Away from the clutches of Adrik and Alvira.

"We can fly or fold them to the bottom of the Chasm," Ryon nods. "It will be difficult, but if they can be convinced to go, then it may be done."

"And then they will walk," Dawsyn agrees, her mind racing ahead to other plans. What provisions to take. What to leave behind.

"The Chasm is filled," Yennes repeats, an echo of a faint

uttering. Her voice shakes as she says it, but she is still louder than Dawsyn has ever heard her. "The path is not empty."

Dawsyn analyses her. Her eyes are wet with fear, her hands in a free-fall tumble she can no longer control. This is it, then, the thing that changed her. A ferocious woman of the Ledge turned withering and fragile.

"What," Dawsyn begins slowly, her eyes narrowing, "is in the Chasm?"

Yennes swallows convulsively, her eyes closing against the moisture. "I've spent years forgetting... *years*."

Dawsyn sighs. More monsters. More beasts. Things of the mountain worse than Glacians. She stands and goes to the woman. She takes her trembling, flighty hands into her own. She feels the way those fingers twitch, desperate to be free, and waits until they relax, waits for Yennes to open her eyes again.

"I am sorry," Dawsyn says softly, and she means it. She is sorry for all this woman has endured alone. For all of Dawsyn's ordeals, at least not all were faced in solitude. "But our people don't deserve to remain on the Ledge."

"I know." She nods fervently. "I know."

"So, we will take them into Chasm," Dawsyn continues. "Whether we know what awaits... or not."

Yennes nods again, her head bobbing with deranged compliance.

"Into the Chasm," Dawsyn says to them all. "And then through it to its end."

Chapter Fifty-Seven

Dawsyn's plan is uncomplicated, and yet still fraught with a million divinations of failure. Those that are willing will return to the Ledge once more. Dawsyn, with the help of Hector, will say that precise thing that will convince a hundred or so people to go into the Chasm – a chasm they have watched and leant away from for half a century. Ryon, Rivdan, and Tasheem will fly the humans to the bottom, two at a time. Baltisse will fold as many people as she can, without debilitating herself.

"Don't speak to me as if I don't know my own limits," the mage says icily. Dawsyn rolls her eyes but continues her speech to the rest of the group, who stand in a loose formation at the shoreline, eyes on the end of the Chasm.

"How will we avoid the notice of Adrik and the rest?" Tasheem asks. "The palace isn't so far away."

"We go at night," Dawsyn says. "We stay quiet. They are not likely to notice a single Glacian and two humans slipping over the lip. We will be careful."

"And then?" asks Esra, his eyes round and astonished.

"And then we walk through the Chasm," Dawsyn says. "And pray we reach the end."

"We pray there *is* an end," Yennes corrects.

"There is an end," Dawsyn says assuredly. "There must be."

Ryon speaks now. "You must all choose whether you join

us or stay. The Chasm is not free of threat. There are… things lurking within that will give us no small amount of trouble, should we meet them. Salem, Esra," Ryon says, dragging the men's eyes from the Chasm's maw. "You needn't come and put yourselves at risk for this quest. You should stay with Yennes in this cove. Build your own home…"

"I won't be staying," Yennes says suddenly, the words dry on the breeze, shaky.

Dawsyn frowns at the woman. "Where will you go?"

"To the Ledge," Yennes says, standing a little taller. "I can fold, so I will come."

"Yen–"

"I will come," she says once more, with force this time. She eyes the Chasm's opening with something that resembles animosity – a threat she has kept in her sight all these years.

"What did you mean, dear Ryon?" Esra asks, his arms crossed. "When you said we should stay? Salem might be two hundred pounds of imbecile, but *I'm* not fucking useless!"

Ryon groans. "Es–"

"I'm not the dimwit in the *velvet frock*, yeh benign lump," Salem huffs.

"Salem, your pants gave up on your waistline a long time ago and we've all been subjected to a very different sort of chasm these past weeks. Do not lecture me on the functionality of fashion."

"*Fine*," Ryon intervenes. "You'll come, Esra."

"And I'll be useful, too," he says, rubbing his hands together. "What weapons shall I procure for the Chasm beasties then?"

Dawsyn smiles at him. "Whatever you can find."

"Whatever can be carried," Ryon adds.

"What can I do, Dawsyn?" Salem asks now. "If this moanin' blob is goin', then I best be at yer disposal too. I'll make meself handy."

"You needn't, Salem."

Salem hesitates for a moment, glancing around their mob,

eyes sticking first to Ryon, then Esra, Baltisse, and finally back to her. "My family is here," he says simply, then says no more.

Dawsyn swallows the tightness gripping her throat, then nods. "If the people on the Ledge can be convinced, I'll need your help sorting their provisions. Preparing them to leave."

"I'm yer lad," he says, squaring his beefy shoulders.

"We might not make it so far," Dawsyn remarks, turning her back on the others to face the Chasm's end. "They might not be persuaded."

"Maybe not," Hector answers. "But we must try anyway."

Dawsyn grimaces. "We must try anyway."

And there is a piece of Dawsyn that won't stay quiet, a nagging thought that this plan is suicidal. That they are no more than pests scurrying away. Running from a Queen who ought to die for her misdeeds; running away from Adrik, who should be pulled apart for his betrayal. A piece of her that calls for their demise. For the liberation of more than just one people.

She thinks of Ruby telling her to lead the Ledge people through the Mecca and watch the Queen flounder. Watch her fold at the sight of Terrsaw rejoicing.

But Adrik is in Glacia, drinking iskra with his followers. When the pool runs dry, he will come to Terrsaw. The cycle will continue. How long before Terrsaw stops seeing the return of the Ledge people as a blessing? How long before they start to long for the days where they lived in peace in the valley, while the Ledge lay out of sight above them?

No, there is only one path. One option.

Through the Chasm.

CHAPTER FIFTY-EIGHT

Inside the Queens' palace, Ruby has fallen into a relentless cycle of delirium. The lack of light in the dungeons does not help matters. She is no more aware of the hour than she is of the number of days that have passed since she was locked away. The comings and goings of sentries mean little to her now. She barely notices the changes.

She sings to stay the hysteria. It reminds her of her initiation at the Boulder Gate, when she did the same to quell the helplessness festering inside her.

When she forgets to sing, she thinks of Will Brockner, the young man she had courted before abandoning. How he is now dead because of her.

Incrementally, she is beaten – sometimes with fervour, sometimes with deep, bitter reluctance. One guard or another comes into her cell, they knock her onto the floor and kick her in the stomach. It has happened with enough frequency that her piss bucket contains mostly blood.

After this she cries, then sleeps.

The cycle repeats.

The only other person who comes to call is Darius, the lop-smiled kitchen hand. He brings extra meals to her cell, just as Ruby once did for Dawsyn.

She awaits her death, a torturous preoccupation all on its

own. Alvira has not come to this keep. Wherever she is, she seems content for Ruby to slowly go mad.

Only small snippets have reached her ears from the guard's conversations.

...Deployed half the army into the forest to search...

...The Sabar girl has not shown her face. You don't think...

...A guard crushed to death. Another swears he saw Sabar and the half-breed...

They haven't been caught – of this, Ruby is convinced. And she is ever-so-slightly mollified to know that her unfortunate capture in that forest did not lead to that of Dawsyn and the others.

At some point in this cycle of misery, a grating sound reaches her. Her eyes fly open, and she thinks, *This is it.* And then, *Thank the mother.*

Her cell gate slides into its recess, and two guards wait on the other side. They bear down on her, take her upper arms in their grip, and hoist.

She is lifted to stand, her legs barely able to comply.

She blinks rapidly, trying to bring to focus the shifting vision before her. There is someone else standing beyond the gate. Someone who waits expectantly.

"Hello again, Captain," says Queen Cressida.

CHAPTER FIFTY-NINE

It takes two days for Baltisse and Esra to return from their scouting trip. When they unfold back into Yennes's cove, as Dawsyn has come to call it, Esra's back is laden with a dozen sheathed swords and a bag of blades, varied in both size and degree of disrepair.

"Come, Dawsyn Sabar," says Baltisse, taking the bag from Esra. "I will show you how we mages prepare our weapons."

Dawsyn follows her into the long grass, swaying languidly toward the sea, and sits cross-legged opposite her, frowning with suspicion.

"Take this," Baltisse says, putting a particularly rusted dagger in Dawsyn's hand. "Do you remember the incantation for fire?"

Dawsyn thinks. "Igniss," she says. "I remember."

"There are many others. If you can continue to make those two competing powers play nicely, you can use your magic as you wish. Tell me what you were feeling when you merged your power to save Ryon."

Dawsyn tries to remember, but it was a medley of thought, all at once. "Panic," she says.

"That won't do." Baltisse shakes her head. "I know that you are capable, Dawsyn, but you must try harder to isolate it. What did you feel when you thought Ryon might die?"

Dawsyn sighs but closes her eyes. She brings back the image of Ryon taking out a guard while the other brought his sword down toward his neck. She pictures her ax flying through the air, too slowly, and she felt… she felt…

"Determined," Dawsyn says, her hand gripped tightly around the knife handle. "I felt… pure refusal. I saw that he would die and I… couldn't allow it."

Baltisse narrows her eyes. "Those two powers are opposite, and yet alike. One thrives on pain and anger, and the other on joy. But you are stronger than either, Dawsyn. Mages must be, to hold them inside our bodies. Use your mage magic and stay determined. Do not allow it to stamp out the iskra."

"But you told me never to force it? That it had its own mind."

Baltisse looks away. "This is the only time you will hear me say this, but I was wrong. You are different, Dawsyn. If there is one thing I know of your mind, it's that you will force your way through whatever barrier dares to thwart you."

A thread of connection holds them silent for a moment. The sea rolls to shore, the grass whispers against their legs, but the two mages only look at each other, their thoughts aligned.

Forgive yourself, Dawsyn thinks, knowing Baltisse will hear it. *You're not the harbinger you think you are.*

Baltisse's eyes don't move in their ethereal way. That burning colour does not morph at all. For once, they are calm. And silently, astonishingly, they become filmy. Wet with centuries of blame. Dawsyn did not ever imagine she might see the almighty mage, the all-powerful sorceress cry. Her jaw remains still, her lips pressed together in resolution, but tears threaten to spill, and she looks dangerous and miserable all at once. "I am the maker of the pool," she says simply. "It cannot be forgiven."

Dawsyn knows a fraction of that pain – being the custodian of unforgivable sins. She sighs. "You would have been a fitting addition to our den of girls," she tells her. "We do tend to carry burdens not our own."

Baltisse raises her eyebrows. "I fear your grandmother would have thrown me into the Chasm."

"Undoubtedly," Dawsyn says through a smile. She takes the mage's hand in hers, and squeezes.

They spend the afternoon in the grass, reciting incantations to clean the knives by magic. "Cistique" to clean. "Ishveet" to repair. "Lussia" to tie. "Bruvex" to break. Dawsyn uses each without her magic threatening to buckle her. That golden glow does the work, and pays no heed to the iskra lurking quietly within.

"And now you will learn to fold," Baltisse says finally, dumping the last of the sharpened knives into the bag.

Dawsyn looks up. "Can it be learnt in a day?"

"Certainly not," Baltisse says. "But we are running out of time. There is none to waste."

"We leave in three days," Dawsyn says quickly. "Can I master it by then?"

"It is not likely," the mage answers, brushing sand from her skirt as she stands. "But 'unlikely' seems to inhabit your entire persona, Dawsyn. Get up."

The next hours are spent in a brutal battle between time and space as Dawsyn learns to think of a desired destination, let it fill her mind entirely, and then will her magic to collapse into something as fine as air.

It is infuriatingly painful and difficult, but she continues to work until long after Baltisse has left, until Ryon comes outside to collect her from the dark. He takes her hand, pulls her into the cabin to eat, to rest, before she must start again.

CHAPTER SIXTY

The night before they're to leave for the Ledge, Dawsyn is standing amongst the thin trees, attempting to fold herself from one place to another, just a short distance away. Thus far, she has done nothing more than manage to disappear and reappear in the same place, gagging and panting, her muscles screaming.

She hears footsteps in the dark long before they reach her, and she stills. Logic tells her that whoever approaches is a friend, but experience tells her not to trust it. Suddenly, the footfalls cease. There is a rush of swooping wind, and then the moonlight disappears. Something descends upon her.

Dawsyn takes her ax out in time for her arms to be pinned at her sides. She is hauled backward a foot to the trunk of a tree, her back pressing into the soft, papery bark, while the mass of a great hulking hybrid holds her there, his face a picture of victory.

"Well," Ryon says, leaning to kiss the underside of her jaw. "I never thought I'd succeed in sneaking up on the infamous Dawsyn Sabar."

"It would be more impressive without the damned ring on your finger."

But Ryon holds up a bare hand. "Yennes wanted to inspect its magical properties," he explains. "The victory is all mine."

"I heard you," Dawsyn mumbles, distracted by the closeness of him. "Hardly constitutes as sneaking if I was aware of your sneaking, does it?"

"I'll have to keep practicing." He grins, loosening his hold on her arms. He touches the soft skin beneath her eyes, which must be black with weariness by now. "Come with me," he asks her. "Sleep by my side."

Ryon's face is etched with something like worry. Worry for the task ahead, worry for her, maybe.

She worries too.

"I don't want to sleep," she tells him, taking his hand. She leads him toward the trees, toward the water. "I have something else in mind."

His face transforms into something wicked. "Perfect."

"Not that," Dawsyn shoves him. "You can tell me a story."

"Riv is the Storyteller."

"A story that is *yours*," she presses.

Ryon groans, but it is performative. When they reach the beach, he sits on the warm sand and pulls Dawsyn down until she is settled with her back to his chest, her head nestled in the crook of his neck. They've rested this way before, in a cave on the mountain, where he whispered a story with his lips at her ear.

He does so again now.

He tells her of bonfires that turned the ground to sludge, where the mixed-Glacians danced and sang around the flames. He sings her a song of the Colony. He talks of Tasheem and his other childhood friends. Dawsyn savours the tales as she once did her grandmother's, letting them fill her mind until it quiets.

It feels right to know him.

It lulls her, to hear him speak.

When the favourable stories are spent, Ryon speaks of darker things. The beatings. The displacement. The way Adrik had shaped him into a weapon and cast him aside once used.

"With no humans on the Ledge, Adrik will move upon the Valley," Ryon murmurs, his tone hollow. "Just like Vasteel. He will find his iskra... one way or another."

The ocean is reflected in his eyes. It claws its way to the shore. On the outside, he appears nothing but stern, contemplative, but beneath it is a man burning from a lifetime of betrayal.

"One day," Dawsyn vows, "when we have settled the humans, we will come back for the mixed."

Ryon nods. "Indeed. Adrik has earnt a slow death."

There's a knot in Dawsyn's gut that has little to do with the danger ahead. It grows tighter when she thinks of the loose threads still to be cut. When they leave tomorrow, they leave knowing that Adrik is seizing his empire, the Queens still wear their stolen crowns, and that somewhere, in some dark corner, lurks Vasteel, biding his time.

Like sores that she ought not pick at, though they are difficult to ignore.

There is one thought, however, that staves off her turmoil. The people of Terrsaw were once content to let her live and die on the Ledge. Maybe it is fitting that she untwines her fortune from theirs.

The people on the Ledge will be saved tomorrow, and the rest can flounder.

Ryon and Dawsyn remain on the shores of Terrsaw, his fingers tracing hers, until the sky is anaemic and starless. When they rise, it's with the willingness to forge ahead. Again. Together.

They will fly through the Chasm. It will guide them back to the Ledge.

The Chasm's walls will provide the cover they need to arrive unnoticed, but they will stay near the top to keep track of their whereabouts. It took Yennes five days to reach the Chasm's end on foot. Ryon believes he can approximate the time back, retracing Yennes's path in the sky. Less than a day.

Dawsyn stares at the Chasm's end, the steep walls of the mountain stretching endlessly skyward. It spits the sea from its mouth, back out to the depths, where Garjum fights the tide.

"I couldn't swim," says a soft voice from behind her. Dawsyn turns to find Yennes dressed in hardier garb. She has replaced her thin shawls with heavy, hooded fur, leather breeches, and boots. She looks like a Ledge woman. "When I finally reached the Chasm's end, all that water rushed in to meet my feet and I could see the ocean. But I knew I couldn't swim. It stretched on endlessly. The water rushed through and out again, over and over and I stood paralysed with fear. I couldn't see beyond the walls, and I was born up there, on the Ledge. I had no perception of Terrsaw. I thought the water might stretch on all sides, forever. I considered if it were better to simply stay there in the Chasm."

"But you didn't," Dawsyn reminds Yennes. So often it seems that the woman's mind has carried her back to a place she fears.

Yennes startles. Blinks. "No, I didn't. I decided I would rather die than stay in that Chasm," she says, adjusting the strap on her shoulder. The satchel on her back must be heavy with the waterskins and food within. "I let the water carry me out, and as soon as I was beyond the mountain, Terrsaw was there, waiting. I almost drowned, swimming to shore. But the waves spat me out."

Dawsyn sighs heavily. "Valma Sabar would have said the Mother had plans for you."

"If that is true, then I have disappointed Her thus far, I'm afraid."

But Dawsyn sees the fear in each spasm of her fingers, the determined set of her jaw, and thinks differently. "Perhaps they are yet to be realised."

"Perhaps," Yennes concedes. "But I must tell you, Dawsyn Sabar, if the Chasm does not spit me out on the other side on this journey, I will forfeit any plan the Mother might hold for me."

Two paths. Both are filled, says an insistent voice. It sticks to the forefront of Dawsyn's mind. The iskra in Dawsyn, the magic that seems more in tune to threat, uncoils with growing disquiet. Dawsyn ignores it. "Whatever lurks in the Chasm," she says, "will be no match for us."

"Dawsyn?" calls a man's voice, one she could pick blindfolded. Hector is striding toward where she and Yennes stand on the shore, his arms laden with Esra's black market weapons.

Yennes nods to Dawsyn and takes her leave, striding along her beach one last time.

Hector jostles the steel. "Take your pick," he says, rattling the swords enticingly.

"None for me," Dawsyn tells him, reaching over her shoulder and grasping the neck of her ax. She brings it forward, blade first, and turns it in her hand until the woodgrain slides through her fingers and the handle settles in her palm. The oldest ritual her body remembers.

"You are so strangely attached to those things." Hector scowls. "Take a sword, Dawsyn. We both know what will meet us up there." He juts his chin to the mountain as he speaks, his features sharp.

She can taste the bitter bite in his tone. There are a thousand healed cuts on his skin that still ooze his resentment. "We don't know that it will turn to battle, Hector. Perhaps with you and I returning once more, they will be persuaded."

Hector huffs. "Or perhaps they will chase us into the Chasm themselves."

"Fear is dangerous," Dawsyn says. "Our people are not violent by *choice*."

"But they are violent, all the same," Hector says bluntly. "I know you feel… obligated," he says carefully, as though he weighs each word. "Loyal, even. But if they do not come, Dawsyn. If they won't listen–"

"Then I will come back again," Dawsyn says forcefully. "I

will come back over and over, if I must. Those people are not resources for Glacians. They are not the bargaining chips of queens. They aren't cattle, or currency, or a fucking lesser class of human. They are simply *trapped*. They act as the trapped do." Dawsyn pauses to draw breath. She is surprised at the vigour coating the words. "*We* acted as trapped creatures do," she reminds him. "And we have earnt our liberation."

Hector watches her for a moment, then nods in a resigned way. "Most of those people would have watched you and I starve to death, Dawsyn. I'm just asking you to remember it before you throw your neck on a blade for them."

"You don't need to accompany–"

"Yes, I do," he says simply. "You and I were never more than friends. Companions. But you're a part of me. And I'm a part of you." He does not meet her eye as he says it, readjusting the weapons in his arms. "We are family. Where you go, I go," he says, and turns his back on her.

Dawsyn watches him retreat. She stays on the beach as the others gather their supplies and go over final plans. She contemplates loyalty.

Hector had used the word. The elusive pull that drives her back to the Ledge time and time again. The binding that exists between Ryon and her. It's the face behind the guilt that plagues Terrsaw. Dawsyn sees her friends coming toward her, ready for the journey ahead, and wonders if loyalty isn't the greatest hindrance of all.

Chapter Sixty-One

Ryon holds out his arms to her, but his expression stops her from going to them.

It is a fracturing glass. The incremental splintering of ice. She can see his jaw working beneath the scruff, his eyes becoming carefully blank, disguising the fault lines.

Despite the vastness of him, the obvious strength he possesses, it seems there is something that can breach it all. She is not dense enough to believe it's the threat of the Ledge.

Dawsyn's eyes prick, and she means to withdraw from the discomfort of it. There is a task ahead, and that callous part of her shies away from the thought of being made to feel. Perhaps she would do just that, if Ryon didn't look so anxious. Perhaps she'd wrap an arm around his neck and tell him to hurry up and untuck his wings. Perhaps she would have shunned any emotion of her own, preferring to live out the next few hours with a prickling throat and a heavy heart.

But she is growing more and more certain that this hybrid was sent here to humble her. She cannot bring herself to ignore the stress in this face she has come to... love.

The word startles her still.

Instead of climbing into his arms, she places her hands in his.

He sighs. "You're not about to coddle me, are you, malishka?"

She chews on the inside of her cheek for a moment before answering. "I do not know how."

He gives a deep, rough laugh, then pierces her with his fathomless stare. "Do not die." His fingers tighten almost unbearably around hers.

"I never do," she says. She takes one hand away and places it on his cheek. She feels the roughness of his stubble, the smooth plane of his skin.

"Say the word," he says. "And I'll take us across this sea. Now."

Dawsyn smiles, despite the seriousness of his pledge. She can feel him almost begging her to agree. She steps in and lays her head against his chest instead. An apology, of sorts. "Not yet," she whispers. Words echoing a time and place much like this.

She hears him grunt into her hair, his lips at the crown of her head. "One day, I'll insist," he says. And then his arms wrap around her, and they leave the ground behind.

With the Chasm before them, they follow the sea into its opening and then ascend, flanked by its dire shelves looming just above. The tide does not reach far into mouth of the Chasm. Soon, the glinting water below resembles a narrow vein, creeping out into the ocean's waiting grasp. They climb with the mountain, until the Chasm becomes the black pit she recognises. The Chasm of her darkest, most hopeless remembrances.

Before long, the wind finds them, and though it does little to deter the strength in Ryon's wings, or that of the other mixed-bloods following close behind, it forces Dawsyn to turn her face into her hood.

She can smell the mountain, smell the onset of the hostile season in the wind. She has lost track of the days. She wonders if the people on the Ledge will be preparing for the coming of a new season or a new Selection. She wonders if the Selection rituals will be different now, with Adrik leading the invasion. Perhaps he has already begun taking what he wants.

Ryon banks from side to side as the Chasm weaves through

the mountain, and when night begins to fall, Dawsyn turns her face outward again. They must be near.

The Ledge approaches, Glacia on the other side.

"Ready yourself," Ryon says to her as they bank heavily around a bend. At a point of no discerning marks, Ryon grips Dawsyn tighter. He grunts as his wings swoop downward. He hurls them at an angle, the lip of the Chasm ahead, set to meet them head on.

Skirt the lip and keep to the ground, Ryon had directed Rivdan and Tasheem in the cove. *Don't break until you reach cover.*

Dawsyn flinches, nails digging into the insides of her gloves as they evade the brink, so erringly close that Dawsyn feels the ice reaching out to snag her clothes. Then they are gliding over it – the Ledge.

Ryon stretches his wings as they sail over the snow, trapping Dawsyn's limbs to her body to keep them from hitting the drifts. They soar above this ice and powder until the night becomes impossibly darker, the pine grove shadowing everything.

Ryon swoops up, landing them as quietly as he can, shin deep in the drifts. The heavy armoury on his back sinks him.

The others arrive in quick succession. Rivdan with Salem. Tasheem with Hector.

For a moment, all stand silent. They wait for the sounds of approach and hear none. They turn and look through the trees to the kingdom beyond the Chasm, its castle turrets only just visible for the white snow heaped on their eaves. It appears quiet. No one descends upon the ice or takes to the sky. They have arrived unseen.

"No sign of the witches?" Tasheem murmurs, and Dawsyn shakes her head. They had agreed to fold here once the sun had descended completely. "Any moment now."

As though she had summoned them, Dawsyn feels the thin air collapse momentarily. Yennes appears alone, her eyes on her feet as they sink into the snow. She gasps as the cold finds her, reclaiming the woman who dared to escape it all those years ago.

"Yennes," Dawsyn calls to her, the wind nearly swallowing the sound. "All right?"

The woman balls her hands within her gloves and lifts her feet from the drift. Though her eyes are far away with what Dawsyn imagines are a thousand lived memories, she nods. She lifts her face to see the tops of the pine.

Baltisse appears a second later with Esra. A length of fabric tied around his mouth and hands.

"You gagged him?" Ryon murmurs to Baltisse.

The mage tucks her hair into her hood. "He cannot be trusted to shut up," she says. "He squawks so."

Esra is indeed mumbling incessantly beneath the gag. Growing more and more infuriated by the moment.

"Es, shut the fuck up like Baltisse says, and we can unbind you," Ryon tells him.

Esra complies, albeit unwillingly, and Ryon pulls the binding from his mouth.

"*Oh, mother of hell my cock has pruned to the size of my smallest toe*–"

Baltisse snaps her fingers and the sound of Esra's whispered ramblings are cut off. He simply gapes like a breathless fish.

Tasheem grins. "Why bind him in the first place if you could have done that?"

"For the deep satisfaction of it."

Salem groans at the mage. "Yeh could've saved me years o' his nonsense, Baltisse. It's been right torture."

"I find satisfaction in that, too," she quips, pulling her cloak tighter.

"Enough," Ryon says, rubbing a weary hand over his eyes. "If there's a wit between any of you, ready it. Baltisse?"

The mage raises her eyebrows at him.

"You and Yennes both must mind your limits as you fold in

and out of the Chasm. If either of you begin to feel any strain, you should–"

"The bounds of my magic are no business of yours, Ry," Baltisse interrupts. "Stop worrying about us. We will all face challenges tonight."

Ryon nods, looking once to the others, and then to Dawsyn. "Time to go."

"Hector?" Dawsyn calls "Are you ready?"

Hector's gaze is far away, and Dawsyn knows the feeling – to be sent back to this mountain after knowing the ground. He sighs, takes out a long knife. "After you."

The walk through the grove is shorter than Dawsyn remembers. Strange how small this shelf seems, now that she's seen how far the world stretches. The virgin snow does not seem so endless, the pine does not tower as it once did. She and Hector turn the trail they always have, their feet knowing it by heart. Around the pocket of Edgarton trees, marked with an E. Through the copse of the Dervichs' claim, then the Tarrows. When they reach the end of the rows, with the cabins pocketed in a long line before the Face, they stop.

Ryon and the rest are nowhere to be seen. She cannot hear them.

Hector reaches over and squeezes her hand with his, just once. They breathe together. Once more they stand on this treeline looking out on the shelf they were once confined too. They see the flickering glow of firelight illuminating the tiny windows. See the chimney smoke quickly claimed by the eddies of frost in the air.

Then, just as they did as children, Dawsyn and Hector step out from the cover of trees together, and advance into the open.

There are only two others who brave the cold this night. The two forms huddle in their furs over dark lumps upon the snow. Bodies.

Two slowly freezing bodies, left out in the night before they are thrown into the Chasm come morning. The two hovering figures are either mourning, or scavenging. Both eventualities are just as likely as the other.

When Dawsyn and Hector come closer, the pair straighten, like animals caught unawares.

"Nevrak," Hector murmurs to Dawsyn. "The Splitter."

"And his son," Dawsyn returns.

Nevrak earnt his moniker for the way he aptly splits people the way one would split wood. His son is the one Briar Sabar referred to as 'weasel,' though his name is Wes.

"Back you go," calls Nevrak evenly, his beard covered in frost. Frozen tears, Dawsyn realises. So, they are mourning. One more glance to the ground before them tells Dawsyn that these bodies are those of his daughters. Neither could be older than ten.

The way the children are bound in hide, their limbs tied to their bodies, Dawsyn knows Nevrak is preparing them for their eternal rest at the bottom of the Chasm.

Another two she was not fast enough to save.

Dawsyn swallows, then lifts her hands in a show of peace.

This is the moment recognition comes. Nevrak's thin face goes slack with disbelief. He readies his stance.

"We did not come to fight," Dawsyn says clearly. But his son is already raising a knife, throwing it through the air.

Dawsyn watches it flip end over end. She reaches up to catch it before it can glide over her. Though she is reticent to, she throws it back, letting it land blade down in the snow before Wes's feet.

Nevrak and Wes stare at it, their expressions bewildered.

"As I said," Dawsyn calls, louder now, "we did not come to fight." Dawsyn's eyes slip to Wes, who seems to be palming his belt for another weapon. "Tell your boy to call in reinforcements, Nevrak. Perhaps it will ease his nerves."

Nevrak hesitates. "What do you want?" he asks, pulling his only remaining child behind him.

"To speak," Dawsyn answers, and prays her words are beseeching enough. "That is all."

Nevrak appraises her for a moment, likely sizing up his chances of defending himself alone against both Dawsyn and Hector. But in the end, he must decide that sending Wes away is of more importance, and so he nods to the boy.

It takes mere moments for others to begin to converge. Word travels quickly along the Face.

The Sabar girl has returned once more. She brings Hector with her.

Two of their own people, taken and returned unharmed. Dawsyn hopes it will be enough to sway them.

They come from their homes – the ones strong enough to stand in the icy wind – several feet from the corpses of children, eyes averted. All have come with one weapon or another. None are so naïve to think that Dawsyn and Hector have come alone. They remember who she was last accompanied by: strange-looking Glacians. Glacians with human resemblance. Their eyes flit over the grove, looking for signs of movement or shadow, ears pricked for the sounds of wings.

"Now or never," Hector murmurs to her, and Dawsyn has never seen him warier. He shakes his head slightly at the sight of the crowd. "Mother help us both."

"Hope you haven't come back for your cabin, boy," calls Nevrak, still hovering protectively over his girls. "Cabin's been occupied."

Dawsyn can hear the way Hector's breath shakes as he exhales.

"No," Dawsyn says. "We've come with the same offer as before." A deep breath. "We've come to help you escape the Ledge." She lets her voice ring out into the cold, bitter night. The words hover in the air briefly, a tangible, visible thing, before the fine wisps of them are swept away.

She ensures all can hear her, perhaps a hundred of them, ragged in their layers of fur, weather-beaten faces grim and bony. She recognises the desperate tang in the air. They are hungry. Adrik still tarries to make the Drop.

"When was the last time the Glacians came?" Dawsyn asks now.

"Why don't you ask your friends?" calls a woman, her voice shrill but tremulous. She is afraid.

Dawsyn raises her hands again. "Hector and I have been in the valley," she says. "We know very little of what the Glacians have been doing on the other side of this Chasm."

The crowd rumbles quietly, disbelieving.

"The valley is… beautiful," Hector offers, almost trance-like. "Sunlight. Flowing water. Soft ground. Flowers," and with this last word he pulls a hand from his pocket and holds it aloft. His fingers slowly unfurl, and with them, the bright pink petals of primrose are collected by the wind and carried past the eyes of the Ledge people.

They look to one another.

Dawsyn speaks again. "What I said before has not changed. The Glacians have a new king. He will come here and reap whenever he chooses–"

A laugh, hollow and deadly. Nevrak. "You come back to preach what you do not know, Sabar. The strange Glacians… they have already come. They come when they choose now. Day and night."

Dawsyn's throat closes. She looks amongst the crowd at the shaking heads, the eyes on the sky. If there is a way to make the Ledge worse, it's to make every day a Selection Day.

She trembles, feels the iskra wind its way from her gut to her hands.

Dawsyn suppresses it. She must stay the frost.

"The Glacians I brought with me… they are rebels. They have been with us in the valley, and they want to help. Please–" Dawsyn breathes, her lungs shrinking. She has grown unused to the mountain air. "Let them."

There is silence. A strange, almost hopeful yearning in

the space between them. And in the lag between words, Dawsyn sees clearly how desperate they are. They are starving. Dying. Living in a constant state of defence. This is what will bring them into the Chasm, she realises. Dawsyn can see it. These people know now what they did not before – they can no longer survive on the Ledge. Every day, more people will fall.

Dawsyn fills her chest with all the air she can manage and sends a prayer skyward. "At the bottom of the Chasm," she says, "is a path. I have seen it." She lets the message reach them. Lets it stick in their ears and watches their eyes widen. "My friends are waiting in the woods, but I assure you, they mean only to help you get to the bottom of the Chasm. We can walk to its end. We can be free. And if you won't let us–" here she pauses. She prepares the words. "Then you will *not* be forced. We have brought food and we will leave it here. Weapons, too. There aren't enough rations to last more than a day or so, but if that is what you choose, then you may have it. We will take our leave to the bottom of the Chasm. You won't be harmed."

More silence. More restless desperation. "We don't belong here!" Dawsyn cries out, imploring them, one by one. "All the hostile seasons we've survived with so little to eat. Every Selection that stole more of us to Glacia. This *fucking shelf* that tries to tip us into the Chasm," Dawsyn heaves, but does not remove her gaze. "You do not need to choose fear and death." She looks back to the crowd. "Choose to find a way out. Come with me," she says. "Please."

The wind whispers threats into their ears, but these are Ledge people, and they have long since learnt to ignore them.

Nevrak is silent, looking down at his daughters, shrouded in their lumpy hide. The cold has already found them. Next, it may find his son.

The crowd tarries. Waiting for someone to speak. Waiting for the first crack.

"How will we all reach the bottom?" comes a voice, the same woman who spoke with quivering lips. Now, her voice is lifted, rallied with something like possibility.

Dawsyn almost laughs, almost falls to her knees with the weight of unfettered relief. The iskra in her stomach becomes languid. The glow in her mind burns brightly. "As I was saying," Dawsyn says. "I have friends."

When Ryon, Tasheem, and Rivdan appear, they do so slowly, carefully. When Dawsyn nods to them, they summon their wings. Angels of death in a place for the dead.

Dawsyn turns to the Ledge people, expecting to see weapons raised, fear replacing the looks of hope. But they are either too hungry or too desperate to quail at the sight of these three mixed-blooded, who neither advance nor speak, and Dawsyn's shoulders sag, relieved. *This will work,* she thinks.

Dawsyn explains the way they will be carried down into the Chasm – not with talons, but in the mixed-Glacians' arms. Baltisse demonstrates the way she can fold and unfold on the spot, earning gasps and low oaths. She curtsies with a wicked sneer. Yennes remains behind the others, but Dawsyn explains her ability to fold similarly. She orders those willing to go into the Chasm to collect their belongings and dress for the journey.

She allows them an hour. An hour to reassure the children that all will be well. An hour to make peace with the unknown that lies ahead. An hour to collect whatever food and clothing they might possess, and pray that it's enough.

Dawsyn is not so hopeful to expect that all are convinced to come with her, and indeed, she sees several cabin doors swing shut with grim reproach. They do not reopen.

Salem, Esra, and Hector organise the supplies where possible. Dawsyn does not trust that some advantageous idiot won't be tempted by the proximity of a mixed-blood's throat when they are carried into the Chasm, and so Dawsyn orders that their weapons be handed over. Yennes and Baltisse will fold those into the Chasm and return.

There are perhaps ten hours left in the night. Ten hours to move a hundred people into the Chasm, two at a time. When Ryon, Rivdan, and Tasheem take the first six, Tasheem grins widely, turns to Ryon and says, "Now this here, Mesrich, is real Izgoi shit." And then takes off.

Dubious tension mounts when the Glacians return a good chunk of time later without their encumbrances, having safely displaced them to the bottom of the Chasm. When Dawsyn calls for the next six to step forward, no one does.

Baltisse huffs impatiently, and abruptly folds, leaving everyone to stare dumbfounded at the place she disappeared. A moment later she reappears, holding the wrist of the man Ryon had just taken over the lip, and waving it in the air the way one would a rag doll. "He lives," she says in a bored voice.

The man gasps in great dry gulps. "It's... safe," he nods, though his face is grey. "What they say is true. The bottom of the Chasm... it's safe. A path."

"Fantastic," Baltisse mutters. And folds them both away again.

The people go more willingly after that. Some of the children scream and cry, but as soon as the Glacians leave the ground, they become stricken and quiet, hurtling away through the pine grove.

Hector and Dawsyn light a fire for the people that remain on the Ledge awaiting their passage. She walks to and fro between the people. Eyes sliding over their bodies for any weapons they might be concealing. She answers the hundreds of questions when she has answers and determines which of them seem strong enough to withstand being folded by Baltisse or Yennes.

Otherwise, Dawsyn feels useless. She watches Ryon, Rivdan, Tasheem, Baltisse, and Yennes come and go, over and over, growing wearier with each passage. The mages must rest after each journey to the Chasm and back. The distance to the bottom is great. They must allow their magic to regenerate after each expenditure. After several hours, Yennes simply stops reappearing. She remains at the bottom of the Chasm. She can fold no more.

The mixed-bloods are strong, but the strength needed to raise themselves from the Chasm wanes them. They sweat, bodies slick with exertion. Their shoulders begin to sag.

But the numbers on the Ledge are dwindling. Another few trips will be all that is needed before it is just her and Hector that remain. The night wears on, but the skies remain a depthless, inescapable black.

The sound of wings on the wind is the only sign of Ryon, Tasheem, and Rivdan returning, but when she hears it again, something makes Dawsyn turn.

Perhaps it is a quarter century of instinct. The sky and snow look no different when she turns. But the hair rises on the back of her neck. Her hand reaches for the ax.

The sound of displaced air fills her, the way it always did in her youth on the day of Selection, when the white-winged Glacians filled the sky and began their circle, picking their prey long before they swooped.

As one, the Ledge people that remain look not through the pine grove, but to the sky above.

The ink-black clouds turn to whorls, churning as wings descend from their midst. Six, seven, eight, nine of them.

Nine Glacians. Pale, but not yet bleached of all their colour, circling above.

"Adrik," Dawsyn breathes, spinning her ax once in her hand. Then she turns to her people. "Run for the grove."

They comply. As one, they sprint across the drifts to the treeline ahead, disappearing in the neat rows of pine and becoming lost in their maze. Dawsyn feels the sting of wind on her cheeks as her hood falls back. Her footfalls are slower than the rest. She remains just behind, watching them scatter like field mice around the trunks, down the tilt of the Ledge, closer and closer to the Chasm.

She hears the snapping of branches above, and then the reverberation of feet falling to the ground behind her. Dawsyn spins.

The nine Glacians sink into the drifts, the disturbed powder throwing them into mist. Adrik himself is before her; he is much changed.

Gone is the scruff that once covered his jaw. In its place is smooth, pale skin. His cheekbones are pronounced, his brow more prominent. His grey hair has lightened to bone-white. The most startling of changes, however, are the two wings now fanning out from his spine.

"Dawsyn," he says. His voice is coloured with the same grating lilt as she last heard it, but his expression reveals what is left of his soul. His lips curl back to reveal his teeth, glinting with their hidden poison. His skin pulls taut along his collarbone as he poises his wings for attack. He is a creature of the cold, more beast than not. "You," he says, "are not what I expected to find."

"Adrik," Dawsyn says, planting her feet a little wider, ducking her forehead a little lower. "Little early for Selection, aren't you?"

He pauses momentarily, then smiles. "Well, I won't deny it. I never much saw why Vasteel felt the need to set a date. Why should a king," he says, grinning at the word, "appease the stock?"

Slow-moving wrath builds inside her, the iskra with it. Despite it, Dawsyn laughs through her nose.

"Something amuses you?"

She clicks her tongue, as though blood-lust is not consuming her where she stands. "I've seen men do a lot of strange things to make peace with a small cock," she jeers, pointing her ax at his crotch. "But I've never seen one grow wings and demand to be called a *king*."

His lip twitches. A small reaction, but one that doesn't escape Dawsyn's notice. "Where is Mesrich, girl?"

Dawsyn's hands become ice. The spark in her mind burns. "Hoping to compare?" she defers. "I wouldn't."

Adrik smiles in response. Dangerously. Promisingly. *"Where is he?"*

"You need not concern yourself," she says clearly, enunciating each word. She rouses the iskra and mage magic both. Light and dark, intertwining. "You won't live long enough to reunite."

Adrik's sneer falls, and Dawsyn waits. She waits for him to do what all the weak ones must do when a girl with an ax challenges them.

He rushes forward.

Dawsyn falls to the forest floor as he dives for her. Her knees hit the snow and she bends backward, watching as his wings sail over her body, watching her ax slice a hole through the translucent leather. His cry rings out through the forest.

Adrik's men, no longer awaiting their master's orders, come for her.

She runs. She hopes she has stalled them long enough. Long enough for the remaining to be taken into the Chasm.

She breaks through the treeline, the snow turning to ice before her.

Six humans remain before the Chasm, including Hector. All of them stand with their blades and axes and swords ready.

Too many. Too many to save.

CHAPTER SIXTY-TWO

"There's nowhere to run, Dawsyn," Adrik calls tauntingly, dragging his feet through the grove.

Blood traces his path through the woods. He and his men approach. They clear the treeline, closing the space left between them and the precipice, with the remaining humans caught between. "Tell me where you have taken the rest," Adrik growls, spit flying from his mouth.

Dawsyn does not answer. She stares with hard, stony silence.

"TELL ME!"

His roar is interrupted.

Behind Dawsyn, in that gaping abyss she has always loathed, sounds reach her.

The Chasm sings.

It is not that same whispered siren call from her dreams. Carried to her on a gust of wind is the sweet, melancholic sonation of wing song.

Ryon, Rivdan, and Tasheem appear from nothing, up out of the endless inky black.

They land with resounding cracks as their talons gouge into the ice.

They appear readied, their swords drawn in flight. Eyes pinpointing each of the assailants before them. Dawsyn can only imagine that Baltisse had warned them, there at the bottom of the Chasm.

"Adrik," Ryon says darkly, stalking closer. His eyes slip to Dawsyn's and away. "You seem changed."

"Hiding in the Chasm, Mesrich?" Adrik calls, his voice a thunderous vibration. "Perhaps I am not the only one so changed. I did not raise you to be coward."

Ryon's eyes become fire and brimstone, the muscles of his arms roiling as he tightens his grip on his swords. "You did not raise me at all," he returns. "That credit goes to much nobler folk."

Adrik laughs, though Dawsyn hears the insatiable thirst in its rasp. The eviscerating madness. "It is your very penchant for nobility that made you my best apprentice, Ryon. I must thank you. Without you and your dim-witted aspirations for the good of all, I would never have known the pleasure of sitting where the Glacian King once sat." Adrik looks to the shadowy outline of the Glacian palace across the Chasm. "Of drinking life as he did."

Tasheem shakes her head wildly, her anger a loosely tethered creature. "You fucking traitor!" she spits.

"Me?" Adrik asks. "For wanting what was withheld from our kind? For claiming what our heritage demands?"

"For pitting your worthless, self-serving life above others," Ryon says evenly, the words striking like serpents. "You are not worth the iskra you were born with. Stealing another's will not save you."

Adrik's eyes flash. "Where are my humans, Ryon?"

"Long gone," he answers. "I'll give you the mercy of returning to Glacia, while your remaining wing might still carry you. Though, I doubt it will."

The moment lengthens, stretching to its limits. Adrik's eyes move to the humans left on the Ledge, who stand erringly close to the Chasm. His lips pull back over his teeth.

Dawsyn braces.

"Kill them," Adrik instructs, and the Glacians at his back lurch onto the ice.

Ryon, Tasheem, and Rivdan charge forward, their wings lifting their feet from the ground and carrying them onto the backs of the first Glacians. They drive their swords into their necks, backs, stomachs.

There is no time to think or feel. No time to strategize. Battle rarely allows it. There is only the spray of blood, the brutal unscrupulous breaking. Dawsyn throws herself into the fray, ax swinging.

She sees Tasheem's jaw crumble against an elbow. Ryon ducks beneath a sword that narrowly misses his scalp, and he drives his own into another's stomach. Dawsyn sinks her ax into an unsuspecting back and pulls it out before the Glacian can fall to the snow. Rivdan tears through them, cutting and slicing without discipline, only strength. A knife sinks into his shoulder and he drops one of his swords but remains standing.

Suddenly, Adrik is before Dawsyn, one wing torn open and drooping, the other whole. He vanishes them, as though not wishing to tempt her twice.

As the sounds of battle ring out around them, he somehow makes his voice loud enough. Even the wind cannot carry it away. "I can't wait," he sneers, "to drink your soul." He then pulls his sword over his shoulder and advances.

Dawsyn blocks the first blow and spins, trying to catch his calf, but Adrik is too skilled a fighter. He kicks her in the stomach, sending her to the ground. Dawsyn tumbles backward and lets the momentum put her feet beneath her again. She pushes herself upright once more.

But Adrik is already there, already shoving her back. He pushes her to the ground again, his body trapping hers, the ax trapped between them.

She can hear Rivdan groaning in pain. Tasheem calls his name in a panicked voice. She cannot see Ryon.

They were already too fatigued for this fight. They are outnumbered.

They will lose.

They will all die.

"I can see why he likes you, Dawsyn," Adrik pants, his cold breath filling her own mouth, sickening her. "You have a certain spirit about you."

Dawsyn turns her face away, and there is Baltisse.

Weary Baltisse, her body slumped. Appearing at the lip, unnoticed by those amid their fight. With a desperate look at Dawsyn, she takes two humans and disappears.

The mage, still saving the remaining. So perhaps they won't all lose. Perhaps some will die for the survival of the many, as it was proclaimed by Queen Alvira all those years ago. They only need to stay alive long enough to hold off Adrik and his men. Just a little longer.

Dawsyn's stare returns to Adrik. She remains still as the Izgoi-turned-king brings the edge of his sword to her throat. "I'll cut your throat enough that you'll bleed," he says to her now, "but not enough that we can't throw you into the pool. You can spend the rest of your existence as an empty shell, wandering the dungeons of Glacia, where I can lie on top of you any time I please."

There have been many times when men have devolved to threats of abuse and torture in Dawsyn's life. All have died soon after.

Inside her, the light and dark magic knit as one. Two threads bound together. They weave through her now, filling every crevice of her, every fibre, until she is painfully full. If these are to be her last moments, they will not be spent beneath this Glacian with wings as pitiful as the rest of him. If she must die in this place of her birth, it will be for the lives of her people, and not for him.

Dawsyn fills her lungs with all the breath she can muster. She commands every tendril of pain and hope and love and hatred to detonate, and then screams.

"IGNISS!"

Red. The Ledge turns red.

Dawsyn becomes fire, combusting with light and heat. The burn of the iskra and the fire of mage blood combine in a cosmic surge that blinds her. Adrik is gone, flying away from her, his wings and hair alight in flame.

Bodies everywhere tumble away from the fire into the mercy of snow. Dawsyn lets her ax fall into the sweet spot of her palm, looks to it once, and stumbles forward. She brings it down into the neck of a Glacian with all the force she can muster. She sees Ryon slam his hands over the sleeve that caught fire and then drive his fist into the face of another.

Dawsyn glances to the Chasm and sees that only two humans remain. *Only two more.*

Tasheem lies face down in the snow. Dawsyn cannot tell if she is alive or dead. She yells to Rivdan, who is bringing himself to stand, but stumbling. "Take Tash!" Dawsyn gasps. "Go!" she shouts. "GO!"

He listens. Hastening over to Tasheem, he hefts her into his arms and lifts them from the ground. Tasheem does not rouse. Groaning in pain, Rivdan flies them over the lip and disappears into the Chasm.

Adrik howls in the distance, his body falling again and again into the snow. He tries to let his wings carry him into the sky, but they are torn and burned, rendered useless.

Dawsyn sees Baltisse reappear on the ice, slipping and falling to her hands and knees. She can hear the mage's pained rasps from where she stands. "Baltisse!" she calls. But the mage only stands, shuddering violently. She takes the hands of the remaining two, and with a wracking breath, folds them away.

All of them, Dawsyn thinks. *We saved all of them.*

A cry rings out. One Dawsyn wishes she did not recognise. But she has heard this sound of pain before. In the Glacian palace, when talons had ripped through Ryon's shoulder amidst a battle just like this.

Dawsyn sees Ryon's knees buckle, sees the spray of blood beneath him in the snow. She sees the knife sticking out of his back. The last of Adrik's Glacians stands behind him, his sword rising above Ryon's head.

And Dawsyn has no more store of power. It is gone. Depleted.

From over the Chasm, comes the sound of dozens of wings taking to the sky.

A battalion of Glacians taking flight. Coming for them.

Ryon sees them just as she does, and then his eyes lock with hers.

He pushes himself to his feet with gruelling difficulty. He runs for her, just as she runs for him. Desperately closing the space between them.

Ryon lunges for her at the same moment that she reaches for him. They collide in the middle.

Ryon tries to throw them into flight, their very last bid for survival, but the knife in his back brings them down, and Ryon falls heavily onto the ice.

They slide faster and faster, down the icy slope toward the Chasm's edge, while the sky above them is obscured by descending Glacians.

Ryon roars as he tries to use his talons to clutch the ice. They do not catch. They are slipping away too quickly.

The Glacians are diving toward them.

It is an end so very like and unlike Briar's.

An end filled with ice and fear.

But better this. Better they go into the Chasm, than die at the hands of the enemy.

The lip appears before them, and Dawsyn shuts her eyes. She waits for the feeling of weightlessness, waits for the world to fall away and take her with it.

But suddenly, impossibly, a hand clutches her wrist. And then the Ledge disappears.

Chapter Sixty-Three

She is suffocating, being crushed from all angles. Her entire being reduced to a pinprick.

And then she is unfolding. Not slowly, but all at once.

The air whips her face and Dawsyn hits solid ground with startling force, the breath pushed from her lungs.

Her wrist is still trapped in someone's grasp, though the fingers have become loose.

"Dawsyn?" someone calls. "Ryon? Baltisse!"

And then again. "Baltisse?"

Again. "Baltisse!"

"*Help her!*"

Dawsyn's eyes open.

Black earth beneath her face. Its particles scurrying into her nostrils when she inhales. Darkness presses in all around. There are only a few weak flickers of light – torch flames, she realises. They throw into relief the hand clasped in hers: Baltisse's long, elegant fingers, the nails crusted in soil. She can make out the curve of Baltisse's profile, her face so close to Dawsyn's. Close enough to feel the mage's hair against her cheek. Close enough to smell her skin.

"Bring a torch," Ryon rasps. "Baltisse?"

Dawsyn groans and heaves herself upward by degrees, enough to see the face of the mage who saved her. Enough to look her in the eye and thank her properly.

But the mage is sightless. Her eyes are already far from here, staring up, up into the snaking light above them. Those roiling, ever-changing eyes, now still and human, turned grey.

"Baltisse?" Dawsyn murmurs. And the mage doesn't stir. She won't turn derisive eyes to hers and lash a cutting word.

I know my limitations, she had told them.

Dawsyn lays a hand to her chest and closes her eyes. "Ishveet," she says out loud. Then again, "*Ishveet!*"

Nothing stirs.

"ISHVEET!" Dawsyn shouts. "FIX HER!" But it comes breathless and cracked. She is no sorceress. No great and powerful wielder of magic. She is spent. She is useless.

Neither side of her magic rises to her call.

A hand comes to rest on Dawsyn's shoulder. "She wanted to go back for you," Yennes's voice says. "She couldn't leave you there."

"Fix her," Dawsyn wheezes, her head lowering. Her vision spins in tightening circles, bile climbing her throat.

A broken sigh. "I cannot."

"*Heal her,*" Dawsyn says again, only this time, the words tremble. She blinks and blinks until the spinning subsides enough to make out the parts of the mage, the parts that saw her through hundreds of years only to bring her here, to the bottom of the Chasm.

"She knew her limitations," Dawsyn murmurs. "She… she…"

Salem's voice now, gentle in her ear, wet with sorrow. A heavy hand rests on her shoulder. "She couldn' leave yeh there, lass."

Ryon leans forward slowly, as though it takes all his strength. He whispers something into the mage's ear, his throat straining with unspent emotion. Ryon, who knew far more of Baltisse than Dawsyn ever will.

Because the mage is dead.

Yennes shuts her lids.

Salem folds her hands.

Ryon kisses her forehead.

The mage is dead.

An immeasurable time passes. A time where Dawsyn cannot assemble fragments of thought. She does not dare to see what other carnage might be waiting in this pit. Instead, she swallows each sob that stubbornly attempts to breach. She lets the image of Baltisse's broken eyes blister the inside of her mind. She waits impatiently for that reliable thing within her to usurp the pain, the anger to quell the sorrow. Stifle it.

She begs for it, pleads for the shock to be swallowed within her and be replaced with something hard and bitter.

It is Ryon's swaying form that brings Dawsyn back. As though her ears were unclogged, her brain unstuffed, she can suddenly hear something other than an inward screaming.

Ryon kneels before Baltisse's body, but his stare wanes. His eyes hooded, head bobbing with delirium, he pitches forward.

"Ryon?"

The knife in his back, Dawsyn thinks. She sees it now, where it lay bloody and discarded beside him.

Ryon groans.

"Yennes!" Dawsyn calls, her voice one of a thousand shards of ice, scratching her lungs as they pass. Her ribs are likely broken. "Yennes?"

"I'm here," she says suddenly, appearing from the loud, echoing darkness with a torch.

"Ryon," Dawsyn tells her, trying to stand. Trying to go to him. "His back."

She watches the woman hover over Ryon's slumped form. Watches the white light glow from her hands as she presses them to his back. The light is feeble. It does not last. Yennes's magic is expended, just like Dawsyn's, just like…

"The wound is… sealed," Yennes says, panting. "That's the best I can do for now."

"Thank you," Ryon mutters, sighing in relief. He falls back gingerly, wincing.

Yennes averts her eyes, begins to move away. "There are many others with infection, lung sickness," she says. "I will need to do what I can for them as well, before they can travel… if the iskra allows me to."

Dawsyn can hear them – the many, many others. Crying, arguing, bustling in the dark. She gestures for Yennes to pass her torch.

Dawsyn lifts the flame high, casts its glow further.

The Chasm is filled.

The Ledge people are all around. Masses of them. Stepping over one another to find space on the ground or milling through the crowd like rats. Along the middle, that thin vein of shallow water creeps through, travelling a path they will not follow. They are trapped in darkness. Fearful. Uncertain.

But free.

"We did it," Dawsyn says to no one, to herself.

Ryon comes to stand beside her, his steps slow and stiff. She takes his hand, intensely relieved to feel it in hers. A remnant of something good.

"*You* did it," the hybrid says.

They say little else. They simply stand amongst the ancestors of the Fallen Village, once again returned to ground, and contemplate the days ahead. The unknown path that must be travelled. The path that leads to somewhere or nowhere.

Two paths, a voice reminds her.

Both are filled.

Acknowledgements

So much has changed within the last year.

This time in 2022 I was pacing nervously, pouring over edits for Ledge and beating back a foreboding sense of ruin. I was bricking it. So badly did I want readers to like Ledge. At least enough to pass it on to a friend. Enough for me to be allowed the pleasure of continued writing. Enough that the book industry wouldn't suddenly wash their hands of me and call it a failed experiment.

Right before the release of Book One, it occurred to me (as it often does now) that this was a monumental shift from my wishes a year removed. In a short space of time, I had gone from wishing for readers in any amount, to already having a queue waiting to give me a chance.

I don't hope for approval anymore. This year, nearing the release of Chasm, I am simply grateful for all the chances that were taken every time someone picked Ledge from the shelf. In my head, the romantasy lovers and I are raving in some dark dungeon with lutes and tankards and bards. The women have daggers under their skirts and the guys are wearing slutty peasant tunics and everyone is the chosen one.

So, first I must thank my people. My online community – I am so glad to be here, and I'm glad you're here too. I hope you had fun. I hope you felt something. I hope it brought you something this non-fictional world neglects to. Thank you, eternally, for your support in every form it comes.

To my intrepid agent, Amy Collins of Talcott Notch Literary Agency, thank you for kicking away each hurdle that means to trip me. I would be a stumbling mess if I had to navigate this plane without you. You are a living, breathing angel.

To the people with the best literary taste in the world – Angry Robot Books. Gemma Creffield, Caroline Lambe, Desola Coker, Amy Portsmouth and the team. Your enthusiasm for this trilogy is a constant source of reassurance. You never fail to galvanise me. I am so fortunate to have such a wonderful and talented bunch of people to collaborate with. Even when you're angry with me for killing off your favourites, the love is always felt.

To the McCallum originals, my parents – Andrew and Julie, and my sisters, Alycia and Teagan. You are forever my biggest champions. Thank you for your collective anger every time a negative word is taken against my name, and your shared love for me. You got really lucky the day I was born.

To my found family, I would like to find whoever divined our meeting and kiss them right on the lips, because they found everything I'll ever need in a friend and wrapped it in a bow. Hannah Maeher, Kaven Hirning, Amber Nicole, Samantha Ferrand and Maggie Siciliano, you have my unending love.

To my husband and children, every day I wake up and I worry. Not because of this book. Not because of money or errands or the labours of each day, but because I hit the jackpot when I married you, Michael. Then I cashed in again when we found ourselves parents to those perfect kids, and the burden of the blessed is worrying that maybe our fortune is too great to last. I guess we'll just have to hold tight, and make sure it does. I love you.

Finally, to you, dear reader. I hope Dawsyn encompassed all of the anger we cannot release in public, and that Ryon epitomised the partner you deserve. I hope you got to put down all the heaviness of your day and pick up a world that feels lighter than our own. I hope you found a measure of peace there.

Apologies for the ending, though. That fucking sucked.

Stacey x